THE SEPTEMBER GARDEN

Nell and Sylvie grow up quickly during the early days of rationing, blackouts, and the arrival of RAF planes in the skies. Sylvie is desperately worried for her parents in Nazi-occupied Normandy. Nell, meanwhile, witnesses the crumbling of her parents' marriage. When the girls fall in love with the same man, the brave RAF officer Alex Hammond, he is spared having to choose between them as the war changes the course of their lives. For Nell, the only place she can ever find solace is inside the September Garden, it is the only place she feels safe, and where she decides to hide her most dreadful secret...

THE SEPTEMBER GARDEN

by

Catherine Law

Magna Large Print Books
Long Preston, North Yorkshire,
BD23 4ND, England.

British Library Cataloguing in Publication Data.

Law, Catherine
    The September garden.

    A catalogue record of this book is
    available from the British Library

    ISBN   978-0-7505-3780-3

First published in Great Britain by Allison & Busby in 2012

Copyright © 2012 by Catherine Law

Cover illustration © Hayden Verry by arrangement with
Arcangel Images

The moral right of the author is hereby asserted in accordance with
the Copyright, Designs and Patents Act, 1988.

Published in Large Print 2013 by arrangement with
Allison & Busby Limited

Magna Large Print is an imprint of Library Magna Books Ltd.

Printed and bound in Great Britain by
T.J. (International) Ltd., Cornwall, PL28 8RW

For Jennie and her girls

Prologue

1945

Nell

The turn of the season greeted her that morning as she left the house and walked the lane that hugged the side of the valley. She stopped still for a moment, listening, breathing in the first earthy trace of autumn. Mist, caught at waist height between the beeches where the little river glided, was vaporous, drifting like phantoms. Drifting, like her memories.

On the horizon, above smouldering golden woods, the hills were sleeping. The summer season clung on: the earth still warm; the sky, empty. The war was over, and the planes had stopped coming. A red-brown kite had the clear blue to himself. He wielded his wingspan, testing the air high above her head, his cry like that of a frightened child.

She stood there and took her fill of Lednor valley; all that was familiar, everything that was her home. She thought of the people who had come here and then had gone. The people who had disappeared, as was the custom in war, like waves from a beach, like clouds from the sky. She thought of cousin Sylvie, and then of Alex. He walked through her mind steadily and inevitably; a passing tangible sweetness. The memory of her happiness teased and haunted her. Then left her alone. She turned around and made her slow way back to the house.

Her footsteps crunched along the gravel drive that wound its way home. The late rose clinging to the red-brick facade dropped its last baby-pink petals like tears. Her Alsatian, Kit, was waiting for her on the step. He raised his head to watch her approach. Just inside the front door, packed and ready, was her battered suitcase, the one her mother had bought her from Peter Jones before the war. She lifted her hand and the dog came to her side, trotting beside her as she made her way around the west wall of the house where a honeysuckle rambled, exhaling perfume.

She wandered inside the walled garden that had been named by her father for the end-of-summer flowers that colonised its four quarters. Globes of dahlia rose above golden chrysanths. The sunflowers – ruddy-brown and gigantic yellow – were on fire. Nasturtiums and snapdragons crowded the beds, while butterflies, early risers like herself, bobbed over them like tiny beacons. Here, in the sharp slant of the sun, the garden was bedraggled and overblown. The other day, her mother had described it as *rampant*, referring darkly to the fact that no longer was her father – or indeed any man – around to tend to it. Even so, she relished the peace and the familiarity of the garden: the September Garden. The crooked apple tree was plump with russet fruit and the brambles heavy with black jewel berries. She plucked a berry and popped it in her mouth. It was sour, unexpectedly so.

She had been persuaded by cousin Sylvie to accompany her back to Normandy. And last night she had packed her suitcase with a resentful and reluctant drag. She and her cousin had barely spoken in the last four years. The idea of this trip was disturbing and provoking, she thought, to say the least. And what of the icy bitterness, the painful breach between them?

In the chill of this first morning of autumn, contemplating the journey back to the place where her cousin was born, she knelt down in the September Garden, in the corner where the big-faced daisies grew, and began to shiver.

Kit shuffled onto the ground beside her, his flank heavy against her ankle. He let out an elongated sigh that sounded almost human as he rested his snout on his paws. She felt her dog watch her as she pulled some weeds away to expose a little patch of short turf. The ground, she noticed, had sunk a little. Some sort of marker, a gravestone, was needed. Something had to be done.

The taxi hooted at the front of the house and she glanced at her watch.

Blunt sorrow burrowed down inside her, fixing her to the ground. She stayed there, crouching, hiding her face with her hands. Kit wriggled his nose, sniffing out her tears, shifting himself closer.

She pressed her hand to the strip of grass. It felt springy, alive. She whispered to it, to the patch of earth, *It is time to go.* Her tears incapacitated her for some moments, ripping her body apart. When at last she could speak, she said, *My little boy, I promised I'd never leave you again. Not ever, not until I die.* Her voice cracked at the back of her throat. *But sleep well, this time, and I promise you, I will be home soon.*

Nell got up and walked away from the unmarked grave, glancing back just once over her shoulder. *I will be home soon.*

Part One

1938–1939

Nell

She squeezed the brakes and came to a halt at the top of the hill, lifting her feet off the pedals and scuffing her heels along the road metal. Her knees were scabbed and her socks were baggy. She rode like a boy, her mother told her. And should know better for a young lady of nearly fifteen. *I dress like a boy too*, thought Nell, wiping the curls out of her eyes with the back of her hand.

This was the best spot. She could see the whole of Lednor valley, *her* valley, from here: the lane that looped through tunnels of hawthorn and beech; the silvery River Chess; the glittering ford at Lednor Bottom. Without the clattering of the bicycle wheels, the rushing of air past her ears, Nell could listen to the day. Over in the copse a wood pigeon purred and then a cuckoo piped – so cheerful and innocent-sounding for the wicked interloper that he was. She must tell Dad, so he could write it down in his notebook. The field of wheat behind the gate was turning to gold. Blazing scarlet poppies, paper-light in the breeze, invaded its bounds.

She saw a sunshine-yellow bird hop, pause, then flee into the sky.

'Dad would know,' she whispered, straining her eyes against the blue. 'He'll know what sort of bird that is.'

She rested her bike on the ground and hooked

her leg over the stile, pulled her knickers down and squatted in the pasture. As she peed, she watched the winsome sheep, now bereft of their lambs, chewing blank-eyed in the shade of the oak.

'I hope you've forgotten your children already,' she told them. 'Otherwise, it's far too barbaric for words.'

Sitting back up on the stile she drew an apple from her pocket and bit into it noisily. She drummed her feet on the crossbar.

The valley was laid out peacefully below her like one of her father's paintings; the sun sharpened the shadows and the heat subdued the birds. A woodpecker hammered away in the wood, then fell silent. Three miles away, behind banks of sultry trees and concealed by the bosomy curves of the fields, lay the village of Great Lednor, revealed only by a shimmering grey church spire. Beyond there, in a distance unimagined to Nell, eventually, lay London.

She peered down the valley, shielding her eyes. There it was, her mother's car in miniature, coursing through the ford on its return from the station, her shopping trip to London, leaving waves and ripples in its wake.

'Better go home,' she told the uninterested sheep.

She chewed the last of the apple and flung the core into the hedge.

Her jaw, her teeth, her bones juddered. She lifted her feet and began to squeal as the lane fell steeper, the bends sharper. She laughed, and her

18

breath was snatched away. One more bend. One more dip. The speed never failed to shock her. Her brakes screamed for mercy.

With a war cry, she plunged through the leafy tunnel and broke into sunshine, straight over the gravel, scattering stones. Her father's doves flapped in an agony of terror up to their cote. The car was already parked, its radiator tinkling as it cooled. The boot was open and Nell half glanced inside. There it was, just as her mother had promised, the brand-new suitcase.

'Only the best, from Peter Jones.'

Her mother had conjured up the holiday plan with her sister, Auntie Beth: this summer, Nell should go and stay at Auntie Beth and Uncle Claude's all the way across the sea in France.

'You can spend your time with cousin Sylvie. Get to know her better. Learn from her,' her mother said, unreasonably. 'She is growing into a fine young lady, by all accounts. And her accent, oh, divine.'

And next year, it was decided, Sylvie would come and visit Lednor and so on and so forth. It was not to be argued with. It was, Nell suspected, a way for her mother and Auntie Beth to have the gift of 'six weeks without the child' every other year. It was no use denying this; Nell heard her mother say those actual words.

She was, her father explained patiently to her, to be packed off on the boat-train from Waterloo to Portsmouth, to cross the Channel with a chaperone. Then she'd be shunted from Cherbourg onto an *autobus*, and finally a horse and cart to reach the Orlande house in the village by the sea.

19

Uncle Claude was a gendarme, her father reminded her; a pillar of the community.

'What an adventure you'll have,' he'd said to cheer her up.

How appalling, Nell had thought. The thing was that whenever she thought of Sylvie – one year older than her, brutally confident, with unforgiving violet eyes and a sharp face of incredible beauty – she felt queasy, belittled and she quite simply disappeared.

'Ah, there you are,' announced Mollie Garland, coming out through the front door. She looked beautiful in her red suit for town, clinched in at the waist, and with her little hat perched on her rolled-up hair. 'Well, aren't you going to say something? What do you think of it?'

'I don't know, really...' What could she say about a suitcase?

'Oh Nell, have some enthusiasm, do. It's all rather irritating. Come on, help me with the shopping.'

Mollie began to hand Nell large stiffened paper bags emblazoned with smart London store logos.

'Did you get me anything else?' she asked. 'Apart from the suitcase.'

'No. Everything you have already is perfectly adequate for Montfleur. You won't be going anywhere special.' Her mother glanced at her. 'Oh, but look at the state of you. What a fright you are. You've been out all day, haven't you? On that blessed bike. I tell you, you'll certainly be learning a lesson from Sylvie this summer, learning to be more ladylike. Just like her. You know she plays the violin. It's a wonder you are

20

so unmusical.'

Being compared to perfect Sylvie was absolute torture.

'Is this everything, Mother, because I really have to go to the bathroom?'

Nell turned on her heel, ran into the hallway and unceremoniously dumped her mother's shopping bags at the bottom of the stairs.

She could hear music straying from her father's study overhead. She went upstairs and along the landing, hearing the pristine notes of Debussy drift from the gramophone and through the air. She may not be able to play a note, but what she heard was beautiful; made her ache.

She poked her nose around the door and asked her father if she could come in.

Marcus Garland was sitting by the window, his chin down, staring up at the easel before him. His paints were scattered on the table – twisted tubes of carmine and crimson lake. Nell loved to line them up, tidy them away for him; press the ends so the paint rose to the top, and not a drop wasted. Sunlight glimmered through his jam jar of water; his brushes were idle.

'Bit shaky at the moment,' he told her. 'Can't quite pull it together.' He kept his hands, stained with paint, tightly clasped in his lap. His buttoned-up waistcoat seemed loose on his frame; his rolled-up sleeves revealed wiry tanned forearms.

Nell asked him if she should mix some paint for him.

'No, not today.' He turned now and threw a smile at her. His eyes were distant, as if he was forever witnessing some other world behind them. 'I thought you were helping Mother.'

She drew closer and peered at the canvas.

'Roses,' she said. 'They're nice.'

'Half done,' he said, 'but I can't see me finishing it now. I can't see them any more.' He tapped the side of his head. 'Can't see them in here. They're gone now. Faded away until next year.'

She reminded him that there were roses still in the garden. Why couldn't he paint them?

'But these are the *dog* roses, Nell, in the lanes. I started this painting a few weeks ago. Those roses are gone now.' He pressed his fingertips between his eyes. 'And I can't remember them.'

Nell heard a shake in his voice. The wild roses of the hedgerows were her favourites, with their open faces the colour of a baby's fingernail. He was right: they had faded, and the hedges were now a richer green; a deep, summer green.

The music finished and the arm on the gramophone lifted with a click.

'Shouldn't you be downstairs, helping your mother?' he asked again, screwing the cap onto a tube of permanent rose.

Nell scuffed her feet on the carpet. 'I'd rather be up here with you. Can I help you? Tidy your study?'

'No, Nell, you have to...' He cocked his head towards the door, towards the world outside his study.

'Do I have to go to Auntie Beth's? Do I *really* have to? It's such a long way. All that way across the sea.'

He insisted that she would like it, that she

22

could improve her French. He said it again; it would be an adventure.

'But I can do that here...' Nell heard her voice whine, sensitivity rising like mercury through her blood. 'I want to stay here.' *With you.*

'Your mother thinks it will do you good. You're fourteen, nearly fifteen. Perhaps it's time to stop racing round the country lanes.'

Nell mumbled, 'Oh, and be just like Sylvie?'

The smile reached his eyes this time.

'You don't have to be anything like her,' he said. 'Just be good.'

Uncle Claude called it *le petit sommeil.* In the weary heat of the afternoon, the seaweed on the harbour walls baked, the tall blue shutters of the house were closed, the street was empty, silent. A solitary dog trotted by.

'Mad,' Uncle Claude would have said if he had seen the dog. And to tease Auntie Beth, he'd have said: 'Mad just like the English.' But he and Auntie Beth were closeted away in their room at the back of the house. Sylvie was in her own *boudoir,* dreaming sweet dreams, no doubt. Nell could hear the house at rest as she lay on top of the white ruffled bedspread in the guest *chambre.* Behind the closed shutters the room held a grey half-light. Nell listened to the cry of seagulls over the rooftops, the ticking clock, a rumbling water pipe. She twitched, her legs excruciatingly itchy, unable to find a comfortable spot. Here at the front of the house, facing west, her room was an inferno. Her own 'little sleep' evaded her.

She went to the shutter and opened it a chink.

The hard sunlight made her screw up her eyes and she retreated. She thought of the still, deep-green water in the harbour and imagined its coolness. She thought of the steps that led down into the water that were still visible in the quiet underworld beneath the surface. She had no desire to dip her toes in. Instead, she yearned for the bourn back home. And home, with its twisted russet-brick chimneys and friendly little casements, two storeys high, spreading itself wide, hugging the earth. She liked the way she could ramble through the long passageways at home, walking the breadth of the house past the displays of her father's less successful watercolours. But here, at Auntie Beth's and Uncle Claude's, everything was crammed in, built upwards, four-floors high. Oh, it was all very grand. The blue-painted gates that fronted the street loomed over her, shut her in; the metal floor-to-ceiling windows were narrow, creating a very elegant, very beautiful cage. She must always climb upstairs and downstairs to get anywhere.

Fidgeting and wretched, she heard the clock chime on the *mairie* across the way. Half past two. Auntie Beth said that she and Sylvie must not emerge until four. *Four?*

Nell sat up and sipped the lemonade that Adele the maid had left her. It was syrupy and warm. She dared herself. Getting up, she slipped barefoot across the floorboards and twisted the doorknob. Silently she emerged. How cool the landing was, facing the north side of the house. A long lace curtain drifted in the scanty breeze. Through the tall landing window, the garden

24

beckoned her.

The house was airless, silent now. Holding its breath just as Nell did. Something creaked behind her. She turned to see the bulk of Uncle Claude in his dressing gown and slippers emerge from behind a door. He closed it with a gentle click and paused to groom his large moustache with his fingers, looking, Nell thought, mildly pleased about something. He spotted her and Nell flinched, wanting to duck, expecting him to bellow. After all, Auntie Beth had said: *Not till four o'clock.*

Her uncle glared at her momentarily, his mouth clamped shut, looking suddenly rather befuddled. And then his face rounded into a smile. He put his finger over his hairy top lip as if to shush her. He turned on his heel and went up the stairs to his own bedroom, the belt of his dressing gown flapping behind him.

Euphoric, suddenly, that her misdemeanour had been brushed aside, Nell ran swiftly, lightly, tiptoeing down the stairs, and down again, along the hallway. Glancing into the darkened salon shuttered from the sunlight she saw oak furniture like sleeping monsters in the gloom. She caught a glimpse of herself in the mirror in the hall: dishevelled curls, a mischievous face and a glint in her eye. Very nearly fifteen, she thought, and still looked like a tomboy. The stone floor of the vestibule was blissfully cold under her feet. Through the back door and down the steps, the garden, enclosed by high mellow-stone walls, was a scented heaven. The air vibrated with the sound of bumbling insects. She ran now in delight, past clumps of lavender and tarragon, past bean frames and rows of onions. By the high wall, against which grew a clump of profoundly blue delphiniums, she stopped.

'*Qui est-ce? Qui est-ce là?*' came the small voice above her.

Nell glanced up, startled, believing she had the sleeping afternoon to herself. Peering over the top of the garden wall were two children, a girl and a boy. Their hair was black and their skin pale, their faces tiny. They were identical, like a pair of dark-headed sprites.

'*Bonjour, mademoiselle, comment ça va?*' the girl greeted her. Her glasses were wonky on her face, her eyes were like saucers.

'*Bonjour,*' replied Nell. 'How are you able to see over the wall? Are you standing on a ladder?'

The children's faces fell. They did not understand. Nell took a deep breath and tried her French: '*Etes-vouz sur un...*' What was the French for 'ladder'?

She wanted to ask them if they, too, could not sleep. She wanted to ask them if they wanted to come over to her side of the wall. '*Voulez-vous aller ici, avec moi?*' she tried.

The boy and girl glanced at each other.

'*Non,*' said the boy, '*On ne nous permet pas.*'

And then Nell remembered. Estella and Edmund Androvsky next door were different, Sylvie had told her, and they were not allowed to visit. Nell stared at them. What was wrong with them? They were only the neighbours' children.

'*Au revoir, mademoiselle anglaise.*'

Edmund and Estella ducked back and Nell

padded along the path. She lifted the iron latch on the door in the back wall and sneaked into the cobbled yard. Opposite her was the old barn, now used by Uncle Claude as a garage for his car; next to it, the two stables built of silvery Normandy stone, commandeered as sheds. These stables didn't have the doors she was used to, cut in half so that the horses could peer over. Here, at Uncle Claude's, the doors were like any other door, solid but with a metal grille for the top half. They had once been deep cherry-red, Nell guessed, but the paint had faded long ago. Above each was an old painted sign, nominating long-departed horses: *demi-sang* Tatillon and *demi-sang* Ullis. Between the two stable doors a narrow set of steps led up into the darkness of the hayloft above. She opened the door to Ullis's stable and entered its cave-like chill. Whiffs of hay, leather and horses, as if their ghosts still lingered, greeted her. Nell imagined Ullis's heavy iron-shod hooves ringing on the cobbles and, in the stable next door – now Uncle Claude's carpentry workshop – Tatillon's soft pliable lips pulling hay from the iron hay-rack still there on the wall. She blinked her eyes in the gloom and saw Sylvie's lop-eared rabbit peering out from his hutch in the corner.

'*Bonjour, Monsieur le lapin,*' she sang. 'You understand me, don't you? What a fat, overfed, spoilt French rabbit you are.' She reached for a carrot from the trug on the floor and, squatting down, pushed it through the chicken wire. The rabbit shuffled forward and reached with yellow teeth. Chewing steadily, the creature took so long to devour the carrot that Nell soon grew bored. She sat back on her heels and looked around her at Uncle Claude's polished garden forks and spades lined up against the stone wall. Cobwebs, grey with dust, choked the corners; fronds of ivy crept through a gap under the eaves. Above the beams in the ceiling, the old hayloft, reached by those narrow steps between the two stables, Nell guessed, colonised by rats and spiders. She listened to the snuffling and chewing of the rabbit as she breathed in the earthy smell of the stable, counted the onions strung from the beams and watched a solitary cloud drift overhead through the tiny window.

Then, suddenly, an unearthly shriek. The rabbit threw himself against the door of the hutch. Nell stared, her scalp shrinking tight to her skull, as he turned violent circles, his claws scratching, his rump banging the sides. She took a step towards the commotion, but then, terrified, turned instead and ran. She slammed the stable door shut and raced back through the garden door, up the path, ignoring the calling of Edmund and Estella from behind the wall. Breathing hard, her curls plastered to her scalp, she slipped quietly back into the vestibule and up the stairs to the inferno of her room.

In the stifling shuttered dimness, Nell finally slept, dreaming of Lednor Bottom, of her green valley, of her tree house above the cool bourn, of her father's gramophone music. She was jerked awake by the screaming. Pulling herself up, groggy and confused, she went back downstairs, meeting a sleepy Adele in the vestibule.

'*Qu'est-ce que c'est maintenant, ma petite Nell?*' the maid asked, rolling her eyes, wiping a plump hand over her hair in a brief effort to tidy it.

They hurried along the path towards the crescendo of cries, the banging and crashing from the stable yard. Edmund and Estella's faces appeared once again over the wall and Adele told them to go away. Sylvie was pummelling the door of Ullis's stable with her fists, her face red and enraged, her eyes flashing with fury. Her dark ponytail swung like a whip over her shoulders.

'*Monsieur le lapin est mort!*' she screamed. '*Il est mort!*'

Adele thought that she'd better go and find Madame and hurried back to the house.

'Dead?' Nell asked her cousin in wonder, feeling a strange twisting in her stomach. 'When I left him, he...'

She was going to say 'fine' but realised he'd been somewhat deranged. She peered into the gloom of the stable to see the door of the hutch wide open, the fat, limp, brown body of the rabbit, his ears crisscrossed. The partly digested carrot amongst the straw.

'When you *what?*' asked Sylvie, turning on her, her cheeks brick-red. Tears squeezed from her eyes; her perfect teeth gritted in startling whiteness. She poked Nell in the chest.

'I came to see him,' said Nell, 'when everyone was asleep. He ... he ran about a bit.'

Sylvie took a sharp breath through her teeth. 'You murderer!' she screamed. 'You killed him. You killed *Monsieur le lapin!* You just looked at

29

him, and killed him! What did you do, what did you do? You killed him.'

'No, no I didn't,' Nell countered.

Sylvie picked up the trug, scattering carrots, and hurled it at her. When Nell ducked and it hit the wall behind her, Sylvie lunged forward and smartly slapped her face.

'Don't come near me again. I don't know why you came here. I don't want you here. Get away, don't even look at him. Look what you've done!'

Eyes watering, her cheek burning, Nell turned, bumping into Auntie Beth, who was followed by a panting Adele. Auntie Beth brushed past her and gathered Sylvie up in her arms, planting kisses all over her head.

'*Oh, ma chère, ma chère.*'

Choking on her tears, her mouth pressed to her mother's shoulder, Sylvie cried, 'She killed him, she killed him!'

Auntie Beth swept her hands over her daughter's forehead as if to iron out the agony. She looked over Sylvie's head and gave Nell a dark stare. She gave her a quick and critical shake of her head. But all Nell could think of was how her mother never held her in that way, or in any way at all.

Nell watched from the landing window as Uncle Claude brought out the small wooden coffin containing the body of *Monsieur le lapin*, which he had spent a whole day making in Tatillon's stable. Sylvie clung to her mother's sleeve, wiping her tears, as the box – complete with dovetail joints – was placed in a hole dug behind the bean frames.

Adele was standing to one side, looking bemused, while the dark heads of Estella and Edmund bobbed up and down above the high garden wall. Nell could see, from the landing window, that they did indeed have a ladder and were taking it in turns.

They saw her at the window and Nell excitedly exchanged their waves, bubbling with giggles. She put her palms above her head to indicate bunny ears but stopped abruptly when Adele sent a frozen glare up from the garden. Adele was trying not to laugh.

Within days, Uncle Claude bought Sylvie two new baby rabbits; they were duly installed in Ullis's stable. At the quiet breakfast table the next morning, Nell sat alone with Sylvie, who was spreading thick butter over a chunk of bread.

Her cousin glanced slyly at her. 'So, do you want to see my rabbits, then? Do you want to stroke them, cuddle them?'

'Oh ... yes. I do.' Nell was confused and re-lieved. She brightened. 'They're babies still, aren't they? Are they very sweet?'

Sylvie shrugged and sank her teeth into the bread.

The door opened and Auntie Beth came in arm in arm with Uncle Claude. They poured their coffee, opened their newspapers and ate in silence.

'*Maman*,' said Sylvie.

'What is it?'

'*Maman*, Nell wants to see the rabbits. She wants to hold them. She told me, she wants to pick them up and squeeze them.'

Auntie Beth's newspaper crumpled with a crunching noise. 'What? Oh, no. Not at all. No.'

Uncle Claude looked befuddled and bored, and snapped his paper to shield his face.

'It won't be safe for them, will it, *Maman?* Nell is not safe with them,' Sylvie insisted. 'Isn't that right, *Maman? Papa?*'

But her parents had stopped listening to her and returned to their newspapers. Sylvie sank her little white teeth into the crust and chewed laboriously, fixing Nell with a hateful stare.

Nell's morning cup of chocolate clattered back into its saucer. The cold feeling returned, fingers dragging at her stomach. She felt queasy, belittled and as unwelcome as the cuckoo in Lednor woods.

The weather in Normandy held throughout August and grew hotter, clinging to Nell's limbs and the back of her neck with a sultry embrace. She circled Sylvie, kept out of her way. She rode the spare bike alone in the cool early morning through the village and out to the rolling, impossibly green fields where creamy-brown cows lumbered peacefully and stared at her with luminous eyes. She read her book in the deep-green shade of the bean frames in the garden before noon and ate in unbearable silence at the table, politely, just as Mother and Dad would have wished. And then she endured afternoons cloistered in her stifling bedroom for *le petit sommeil* – supposedly sleeping.

The days dragged on like this until, one early

evening, Auntie Beth called Nell and Sylvie down to the salon after *dîner*. She sighed up at them from her newspaper, appraising them over the rims of her reading glasses, making Nell's skin prickle with discomfort. Beth told them to stop their sniping and just be friends, for goodness' sake.

Beside her, Nell could sense Sylvie bristling; she could feel the buzzing of her protestation and her suffocated anger. But her cousin mumbled obediently, '*Oui, Maman,*' scuffing at the carpet with the toe of her shoe.

Auntie Beth threw a silent demand at Nell who also nervously uttered her compliance.

'Go out for a walk together before bedtime. Get out of my sight,' said Beth, but smiling a kind smile. 'You girls can't stay cooped up in the house all day long.'

Nell wanted to correct her, and tell her that, actually, she managed to escape the house every day. But she lost her confidence beneath the onslaught of her aunt's harrying.

'You girls need more exercise. And it will be better for you, in the cool evening air. But don't go too far, stay on the pavements, don't go near the boats and don't annoy the fishermen. Half an hour. Now, go on with you.'

Nell did not need to be told twice. She ran, released, down the hallway, hauled open the great front door and scooted across the court-yard. But Sylvie soon caught up with her, and rapped her hard between the shoulder blades just as she reached the tall blue gates.

'We're going to the harbour,' she told Nell as

33

she barged through and turned the heavy metal handle.

'But what about what Auntie Beth said. We're not allowed. I want to go out to the woods. Anyway, the harbour stinks. Have you seen what they use for bait? In this heat it will be rotten.' Nell considered the broken crab shells littering the bottom of the fishing boats; the pungent nets tangled in piles; lobster pots reeking.

Sylvie gave her arm a vicious pinch. 'After what happened to *le lapin*, you have to do as I say. Never mind my mother.' Nell rubbed her arm, wincing with delayed pain. Sylvie pushed her through and slammed the gate shut behind them. 'I want to go to the harbour. We haven't time for the woods, you imbecile.'

Nell heard the *mairie* bell toll eight-thirty as she dawdled reluctantly along the narrow pavement, following her cousin, trailing past the high garden walls of Montfleur.

'We *are* devils!' said Sylvie. 'Out so late.'

'But it's still so light,' said Nell, in awe of the sublime evening. She thought it so beautiful that the throbbing in her arm soon faded. She watched swallows swoop and dive in a pearly sky, carousing in little gangs. The stone houses of Montfleur glowed like silver in the soft light. Windows tucked under the eaves of steep roofs were shuttered. Great doors were closed, sheltered courtyards quiet; even the little stream under the stone bridge was drowsy after the heat of the day.

Nell guessed that everyone else was asleep.

'Course they are not,' snapped Sylvie. 'Don't be such an idiot. Ha, see how many English words I

34

know to describe you. All the *other* children might be asleep but *we're* not because we are nearly grown-up, and the adults aren't either. Look over there. There's Madame Androvsky.'

Estella and Edmund's mother was walking along the pavement towards them, her red head-scarf bright in the fading evening. Her dark hair made her face seem paler, as radiant as a bride's. She said good evening, her smile broadening.

Sylvie folded her arms and Nell heard her mutter 'good evening'.

Madame Androvsky continued to smile and speak, although Nell could not grasp all of her gentle, rapid words.

Sylvie retorted, shrugged and pulled Nell on.

'Oh, what did she say?' asked Nell.

'That shouldn't we girls be in bed,' complained Sylvie. 'And I told her to keep her big nose out of it. I told her we were old enough to do whatever we like.'

Nell glanced back and, with a strange sour grinding in her stomach, watched Madame Androvsky hurry across the street with a humble dip to her head.

'Come on, run, and don't tell *Maman* what I said. It's only Madame Androvsky. Don't waste time. We only have half an hour.'

The terracotta-brick church stood at the entrance of the harbour, with curving domed roofs and rounded buttressed walls. Fishing boats, with lights swinging, made their slow way out to sea. Sylvie walked over to the harbour wall and waved at the fishermen.

'*Au revoir, messieurs. Bonne chance ce soir! Bonne*

chance! That man there,' she told Nell, 'on the *Orageux Bleu.* That's Simon. And his mate is Adele's beau. He is very handsome, isn't he? His name is Jean. I often wonder how Adele can have such a handsome boyfriend when she's so fat.'

The light finally, by degrees, started to fade. On the war memorial by the church the stone soldier bowed his head over a list of carved names. The men of Montfleur, Nell read, who fell in the Great War. There weren't that many, perhaps twenty. But for a village this size, Nell pondered, that might be one from each family. She ran her finger over the list. She could not see an Orlande, but there was one name she recognised: Androvsky. Androvsky, Francis.

Sylvie sauntered over and nudged her. 'Don't dawdle, come on. What are you looking at?'

Nell opened her mouth to explain, but her thoughts collided in confused misery.

'My dad was in this war,' she said at last. 'That's why he digs his September Garden. That's why he paints. Why Mother says we need to be careful what we say.'

And that, she thought, is why I don't want to be here. I want to be home.

The hesitant scratching and keening of Sylvie's violin forced Nell to cringe back into her chair in the salon with her fingers in her ears. Above her, the teacher thumped his cane on the floor of the music room, making the salon chandelier quiver.

'Recommence!' came his disembodied bark. 'Start again!'

'Start again? Oh, please no. No more,' Nell

whispered and glanced up to see Adele in the doorway, her face bright with amusement.

'Go and take a walk outside, *ma petite,* where it's more peaceful. And then, later, I'll help you pack your suitcase.'

Nell brightened, casting a happy smile across the room. In two days' time, she'd be on the ferry. In two and a half days' time she might just be home. She thanked Adele and made her quick way along the garden path and out of the back gate, thinking, now that the weather was cooler, she'd go to the harbour and look at the stone soldier one more time. Ignoring the stables, and their forbidden inhabitants, she walked across the yard and around the back of the Androvsky garden wall from where the rhythmic clunk of spade against earth issued. She stopped in her tracks, exhausted with homesickness. In her mind's eye, she saw her father weeding the golden beds in the September Garden. By the time she got home, it would be in all its blazing glory.

Enticed by the sound of laughter, she went over to the garden door and peered round it. Monsieur Androvsky was digging a cabbage, while Estella and Edmund, heads together, squatted beside him squealing at the worms he unearthed. Her French was improving – Mother would be pleased – and she could understand.

Monsieur Androvsky teased his children, telling them they had to put the carrots they had dug up back in the soil. They'd also, he said, have to put the worms back into their holes.

'Take this cabbage to *Maman,* and she will boil it up,' Monsieur Androvsky told Edmund.

'Are you staying for *le déjeuner?*' asked Estella. He said, no, he had to go to work.

The boy and girl chorused their disappointment but Monsieur Androvsky kissed both his children on top of their heads and took up his bicycle. He snapped on his cycle clips.

Estella begged him not to go.

'Do you want a new dress?' he asked her. The girl nodded, her glasses wobbling on her pale cheeks. 'Well, my pupil needs tutoring in maths. And you want a dress. That's why I have to go. You also need new glasses, my girl.'

Monsieur Androvsky wheeled his bike along the path, his fringe of dark hair flopping over his forehead, and spotted Nell. He called hello. He pulled his folded cap out from his top pocket and settled it on his head. His dark eyes in his narrow face glittered at her. Nell suddenly felt ashamed; if she was not allowed to talk to Estella and Edmund, then she was surely not allowed to speak to their father.

'I was just...' she glanced around her '...just looking at the stables. At the signs, I mean. Not actually *in* the stables. I wasn't *in* the stables. I was reading the horses' names...'

'Ah, yes, I remember the horses.' He spoke beautiful English. His smile was bright and attentive. 'They lived here when I was a young man. It was a pleasure to see them every day. Ullis was white,' he told her. 'You English say *grey*, don't you? Tatillon was a deep glistening brown. Like mahogany. They went to Flanders in 1915.'

Something in his voice drew a melancholy line

down her spine. She hesitated, thinking of the stone soldier by the harbour wall. 'Didn't your ... did not someone who ... in your family also...?'

Estella and Edmund ran up the path. The boy accused him, *'Papa,* you have not gone yet.'

Estella wondered if this meant her father was going to stay. She pleaded with him one more time.

Mr Androvsky looked at Nell. 'You're talking of my older brother, Francis. He also went to Flanders. And, just like Ullis and Tatillon, he did not come home.'

Mr Androvsky said goodbye, wheeled his bike across the yard and down the narrow passage-way towards the street.

'Au revoir, Papa!' cried his children.

'Au revoir, mes enfants!'

And their calling continued, repeating, echoing along the passageway, until they could no longer hear each other. Quiet now and subdued, Estella and Edmund said goodbye to Nell, slipped back into their garden and closed the door.

Nell waited a moment and then followed Monsieur Androvsky's tracks, down the passage-way to the street. She caught sight of him at the end of the road, wobbling off on his bike around the corner. She heard him shout goodbye, once more, even though he was out of earshot of his children and they'd never hear him.

1939

Nell

Mollie Garland, standing with hands on hips in the hallway, was furious.

'I told you, midday, Nell. Be back here by midday. How *dare* you behave like this the day our visitor arrives. Are you going to go upstairs and wash and change?'

'It's only cousin Sylvie,' Nell retorted.

'Get up those stairs at once and make yourself presentable.'

Nell shuffled reluctantly up the stairs, glancing down through the banisters to the drawing room where she glimpsed her cousin sitting patiently, knees together, hands folded on lap. Her white socks were pulled up to just below her knees; her patent shoes were prim on the carpet. A year older, Nell thought, and she looked taller, there was more to her; her cheekbones more defined. She looked like she had a bust. Sylvie turned her head away and Nell knew, by the very tilt of her head, that she was pretending not to have heard the telling-off.

Up in the bathroom, squeezing out the flannel, Nell dabbed half-heartedly at the smudges on her face. She had been out on her bike, as usual, and had dawdled all the way home. In the bedroom, where the usually empty twin bed was now made up, ready for her cousin, she changed and found her best blouse, thinking, she still hates me, she still hates me.

'There you are at last,' said her mother downstairs in the hallway. 'Sylvie's in there waiting for you to come and say hello. I've given her some squash. If you want some, you'll have to make your own. Mrs Bunting's busy with the dinner.'

Nell slipped in to the room. The French doors were open to the garden and through them blew the breeze scented by *Boule de Neige* roses. Long slants of sunlight threw rectangles over her mother's Aubusson rug. Occasional tables were polished to the depth of golden syrup by the girl from the village who 'does'. In the silence, a leaf from the dried-flower arrangement in the fireplace fell with a surprisingly loud, crisp sound onto the hearth. Nell peered at her cousin. Sylvie was sitting primly on the sofa, her face concealed by the large glass of squash from which she drank deeply. Nell's eyes rested on the long midnight-black hair held back with an Alice band. In the face of her poised beauty, envy nudged her. She shrugged it off and moved forward across the rug until her favourite photograph of her father on the occasional table came into view. There he was: young and clear-eyed in his old-fashioned uniform. The photograph was brown-tinged, just like the war into which Ullis and Tatillon and Monsieur Androvsky's brother disappeared. The 'hell' her father went through all those years ago was only ever referred to by her mother in hushed whispers. And now, Nell sensed with a creeping discomfort, a new war was spoken of in a fresh urgent way. Only yesterday, she'd heard her father say,

'I can't face another one,' and her mother reply, rather cuttingly, *'You* won't have to.'

Nell watched as Sylvie set the empty glass down on a coaster. For the first time in a whole year, Nell looked into her violet-black eyes.

'Bonjour, Sylvie,' Nell said, queasy again, and awkward.

'I've got to speak English,' Sylvie said, bluntly, 'Maman has warned me. And Auntie Mollie is going to monitor me. So I will be grateful if you don't try to speak French.' Sylvie fixed her with a narrowed stare. 'You were never that good anyway. We all had to make a huge effort to speak English last year, you were so bad.'

Nell said that she thought she'd done all right.

'Not really. Anyway, it helped me to learn better English. More fool you.'

Nell, disgruntled, opened her mouth to respond, but was interrupted by her mother rushing back in.

'What are you two still doing inside on such a lovely day?' Mollie demanded. 'Nell, take Sylvie round the garden. Show her the tree house.'

Sylvie said brightly, 'That sounds like fun, Auntie Mollie.'

'What's for dinner?' Nell asked.

'That's all you ever want to think about – food. Mrs B has told me that the last of her Victoria sponge has disappeared. I think I can take a flying guess who the culprit is. Dinner is a surprise, something special for our visitor's first evening. You girls will have to wait and see.'

Nell led the way down the terrace steps, across the

lawn, past the high wall to the September Garden – there was no way on earth she was going to take Sylvie in there – past her mother's herbaceous borders where lanky hollyhocks were alive with bees, and where Mr Pudifoot, gardener and general handyman, stood leaning on the handle of his fork, listening to birdsong. He doffed his hat to them.

'Afternoon, young ladies. Fine afternoon, innit? Where you off to, then?'

'We're going down to the bourn. We're going to go up in the tree house,' Nell piped up. 'I've got to show her the tree house. This is my cousin Sylvie. She's French.'

'Half French,' snapped Sylvie.

'Welcome to Lednor Bottom, *maddy-mo-selle*,' chuckled Mr Pudifoot. 'Pleased a meet you. You ladies take care. Don't get wet now, French miss. Ha!'

They set off again, following the long path that wound down to the back of the garden.

'Who's that and what did he say?' asked Sylvie.

'That's our gardener, and he has a lovely voice,' Nell said, thinking of Mr Pudifoot and his soft Chilterns twang. 'He's a nice man.'

'A simple man,' said Sylvie.

Nell ignored her. They came to the bourn, which formed the boundary of the back garden where silvery willows overhung the water, and rushes created a spiky margin. Pebbles under the clear current made the water burble and sing, made it froth and bubble. Long weeds streamed under its surface like green hair. Watercress choked the flow further upstream and occasion-

46

ally Nell would spot the heron stalking the stiff velvety-brown heads of the bullrushes. Often, ducks would quack their way through the current and, once or twice in springtime, they were rewarded with a family of swans nosing against the flow.

'Why don't you call it a river? Or a stream?' demanded Sylvie, standing back from the water's edge as if she was compelled by Mr Pudifoot's warning.

'Because it's a bourn. And a bourn is a chalk stream,' said Nell, feeling momentarily superior. She peered down. A school of tiny brown minnows froze in the shallows when her shadow fell over the water. 'The water comes down from the chalk in the hills to join the Chess in the valley. It rises in the winter. Some summers, this is just a dry bed. You only get bourns in the Chilterns.'

Sylvie wondered what on earth they were going to do next, her face pouting with boredom.

Nell turned to the biggest willow and reached up for a rope hanging from a branch that stooped over the water. She pulled, and a rope ladder unfolded down the trunk.

'We're going to climb up here.'

'It's not very ladylike,' complained Sylvie. 'I'll ruin my shoes.'

'Take them off, then.'

Sylvie unbuckled her patent shoes, rolled off her socks and stuffed them neatly inside. She lined them up at the base of the willow trunk. Nell, not bothering to undo her sandals, pulled them off with her socks in one go and left them where they fell.

'Come on, then,' Nell said, folding her bare toes around the first rung. 'Follow me.'

When she got halfway up she felt Sylvie's weight pulling on the bottom of the rope ladder, making it swing and crash back against the trunk.

'Ouch! *Merde*,' swore Sylvie below her.

Suppressing her desire to laugh, Nell climbed quickly through the willow boughs. She eased herself up into the tree house set into a crook where the trunk split into two. The ceiling was too low to stand up. When her father built it he had miscalculated and was loath to cut away any more branches, leaving it with Lilliputian dimensions.

It will be fine, he had told her. It's only meant for children. Grown-ups not allowed.

Nell wondered for how many more years she would be able to squeeze inside. She sat down and shuffled across the floor to the window – little more than a gap in the wall of rough boards. From her perch, Nell could see clearly across the garden and towards the back of the house. Mr Pudifoot was wiping his forehead with his handkerchief. She spotted Mrs Bunting, cook and housekeeper, flinging some potato peelings onto the compost heap. Through the french windows, she saw her mother, in short-sleeved blouse and wide linen trousers, walk across the Aubusson rug with the folded *Times* and sit in an armchair out of sight. Only her long crossed legs were visible. Now and again a leg bounced, the ankle circling. From below, Nell heard Sylvie puffing and straining, muttering on the swinging rope ladder.

'Not long now.' Nell called encouragement over her shoulder. 'Nearly there.'

She turned again to the house and saw that the window of her father's study was still open. In the dimness of the room behind it she could just make him out, turning the dial on his radio set. He sat by the window listening and shaking his head. Nell watched him light a cigarette and smoke it as if it was the same as breathing.

Sylvie rolled into the tree house, exclaiming in surprise that she'd made it.

Nell was surprised by the pleasant expression – she couldn't really call it a smile, more of a glow of triumph – on her cousin's face.

'So, now we're up here,' said Sylvie, dabbing her glistening forehead with a lace-edged handkerchief. 'What on God's earth do we do?'

'We could play cat's cradle,' Nell said, reaching for the old biscuit tin in the corner where the pitched roof touched the floor. She fished out a piece of knotted wool.

Sylvie crowed, 'I am not a baby. I am sixteen.'

'Well, we can spy on my parents.'

Sylvie said that that was more like it.

The girls knelt at the squat window and peered through the canopy of leaves.

'What does Uncle Marcus do all day, up there in his room?' asked Sylvie.

'He paints,' said Nell, 'and listens to music. He has exhibitions. He has sold his paintings. There was even one up in London. And when he's not painting he tends the September Garden.'

'The what? What do you mean?'

'Shush, Mother's coming out.'

49

Mollie walked over to the herbaceous beds.

'Mr Pudifoot,' Nell heard her call, 'Will you make a start on the ivy. It's in a dreadful state.'

Nell glanced up and saw her father look out of his window at the sound of her voice. He pondered over his cigarette, then turned and switched off the radio.

'Your parents are strange,' mused Sylvie, sitting up and rubbing her knees where the wooden floor had embedded marks in her flesh. 'Whenever *my* parents are at home, when sometimes *Papa* is home early from work, they go to their room together. If I'm at home, on school holiday, or whatever, they send me out to the shops with Adele.'

'My parents don't have a room together.'

'How do they make babies, then?'

Nell shrugged, loath to admit she did not quite understand.

'Do you still have to have "the little sleep"?' she asked.

Sylvie told her that was an idiotic question. 'Ice-cold English,' she muttered and glanced back out through the branches. 'My *papa* says your *papa* is soft in the head.'

'Soft? Oh no,' said Nell, bristling in defence. 'He is very clever. He has a *condition*. He is *shocked*.'

'Shell-shocked do you mean? Don't they say there's going to be *another* war?'

Nell felt a sudden cramp of fear. She picked at a loose piece of bark with her fingernail.

'Anyway, who knows. Only those grown-ups know,' Sylvie went on. 'We just have to do what

50

we're told. Don't you hate that? The grown-ups tell us what to do. Even when they're stupid, they still rule everything...'

Suddenly there was a terrific clanging sound coming from the house. Mrs Bunting was standing outside the kitchen door banging a wooden spoon on a saucepan.

'*Merde!* What on earth...?'

'Dinner time,' said Nell.

The girls ran barefoot across the lawn until Sylvie suddenly stopped and, chastising herself, sat down to put on her socks and shoes.

Nell waited for her, wriggling her dirty toes in the grass.

'I must be ladylike at all times,' said Sylvie. '*Bien élevée.* That's what I must be – and so you should too.'

Nell ignored her. She was hungry. The smell of Mrs Bunting's dinner wafted from the dining room.

As they walked into the room, hands washed and hair brushed, her father, already seated at the table, was saying, '...the belligerent madman is not giving up on Poland. Have you heard what he's done with Danzig? He'll want France next, you'll see...'

Mollie suddenly hissed, 'Marcus! The girls!'

Marcus Garland turned round in his chair with his particular false gaiety and cried, 'Well, well. *Ma petite nièce. Comment vas-tu?*'

Nell broke in, 'She's not allowed to speak French. Auntie Beth said so.'

'There's no need to interrupt, Nell,' said her mother, 'while your father is talking.'

51

'That's all right,' said Sylvie sweetly, sitting at the table, in the centre of which stood a steaming pie, and shaking out her napkin. 'I'll speak French with you, Uncle Marcus, if you like. It's been a long time since I've seen you. Don't you think I've grown?'

Nell, her eyes fixed on the tiny breasts swelling under Sylvie's blouse, began to giggle.

'That's enough, Nell. Remember your manners,' said Mollie, pulling the pie towards her and brandishing a serving spoon. 'Now, Sylvie, I hope you are hungry, for we have the best of Mrs Bunting's culinary efforts before us. Well, the best of her weekday fare, anyway. Marcus, the plates?'

'Now, what would you girls like to do this summer?' asked Nell's father. 'There may be a play up in town you'd like to see.'

Nell turned to Sylvie. 'When he says *town*, he means *London*.'

Her mother said quietly that in the circumstances, perhaps a trip to London might not be a good idea. They'd have to wait and see.

'Because of the belligerent madman?' asked Sylvie with a glitter of defiance.

'Only pleasant talk at the dinner table, please, Sylvie.' Nell's mother cut into the pie and spooned the slivers of meat dotted with carrot chunks onto a plate and topped it with a slice of crust. 'Here you are, dear. Do help yourself to vegetables.'

Sylvie waited politely while the other plates were filled and passed around. Mollie poured water into the girls' glasses, and then splashed wine into hers and her husband's.

Looking satisfied, Sylvie forked a morsel of meat into her mouth and delicately chewed.

'Oh, my favourite,' announced Nell as she cut through the crust on her plate.

'Mmmm, it is lovely. What is it?' asked Sylvie.

'Rabbit pie,' said Mollie.

Sylvie's shriek was eclipsed by the crash of her plate as she upended it and it splintered on the floor. Gravy splashed up her socks. Expletives flew from her mouth.

'You did it on purpose!' Sylvie screamed. 'You spiteful, *nasty*...!'

Nell covered her mouth with her hand to muffle her giggle of shock.

Marcus grabbed his wine glass and pulled it out of reach of Sylvie's flaying hands.

'Well, really,' exclaimed Mollie, her fork stopped halfway to her mouth. 'Whatever's the matter?'

Sylvie's dark eyes, bright with tears, flashed venom. 'My rabbit. She killed my rabbit. And now you make me eat a rabbit! How could you! You ice-cold English *bastards!*'

With a throaty sob she turned, grinding cooked rabbit flesh into the carpet with her heel, and fled from the room.

After a moment, Marcus cleared his throat and said quietly, 'I'm not one to profess to being an expert at French, but...'

Mollie took a great gulp of wine.

Nell lifted her fork, not wanting to let any of her favourite meal go cold and said, 'Yes, Dad, I don't think that was very ladylike, do you?'

Far into the evening, Sylvie wept, her eyes swollen, her nose the colour of Marcus's red madder paint. Nell, from her own bed, watched across the lino bedroom floor, with the knotted, circular, wool rug dead centre, as her mother knelt by the head of Sylvie's bed. Mollie smoothed her niece's hair over her forehead. She never does that for me, thought Nell, even when I'm being sick. Dad always looks after me, and gets me a bowl.

'Come now, Sylvie. No more tears,' said Mollie, trying her best to sound soothing.

'I don't like it here. I don't like *her!* I've *never* liked her.'

Nell cringed and pushed her head under the pillow.

'Try to sleep and you'll feel better in the morning,' Mollie sighed.

'Bring Uncle Marcus in,' demanded Sylvie. 'He should tell Nell off.'

Mollie said, 'Uncle Marcus is indisposed.'

Probably, thought Nell, with his head under *his* pillow.

Mollie tried again, reminding her wearily that it was getting late. She reached out and switched off the bedside lamp.

In the now darkened room, Nell saw that the moon'd risen, the big, white, summer moon, and it was sending a silver pathway across her bed.

Sylvie relented. She snuffled, blew her nose loudly and turned over to face the wall, muttering in French as her sobs faded.

Nell looked up to see her mother standing over her, her face in shadow but her anger fizzing from her fingertips. The light from the landing behind her made her silhouette enormous.

'You really, *really* should have told us about the rabbit.'

Sylvie

The seagulls' cries were sharp and melancholy over the rooftops and a faint tang of the sea drifted through. Drenched by sleep, her eyes tightly closed, she imagined the gaps in her shutters letting in crooked beams of light. She smelt the lavender-soap scent of her boudoir, fleeting but pungent. Wobbles of sunlight danced across the honey-coloured puzzle of the parquet floor. Occasional muffled footsteps fell along the corridor outside her door. For one clouded, confused moment she was there. Right there. But then, she dropped like a stone back to reality and lay pinned to the spare bed in her cousin's meagre little room.

She had slept for far too long; her face, covered with a fine film of dampness, had sunk into the pillow. Her scalp was soaked with perspiration, her temples ached and her mouth was dry from weeping. She squinted across the room she was resigned to share with Nell for the summer. Where was the lace, the delicacy, the flowers she was used to? The rag rug had seen better days, the grey lino was split here and there, and the crocheted patchwork quilt that Nell boasted she'd made last winter was rumpled at the end of the empty twin bed. And it looked like it would smell of mothballs.

Sylvie fingered the thin cotton sheet and compared it to her lace-edged counterpane. Her insides emptied in loneliness. She begged herself not to think of her mother. She got out of bed and grabbed her silk dressing gown, wrapping it around her nightgown which had been stitched by the nuns of the Abbaye du Mont-Saint-Michel. She sat down at the kidney-shaped dressing table which Uncle Marcus had made in the year after the Great War, Nell had told her proudly. It was a way of keeping himself occupied. He made lots of things, apparently, painted a great deal of pictures, and dug in his September Garden. It was a child-size dressing table, really, and Sylvie's long legs poked through the gap in the seersucker curtain at the front. She knocked her knee and sucked an oath through her teeth.

The mirror was foxed around its edges. It could do with a polish, she thought as she leant forward.

'*Zut,*' she whispered, staring at her puffy eyes and crumpled skin. Her pillow – rough linen, not the fine silk cotton she was used to – had marked her cheeks and forehead like a road map of Normandy.

Tears returned to singe her eyes. How could they? How could they make her eat *lapin?* Nell knew. And Nell had *laughed.*

Sylvie brushed furiously at her hair and reached for her pink ribbon to make a ponytail. *Maman* said her hair was as dark and as glossy as the midnight hour. *Papa* said so also. *Maman* said that that particular shade of ribbon contrasted so

56

beautifully with the colour of her hair. She shook her head, whipping the sleek lock of hair over her shoulder, irritated now by the thought of her mother and the way she said things. Irritated by her ineffectual presence.

As Sylvie fumbled with angry fingers at the ribbon, retying it tight and low at the nape of her neck, she heard her uncle and cousin's voices lifting from the hallway below. The morning was moving on without her, and she wanted to be part of it.

Her suitcase was on the floor, its open lid resting against the wall, her clothes still unpacked. Adele would have sorted her out by now. Adele would have hung her clothes, pressed her clothes. Folded them neatly in drawers. She knelt to extract her underwear, summer dirndl skirt and third-best blouse, her stomach empty and yawning with hunger. She'd eaten just one mouthful of rabbit flesh many hours before.

At last presentable, Sylvie left the bedroom and quietly walked along the landing floor, loose boards heaving under her feet, towards the sunlit well of the stairs. She stopped. She could see the top of Nell's curly head below her in the hallway. Her cousin was speaking excitedly as Uncle Marcus, in tweeds and a jacket with leather patches on the elbows, packed his knapsack by the front door, saying, 'Pencil, notepad, field glasses, flask.'

'Oh Dad, you're going birdwatching.' Nell was particularly bouncy. 'Can I come? Please, Dad. I want to see if we find the yellow bird again. Do you remember, last year I saw it? Maybe we'll see it again.'

Uncle Marcus told Nell, 'I overslept. Should have been out hours ago. Where's Sylvie?'

Sylvie got back into the shadow of the landing, suddenly, inexplicably desperate to melt away.

Nell mumbled something about her, surely, still being asleep.

'We can't go without her,' said Uncle Marcus, 'she'll be upset. Even *more* upset. You better stay here and wait for her to get up.'

Sylvie's throat contracted at his kindness. Uncle Marcus, as lean and wiry as a willow osier, was kneeling down and checking his knapsack on the floor. What slender wrists he has, thought Sylvie, for a man. She thought of her father and his paunch and his drooping moustache, his ruddy nose. He had particularly fat wrists.

'Will you take your rain thingy?' Nell was asking, extracting a green rubber jacket, crumpled and stiff, from the hall cupboard.

'No thank you, Nell. It isn't going to rain. Now give me a smile, and hand me my book of British birds. There, look, on the hall table. Now go and see if Sylvie wants some breakfast. I hear Mrs Bunting has some duck eggs.'

'Don't want duck eggs.'

But I *love* duck eggs, thought Sylvie, swallowing hard on a twist of hunger.

Sylvie ate her breakfast alone at the kitchen table. Mrs Bunting had left out dry toast and a dab of jam. Not a duck egg in sight. Afterwards she went into the drawing room where her auntie was taking her morning coffee.

'Ah, there you are. Go and find Nell,' said

Mollie, barely glancing up from *The Times*. 'I think she's sulking in the tree house.'

'I'd rather sit in here with you and read the paper...' Sylvie began, liking the grown-up scent of the coffee, the sedate rustle of the newspaper. She often sat with *Maman* on quiet mornings, just like this, when *Papa* was on his shift at the gendarmerie. Just the two of them.

'Nonsense, I won't have *two* girls sulking. And anyway, it's all rather grim today...' Mollie folded the paper and looked up at Sylvie. 'Have you breakfasted?'

'*Oui* – ah, yes.'

'Well, get yourself outside into the sunshine. If Uncle Marcus had had his wits about him he'd have got you girls up early with the lark and taken you with him. As it is, he is very self-absorbed these days.'

How curiously like her mother Auntie Mollie was, Sylvie thought. And yet, at the same time, so very different. Yes, they were both slender and long-limbed, and yet her own mother's attractiveness was hidden behind large aprons, severely tied-back hair and stout shoes. Auntie Mollie's allure was blatant, gorgeous and imperious.

Sylvie wandered out through the french windows and across the lawn. A warm and pleasant odour emanated from Mr Pudifoot's herbaceous beds where bees were congregating in the morning sun. She was conscious that Nell would have spied her already from the tree house and was possibly descending the rope ladder, to escape and vanish for the rest of the day. She wouldn't blame her after the names she called her yesterday.

But to her surprise, when she reached the willow tree, her cousin's sandals and socks were still there in an untidy telltale heap on the ground.

She grasped the rope ladder and pulled herself up, relishing the pleasure of suddenly getting the hang of it. Nell was lounging on an old mildew-reeking eiderdown laid across the floorboards reading *Adventures of the Little Wooden Horse*. At Sylvie's sudden, stealthy approach, Nell turned on her, her green eyes like shards of glass, and the book was swiftly hidden under a fold in the quilt.

Ducking her head and crawling into a sitting position, Sylvie brightly said hello and asked her what she was hiding. She wanted to forget her rage, forget the rabbit pie. She was tired of being angry and so out of place.

'Aren't you a bit old for it?' Sylvie observed, moving closer, trying to be friends. 'Isn't it a children's book?'

Nell retorted that she liked it, that she read it over and over again. And, anyway, it was none of Sylvie's business.

'Even though you know what's going to happen?'

Nell tilted her chin, her innocence brisk and pert. 'I like to know what's going to happen. I like the way the little horse keeps trundling on even when he goes down the mine and the children try to drown him. Even when his wheels fall off. I want to write about a horse one day. Like the horses who used to live in the stables behind your house.'

Sylvie told her that she had never really

thought about them and, anyway, weren't they dead? Then, unable to stop herself, boasted, 'I've read *Pride and Prejudice* and I'm now on *Rebecca* – in *English*.'

'Well, I will be soon. If Mother can't find her old copies, then Dad is going to borrow them for me from the library.'

Sylvie, weary of competition, tried for something more cordial and told Nell she was hungry. Without a word, her cousin reached over to draw out a biscuit tin from under the tree house eaves. She popped the lid off and Sylvie peered in, catching a peculiar dusty, sweet smell. Among her cousin's treasure – jacks, tiddly winks, the cat's cradle string from yesterday, plus some scurrying woodlice and a transparent dead spider – was a haul of toffees.

'I stole these from Dad ages ago. He's never noticed.'

They certainly had been in there a long time. Some of them were fused together. Nell snatched one up and began to unwrap it. Sylvie copied her, peeling with fingernails at the sticky paper, popping one after the other into her mouth until the sugar made her giddy.

Digging toffee out of her back teeth, Nell asked her if she was homesick.

'That's a stupid question.' Sylvie watched the flickering willow leaves surrounding the tree house. She liked the way the branches seemed to hold her in a haphazard yet sturdy embrace. At that moment, she knew, her mother should have come with her.

Nell said that she hated staying in Montfleur.

'And I hate it here,' Sylvie snapped back.

The sun came out then and the tree house was dazzled suddenly with droplets of yellow light, vibrating through the leaves. Sylvie could hear the bourn splashing and bubbling below. It rested on her ears, settled her.

'But it feels good up here in the tree house,' she ventured, confused and hesitating over the truth.

'Well, I liked it a *little bit* by the harbour,' Nell conceded. 'The church and the statue. So we're even, then.'

She put the lid back on the tin and reached for an exercise book with curling pages and ink stains on its cover.

'I want to write in my diary now,' she declared, fishing a pen out of her pocket.

'What will you write about?'

Nell supposed that she might write about the horses.

'How can you, when you didn't even know them?'

Nell told her to not be so nosey. Sylvie recoiled and her anger bubbled. Unlike their mothers' similarities, she decided, Nell was *completely* different to her. Nell did not know she was pretty. Nell did not care. Her hair was so very curly and everyone loved those curls. They would never be alike, they would never be friends.

'I'm going back down,' Sylvie said, shuffling awkwardly to the top of the rope ladder.

Nell immediately brightened, not bothering to rein in her relief. 'Take the *Little Wooden Horse* if you like.'

Sylvie took the book and withdrew in silence.

As she inched her way down the rope ladder, the bourn chattered below and the breeze twitched her hair. She held on tightly to the rungs and felt her body floating in a restless limbo. When the ladder swung and she grazed her knee on the bark she barely felt the sting of it.

She sat down at the bottom of the tree and opened the first page of Nell's book.

'Tatty old thing,' she muttered.

Years before, Nell had written her name in large looping letters, *Nell M. Garland, aged 9.* Her book. Slowly, with great care, Sylvie began to tear up the book, page by page, and scattered the pieces into the bourn.

Long weeks passed at Lednor Bottom. Long weeks of sunshine and showers. Time was drawing on and Sylvie noticed a gentle slipping of the sun. The season was changing, the light had altered a degree, slanting golden yellow over the front of the house. By now, she should have been home. By now she should have crossed the water on a cross-Channel steamer. There should have been a great expanse of choppy grey water between her and Lednor, between her and Nell; a great distance between their squabbles and spats. But the letter that arrived last week from her mother changed everything.

...Sylvie, ma chère, children are being evacuated from Paris, the whole of France is in turmoil. Your father and I feel it's just not safe for you to travel back home. Who knows what the ports will be like, what the state of the roads will be? Stay with Auntie Mollie, and we'll think of something, ma chérie ...

we miss you so dreadfully.

Next week, she and Nell would be at school together. She would be sitting in an English classroom, with English girls, and all because the Germans were getting *tetchy*, as Uncle Marcus put it.

The doves were purring contentedly, obliviously, on the cote. She counted the windows along the front of the house, all with their blackout curtains. It had taken a week to do; even Uncle Marcus had got out his stepladder, hammer and tacks in the end because Mr Pudifoot couldn't do it all himself. Uncle Marcus's involvement had saved the day and made it all far less boring for everyone. A few fractious words from Auntie Mollie, but that was to be expected. Each and every pane was crisscrossed with paper strips; that had been yesterday's task. The house now had a dismal, patched face.

Amid the languid morning, she heard the clatter of pans from the kitchen. Mrs Bunting had started a roast dinner. She thought of Adele's deep, rich pork casseroles, laced with cream and cider; the fish that Jean brought to the house, which Adele sprinkled with tarragon; the sweet butter her mother made. She thought her stomach would split open with longing.

Spotting Uncle Marcus and Auntie Mollie through the open dining room window, lingering over breakfast, Sylvie tapped on the pane and gave a feeble wave. Uncle Marcus came to the casement. Auntie Mollie was hunched close to the wireless, her manicured fingertips tenderly on the dial.

'How are you this morning, Sylvie?' he asked,

wiping toast crumbs from his fingers, his ear still cocked to the clipped tones of the announcer on the radio behind him.

Please don't ask me, she thought. She told him she missed home. But, really, all she could think about was her mother.

'You're bound to,' he said, cheerfully, as if he had barely heard her. 'It's all very worrying, isn't it, but you'll be safe with us here.'

'But, Uncle Marcus, is *Maman* safe...?'

'What's that?' He was distracted.

Auntie Mollie cried out, 'Marcus, quickly! It's Chamberlain.'

Marcus turned abruptly away from her.

Sylvie stood open-mouthed, insulted, for a moment but then hurried around and through the front door nearly bumping into Nell and Mrs Bunting who were also darting in from kitchen to dining room, drawn by Auntie Mollie's shouting.

The radiogram crackled. And the newscaster spoke his grave, measured words.

Mrs Bunting backed into the corner, her face wide with shock. Mr Pudifoot, in his green gardening overalls, came in and stood to attention by the dining table, his chin tilted as if he was on parade. Nell impatiently jiggled on the spot. Sylvie, sensing the seriousness, held her breath and listened.

'...*now at war with Germany,*' came the voice from the radio, small and tinny in the hushed silence of the room. '*We are ready.*'

'By golly we are,' Auntie Mollie said stoutly. 'No more shilly-shallying around. This is it.'

The room suddenly seemed darker, as if the sun

65

was snuffed out. Sylvie pondered on how the paper strips on the windows blocked so much light. Then the words from the radio sank deeper. Her uncle sat down as if suddenly exhausted, drooping over the table, shoulders hunched.

'Not again,' he muttered. 'Here we go again.'

Mr Pudifoot cleared his throat. 'National honour is upheld at last,' he announced curtly. 'We'll show the Bosch. They can't do it again.'

'Looks like they'll give it a bloody good try,' replied Mrs Bunting, rolling her forearms in and out of her apron.

Sylvie looked from one perturbed face to another and a bewildering wave swung through her body, making her dizzy. She fought it hard but it beat her, made her cry. Uncle Marcus got up from the table and walked over to her to put his arm around her shoulder.

'What does it mean? What does it mean for *Maman* and *me?*' Sylvie cried, her sobs muffled by her uncle's shirtsleeve.

'Oh dear, dear,' muttered Auntie Mollie, biting the corner of her handkerchief. 'What will they *do?*'

'Who?' Nell piped up. 'Who, Mother, what will *who* do?'

'Uncle Claude and Auntie Beth, of course. Oh my God, my poor Beth. War in Europe *again*. It's too bloody for words.'

'Really, Mollie,' Uncle Marcus barked. 'Keep a lid on it! For Sylvie's sake.'

The beast of reality bit Sylvie, suddenly, with brutality. Her mother was so far away, in that instance, so out of her reach, that she couldn't re-

66

member what her face looked like. Panic gripped her, like a cramp. She should have come with her.

'She should have come with me,' she said out loud, but no one heard her.

'Well,' Mr Pudifoot boomed, making her jump. 'I'm going straight out there to turn those beds over. Got to keep myself busy. We've all got to.' He slung his cap back onto his head. 'Either that or we'll all go raving mad.'

Sylvie took a breath. There was only one way to fight this, she decided. She would harden her skin, keep herself upright, fix a smile firmly on her face.

Nell drew close to her and put her hand on her arm, but Sylvie couldn't bear to look at her. She knew her face would be sweet and forgiving, despite everything. She resolved that she would change; she would try hard, try especially hard to be her friend. She thought of the *Little Wooden Horse* and the way Nell told her that he'd kept trundling on through adversity, through terrible things. But of course, she hadn't read the damn book. She'd ripped it to shreds.

Nell

Her mother stood in front of the hallway mirror, applying red lipstick. She perched her best hat, the one she wore for shopping in London, over her neatly rolled hair. Tugging at the hem of her jacket, she stepped back to appraise herself.

Nell sat on the bottom stair with Sylvie, thinking that her mother looked just like Rita Hayworth. She asked her where she was going.

'Great Lednor village hall. I am now billeting officer. They are arriving by the trainload at Aylesbury and the buses will be bringing them out to the villages. Lots of them. They've all got to go somewhere.'

'Not here, surely?'

Mollie turned her bright stare on her.

'Yes, *here*, Nell. How can you be so selfish?'

'We have Sylvie,' Nell nudged her cousin. 'She's our evacuee.'

Mollie pouted at herself in the mirror and reminded them that they also had four other empty bedrooms. 'But don't worry, we'll get two nice girls, from Marylebone or Mayfair. Not boys. We don't really want *boys*, do we?'

Nell shrugged. 'But the war only started yesterday.'

Mollie checked her teeth in her compact. 'Yes, and we're all going to have to get used to it. To rally round, aren't we, Sylvie?'

Mollie glanced at her niece and Nell followed suit. Sylvie was miles away, staring beyond the hallway, beyond the house. Nell nudged her and Sylvie seemed to draw herself together with a slow weakling smile.

'That's more like it,' said Mollie. 'Now,' she snapped her handbag shut, 'according to *Public Information Leaflet Number Three*, petrol will be the first thing to be rationed, so I will do my duty and cycle down to the village.'

'In that suit, Mother?' said Nell.

Mollie paused and brushed her hands over the padded shoulders. 'You're right,' she said. 'But we must keep up appearances, even though there's a war on. I'll get Mr Pudifoot to back the car out. Use a bit of petrol. Just this once. This is my national duty, after all.'

The girls had had their tea hours ago and, as evening fell, Nell went up to the bedroom. Outside the open landing window, the birds changed their key, settling down for the night. Sylvie was lying on her side on her bed, chin propped on her palm staring at *Rebecca*. Nell began to sort out a pile of school books.

'Your school had better be nice. They'd better put me in the right class,' said Sylvie, closing the book and throwing it onto the nightstand. 'I've tried to read that page about a dozen times.'

'Are you all right today?'

Sylvie told her to stop asking. 'You're making it worse.'

'It's just a school, an ordinary school. We have to get the early bus from Great Lednor to Aylesbury. You'll be top of the French class, at least.' Nell made a pile of exercise books from last term and began to sharpen her pencils. 'Girls only. I wonder who Mother will bring back from the village hall. What would you prefer?'

'Boys, definitely boys.' Sylvie yawned. 'Then we won't be expected to play with them. And we can flirt with them if they are handsome enough. *Merde*, is that the time? It's getting dark. I don't know how you can see what you are doing.' She reached to put on the lamp.

69

'Sylvie! The blackout!' cried Nell.

'Oh, this is going to be such a bore.' She hauled herself up off the bed to pull the curtains. 'Whatever happens, I want to be home for Christmas. Adele makes the best Christmas dinner ever, with *Maman's* help, and sometimes mine. We have goose. Have you ever tasted goose skin? And Calvados apple sauce. Oh look, Auntie Mollie's coming up the drive.'

The Ford rumbled over the gravel, its dipped headlights two feeble beacons in the near darkness.

'Boys or girls? Boys or girls?' wondered Nell.

Her mother parked the car and emerged, her suit rather crumpled. Then the passenger door opened and both girls gasped in surprise. There was a woman – youngish and bookish – with a drooping hat and saggy skirt. She stopped, perplexed, and gazed up at the front of the house. Nell could see her mouthing as she counted the windows, a hand pressed with surprise over her throat.

Mollie sounded cheery, even though Nell knew she'd be all in. 'Come on, miss. Do come on. Here we are. Meet my husband. Meet the family. Welcome to Lednor.'

The girls hurried downstairs and passed a dented cardboard suitcase, tied with rope, that had been left at the bottom of the stairs. They followed the sound of voices from the drawing room where her father was just getting to his feet to shake hands with the stranger, while Mollie stood next to him, her hand proprietarily on his arm. He towered over the younger woman, who, Nell noticed, almost did a curtsey.

'Ah, and here are the girls,' Marcus said. He introduced them. 'This is Miss Blanford.'

'Please, *Diana*,' said the woman, blushing and flicking her eyes sideways and up to Marcus's face.

'She's the teacher,' announced Mollie, still relishing her billeting officer authority. 'The school has been evacuated from Harrow to Great Lednor. And she is billeted with us. Isn't that nice, girls? Say hello to Miss Blanford.'

'So no boys and no girls,' Nell observed.

'What? Oh, my daughter is so fanciful some-times, Miss Blanford. You might have to ask her to repeat herself many a time before you actually understand her. Head in the clouds. As for my darling niece, Sylvie. She's all rather sad, having to stay here with us. She came over for her summer holiday and now she's our evacuee. Our *other* evacuee.'

Diana Blanford said how very pleased she was to meet them and what lovely girls they were. Her gushing made Nell positively twitch.

Nell appraised her flattish shoes, heavy calves and large behind. She was rather short standing there next to her mother and father. Miss Blanford's pale face, tired and angular but verg-ing on pretty, was framed by a softly dishevelled hairdo of glossy brown hair. Her smile was nervy but her eyes sparkled.

'Oh, you can have the Lavender room then, Miss Blanford,' said Nell. 'That's the nicest room.'

'We'll see about that,' interjected Mollie. 'I was

71

expecting at worst some ruffians from the city so made up bunk beds in the Blue room, but I think things have worked out rather well, haven't they? Ah, here's Mrs Bunting.'

The housekeeper gave Miss Blanford a blunt good evening.

'I hear from Margery Trenton that the children are having the shock of their life,' said Mrs Bunting. 'Some of them have never gone further than ten streets and now they're right out here. Going to have to get used to us and our country ways.'

'Poor lambs,' offered Miss Blanford. 'Some of my children–'

Mollie interrupted, 'I hear that some of them are regular little criminals. Only tonight the Olivers in the village reported shenanigans already with their three from Wembley...'

'And *lice!*' said Mrs Bunting.

Marcus interjected. 'Thank you, Mrs Bunting. Shall we have some tea? Miss Blanford here ... oh sorry ... Diana, will be parched and famished. Maybe even a nightcap, Diana? As for you girls,' he said, 'bedtime.'

Nell pronounced that she wanted to stay up. After all, Miss Blanford was here.

And her mother wearily reminded her, unlit cigarette between her now unrouged lips, that it had been a long day, that they were all very tired.

'Can't we just show miss the Lavender room?' asked Nell.

Mollie conceded with an exhausted shrug that said, 'I'm too beat up to argue with you,' and bent her face to her lighter.

Within moments, the two girls and Miss Blanford stood on the threshold of the best spare room.

'Is this for me? On my own?' The teacher's face billowed out, round and happy, as she stared into the softly lamplit room.

Nell wondered if it was all right for her.

'It's a palace,' she breathed. 'We were warned that we would have to share. That we might be put up in draughty attics, or garrets or suchlike. But this is just heaven.'

Diana Blanford walked over the cream rag rug and sat down on the edge of the bed where the satin eiderdown created a gleaming expanse of luxury in the lamplight. Mrs Bunting came in with a vase of Mr Pudifoot's purple chrysanths and set them down on the side table, next to the wash bowl and jug.

'You are all so very kind.' Miss Blanford's middle seemed to collapse and she looked quite teary. 'It's been a long rotten day. You girls must call me Diana. I insist. And you, Mrs Bunting,' she said, 'what may I call you?'

'Mrs Bunting,' the housekeeper replied.

Diana plucked out her tiny pearl earrings and placed them in the porcelain dish on the bedside table. 'Everything's so pretty,' she yawned and pulled her blouse over her head. 'I'll just change out of these things and be downstairs in a jiffy.'

'Don't you have a dressing gown, miss?' Mrs Bunting asked hurriedly, evidently outraged.

'Why no.'

'If ... if you need more clothes,' said Nell, trying not to look at Diana's bosoms spilling out of her stained bra – such a large chest for such a

73

little woman. 'Miss Trenton might have a pile of jumble. She's the matron at the boys' school.'

'Oh, I wouldn't go anywhere near her jumble,' observed Sylvie dreamily.

Nell, fearful that Diana was going to peel off her brassiere too, grabbed Sylvie's arm and headed for the door.

Bright and early, Nell ate breakfast in the kitchen. The start of school was delayed by one day because of the evacuees' arrival, and the hours lengthened ahead of her like a curving Chiltern lane, enticing and full of mystery.

'Did I hear the kettle? Time for a cup of tea, is it?' Mr Pudifoot was at the back door, slipping off his cap and settling beside Nell at the table. 'Where's our French miss? And where's them refugees?'

'*Evacuees*, Mr Pudifoot,' Mrs Bunting at the range corrected him. 'And *evacuee*, actually. Just one. A lady teacher. Strange sort. Bit over the top if you ask me. Still fast asleep.'

'Strange you say?' Mr Pudifoot said, nudging Nell. 'If she's strange it's cos she's a *stranger*. Make her a boiled egg, Mrs B. Make her feel at home. Perk her up.'

Muttering, Mrs Bunting reached for Miss Blanford's ration book on the dresser.

Nell piped up, 'When are you two going to get married?'

'The cheek of it.' Mrs Bunting tried to look cross but her face turned an extraordinary shade of red as she flicked through the buff empty pages of the ration book as if fascinated.

74

'Lost count the amount of times I've asked 'er,' stated Mr Pudifoot, sipping his tea from his saucer. 'Still, there's always the next time.'

'Oh, I wanted an egg,' said Nell, looking hopefully at Mrs Bunting.

'You'll be lucky, Miss Nell.'

Mollie appeared at the kitchen door, rosy-cheeked and bright-eyed, searching her long dressing gown pockets for her cigarettes. Nell wondered idly if her father had spent the night in her room last night. She always looked vividly happy and beautiful on those rare occasions.

'Morning, all,' said Mollie, languidly lighting a cigarette.

'Sorry to intrude, Mrs Garland, just 'avin me tea,' Mr Pudifoot said.

'Oh, think nothing of it. I'm just desperate for coffee. Anything on the go, Mrs B?'

'There's always *something* on the go.'

Nell saw her throw a whisper of a smile at Mr Pudifoot.

Mr Pudifoot got noisily to his feet and doffed his hat to Mollie. 'That spud bed won't dig itself, Mrs Garland.' And he left with a badly disguised wink in Mrs Bunting's direction.

'Shame about the hollyhocks.' Mollie drifted through and reached for an ashtray from the dresser. 'But that's what this war is all about. Veg has to come first. Oh, and next time you see grouchy Trenton, Mrs Bunting, tell her I've resigned as billeting officer. I'm not putting myself through that again. You can serve me coffee in the drawing room. Where is Miss Blanford? I thought I–'

She was cut short by an inhuman wailing. It pierced the glass in the windows and the plaster in the ceiling and just about penetrated the bones of Nell's skull. She ducked, pressing her hands to her ears.

'Oh, Mother! Dad!' she cried.

'Oh, Christmas!' shrieked Mrs Bunting, grabbing Nell by the arm and tugging her down. 'Quickly under the table. Everyone, quickly. Where's Sylvie?'

Nell ducked under the table, crouching as tight as she could, followed by her mother and Mrs Bunting.

She heard Sylvie call out excitedly, 'Merde! Our first air raid!' as she burst into the kitchen and dived under the table.

Knees and elbows bumped painfully. Nell cracked her head on the underside of the table. Mrs Bunting shuffled her behind towards her, exposing an unflattering glimpse of her white gusset. And all the while, the siren continued its strange unearthly scream.

'I can't get used to this,' uttered Sylvie.

'Heads down, everyone,' cried Mrs Bunting.

Mollie wondered where on earth Marcus was. Then Nell saw, through a gap in the confusion of table legs and bodies, her father, shirtless and in his underpants, with socks and gaiters over tanned spindly legs, squeeze into the cupboard under the stairs, followed by Miss Blanford in a nightie with a threadbare cardigan thrown over the top. They shut the door.

'Are we all here?' asked Mrs Bunting. 'Pudifoot's outside.' She was breathless and more

76

frightened, Nell could sense, than she was letting on. 'Oh, I see Mr Garland and Miss Blanford have used their head. We must get a proper shelter, Mrs Garland. An Anderson for the garden. We must be the last people in the whole of Great Lednor not to have one. Mr P won't mind if we dig a hole in the lawn.'

'Oh, but I will,' muttered Mollie, holding her hands over her ears.

'I thought the war came first over the garden,' Nell observed and her mother hissed at her not to be so pedantic.

'What about the September Garden?' she protested with a trembling voice, her mouth pressed close to her knees. 'Don't let him dig that up.'

'*Merde*, Nell,' Sylvie muttered. 'Your elbow is right in my–'

'Oh, my life, the gas masks!' cried Mrs Bunting in Nell's ear. 'Where are the gas masks?'

Marcus's muffled voice came from the understairs cupboard. 'In the shed, Mrs Bunting. Waiting to be unpacked.'

'And what good is that, Marcus?' said Mollie looking up and knocking her head on the table. 'Christ.'

Silence. The siren ceased, cut off mid wail, but the hollow void it left inside Nell's head was equally alarming.

Birds began singing outside in the garden again and Nell gradually sensed that life was perhaps normal beyond the cramped table, beyond the four walls of the house.

'Where's Mr Pudifoot?' asked Sylvie.

Suddenly, another siren but this time in a

different key.

'The all-clear,' someone said.

Nell peered up to see her father emerge from the cupboard with Diana Blanford, who was pink-faced, her skin exceptionally dewy. Nell thought how straight her nose was; as perfect as the Queen of Diamonds' on her mother's playing cards.

Out in the hallway, Mrs Bunting put down the telephone receiver. 'The Olivers say it was a false alarm. Just testing, evidently.'

Nell thought, but the next one might be real. How long would this go on for? How long were wars, anyway? Her father left her mother at the bottom of the stairs looking frazzled and exasperated, her earlier beauty vanished, while he went upstairs, into his study, and shut the door. At least that was normal.

Mollie threw the teacher, who was loitering in the kitchen doorway, a rather hard look.

'Nell, why don't you show Miss Blanford around Lednor, take her for a walk,' her mother said. 'Go on, both of you. And you, Sylvie. Show her the September Garden.'

'Oh, what fun,' cried Diana, showing symptoms of exaggeration. 'Don't tell me you have a garden for every month of the year?'

Nell patiently explained that all the flowers come out at this time of year. 'My father planted it years ago in the walled garden. He likes to keep himself occupied. It stops the shaking and the—'

Nell was stopped by her mother's headlamp-like glare.

Diana brightened. 'Oh well, show me, you must show me. Mr Garland's very own garden. How very exciting.'

Outside was hushed, the air serenely calm. The teacher gazed around at the towering beeches at the end of the stretch of lawn, the voluminous herbaceous borders along its edges, exclaiming at the size, the beauty, the variety of plants.

Nell pointed out that there was a bourn at the end of the garden and the door, over there to the left, led into the walled garden. But she was loath to take Diana straight there. She felt she had not earned the right to sit and contemplate its golden beauty.

'I wonder where Mr Pudifoot went?' Nell asked, playing for time.

'I think he probably ran off home to his own cottage when the raid started,' said Sylvie.

'I'm to meet this Mr Pudifoot today?' asked Diana.

'If you're lucky, he's our gardener and our handyman. He is part of the furniture, Mother would say.'

As they began to walk across the lawn, Sylvie asked Diana about the school and she told her it was quite a large one, in fact, in the London suburb of Harrow.

'"Metro land" we call it. The children's fathers take the railway every day up to London and back again. What a change for the children to be out in the country. We have a playing field and a park, but of course nothing like you have here. And you girls go into Aylesbury for school? Have they built air raid shelters? They dug ours in our playing field over the summer holidays. Long tunnels where the children can sit in rows. We practised last term. Gas masks and all. The ones who stayed behind will have them to themselves– Oh, is that a pair of feet?'

Nell peered at where Diana's chubby manicured finger indicated and let out a hard shriek. Then she streaked towards the dug-over hollyhock bed. Among the mounds of turned earth and exposed roots, among the fallen flowers, lay Mr Pudifoot, spreadeagled, the toes of his great boots pointing to the sky. His grubby hand clutched the handle of his spade, which lay over the ground, twisting his wrist unnaturally. His eyes were open, staring at the sky.

'Is he asleep?' asked Sylvie, panting up behind her.

'No, I fear he's not,' said Diana Blanford.

Nell felt queasy, looking at the man's contorted hand. 'Mr Pudifoot! Mr Pudifoot! He won't wake up!'

'I think he's dead,' whispered Diana. 'He must be dead. He looks dead.'

Sylvie's scream pierced Nell's ears.

'He can't be,' cried Nell. 'It's Mr Pudifoot!'

Mollie and Mrs Bunting came running from the house.

Nell backed away as Mrs Bunting knelt in the dirt of the flower bed and tenderly touched Mr Pudifoot's forehead.

'Whatever happened, girls?' Mollie asked, her voice tiny and timorous.

'Call the doctor,' the housekeeper sighed. Then she cried out, 'Fetch the doctor. Now!'

Diana turned and ran back to the house.

Mrs Bunting raised her face. It was white, crumpled. Her eyes had disappeared. Her mouth gaped. 'You children. Go away! Get out of here. Go! Go!' she bellowed. 'Please, let my man have some peace!'

Sylvie said, 'Did you see poor Mrs Bunting?'

'What killed him?' asked Nell. 'Nazi bullets? Gas? A bomb?'

Sylvie said, 'There weren't any planes. It was a false alarm.'

'Where are we going?' asked Diana.

They were on the lane by now but shock still pursued Nell with punishing speed.

'Let's go down to the river,' she said, fighting nausea and dismay. 'At least we can paddle. We have stepping stones, and bullrushes and ... Miss Blanford, do you want to paddle?'

The teacher was happy to do anything, anything at all, she said, blowing her nose with a handkerchief damp and screwed up in her pale shaking hand.

Below them lay the flat-bottomed valley, with the River Chess broadening through the shallows and the still water of the ford reflecting the clouds. Beyond, in the water meadows, brown cows languished up to their knees in tall grass. One by one, they raised their chewing faces to observe their approach. Further on up the sides of the valley, golden fields had been shaved to stubble.

'Oh my goodness,' exclaimed Diana. 'A great big eagle.'

'No, it's a kite, miss. They live all over the Chilterns,' Nell corrected her, gazing upwards at the magnificent bird, thinking, but this lady is a teacher. She should know.

'No, it isn't a kite,' Diana said lightly, her voice breaking. 'It doesn't have a string.'

They laughed a little. The kite glided effortlessly on its great red-brown wingspan through the warm air over the valley. Cloud shadows were chasing themselves over the hillside.

'Oh, girls, I must confess, I've hardly ever left my hometown,' announced Miss Blanford, 'and now when I do it's because of the horrible war. I'm in charge of all the pupils, their welfare and everything, and yet I can hardly cope with any of this myself.'

Nell worried that she was going to start crying. Sylvie asked her how old she was.

'Twenty-five,' she replied. 'Not that you're supposed to ask a lady such questions.'

'Do you have a boyfriend? Are you getting married?'

Diana blushed. 'Questions, girls, questions...'

They came to the ford.

'We can do this one of two ways,' decreed Nell. 'We can take the sensible way and cross on the stepping stones. Or take off our shoes and socks and paddle right through. I know what I'm going to do.'

'Me too,' said Diana, slipping off her shoes and reaching under her skirt to unclip her stockings.

'I'm being sensible,' said Sylvie unsurprisingly, and began to pick her way across the stones, her patent shoes as pristine as ever.

Miss Blanford shrieked as she dabbed her toes in the water. 'It's ice-cold!' she cried, laughing. 'Oh my goodness. This is a first for me. Would you ever! This is unbearable, oh goodness. But somehow, rather splendid.'

On the other side of the river, the short willows on the banks grew thicker, the dells deep and secret, the pathways more secluded. Nell guided them, ducking under draping branches, pushing through the green-scented undergrowth of wild flower and reed, avoiding the webs of golden-yellow spiders fat from a summerful of flies. All the time the river sang beside her with a fresh burbling tune.

'The war is far away now,' Nell said as they settled on a grassy bank in the broken shade, under a flickering canopy of willow leaves. Her sick feeling faded as she breathed on sweet river air.

'This is bliss,' sighed Miss Blanford, wriggling her toes. 'What a marvellous place for you girls. Yes, the war all seems such a long way off now.'

And so, thought Nell sadly, is Mr Pudifoot.

Debussy drifted down the stairway from her father's study as Nell walked back into the hall with Sylvie and Diana. She knew each pondering note so well. She headed for the kitchen, hoping for a cup of milk and a biscuit, and stopped on the threshold. There was her mother, her hand on Mrs Bunting's shoulder. Mrs Bunting was sipping a cup of tea, shaking her head, a sort of quivering attacking her plump body.

'Oh, there you are, Nell,' said Mollie, her eyes

dark and unreadable. 'I'm afraid I've got some bad news for you. For you all.' Her tone made Nell uncomfortable, as if she was in some way responsible. 'Mr Pudifoot died, I'm afraid.'

'George, my poor George,' Mrs Bunting sobbed into her hand.

'The doctor's just left,' said Mollie. 'He said he had a bad heart He thinks the siren frightened him. Made him have a seizure.'

'Bloody, *bloody* war!' snapped Mrs Bunting, her sobs bitter. 'He survived the last lot. Was going to do his bit this time round if he could. Now look... What a mess. What a bloody *mess*.'

Upstairs, Marcus turned the volume up and Debussy soared.

'Oh, that blessed music,' cried Mollie, 'It's been non-stop.'

Mrs Bunting looked like she was going to break in two. She declared that she could not bear it. Couldn't he play something else? Better still, nothing at all?

'Go and ask him, Nell,' said Mollie. 'Tell him it's upsetting Mrs Bunting.'

Nell went upstairs, immersed in *'Clair de Lune'*. No more Mr Pudifoot. No more jokes, which weren't actually very funny, but still made her laugh. No more impishness twinkling from his eyes. Where had they taken him? Had they taken off his muddy boots? Had they closed his eyes?

She walked into her father's study. Marcus was painting with a queer energy, absorbed and focused on his canvas. It was a new painting. He had not diluted the colours but was using great daubs of fresh wet paint – crimson and gold – to

84

create a field of wheat dotted with poppies. They were broken and cut down. He jumped when she touched his arm, and Nell was astonished to see tears in his eyes.

'Oh, it's you,' he said.

She went over to the gramophone, eased the volume and lifted the switch so that when the record finished, the needle would return and not start playing again. Finally, the last melancholy piano note faded.

'He was in my regiment,' said Marcus, wiping his brush with a rag. 'Second Battalion, Buckinghamshire Yeomanry. He was Gunner Pudifoot. I was his captain.'

'Did you know his name was George?'

'Of course I bloody did.' Marcus was momentarily angry. He reached out with a finger to the painting and swiped a dab of blood-red paint from it. 'Did you know, Nell, that he loved Mrs Bunting but she married someone else while he was in Flanders?'

Nell, perplexed, asked who did she marry.

Marcus shrugged with a strange comical smile. 'Why, Mr Bunting, of course. But he left her.'

Nell pondered on this, bit her lip and said, 'That's new,' nodding at the painting.

Marcus picked up his paintbrush and executed an exquisite flourish to create yet one more broken ear of wheat. 'New, yes.' He gestured to the painting, to the world outside the window. 'In future, you will find many things are new – for all of us.'

Sylvie

A few weeks ago, the first autumn storm had whipped the leaves from the beeches revealing their skeletons, their true selves. Scraping frost from the inside of the windowpane, Sylvie could see right through the naked branches across the valley to the quiet brown fields on the other side. Mist from the River Chess drifted low along the bottom.

'*Merde,* it's like the outside is on the inside in this house,' she muttered, shivering as she plunged her arms into her cashmere.

When she first arrived at Lednor, the valley had been shielded from her by rich summer-green trees; but now this bare frigid landscape was her winter view. The earth seemed to sink into the peace and serenity of the dead end of the year. She thought of home and the endless impenetrable *bocage* that surrounded Montfleur and guarded it. A sudden uproar from the rooks that circled over the beeches brought her back to Lednor with a start.

Auntie Mollie called up the stairs, 'Time for our walk, Sylvie. Shake a leg!'

Suitably attired – she'd reluctantly borrowed Uncle Marcus's green rubber coat from the hallway cupboard – Sylvie walked with her aunt and cousin, breathing in the new earthy smell of the season. The way through the beech woods was muffled with bracken. Deep-green moss furred the grey trunks and fallen stumps. Her feet snapped on twigs and crunched on beech nuts. Mist was evaporating on branches overhead and drops hit the top of her head with great wet plops.

Auntie Mollie carried her pannier, her finger-tips, it seemed to Sylvie, twitching impatiently for the hunt for mushrooms to start. Nell, also annoyingly eager, hurried off ahead. Sylvie peered into the false green twilight and caught sight of her cousin's curls as she dipped her head to root under ferns, and tenderly part the leaf mould. There was a peace and stillness between the trees. A pheasant coughed in the valley; a wood pigeon brooded up above.

She asked, 'When you were girls, Auntie Mollie, did you and *Maman* go mushrooming together?'

'Oh yes, of course. All through the woods where we lived. Your mother is quite the expert. She knows her fungi like the back of her hand.'

Of course, her mother still is the expert, Sylvie assured herself, even though she is hundreds of miles away across the sea.

'I love it when we go foraging in the *bocage* beyond Montfleur,' Sylvie mused. 'We make a day of it. Just me and *Maman*. Adele packs us a picnic.' She paused, as her happy memories cascaded through her like warm syrup. '*Maman* always has an absolutely wonderful time.'

Her aunt glanced at her with a ghost of a tear in her eye.

'Well, then, let's have a look round here,' she announced heartily, bending to part the under-growth at the base of a large beech trunk. 'There

87

were lots around this tree last year.'

Sylvie squatted down to look, her own tears fogging her eyes, blinding her. 'Look at these beauties, Auntie Moll.'

Her aunt was at her side. 'Oh, oh no, don't touch that. Destroying angel. That one would definitely floor you. Steer well clear.' Mollie paused and twitched her nose much in the way Beth would when she was on the scent. 'Oh, but here, here now. Puffballs. This is better.'

Mollie grasped a white bulbous stem, laid it in her basket and reached back to pull up its group of mates.

'Now this will be lovely, fried up with some butter,' she said, 'with a dash of parsley and even a splash of wine. We'll raid Uncle Marcus's cellar. What a treat. We can have these tonight, with our steamed meat pudding. Oh now, Sylvie... No more tears.'

A heavy, dank feeling wrapped itself around her as her aunt embraced her, crushing the coldness of the rubber jacket to her ribs, so her chill of loneliness reached deeper than ever before.

In the dining room the small stack of coals hissed in the hearth, emitting a peculiar mineral scent. Sylvie, attempting her English homework at the table while the cold autumn evening fell quickly, decided that the warmth of the fire fell woefully short, not like Adele's great roaring applewood blazes. The blackout was down, and the heavy curtains muffled sound, cloistering the room from the outside world. Opposite her, Nell was doing algebra, her hair brightened by the yellow glow of the oil lamp. She needs to grow up, thought Sylvie, sharpening her pencil. She needs to get over the *Little Wooden Horse* and read Jane Austen.

Miss Hull, the English teacher who used the long hooked stick to ease open the classroom windows and also to bash the desks of those girls who did not come up to scratch, had recently pressed on Sylvie a tatty copy of *Persuasion*. She'd also singled her out in front of the whole class to praise her. Sylvie's skin crawled and her eyes smarted at the thought of that particular ordeal.

'B-plus for your English exercise. A for effort,' Miss Hull had announced. 'Girls, I want you all to look to Sylvie Orlande as an inspiration. Never forget how brave Mademoiselle is in these terrifying times.' Miss Hull's bright blue eyes in her weather-tanned face fixed on Sylvie. 'I must say, Orlande, seeing how you have coped with your lessons here, the French education system must be very good indeed.'

'Oh, yes, Miss Hull,' she had replied, nervous in the face of such an onslaught of praise, 'but *Maman* helps me at home.'

Now, trudging through her homework in the Lednor Bottom dining room, the embrace of solitude was complete. She opened her exercise book and stared at the lessons. She struggled to keep her face composed, not wishing to reveal the pain hammering her insides. What was the use of good marks if she couldn't chat with her mother and tell her all about them?

'A letter has arrived for you, Sylvie.' It was Uncle Marcus, making her jump. He had come in, in his slippered feet, and was looking over her shoulder. He drew an envelope out of his waist-coat pocket. 'Your auntie and I took the liberty of opening it when it arrived this morning. We hope you don't mind.'

A rush of joy swept aside her pain. Her mother's handwriting was beautiful, looped and pretty like notes on a sheet of music. It took her straight back to the salon in Montfleur and *Maman* sitting at the secretaire in the corner writing elegant letters to Auntie Mollie and to all her friends. Sylvie ran her fingertip over the inked page as if to stroke her mother's cheek. She imagined her father reading over her mother's shoulder as she wrote, a heavy presence, preening his moustache. She drew a breath and read quickly, glancing at the last line above the love and kisses. Then she started again, slowly this time.

'A trust fund?' she said. 'They're transferring money for me? To Switzerland?'

Nell asked if Sylvie was going to be rich.

'See it as your Christmas present,' said Uncle Marcus, pulling out a chair to sit down next to her. 'The fund will be secure in a Swiss bank. Safe as houses, so they say. Your parents want to make sure that you have everything you need.'

Everything I need? Sylvie thought. How will they know what I need?

There was nothing in the letter from her father, although she could feel him there, like a stain upon the page.

'As from now on we – Auntie Mollie and I – are to be your legal guardians.'

Sylvie looked at her uncle. *'From now on?'* she repeated. 'What do you mean, *"From now on"?'*

'They are being sensible, under the circumstances.'

'But nothing's happened yet,' Nell butted in. 'At school, they're calling it the Phoney War. They said it would be over by Christmas, and it's like it's never even started.'

'Nothing happening, you say?' said Marcus. He unfolded *The Times* that he'd brought in with him and spread it on the table. 'Let me have a bit of a read and I'll see.'

Sylvie neatly folded her mother's letter in its envelope, and tasted the bitter length of the distance between them.

'Miss Hull likes you, Sylvie,' said Nell. 'You're the teacher's pet.'

'So?' said Sylvie, filling her ink pen from the pot of Quink.

'You know she's a lizzie,' Nell whispered across the table.

'Now really, girls,' Marcus said, folding the paper in half. 'Nell, have more respect, I'm surprised at you. I really am. You're sixteen now. Come Easter you'll have taken your exams and left. I expect more from you.'

'It's not fair. Sylvie is leaving school at Christmas.'

'That's because I have a whole year on you.' Sylvie wondered how much money she might be receiving. A drip of an idea spread over her mind, like the ink stains on Nell's exercise books. An idea of being free, independent and alive. Away from her misery? Away from Lednor?

Uncle Marcus said, 'Now, listen to this. We've had our first casualty on the Western Front, a

91

captain...What else...?' he pondered. 'The Finns are resisting the Soviets. Humiliating the Red Army. Canadian troops will soon begin arriving in Britain, to help us. That's good. That's because they are part of ... what, Nell?'

'The *Empire*. Oh Dad, I know *that* much.'

'And ... oh dear, this is not good.' Marcus scanned a short piece of type on page three. 'It says here, girls: "The Nazis are beginning to deport Jewish people from occupied lands." "Resettling", they say.'

Sylvie lifted her head. 'We have Jews next door to us back home. Maman talked about them in her letter.' She unfolded it. 'Where is it...? Ah yes: *Our neighbours have asked us if we can help them come to England ... asked your father for references... I suspect, as your papa is the gendarme, they think he can help...*'

Nell sat up. 'Do they have to leave, too? Mr and Mrs Androvsky? And Estella and Edmund?'

Sylvie glanced at her uncle to see his face close down behind a mask of ill ease.

Nell persisted, 'But what would happen to their cabbages and carrots? And Mr Androvsky's bike?'

'Oh, do grow up, Nell, and behave,' snapped Sylvie. 'What are you going on about? Cabbages and carrots?'

Her uncle interrupted, brightening with forced jollity. 'Now for some good news. You girls will like this, I'd wager: *"Gone with the Wind* opens in Atlanta, Georgia".'

'How wonderful!' cried Sylvie, her spirits rushing to the sky.

'You can go when it opens in Aylesbury.

Auntie Mollie will take you,' said her uncle, 'and I'm sure Diana would like to go, too.'

Miss Blanford had just let herself in at the front door, her footsteps clicking on the parquet. She stood at the threshold of the dining room, untying her woolly scarf.

'Where would I like to go, Marcus?' she asked.

'You've brought the cold in with you, Diana,' he replied, his voice, Sylvie noted, falling down the scale. He spoke to her as if no one else was there.

'We're going to see *Gone with the Wind*,' cried Nell, giggling with the thrill of it. 'Oh look, miss, come and look at the photograph!'

'My, my, how very exciting,' said Diana as she leant over Nell's shoulder and looked at the newspaper story. Her plump hand with its tiny manicured nails resting on the table was perilously close to Uncle Marcus's and Sylvie realised that she was the only one to notice. However, it was far more exciting to think of the film. Her imagination blossomed and turned a joyful corner. She, too, peered at the photograph in the newspaper of the glamorous film premiere in Atlanta, Georgia. The grainy image showed the actresses in lovely gowns, the men in their dinner jackets.

Nell held on to Sylvie's arm tightly; such was the force of her glee that she knew she'd have little bruises there tomorrow.

'Oh look, Sylvie, look at lovely Vivien Leigh. And look at Rhett Butler.'

Sylvie smiled and silently appraised Clark Gable's grin and his wondrous set of teeth, and her desire for freedom made a circle round her heart. It was a whole other world.

Adele

Tuesday was usually her afternoon off. Even so, as a favour to Madame Orlande, she agreed to fetch the fish. As the hall clock tinkled out the afternoon hour of two, she took her coat from the hook in the vestibule and tapped on the salon door.

'That's me done for the day, Madame,' she said, poking her head around. 'Lunch is cleared and the clean sheets are ironed and folded in the linen press. I'm heading off now.'

Sitting by the fireplace where a small fire flickered in the grate, a magazine over her lap, Beth Orlande was startled, shaken from her thoughts. She looked, thought Adele, tiny within the grand, grey proportions of the room. The marble of the fireplace looked as pale and as bruised as the fragile, translucent skin over her cheekbones.

'Oh! Oh yes. Thank you, Adele. Have a nice– Oh, don't forget the *cabillaud*.'

Madame hadn't bothered to light the lamp, Adele noticed, even though the wintry afternoon was darkening already. Inky shadows filled the corners, like strangers waiting for an introduction.

'*Cabillaud*, Madame?' objected Adele. 'Oh, you mean *colin*, don't you?'

'Yes, yes ... whatever you like...' Madame Orlande trailed off, her eyes returning to the

94

page open before her. Adele knew she had not been reading the magazine but blindly turning the pages.

Madame often seemed nervous, Adele decided, and often a little sad. But, since her daughter had been marooned in England, her distraction and her vacancy had become more profound. Even so, thought Adele as she opened the front door onto the cold day, Madame has lived in France for seventeen years and she still gets the word for hake wrong. She was forever mixing her fish up. This irritated Adele and in the village of Mont-fleur, where fish was everyone's way of life, this was unforgivable. Monsieur was no help, teasing Madame whenever she tripped over her sentences, which was often. He was no help at all.

A frigid, solid breeze came straight off *La Manche* and blustered along the streets. As soon as Adele shut the tall blue gates behind her, she felt it hit her cheeks. She wound her scarf tightly, turning up her collar. The stone-paved streets were quiet and bleak. Dried leaves, bowled along by eddies of wind, made a scratching noise on the pavement.

Of course, she didn't mind doing this small errand for Madame. The *Orageux Bleu* would be chugging back into the harbour very soon and Jean would be busying himself with ropes and boxes of fish and tangled nets, and she would gladly watch and wait for him, and collect the fish for her employers' supper. It was peaceful by the water's edge. She went to the harbour and sat down on the bench near the moorings, searching for the boat, for its lantern swinging out at sea in the smoke-coloured dusk. The dark-red stone of the church near the mouth of the harbour stood out against the sky in the fading light, its blush heightened by the deep, cold blue behind it. Water in the harbour was choppy and sloshing; out at sea white horses hurried to shore.

At last the clanging of rigging, like the repeated metallic calling of a seabird, and the boat emerged suddenly from the gloom, labelled by a trail of hungry pewter-coloured gulls.

'*Bonjour, Adele. Bonjour!*' called Jean, at the prow, a silhouette to Adele in the half-light, raising his gloved hand in salute.

Adele felt the relief, always a surprise, settling deep in her belly. Jean had made it home, the *Orageux Bleu* was in safe harbour once more. Simon, his mate, stood at the helm, his feet planted wide as he steered the boat to shore, his cap low over his large nose. He bellowed, 'I like your scarf, mademoiselle! It's a pretty colour. Suits you so well. Is that a new coat?'

'Unlikely, Simon,' she called back, cheerfully. 'Not on my wages!'

'New shoes, then?' he shouted.

'Not a chance.' She laughed, standing up to watch the boat glide slowly to the harbour wall. All of a sudden it was upon her. Jean threw her a coil of rope, which she caught, expertly, and dipped to wind it round the cast-iron mooring. Jean leapt from the boat and was at her side immediately, taking the rope from her, taking up the slack and fixing it tight. They stood facing each other. Adele felt her face break open with her smile. Simon killed the engine and, in the silence that followed, she heard the familiar creaking and bobbing of the boat on the water. Jean's kiss was full and warm on her lips.

'Two hake please, fisherman,' she grinned at him. 'For Monsieur and Madame's supper.'

'Straight off the boat,' Jean said. 'You can't get fresher than that. You do spoil them. Hey, Simon,' he called over his shoulder, 'find us the hake.'

'As if I haven't got enough to do,' Simon muttered playfully and began to look through the boxes. 'You better pay us, mademoiselle,' he teased. 'And pay us soon.'

'Oh, I will,' she laughed. 'I always pay promptly, Jean knows that.'

Simon wrapped the fish in newspaper. A headline, folded now within its creases, had exclaimed of the German advance through Poland. She sat down again, set the parcel by her feet and watched the evening ritual, watched her man at his labour. The rhythm of the work at sea continued on to the land. Nets were hauled ashore and spread to dry. Ropes were coiled neatly, boxes of fish stacked on the quayside. The fishmonger arrived through the dusk on his bike and began to examine their contents. The business began in low voices, prices were uttered, refused and accepted. The scent of the sea tinged the air around her: sweet then sour with every other breath. There was poignancy in the air, an exquisite pause between day and night. Adele shivered and thrust her hands in her pockets.

'Good evening,' Jean said, at last able to rest, to sit beside her on the bench. His knitted gloves were grubby, silvery with scales. He tugged off his

97

cap, stripped off his gloves and ran his fingers through his hair. 'You look sad all of a sudden. What ever is the matter? I've nearly finished for the day. I'm not going to get anything more out of Simon. You should be smiling. What's wrong?'

'Oh nothing. Something ... nothing.' Adele struggled, not wishing to voice her fear. 'It's just the newspaper. The Germans can't come into France, they can't reach Paris, surely? Our army is there. Between us and them. We have the Maginot Line.'

She stated this, believing it. She watched Jean's face and how his eyes ranged across the harbour and stared at the water below them, avoiding her. She knew he was thinking carefully about what he was going to say. 'Even if they do get to Paris,' he said, 'they can't touch us here. It'll take them an age to reach the end of our peninsula. And just across there,' he pointed beyond the harbour wall, 'are our friends.' He put his arm around her shoulder. She sensed the scent of sea spray crusted on his jacket, the chill of the waves in his bones. He kissed the side of her head, through her hair. 'You're not to worry. I am safe from conscription. And so is Simon. They'll always need fishermen. We'll always need fish.'

She glanced at him. Her face felt tender in the cold air. 'Madame says that Monsieur is worried it will be like '14 again,' she said.

'Oh, Monsieur Gendarme has a lot to say about a lot of things, doesn't he? I don't like the way he marches around the village like he owns the place.'

'He ... he just does his duty.' Adele stood up, a

surge of loyalty making her want to break off the conversation. 'I need to get this fish back to Madame. She is cooking tonight. She enjoys taking her turn on my afternoon off. I will help, though,' she added. 'I always do. But first, I must go to the church.'

'I will see you later?'

Adele bent to kiss him and told him of course he would. She looked into his eyes and realised how well she knew him. She adored him.

Simon, his head lit like a halo by the boat's lantern, made kissing noises from the deck of the boat. He took off his cap. 'One for me, Adele, one for me.'

'Not today,' Adele called, laughing lightly. 'You smell of fish.'

'But I always smell of fish.'

She waved goodbye and headed along the harbour, stepping over ropes, skirting piles of nets and stacks of lobster pots grisly with fish bait.

Inside the sweet-scented church, the air was remote from the outside, as still as an underground cavern. Adele crossed herself and bobbed at the altar and then walked to the niche in the wall. She lit a candle for Sylvie and set it in the tray of sand, among the other dozen or so that burnt erratically, sending thin streams of smoke up into the darkness of the vaulted ceiling. She said a silent prayer for Mademoiselle Sylvie; for Jean; for them all.

Back in the warm kitchen, Beth Orlande said, 'Adele, would you be so kind as to make the sauce for me?'

'Of course, Madame.' Adele took up the knife and began to chop the chervil. She found a bunch of dill on the window sill, and a lemon in the pantry.

'This is Monsieur's favourite dish,' Beth told her.

Adele felt obliged to smile. Every time Madame made hake in cream sauce, she told her this wholly unexciting fact, as if announcing it for the first time.

'How's the fishing?' Madame asked as she washed the hake under the tap. 'How is the fisher*man*?'

Adele blushed. 'The *fishing* is good. The fish*monger* was pleased. I think he bought a dozen boxes. I lit a candle, Madame, in the church.'

'A candle for my Sylvie? Thank you.' Her voice had a brittle note. She laid the filleted fish in a dish and washed the blood, scales and stringy gut off her hands. 'It's better that Sylvie is safe in England with my sister. Better for all of us. We're not so worried now we know she will stay there.'

Adele glanced at her employer, thinking how much she was trying to convince herself. She knew Madame missed her daughter. She saw how tired she looked. Her hair, usually rich and dark, looked drab. Grey hairs peppered it. Madame somehow looked hollowed out. Not like me, thought Adele wryly, I have enough flesh for both of us.

'Of course my sister worries about *us*, but I have written and told her not to,' went on Madame. 'She has a lot on her plate. She has an evacuee teacher from London. Bit of a houseful, really.

And they lost their gardener in September. A lovely old retainer. Popped his clogs – just like that, apparently.' She clicked her fingers.

Adele mused over someone's clogs popping, and let her thoughts drift to Sylvie's cousin, pretty little Nell, and the way her hair curled. She cried suddenly, 'Oh, I forgot, Madame. I need to feed the blessed rabbits.'

'Not to worry. The Androvsky children have been round to do it. They enjoy themselves. The sweet little bunnies, they say. They are quite sweet themselves, really, if a little troublesome.' Beth Orlande pointed to the wall that divided the two houses. She lowered her voice. 'Monsieur Androvsky also paid a call this afternoon, asking again – it must be the third time – if Monsieur could provide references so that he, and his family, can leave for England. He thinks that we can simply send him over to Lednor to live with my sister. I suppose they need teachers in England. He thinks that Monsieur has special powers to help him leave the country.' Madame looked insulted. 'I think it's a bit rich, actually. He's not the only one with problems around here.'

Adele murmured that she was right, that they all had their worries.

'My daughter is hundreds of miles away, across the sea. At least *his* children are with him.'

'So they are ... but you know Mademoiselle Sylvie is in a safe ... a *safer* place than those children.'

'But she's not with *me*.'

Adele glanced up to see Madame Orlande's eyes blazing at her.

'If it was that easy to pack up and leave, like

Monsieur Androvsky seems to think it is, then I'd be the first one on a boat out of here,' she cried. 'I want to leave, Adele. I wish *we* could leave. But Monsieur won't. He simply won't desert his post. And the Germans, when they get here...'

'Oh, come on, Madame, have faith.' Adele tried hard to remember what Jean told her.

'*When* they get here, they will have me down as an enemy in an instant. I *am* their enemy,' she whispered, defeated.

Adele saw an instance of terror flash across Madame's face. She stared quickly back into the saucepan, at the creamy sauce flecked with green. She asked, 'How is your sister, Madame?'

Beth Orlande's sigh ground with sadness. 'I've had no word from her since September. Communication is *kaput*. Ha – see we're talking German already.' She laughed briefly.

Adele did not find it funny.

Madame went on, telling her that she wrote a month ago to inform her daughter that they transferred money to a Swiss bank account for her. And that her sister and her husband will be her guardians. For the *duration*. The duration, she laughed, saying, how long is a piece of string?

'Beth!'

Adele spun round to see Monsieur Orlande filling the kitchen doorway. His eyes were like chips of ice in his red face. His great moustache twitched with fury. In his gendarme uniform, he looked like a giant.

'Oh *chérie*, you're home early,' Madame Orlande cried.

'Come out here, will you?' He left the room,

and, with an embarrassed glance at Adele, Madame scurried after him.

Adele stared down into the sauce, turning the spoon over and over.

Monsieur Orlande's bark reached her through the half-closed door.

'...and how dare you ... our financial arrangements ... Sylvie ... private ... she's our *maid*, for God's sake.'

Madame's quick unhesitant apology was barely audible. Adele heard his boots clip away along the stone passageway and up the stairs.

'Is that sauce ready?' Madame was at her side, peering into the saucepan. Her cheeks were flushed, and her eyes watery. Blue veins traced the pale skin over her cheeks. 'Ah yes, it looks good.' She dipped in her little finger and sucked it. Her hands were shaking. 'Tastes good too. I knew I could rely on you to make the sauce. This is his favourite meal, you know.'

Involuntarily, Adele glanced at the clock.

'Yes, you can go now... Are you meeting Jean? Of course you are. You look so happy. Where are you meeting?'

'At the Petite Auberge. We will have dinner together.'

'That's nice...' Madame's voice trailed off as she spooned the sauce into a jug.

'Oh, Adele.' Her command stopped Adele at the threshold. She turned back to see Madame draw back her shoulders and assume authority. 'I want you to clean Sylvie's bedroom tomorrow. Clean the carpets. Scrub them with soap. I want you to make sure there is not one feather sticking through the mattress that might scratch her. I want everything to be ready for her. Fresh, clean and new for her.'

'But, Madame, surely–'

'No argument. I want her home in the spring.'

Nell

She watched her father pop the cork at exactly twenty to one on Christmas Day. She waited patiently as he went round the room filling glasses, anticipating her first taste of champagne.

'I might put a dash of Angostura bitters in mine,' said her mother, heading for the silver drinks trolley, brimming glass in hand.

'Steady on, old girl,' Marcus said, glancing at his wife with a careworn look. 'Mrs Bunting, here you are. Sylvie? Nell? Just a splash, I think.'

'Put some orange cordial in it,' said Mrs Bunting. 'Might take the edge off.'

'No, that will ruin it,' proclaimed Mollie returning with her flute now cloudy. 'What a waste of good champagne to mix that sweet muck with it. Let them have it straight.'

Nell thought how nice her mother looked in a cream fine-wool dress that flared out prettily over her hips. On her feet were black patent Mary Janes.

'Just the one for me,' said Diana, taking the glass that Marcus offered her. She had borrowed one of Sylvie's peacock-blue silk dresses – as she 'had nothing to wear, absolutely nothing'. The colour transformed her, contrasting with her dark hair so that it gleamed. Her lips were ruby-red, she informed Nell earlier, courtesy of the latest Elizabeth Arden. Diana's parents had wanted her to go home to Harrow for Christmas, and she had chosen to stay here at Lednor. 'Oh goodness,' she giggled, sipping the champagne, 'I've never had the like.'

'Really?' said Mollie. 'You've never had champagne? That does astonish me.'

Nell thought that her mother did not sound at all surprised.

'Port and lemon is my usual tipple. If, and only *if*, I drink. But this is splendid... Ooh, it just went up my nose.'

Nell's father cleared his throat and stood by the hearth, poker-faced.

'I just want to say how delightful it is to have our visitors with us this Christmas. Dear Sylvie, and our new arrival, Diana.' He raised his glass in the teacher's direction. 'I wish us all a very happy Christmas. These are uncertain times and times ahead might be hard...'

'Oh God, morbid,' muttered Mollie.

Marcus glared at her. 'As I was saying, good luck, everyone.'

'Happy Christmas,' they all chimed, raising their glasses.

Marcus paused, his glass in the air. 'Absent friends,' he said.

Nell saw Sylvie's eyes darken. She must be thinking of Auntie Beth and Uncle Claude and Adele's roasted goose. Her mother looked away and dabbed at the corner of her eye with her fingertip.

'Absent friends,' everyone repeated.

Mrs Bunting wiped her eyes. 'I better go sort that turkey out,' she said, and quit the room.

Mollie took her seat by the fire, elegantly stretching out her long legs as she crossed them. 'I was thinking, Diana,' she said, holding out her glass for more champagne just as Marcus walked past her, 'that you might like a little more privacy. It must be hard living with a strange family in this rambling old house. I was thinking you might like to move into Pudifoot's cottage in the new year.'

Miss Blanford perched upright in her chair and began to exclaim and blush, her eyes darting in surprise.

'Really?' interjected Marcus as he caught a drip of champagne from the bottom of his wife's glass with his handkerchief. 'Is it in any fit state?'

'It was in a fit enough state for poor old Pudifoot,' countered Mollie, holding her husband's stare, her eyes inscrutable.

Marcus spoke quietly through his teeth. 'But, Mollie, dear, he was our *gardener*.'

'I don't see your point,' Mollie exclaimed loudly, tapping the side of her glass with her fingernail to indicate that his top-up was ineffective. 'I don't see your point at all.'

Sleepy from the dinner, Nell curled up in the armchair, with the weight of the glorious turkey filling her tummy. The champagne she'd had earlier sat like warm embers inside her head. She closed her eyes for a moment.

'Come on, Nell. Chop chop.'

Nell looked up to see Diana standing over her.

'I need some air. Looks like you do too. Let's go for a walk. I'll just fetch my coat.'

Nell was rather unenthusiastic. The fire in the hearth was radiant; out of doors looked chilly, brown and dead. But, by the time they had reached the September Garden, Nell was filling her lungs deeply, gratefully, as the cold air stopped the swaying effect of the champagne.

A storybook hoar frost had gripped the Chilterns. Inside the September Garden, the bare branches of the apple tree were frozen like the arms of ballerinas in a sheath of white. Red hips and haws glowed through icy fur in the tangle of bushes. The borders were brittle, encased in frost. Diana's red-as-a-fox fur coat glowed against this glistening winterscape. She was wearing a pair of Mrs Bunting's boots and an old woollen hat with ear flaps that she'd found in the hallway cupboard. It used to belong to Mr Pudifoot but Nell dared not tell her so.

Diana was making conversation. 'I read in the paper that meat and sugar will be rationed after Christmas. So we better make the most of it. Doesn't Mrs Bunting do a lovely dinner? She must be so sad. Her first Christmas without Mr Pudifoot. To think I never met him when he was actually alive. Only saw him lying there, dead. Oh, I'm so sorry. Listen to me rattling on.' Diana linked her arm. 'You'll learn that about me, Nell. "Boisterous Blanford" they called me at school. I don't tend to *think* before I open my mouth. Tell you what, show me his cottage.

Show me where your mother wants me to live.'

They walked out of the walled garden, along the drive and out onto the lane. The winter sun was low and slanted like a beacon through the skeletons of the beech copses. A deep winter hush made the hills and valley hold their breath. On the lane, Mr Pudifoot's cottage stood empty, its windows blank and cloudy with frost.

Diana shivered. 'Oh well, I'll make the most of it.' Her frozen breath made it look like she was smoking. She went to the front door, with its peeling paint and mossy step, and bent down and looked through the letter box. 'Get a good fire going in there. Should be rather cosy.'

'I'll help you,' conceded Nell. 'We all will.'

Diana continued to shiver, turning up her fur collar and holding it to her chin. 'Well, my coat will keep me warm. Ha, I must tell you. The fact of the matter is, I stole this coat.'

Nell burst out laughing and admonished that, really, Miss Blanford couldn't have.

'I'm a simple poorly paid teacher. Did any of you think that I could really afford *this*?'

Nell spluttered out her questions of where? How? And what on earth was she thinking?

Diana laughed, her pale face highlighted with two points of blush on her cheekbones. The lipstick was still in place. In the light of the sinking sun, Nell thought, she looked beautiful in a mischievous sort of way.

'I was in Simpsons on Piccadilly, finishing off Christmas shopping for my parents' presents last year. I was freezing. I had got wet waiting for the bus, then I got splashed by a taxi. And I was shiv-

108

ering. I was trying to cheer myself up and looking at the Christmas lights. I went into the shop and walked up this gorgeous curving staircase to the third floor. I just wanted to warm up, you know.'

'You stole the fur from Simpsons?' Nell was incredulous.

'Not exactly. There was a lady looking at woollen coats. You know those long ones with a clinched-in belt and wide shoulders? Latest fashion. The assistant was a bit flustered. I sat on the window seat with a mind to look at the lights on Piccadilly while I dried off. This customer was making a bit of a fuss, raising her voice. Insisted on taking ten coats to try on in the changing room, when I think you are only supposed to take three. She'd discarded her own coat, the fur, complaining at how hot she was. I thought, nice to be too hot. She flung it at the assistant who didn't quite know what to do with it so she laid it on the seat next to me. I gave her a smile. Poor girl hurried off to wait on madam. I waited. And waited, watching the traffic, watching the lights. I reached out to touch the fur. Let my fingers sink into it. Then I stood up, slipped off my own old coat, and slipped on the fur.'

'Goodness, how ever did you have the nerve?'

'Search me. I surprised myself, walking out of that shop, slowly, with dignity. Head held high. Back down that beautiful staircase.'

'Oh dear. Don't tell Mother, she might throw you out the house,' Nell laughed. 'She might not even want you in Mr Pudifoot's cottage.'

'Thing is, it's so beautiful and warm. And I think I can look the part in it,' said Diana, caressing the collar against her cheek. 'Trouble is, it still stinks of that old bag's perfume.'

Nell was back in her armchair, warming herself from her walk, when Sylvie came over to her holding out a brown paper package.

'Happy Christmas, Nell.'

'Oh, happy Christmas...' Nell muttered.

'No,' Sylvie jiggled the package up and down and thrust it on her. *Happy Christmas.* You're meant to open it, Nell.'

She peeled away the paper to reveal a book, a pristine, brand-new copy of the *Adventures of the Little Wooden Horse.*

'I ordered it especially from Foyles,' said Sylvie and she went back over to the card table where Mrs Bunting was setting up snakes and ladders.

Sylvie's gesture left Nell shy and bewildered. She stared down at the cover for a while, relishing the familiar illustration and listening to the tapping of the counters on the board as the game progressed. When she looked up she noticed her father was watching the frosty afternoon grow darker from the french windows. His shoulders were down, his hands were in his pockets. He seemed very relaxed, looking, Nell thought, so unlike himself.

Mollie was lounging on the sofa in stockinged feet, remembering the time Mr Pudifoot forgot to put the handbrake on the car and it rolled back into the dovecote. Mrs Bunting laughed at the memory as she rattled the dice in the cup. Nell exchanged hesitant smiles with Sylvie and relaxed back into her chair.

Diana, in her heels, came into the room and walked over to the windows, yawning and stretching as she went. She stood close to Marcus.

'What a lovely walk I just had with Nell,' she told him. 'Lovely how a good walk refreshes you and makes you inordinately tired at the same time. Just now, when I went upstairs to change my shoes, it was all I could do not to lay down on the bed and fall asleep.'

Diana gazed ahead of her through the misty windowpane. Marcus turned his head and looked down at her for what, Nell decided, was a very long time indeed.

'Parlour games!' cried Diana suddenly and made Marcus jump. 'That will wake me up – wake us all up.'

Mollie put her fingertips to her forehead and muttered, 'Oh no.'

'I've got a good one,' said Diana, excited. 'Sylvie, come on, snakes and ladders can wait. I need your help. Come with me.'

'Don't know about everyone else but I'm ready for a snooze,' yawned Mollie, standing up, 'I'm going upstairs. *Marcus?*'

'Oh, I'm staying here,' he said casually, shrugging his shoulders with a boyish grin. 'I want to see what Diana has in store for us.'

Her mother left the room.

'If looks could kill,' muttered Mrs Bunting, sinking her nose into her champagne glass.

Ten minutes later, Diana and Sylvie carried Marcus's easel into the drawing room, knocking the paintwork with it and grimacing with mirth. Attached to the easel was a large sheet of his best art paper.

'But that's my...!' he started and then sat on the sofa, highly amused. 'Oh, never mind.'

Diana had used charcoal to draw a huge face with squinting eyes, a bulbous nose and a shock of black hair over its forehead. But no mouth.

'Oh, it's–' Nell said.

'Yes,' said Diana, holding up a square piece of black card, filched from Marcus's cupboard. 'And this is his tache.'

She'd taken the scissors to it and cut the exact hilarious shape of Mr Hitler's moustache.

'We're playing pin the tache on the dictator,' she cried. 'All we need now is a blindfold.'

Sylvie relinquished her silk scarf, allowed herself to be blindfolded and the game began. Diana and Nell, giggling together, turned her around and around and led her outstretched arms towards the easel to complete Adolf's face. Sylvie chuckled and protested, muttering in French.

'Hey, Sylvie,' chastised Marcus, 'none of that. Remember where you are.'

'Oh, tell me, have I done it?'

Marcus couldn't answer her. He was laughing hard with Diana, his face open with surprise and utter delight as he looked at her.

Diana said, 'I noticed your gramophone up there, Marcus. Can we fetch it down?'

Nell wondered whether it would wake her mother. Marcus ignored her and hurried upstairs for it, bringing with him a case of seventy-eights.

'Oh Dad, you're not going to play Debussy, are you?' she protested.

'No, I most certainly am not. Sylvie, pull the

blackout. Nell, help me roll back the rug. Mrs B,' he extended his arm to her, 'would you do me the honour of partnering me in the first dance?'

As the jazz beat swung out around the room, Marcus spun the housekeeper across the parquet until she was red in the face, protesting.

'Pudifoot could dance, Nell,' she called out. 'You never would believe that of him, but oh, could he dance.'

Diana clapped them. 'Put something else on,' she urged Nell.

'How about "Okay Toots"? Or...' Nell pulled a disc out of a sleeve and peered at the label, "Anything Goes".'

'Isn't that all a little bit racy, Uncle Marcus?' asked Sylvie.

'Oh, it's all good fun. How about "Cheek to Cheek". That's it, that one.' Then he held out his hand to Diana. 'Put that glass of champagne down and dance with me. Mrs B, you'll have to sit this one out, I'm afraid.'

The housekeeper collapsed into the fireside chair, waving her hand and insisting that he shouldn't mind her.

Marcus pulled Diana into the centre of the floor and twirled her so that her blue silk skirt lifted to show surprisingly pretty knees. He was quite the expert, thought Nell. His back straight, his arm cocked just so.

She remembered her mother telling her how she and Auntie Beth met their future husbands on the same night, at the same ball. The sisters had only just bobbed their hair and Mollie had daringly worn trousers for the first time ever

113

only the week before. The war had been over just three years, and the shortage of men was astonishing. They thought they'd never find a suitable boyfriend, let alone ever be swept around a dance floor by one.

Uncle Claude, blustery and moustached, had just been seconded to Scotland Yard for a year, from the French gendarmerie. Marcus was to be decommissioned and was looking for an army desk job that would allow him more time to paint. Claude's elegant accent contrasted with his stout, imposing figure. He danced very well, was surprisingly light on his feet, said Mollie, and told jokes, which made the girls giggle. Marcus was silent and sensitive. He made sure that their lemonade was topped up and fetched them each a tot of punch. When they danced, Mollie said, she felt like she was flying. She said she felt like a princess in his arms. The sisters made their choices: Auntie Beth to travel to the other side of the Channel to the village in Normandy; her mother to live as the wife of a captain in the Chilterns.

How attractive, how dashing her father'd been in his officer's uniform. Dashing, her mother had said, and yet underneath it all so very fragile.

He didn't look fragile now, thought Nell as she helped herself to another glass of champagne and shuffled back deep into her armchair. She felt her toes tingle from the heat of the fire. Her eyelids fluttered heavily as the warm whirling room closed in on her. And all the time her father laughed and danced in the arms of Diana Blanford.

The cold valley lay in shadow; the trees were silhouetted against the horizon the colour of watery buttermilk. In the silence of the afternoon, Nell strained her ears for the sound of the Chess, sluggish within the wintry chill.

The red-brick and grey-flint walls of Pudifoot Cottage were bright amid the dull landscape as she turned the corner. A lamp was on in the kitchen. Diana had renamed the cottage in honour of its late tenant and Marcus had painted the sign for her; he'd even got out his hammer and nails and tacked it up above the door.

'Here I am,' Nell called, tapping on the door as she went in. 'I come bearing gifts. Put another way, some of our household cast-offs.'

Diana looked up, beaming, her hair tied up in a turban. She wiped her blackened hands down an old apron of Mrs Bunting's. There was a smudge of dirt on her nose.

'I'd make you some tea if I could get this darn range going. Your father promised to look at it for me. Just needs a certain knack, he said. Obviously something I have not. How's Sylvie? She seemed so down the other day. Am I right she has not heard from her parents this Christmas? Tell me to mind my own business if you like, but I do feel for her.'

'Mother's keeping her busy. She's told her she has to take over from Mrs Bunting today and try her hand at rabbit pie. I just left her just now jointing the little fellow in the kitchen.'

'So, you expect to eat dinner some time today, then?' Diana smiled.

Nell handed her a bag, telling her that it

115

contained the last of the sheets, and a couple of pillows that were a bit saggy but she thought they were all right. 'Shall I pop them upstairs?'

Diana handed her a broom. 'You wouldn't give it a good going over for me would you, while you're up there? I'm behind schedule already. I wanted this place shipshape by sunset, but I'm failing admirably.'

Upstairs, Nell opened the window to give the little bedroom a good airing. Diana had hung her clothes in the wardrobe and set out her hairbrushes on the shelf. But the room was a mess. There had been a fall of soot in the little cast-iron fireplace and black footprints pro- ceeded across the lino. It would need more than a 'going over', Nell conceded. She tugged the corner of the metal-framed bed to move it a few feet before running the broom along the skirting. But how nice her mother's old patched curtains looked at the window, she decided. And maybe a lick of paint would do the trick. Diana would be cosy here, in no time.

She heard the clatter of the range lid down- stairs and Diana exclaim in delighted surprise. Then she heard her father's voice.

'How are we doing, poppet?'

Nell propped her broom up against the wall and went out onto the tiny postage stamp landing. The stairs went straight down into the kitchen, the banisters forming a neat little cage for them. She opened her mouth to call 'Yoo- hoo' but stopped in astonishment. Below her, just visible through the banisters, Diana was holding up two ribboned medals to the light.

116

'Guess what,' she said to Marcus, 'I've found Mr Pudifoot's Great War medals. They were here, right here at the back of the dresser drawer. Caught behind a wad of newspaper. What shall we do with them?'

'Oh, let me see.'

Nell crouched down in the shadows of the landing, to peer through the banisters, intrigued by the medals. Mrs Bunting had been searching for them for ages; she was desperate for them. Nell's father had his back to her.

'My, my,' he said softly, an edge of pain in his voice. 'Good old Pudifoot.'

Nell saw Diana's face clearly and it was full of her beautiful mischief.

'Perhaps, Marcus,' she said, 'perhaps they should be melted down for the war effort. They're always banging on about scrap metal.'

Marcus flinched suddenly and grabbed the back of Diana's neck as if she was a naughty cat. In shock, Nell put her hand over her mouth. He spoke low and hard. 'Why do you have to joke all the time? This is serious, serious stuff.'

But Diana was laughing, swaying her body in front of Nell's father, still caught by the scruff of the neck. 'Oh, you are so easy to tease, Marcus. So, so easy!'

Saturated with confusion, Nell's heart rapped in her throat. Why did her father behave like this, always, always around Diana? Why did he never remain still and calm and *normal?*

'I wish you'd shut up,' he snapped, although he was smiling. 'Do shut up, Diana.'

Diana put her hands on Marcus's shoulders,

117

and her face, tilted upwards, was radiant, in her own little world.

She has forgotten I am here, Nell thought with a seething anger. She thinks I don't have eyes to see, or ears to hear them. She must think I don't matter at all.

'I'm pulling your leg, my love,' Diana was whispering. 'Give them to Mrs B. She loved him, didn't she? She loved him very much.'

'I told you to shut up.' Her father's voice was hard, strange, frightening.

'Why are you being like this, Marcus?' Diana's whisper was almost inaudible. 'Why are you so afraid of *love?*'

Nell moved her head for a clearer view. Why on earth were they speaking to each other like this? Diana looked soft, pliant and breathless. Her father seemed tall and powerful. Again, so unlike himself.

He grabbed Diana's shoulders and held her, looking down on her. She is so short, thought Nell, when she is not wearing her heels. Disgust burnt her stomach. She kept her palm pressed to her mouth, her hot breath forced out through her nostrils.

'Didn't I tell you to shut up?'

Diana stretched herself up to retort, her neck long and pale, her chin tilting like a diamond. She half closed her eyes, mocking him, her lips pouting and twitching. Nell watched in dismay as her father leant in and kissed Diana Blanford deeply, so severely that their faces locked and their bodies twisted together, Diana's flailing hand dropping the medals onto the floor.

Part Two

1940

Nell

From the first-floor office of the *Bucks Recorder*, Nell could see through the window and across the cobbled market square. The cloudy sky beyond red-tiled roofs was thick, like the skin forming on off milk. A poster outside the cinema was advertising *Gone with the Wind*. 'The most spectacular film ever made!' it shouted. 'Coming soon!'

She watched the queue form at the bakery: housewives in headscarves and gloves, stamping their feet in the cold, clutching shopping baskets. Reluctant children trailed them, holding their hands or running in short bursts to the kerb and back to keep warm.

Her belly was full of beating wings. She sat up straight. She needed to make a good impression on Mr Flanagan who was seated behind his desk and whose large stomach pressed against the edge of it like a great yielding barrel. His tie was loose, shirtsleeves rolled up, cigarette stuck to his lip. He was reading her letter of application, and his silence was excruciating.

Another group of women began to crowd at the door to the tailor's. Could it be that some new fabric had arrived? From America? Nell looked down at her old school skirt. She'd let out the hem so many times, it looked poor and ragged. But it was her smartest skirt; it would do, her mother had said, for an interview that was likely to be a waste of time, anyway. She wore long boots, borrowed from Diana. They were old, but at least they were ladies' boots, and helped make her look more grown-up. On her way through the lobby downstairs, Nell had caught sight of herself in the large mirror emblazoned with the newspaper's masthead and felt a little closer to growing into a woman. Over Christmas, she had persuaded her mother that she should let her roll her hair and, now that Sylvie had left school, she wouldn't be far behind.

There was something so repressive and redundant about the classroom. Nell longed to be out in the world where she could make a difference; she longed to be noticed. Here in the charged atmosphere of the newspaper office, a strange stew of confidence and fear inside her made her tilt her chin, take a breath and look Mr Flanagan, chief reporter, in the eye.

Mr Flanagan folded up her letter and tossed it onto a mess of papers and galley proofs on his desk. He barely glanced at her. Instead, he sucked hard on his cigarette. The smoke curled out of his ruddy nose. Nell stared at the tufts of hair protruding from his ears.

'How old are you?'

She told him she was sixteen.

'What makes you think you can be a reporter?'

Nell's mouth dried out; her thoughts tumbled. 'Well, sir ... I am proficient at English, as you can see from my school report, there.' She nodded at another piece of paper he had discarded. 'My teachers expect me to get good grades when I sit for my school certificate. I have good grammar and spelling.' Nell thought, thank goodness for Miss Hull.

'I leave the grammar and all that technical stuff to the subeditors out there,' he snapped. 'John Danty's been called up. I want a reporter. Why should I employ you?'

Nell glanced through the glass partition at the main office where a large desk stood in the centre under a low lightshade. Two subeditors – men too old to go to war – sat there in shirtsleeves, wearing visors. They bent their heads to huge page proofs clipped to sloping stands, pens dashing and scratching in peculiar hieroglyphics. Beyond them, a secretary with glamorous red lips and an enormous hairdo of puffs and rolls was tapping at her typewriter; a reporter was on the telephone, writing in a notebook. Suddenly a door on the other side of the office was flung open and a tall suited man marched out brandishing a page proof. He stood over one of the subeditors, raging. Even though Nell could not hear through the glass, she felt his anger. The tall man became still for a second and then purposefully and calculatingly ripped the proof up, scattering paper over the desk.

Nell swallowed hard. 'I observe,' she said, thinking, no, really I'm an eavesdropper. 'I notice everything. I miss nothing. You could say I am nosey.'

Mr Flanagan stubbed out his cigarette. 'Historically, the *Bucks Recorder* has a running battle with the council, with the government. That's our job, to hold them accountable to every little battle; whether it's the dustmen, the street lights, the local constabulary. But these days, that all goes out the window. We all have to stick together. We can't criticise too much. Propaganda.'

He folded his arms and looked at her.

'I understand,' she said, forcing her new maturity forward in place of fear. 'I see how things have to be adapted, when there's a war on.' She paused, feeling even braver. 'But surely that man out there can't get away with wasting paper like that.'

Mr Flanagan smirked. 'That's the editor. He gets away with whatever he likes. Are you sure you want a job here? You look terrified.'

Nell braced herself. 'Of course I do. Yes, I want a job here.'

Mr Flanagan tapped another cigarette from the packet and struck a match. 'Tell me the significance of Bovingdon Airfield for the Bucks community, Miss ... er ... Garland.'

Nell pulled herself upright, her eyes stinging in the fug of smoke.

'Bovingdon?' she said. 'It's the RAF station about fifteen miles from here. I understand it is a good position for an airfield as it is on a ridge, higher than Heathrow or Northolt and so can be used if those airfields are fogbound and...' she warmed to the subject, 'every day, at Lednor Bottom, we see the planes rumbling over. The Wellington bombers. I've seen the officers in the town, in the shops or coming out of the pubs. I can recognise the ranks from the stripes on their cuffs. That's all I know, really.'

'There's a war on, of course that's all you should know. But I see you are observant. You have something about you... You have an interest. You're keen.' Mr Flanagan sighed and scratched his head. 'I don't suppose the womenfolk of Aylesbury mind this invasion.'

Nell was sure that everyone welcomed the RAF.

Mr Flanagan grimaced. 'That may be so. The things I hear about what goes on at the town hall hops, some make them more welcome than others.' He inhaled deeply from his cigarette. 'You seem shocked, miss. I could, of course, have used worse language than that, young lady. That's something you will have to get used to in this office. You won't be spared the bad language. When do you leave school?'

Nell felt her expectation soar as she told him this Easter.

'You can start on April fifth,' he said bluntly. 'Oh-eight hundred hours, as they say. But don't get any ideas about reporting. You will be making tea, filing, watering the plants. Helping Mrs Challinor, the secretary, out there. Sweeping up bits of torn paper.'

The coal fire in the tea room was too far away for Nell to feel its benefit, so she kept her coat on and crossed her ankles to the icy draught under the door while she waited for Sylvie.

'What you having?' asked the elderly waitress, hovering with impatience by the table.

Nell glanced at the chit of paper on which the short menu was handwritten.

'Tea and a bun,' she said. 'For two.'

'There's no icing on the buns. Just to warn you.'

Through the window, Nell saw Sylvie strolling

125

arm in arm with an airman, resplendent in his perky forage hat, across Aylesbury market square. Her cousin stopped, giggling, right in front of the window and kissed the man firmly on the lips. Nell watched her cousin's slender hands pushing the man – a sergeant, Nell deduced, from the stripe on his cuff – away as he leant in for another. He gave Sylvie a humorous salute then, as she turned to the tea room door, landed a slap on her behind before about-turning and marching off across the square, turning the heads of the good people of Aylesbury as he went.

Sylvie burst in, sparkly eyed and breathless. 'Oh Nell, the cheek of it! Did you see him?' she cried, as she inched her way through the tightly packed tables, rotating her hips to fit past the backs of the chairs.

'*Everyone* saw him,' said Nell, lowering her voice and glancing around at the disapproving faces. She was embarrassed, but not surprised by her cousin's behaviour.

'Oh, it's all a bit of fun. Don't think for a moment that he's getting anywhere with me. He's not an officer.'

The waitress set down two teacups slopping with grey liquid and two rather hard-looking buns.

'Forgot to mention,' the waitress said, wiping her hands on her apron, 'we have no currants either. But here's some marg...' She produced a saucer with two yellow curls of fat on it. 'To make up for it.'

'I can never get used to this English tea,' said Sylvie, taking a tentative sip. 'Why do you always go on about it?'

'Well, *this* tea is not good,' conceded Nell, wrinkling her nose over the cup. 'Mrs Bunting makes the best tea, even if she is using yesterday's leaves. And she always, always fills the kettle to the brim before she goes to bed, just in case a bomb falls and cuts off our water. At least, then, we can have...' She paused and Sylvie joined her to say, *'A nice cup of tea.'*

Nell began to saw her bun in half, commenting that it was a bit robust.

Sylvie mused, 'And there is Uncle Marcus worried about not being able to sell his paintings. Doesn't he realise, these days, people haven't even got buns with currants in them? They won't want *paintings.'*

Nell swallowed the dry confection, not wanting to think of her father, his paintings or anything else about him, for that matter.

'Oh, but enough of all the gloom,' said Sylvie. 'Tell me, tell me.'

Nell drew herself up with pride. She beamed, 'Come Easter, Sylvie, I will be able to pay for these horrific buns with my first pay packet.'

'Oh, well done, Nell. I knew you'd do it.'

'Really? You did?'

Sylvie waved her manicured hand. 'Of course, of course. Now listen to my news. I've had word from the landlord in Montague Street. The mews will be empty and ready for me to rent in the summer. Thanks to my allowance I can afford a modest place. And it's a dear little place. Rather like a cottage in a cobbled lane but right in the centre of town. What fun that will be. And the other even more exciting bit…'

Nell sat back, giving in to the onslaught of Sylvie's delight.

'Miss Hull is a genius. Wrote me the most marvellous reference. I've just had the letter. The Foreign Office want me. I'm to be a translator.' She dipped her head. 'Of course, we really shouldn't talk about it, should we? Not here. *Careless talk*, etcetera. But isn't it wonderful?' Sylvie gripped Nell's arm with tight and eager fingers. 'I'm moving to *London!*'

Later on, Nell was upstairs sorting through her wardrobe, wondering what might be suitable for her new job. Compared to Sylvie's, her clothes were girlish and down at heel. What was the use of coupons if she couldn't afford anything nice anyway? The money her parents gave her did not stretch far at all.

She heard the front door and recognised her father's footsteps as he took the stairs, beating his usual path to his study. Excited to tell him her news, she rushed to open her door but then she remembered that her mother had come up earlier and was waiting for him in his study. Peering round her bedroom door and along the landing, she saw him stop at the threshold. His face fell.

Mollie's voice rang out sweetly. 'Darling. I was worried. I didn't know where you were.'

Nell watched him vacillate, his hand on the doorknob.

'Wasn't it obvious?' he replied, spots of colour on his pallid cheeks. 'Diana needed me over at Pudifoot's. There is something wrong with the bathroom tap,' he added quickly. How thin her father's handsome face was, Nell thought, etched with worry lines.

'Oh? Oh yes, poor Diana.' Her mother's voice was all tenderness. 'Come here.'

'What do you mean?' Her father still loitered in the doorway.

'Close the door and come over here.'

Her father walked in but left the door ajar.

Nell came out of her room and hovered on the landing. She was frantic to tell him about the job and half expected her mother to. Perhaps that was why she was waiting for him. Nell cocked her ear, listening for the good news to be imparted, so she could rush along and enjoy her father's reaction.

'Take off your coat,' she heard her mother say. 'I've lit the fire, look. Hasn't been lit for ages. Isn't it gloriously warm in here? Makes a change. I will pour us a whisky. Keep us even warmer.'

'You've brought the decanter up?' Nell's father sounded incredulous.

'Yes. Oops, not the usual routine, is it? What will Mrs B say? I thought we could have some privacy. Away from everyone and everything. There is bad news every time I open a newspaper, or switch on the wireless. And I'm beginning not to be able to stand it. I'm worrying for Beth and Claude so much, it's too bloody grim for words. But we're all right, aren't we, Marcus? We can leave the war behind, can't we, for an afternoon?'

Nell heard a rustling. A weak, false cough from her father. Her mother's voice, low and soft: 'Your coat seems to hold all of the chill of outside. Let me unbutton it. That's right.'

Nell stepped forward now, rather bored of waiting. She reached the door of her father's study and pushed gently on it.

As her mother unbuttoned her father's coat, he tilted his chin away from her. It was as if her presence repelled him. Her fingers stopped near his collar and she appeared to hold her breath. And then she breathed in deeply. 'How *is* Diana?' she asked.

'I told you,' he said, his voice cracking with strain. 'She's fine.'

'Not homesick? In need of comforting?' asked Mollie.

Nell pressed her hand to the door to steady her dizzy nerves. Her eavesdropping was becoming a nasty habit.

'Did she need you to hold her in your arms? To kiss her?'

Nell's blood switched to cold water up her spine.

'Now, look...' Marcus drew himself back. His face twisting, the lines drawn deeper and deeper. 'What's all this about?'

Mollie began to laugh, the sound of it rising to the ceiling in hysterical waves. 'Look at your face, Marcus. What a tease I am. Of course, at a time like this, we all need comfort, a friendly face, a shoulder to cry on.' She went over to the decanter and poured two glasses of whisky. 'And so do I.'

Nell's father breathed out a sigh and rubbed his fingers through his hair. 'Oh, I see, I see...'

Standing behind the half-open door, Nell heard a chink of glass on glass as her mother, out of view, poured the drinks.

'How about you and I locking the door and comforting each other. God knows we both need it.'

'Thing is, Mollie darling, I'm bushed, don't you know. Can we save it?'

'Why save it?' she asked archly. 'It's been a long, long time.'

'Look, sweets. I am pretty worn out, truth be told.'

Nell turned to walk away, disgusted with herself for listening in, and sickened by her father's pathetic sidestepping.

'Take off your coat.'

Her father said all right, that he would, but that's all.

'The perfume is quite distinctive, you know,' Mollie said.

Out on the landing, Nell stopped in her tracks. Her heart iced over.

'Yes. I know, Marcus,' said her mother. 'The "old bag" perfume. Diana has told me all about the coat. The story of how she stole it. Bored me with it the other day. Except now I'm not bored. I'm furious. And the perfume is disgusting. It clings to her, and clings to that dead animal pelt she wears absolutely everywhere. And clings to anything and anyone who gets close to her.'

'Are you teasing me again, Mollie dear?' Marcus was trying to laugh.

'No. Not this time. Are you having an affair?'

Silence.

'Are you having an affair with Diana Blanford?'

'Now, really, Mollie–'

131

A whisky glass slammed down onto the tray.

'Just admit it, Marcus, you utter bloody coward!' Mollie screamed. 'No wonder they wouldn't send you over the top. No wonder you got yourself a Blighty. It's always the same with you. You won't admit it. You won't admit anything. And you keep me here in purgatory. Do you know how that feels? I'm being ripped in two. Do the decent thing, Marcus, God damn you.'

'I'm not sure it's something you'd want to hear...'

'What I want? What I want? You've long ago stopped caring what I *want!*'

'We love each other.'

Nell's blood froze under her scalp as if a cold, tight hood had been placed over her head. She trembled, taking tentative steps towards the study. Cocking her ear, she felt compelled to listen to horrors she did not want to hear.

Inside the room her mother hissed, *'Love?* I thought you were just having sex with her?'

'We're going to leave,' he said, his voice weedy, trembling. 'There never will be the right time. But we will do that right now. If that's what you want.'

Mollie screamed.

Nell, in a rush of brutal panic, leapt forward into the room. She saw Mollie thrust her hands into her hair, wrecking her hairdo. She jerked towards her father, who took a step to get out of her way, and pushed straight past Nell not seeing her at all. She ran down the landing, ran downstairs and wrenched open the door to the hall cupboard. Nell heard the dustpan and brush, the vacuum cleaner, the mop and bucket, everything being hauled out and clattering as she threw it onto the floor.

Nell cried, 'Dad, what on earth...'

Her father looked at her like a beaten dog. He wouldn't say a word, his silence torturous.

Her mother came back up the stairs lugging a suitcase screaming, 'Out! Out! Out!' as she kicked it along the landing.

She flung the suitcase on the floor in the centre of the study and opened the lid. At the cupboard, she yanked out shirts, socks from his drawers, and slung them into the case. Nell's father was cowering by his easel, his paint-stained fingers gripping a handkerchief in front of his chest.

Mollie suddenly looked round and stared at Nell.

'What's going on?' Nell managed to say, clasping the door handle.

Marcus muttered, 'I think you'd better go downstairs.'

'Don't you dare speak to her! You rotten bastard!' Mollie screamed and ran towards him, her hands outstretched like claws. He dodged out of her way. She grabbed a fistful of paint-brushes and another of tubes of paint and slung them into the suitcase. 'You awful, awful bastard! Do you know, Nell, he's been at it with that tramp? What a fool I have been. What a stupid, mad fool. No longer. Not any more!'

Marcus put his hand on her arm.

She reacted as if he'd burnt her.

'Mollie, will you please calm down. Look at Nell, you're upsetting her. Please Mollie, just–'

133

She glared at him. 'Coward,' she spat. 'You let your men down. They went over the top. Not you. George Pudifoot went over the top. Shell shock? Huh! What a joke. You've been milking it for years. Should have given you white feathers instead of marrying you.'

Mollie lifted her hand to strike him. He bowed his head and simply allowed her blows to rain down on his ears, his chest, his face.

A feeling of cold, of death, sank to the base of Nell's stomach and stayed there. It weighed her down, clenched like a fist.

'You pathetic little man,' her mother seethed at him, rubbing the palms of her hands from the impact against her husband's flesh and bone. 'Diana Blanford can have your stupid paintings, your paint, your dirty socks and your blessed *"Clair de Lune"*. She can have you. She can have all of you.'

The floor beneath Nell's feet rocked as if she were still fourteen years old and on the ferry heading for Cherbourg; heading away from home for an endless, lonely summer. Her stomach suddenly filled with hot juice. She turned and ran. She made the bathroom just in time to kneel in front of the toilet bowl. Violent spasms brought the stale bun and the tea up, and in the dreadful, drawn-out, heaving minutes that followed, her world fell about her ears, the walls of her home crumbled. She heard, through her own wrenching sobs of disgust, along the landing, her father close his study door and his footsteps retreating towards the stairs. Down in the hallway, the front door was opened, and then was quietly shut.

134

'What in Mary's name is going on?' Nell heard Sylvie say, her voice reaching her from the hall-way below.

Nell drew herself up, leant on the basin, feeling the cold porcelain against her palms propping her up. She splashed her face with water to erase the tears, the bewildered look that stared back at her from the mirror. She gave up, and made her shaky way along the landing.

'What's the mop and bucket doing out?' Sylvie demanded of her. 'Are we to start spring clean-ing? This early?'

Nell stopped on the bottom stair. She held onto the banister, her knees like straw. Her cousin stared at her.

'Nell, what's the matter? What on earth...? Where's Auntie Mollie?'

'In here,' came Mollie's muffled cry.

In a stupor, Nell followed Sylvie into the draw-ing room. Her mother was on her hands and knees, running her fingertips over the Aubusson rug.

'Just a bit more,' Mollie muttered, plucking at tiny specks of dust. 'Just clearing up.' She glanced over her shoulder at them, knelt up and then sat down elegantly on the rug, gathering a wad of fluff into the palm of her hand. 'I've started in here. We'll have this place clean and free of him, and her, in no time.'

'Auntie Mollie?' Sylvie's voice was a whisper. 'Are you all right?'

'Mother, do you need a drink?' Nell asked, find-ing herself in front of the trolley. Her trembling

135

hands reached out with impulse. The whisky decanter was still upstairs but there was some brandy. She splashed liquid into three glasses.

'What a good idea,' said her mother. 'That's it, Nell. A nice big drink. That's what we all need.'

Nell sat beside Sylvie on the sofa and sipped at her brandy as if it was oxygen. Her mother remained on the floor in front of the fireplace.

Sylvie, cradling her own drink, watched her aunt guardedly. 'Have you had bad news? Is there a letter from the Red Cross? Oh, no. Is it...?'

Mollie threw back her head to laugh. 'No, dear self-centred little Sylvie. Not your poor mother. Not my poor sister. It's all about me this time. This is my *news*.'

The crystal tumbler chinked against Nell's teeth.

Sylvie demanded to know what was happening. She implored Nell to tell her. Nell looked sideways into the ebony of her cousin's eyes and she swallowed on the choking fire in her throat.

'Dad's left.' It felt as if she was telling a great, dirty lie.

'*What?*' Sylvie dipped her head.

Mollie guffawed loudly, making them both jump.

'Tell her the best bit, Nell. Can't leave out the best bit. Ha, if you can't then I will. Guess what, Sylvie, my dear. Your Uncle Marcus has run off with Diana Blanford. That's right. Little miss schoolteacher.'

'But I just saw them,' said Sylvie, incredulous. 'I waved at them. Uncle Marcus and Diana. They were in the Olivers' taxi on their way down the lane. I thought it was strange, for a moment, but you know how it is. I just waved.'

Sweat drenched Nell's scalp, swept over her shoulders and down her back. She stood up and set her glass down with a crash onto the coffee table.

'Where are you going?' demanded Mollie, her voice high on the scale, but Nell had no time, or inclination, to tell her.

She hurried out to the front door and plunged out into the fresh, frigid, heart-stopping air. She ran, hurtling over the gravel, her shoes slipping on sodden fallen leaves. She was chasing the Olivers' taxi, even though she knew they were long gone and it was far too late. Even so, she kept running, wanting to make it stop. To say to her father, 'Don't leave us. Don't leave *me*.'

Her lungs were singed by the cold, the tears on her cheeks ripped at by a wind like invisible ice. As she ran and ran down the valley, the low sun cast her shadow over the lane; but that shadow, she thought wildly, shortened and stumpy in the low sun, looked just like that of a little girl.

Her second week on the *Bucks Recorder* and, like a volley of deadly salvos, something new and unprecedented was thrown her way every single day. Mr Flanagan's warning of only being there to water the plants and pick up torn bits of paper proved to be unfounded.

The unpredictability of everything was sourced by the tension that was centred, as always, over the subeditors' desk. Here Mr Collins and Mr Smith were either screaming for copy, or bent in tense silence over their galley proofs. Every so often there'd be a short burst of shouting, like a break in a dam, peppered with swear words. Nell would visibly flinch at her typewriter as if ducking a bullet. And then Mrs Challinor would laugh and say it was 'tin hat time' and general gaiety would boom around the room in agreeable release. Anthea Challinor, the editor's secretary, was in her middle thirties, all lipstick and painted-on eyebrows, and would not stand for any despondency. She was the paper's life force.

'Come on, girl, look lively,' Nell told herself as she hurried across Aylesbury town square that April morning, mimicking Mr Flanagan's daily bellow.

The blackout was still down at the windows of the *Bucks Recorder,* crisscrossed with paper strips to save them from the bombs. Inside the dim interior of the stairwell, Nell caught a whiff of Anthea's first cigarette of the day. She could hear the secretary tap-tapping away already, upstairs in the main office. As she opened the door, she relished how empty and peaceful it was, such a contrast to the bubbling maelstrom that unfolded each day. Over in the corner, Anthea was working, her cigarette sat in its ashtray at her elbow, sending a stream of smoke up to the tobacco-stained ceiling.

'I'd keep your coat and hat on if I were you,' said Anthea, looking up from her typewriter.

'Yes, still rather chilly, isn't it, for spring?' said Nell. 'But I'll soon warm up by the gas fire.'

Anthea pulled out a sheet of paper from her machine with a satisfying whirring of the mechanism and placed it in her *For Signature* tray.

'No, keep your hat and coat on,' she said. 'Mr Flanagan briefed me last night. You are to be sent straight out on a story this morning. No time for a cup of tea. And no need to look like that, Nell Garland. It's your first assignment and I'm coming with you.'

Nell, surprised, sat down with a thump at her desk.

'Apart from being an excellent secretary,' announced Anthea, plucking a pencil out from behind her ear and checking her lipstick in her hand mirror, 'I am also staff photographer. And I know what you're thinking: desperate times need desperate measures. But our staff pictures man was sent over with the BEF and I stepped in, like us women have to these days. I'd rather do this than work in munitions, wouldn't you?'

Nell rummaged in her drawer for her notebook and pencil and told Anthea that she felt guilty for not doing more for the war effort.

'Oh, but we are, we are.' Anthea stood up and fetched her coat from the hook on the wall. 'We keep morale up. We keep them smiling through.'

Anthea's husband Syd was with the Royal Engineers 'somewhere in France – in the Northern Zone', but she never lost heart, or her smile.

'Our lovely readers all over Bucks,' enthused Anthea, 'will *love* this story Mr F has in mind for you. The RAF over at Bovingdon Airfield have a brand-new mascot. Kit the Alsatian. Mr F's sending out his best tip-top team – that's us, Nell – to cover it. So perk yourself up.'

'An Alsatian – a *German* shepherd? That's all a

bit inappropriate, isn't it? Under the circumstances.'

'The wing commander did have a Jack Russell, but it was a pain. Kept nipping pilots' ankles, weeing in helmets. Mounted the lady mayoress's leg when she paid them a visit. The Alsatian, apparently, is a lot more placid. They tell me he's like a great big rug. He's a stray. They found him wandering in the village evidently. Someone had turfed him out.'

'Probably in revenge for being *German*,' said Nell.

'Those RAF boys are going to love us. You, the gorgeous young girl. Me, the mature woman of the world.'

Mr Collins the chief subeditor walked in, unbuttoned his overcoat and set his hat on the coat rack. Anthea chirped good morning.

'You off to Bovie Airfield?' he asked.

'Yes, it's going to be the scoop of the week.'

His grim face remained inexpressive. 'We need the copy by four o'clock today, Mrs Challinor, if we are to anywhere near meet the deadline.'

'Yes, Mr Collins. Copy. That's Miss Garland's department.'

Mr Collins threw Nell a begrudging look of approval.

Last week he had come over to her desk with a final page that needed proofreading before it went to press.

Nell had wondered why he wanted her to read it.

'We're desperate,' he said. 'We have thirty pages going to bed at the same time because of

140

some mucking cock-up. We're short-staffed here, hadn't you noticed?'

Nell lay the proof before her and began to read. She used a type scale rule to focus her eyes on each line of type. She did her best to shut out Mr Collins pacing up and down by her desk and Mr Smith shouting that he needed the proof ten minutes ago, while Mr Flanagan lit yet another cigarette and the editor slammed his office door. The headline read: *Bucks Munitions Fund-Raising Supper a Success*.

And the story underneath began: *On Thursday last, the Mayor and Mayoress of Buckingham entertained fiends, including Wing Commander Bevin and all the airmen of Bovingdon, to high tea and high jinks at the town hall.*

She found just the one mistake, marked it up and handed it back. There was a frantic flurry of activity as Mr Collins dialled the typesetter's telephone number and bellowed their mistake down the phone. 'This has got to be amended. We have *got* to hit the press!'

Anthea peered over his shoulder.

'Ooh, what an absolute howler,' she said. 'It's a classic. We can't call our lovely airforce *"fiends"*, now can we? Winco would have our guts for shoelaces. Well done, Nell.'

When he had finished berating the typesetter, Mr Collins replaced the telephone receiver, rested his forehead on the desk and shut his eyes.

Now, Anthea was putting on her coat and telling Mr Collins, 'My film for today will be rushed through at the pharmacy on Station Road. But, as you know, you probably won't get

141

the pictures until first thing tomorrow.'

Mr Collins looked disgruntled. 'As usual,' he said. 'These deadlines drive me to distraction. This will be the death of me, this newspaper.'

'Well, at least we're all stood here worrying about print deadlines, and not taking the flak from the Luftwaffe somewhere in France,' snapped Anthea. 'Come on, Nell,' she cried, pulling her hat gingerly over her perfectly set chestnut hair. 'We need to catch the nine-oh-nine.'

The bus bumped along through the Chiltern countryside thick with springtime, brushing the burgeoning hedges with its wing mirrors. The sun was out, warming everything. New leaves bounced merrily in the breeze and cow parsley frothed like lacy clouds along the verges. Through the bus window, Nell could smell air as intangibly sweet as butter icing. She scanned the unblemished sky for kites and warplanes.

'My Syd always loves this time of year,' said Anthea next to her. 'There's such a change in the light, change in the colour. Such fresh hope, he says. But this year, well. Everything is so dreadfully different. Sometimes, I wonder if it will ever be the same again.'

Nell turned up her coat collar and pushed her hands up her sleeve, thinking of her father. She shivered. If he was still at Lednor he'd be out every day in his green rubber jacket with his field glasses now that the hedges were rustling with nesting birds. He knew their calls; he knew every note. How time was passing, she thought, how the year was rolling forward. The fledglings would soon be leaving their nests. And still no word.

'Are you all right?' Anthea asked her, pulling the camera out of its case to inspect the lens. 'You're looking rather pale. You coming down with something?'

Nell glanced at her companion. How could she tell Anthea about him? How could she tell her that her father'd left home with another woman? Her shame simply had to remain a secret.

'Can I have a look at the camera?' she asked instead. 'Show me how you work it.'

'It weighs a ton,' said Anthea. 'Feel it. Government-issue Super Ikonta. My Syd tells me the photographers have them in the army. He says they're sometimes braver than the ordinary Tommies; they never stop clicking even with grenades exploding around them. They have to record what's going on, he says. They have to get the story back to us. Tell the world. I expect you could say, on an infinitely smaller scale, my dear, that this is what *we're* doing.'

RAF Air Station 112 was in the perfect strategic spot, laid out on a flat, wide plateau between the Chiltern Hills. Nell and Anthea had to walk for ten minutes along the lane from where the bus dropped them off in the village.

'We're going to be cooked by the time we get there,' commented Anthea, hitching her camera case over her shoulder. 'I'm breaking a sweat here, lugging this thing. Nell, don't be nervous. Just use that natural inquisitiveness of yours to get the story. It's only a stupid damn dog. As long as I get a good shot, lots of smiling airmen, should keep Flanagan happy.'

143

The airfield stretched wide and open. Three runways formed a triangle, with a cluster of mess huts, offices and control room on one side. Lurking in an orderly line up on the apron were the dispersed Wellington bombers, battle grey, their wheels shrouded by canvas covers. Engineers, equipped with toolboxes and oilcans, worked around them like drones around hard-faced queens. Fuel tanks were parked on the hard-standing, the bomb loaders nearby. The windsock stood out from its pole.

'Crikey, the wind blows hard here,' said Anthea, clamping her hand on top of her hat. 'Looks like we're expected.'

She indicated an airman standing there in his fatigues outside the officers' mess, with the Alsatian sitting alert and proud next to him on the lead.

'Oh, what a lovely dog!' Nell exclaimed, suddenly feeling the day grow brighter.

'Smashing owner as well,' Anthea said out of the corner of her mouth. 'I know I'm a happily married woman, Nell, but heaven almighty, what a lovely looking fella.'

'Anthea, really.' Nell barely glanced at the airman but gazed instead at the dog, whose button eyes were quizzical, his pink tongue lolling and his expressive brow lifting at their approach. The airman saluted and stepped forward to shake their hands.

'Flight Lieutenant Alex Hammond, at your service, ladies.'

'So this here is Kit,' said Nell, kneeling down to pat the dog's shaggy ruff.

144

'He's a huge softy,' the flight lieutenant said, hauling Kit back as he made an affectionate lunge for Nell. 'He is a great morale booster for the boys. We wouldn't be without him.'

'And he replaced the previous mascot, I understand. How old is he?' Nell asked, whipping out her spiral-bound notebook to start her interview. She glanced at the airman for his answer. He held his shoulders with a comfortable pride, exuding subtle energy and poise. She noticed sharp blue eyes under his cap and dark hair.

'No one knows how old he is,' the airman told her with a rather handsome smile. 'Just sort of rolled up here. We couldn't turn him away. I say "we" but Kit was already here when I was transferred. In the two months I've been posted here, we've sort of become inseparable. He sleeps in my room.'

Nell watched the man embrace the scruff of Kit's neck, mock wrestling. She glanced again at his face and suddenly saw what Anthea had meant.

'I want to ask you about Kit's day-to-day routine,' said Nell, remaining professional. 'I want to know what he eats and–'

'Let's get you ladies out of this breeze first,' he said. 'You can ask me as many questions as you like in the mess.'

Anthea said, 'What a blisteringly good idea. So, where are your crew, sir? The rest of your squadron? Can you gather your mates together for a group photograph? I'm the pictures man today. That would be lovely.'

Mr Hammond told them to follow him, asking

145

Nell if she'd like to walk Kit.

She held the dog's lead with pleasure and followed the flight lieutenant towards the mess hut, realising how much she liked the unfamiliar tug of the heavy-pawed, graceful dog.

In the anteroom an orderly made them tea in enamel mugs and showed Nell the way to a seat at the end of one of the long tables. Within moments a group of well-turned-out, eager young men noisily pulled up their chairs, all vying for her attention. Kit barged his way under the table and settled himself down over her feet with a deep, languid sigh.

'He's better than any blanket, isn't he?' Nell said, adding milk from the jug proffered to her by a bright-eyed teenage pilot officer sitting across the table.

While Anthea sorted out her equipment and began clicking the shutter Nell sipped her tea, scribbled some notes and listened to the men chat.

'You see that landing strip there, miss? Over a mile long, it is. But when you're bringing one of our monsters home, and you've got your wheels down and you're trying to keep your nose up, it looks about the size of a doormat.'

'Has to be a mile long, miss, to take the big girls – our Wellingtons.'

'We're training every day. That's what all this is, miss. Training flights, air operations. It never stops.'

'Hope we don't keep you awake at night. Do you live near here?'

'Excuse me, miss, is your friend the one who

looks like Scarlett O'Hara?'

Nell laughed and told him that he must be referring to her cousin.

'We've seen her around the town. She's quite a lady.'

'Now, now, boys. Less of that,' said the flight lieutenant. 'Give Miss Garland a chance. She's here to talk about the dog, not what you fellows get up to in your spare time. Let her ask the questions, and keep it zipped.'

His voice had a soft trace of a London accent. Nell thanked him with a smile for noticing that she was rather overwhelmed.

Anthea raised her voice. 'We really do need a shot of Kit, Nell.'

'He's fast asleep, Mrs Challinor,' called the flight lieutenant.

Nell could feel the weight of Kit over her feet and, with it, pleasant solace settling in her stomach. She thought the flight lieutenant kind. He laughed and leant over to pluck the pencil from her hand and correct a spelling on her notebook.

'It's Hammond with two "m"s,' he said.

She liked the way he sat easily with her, his elbow touching her arm as he wrote his name neatly across the page. Then she remembered with a crippling thump of distress that her father also had nice writing. That her father had gone. She took a sip of her tea and the sudden thought that he'd vanished rushed to her throat like acid. She tasted it and she felt an instant wash of tears behind her eyes.

'Are you quite all right, miss?' Alex Hammond's face was near hers. His eyes narrowed, like two blue diamonds. He dipped his head to peer at her.

He was so kind, she thought, so very kind. 'Feeling a bit hot,' she managed. 'Is it warm in here? I need to go outside, I need to–'

Nell pulled back her chair and raced out of the hut. She ducked around the corner and wept as briefly and as discreetly as she could. Wiping her eyes, her throat was sore and tight and yet out in the mild spring sunshine she began to feel better. The balmy breeze brightened her face and caressed her cheek. She sighed with shuddering relief as the last sob died away, then heard a step behind her.

'It's all right, Nell,' said Anthea. 'I got the shot. You rushing off like that roused Kit. He came out from under the table and the crew were all looking in the same direction at your departing back. A great picture. Flanagan's going to love it. You can file your story through using Winco's telephone. Dictate it to Flanagan. But go slow. His shorthand is crummy. What's the matter, my love?' Anthea Challinor put her hand on Nell's arm. 'Here, wipe your face.' She fished in her handbag. 'Here's some cologne. I'll get you a drink of water.'

'Thank you. Oh dear... What must they think of me in there?'

'They did wonder,' Anthea told her. 'But being gentlemen, didn't like to ask. Are you quite unwell?'

'I feel better now. It's just that Mr Hammond was so ... kind. I've had a little bit of trouble in my family recently. And you know what it's like.

148

One kind word and...' She stared across the airfield, and watched the short clipped grass strain in the wind, the men in overalls bend to their work, the mighty machines of war resting, making ready for their next offensive. 'What must they think of me?'

'Oh, Number 23 Squadron in there are none the wiser. They're all busy talking about your cousin.'

'And I've told them to stop,' said the flight lieutenant, coming round the corner. 'I won't tolerate any gossip like that on my wing.' He looked at Nell. 'If you are more disposed, I'll show you to the wing commander's office. And when you've done, I'll give you both a lift back.'

Flight Lieutenant Hammond pulled up in the RAF staff car outside the pharmacy for Anthea to drop off her film and drove her to her semi-detached home on the outskirts of the town. Then he negotiated the lanes so quickly and expertly that, for Nell, it was like riding on a cloud. What a pleasant change it was, she mused, to be driven like this, instead of trekking home from the bus stop at Great Lednor.

The airman wasn't chatty, which pleased her. She felt perfectly at ease sitting quietly. To amuse herself she watched his hand on the gear stick, the leather strap on his wristwatch, and decided that she liked him. The car turned a corner in the lane and she caught sight of Pudifoot Cottage – empty and in darkness. Only then did her troubles come back to her.

The airman peered through the windscreen. 'I

thought that was the sun setting over there – but it can't be, it's the wrong direction... It's not the sun... Something's on fire. There, behind those trees. Where we're headed.'

Nell jumped with horror. 'But that's my home!'

'Hold on tight.' He put his foot down and took the last series of corners at speed. They roared through the gates and bumped over the gravel drive. The blackout was down and the house looked blind, sleeping.

The airman hit the brakes, and the doves, woken and startled, fluttered from their coop. Nell leapt from her seat before he had a chance to crank on the handbrake. The burning smell hit her immediately. A veil of smoke drifted serenely down from the darkening sky.

'Is it the chimney? The woodpile?' she cried and raced around the side of the house. 'Oh God, where is everyone?'

The airman was right behind her. 'Take care, miss. Take care.'

She was greeted by a ferocious bonfire scorching the centre of the lawn. It crackled and roared like a wild animal. Tongues of flames licked upwards, sending sparks into the sky. Her mother, a slender silhouette against the raging blaze, bent to grasp something from a pile of debris and sling it into the fire.

'Mother, what are you doing?' Nell cried.

Sylvie and Mrs Bunting came hurtling from the kitchen door with buckets of water. They stopped, breathless, then braced themselves to hurl the contents into the bonfire.

'We've got to stop her!' cried Sylvie as she

150

turned to retrieve more water. 'She's gone completely mad! Oh, who's that fellow?'

Nell raced over. The heat scorched her face as she gripped her mother's arm. Mollie turned on her, her face alight and ravaged, her hair and skin and blouse speckled with soot.

'Worthless!' cried Mollie, her teeth gritted. 'They're all worthless anyway. We don't need them any more!' She flung two watercolours onto the fire. 'As for this...'

Nell looked down. Amid the heap of her father's paintings, with frames cracked, canvasses peeling and shredded, was her parents' wedding album. Without hesitation, her mother grabbed it and slung it into the flames, screaming, 'We don't need any of this any more. Just like we don't need *him!*'

'Mother, Mother, please stop.'

The airman was by her side. 'You'll have the ARP round here after us, madam,' he said, composed and quietly authoritative.

'It's like a beacon, a bloody landing strip,' cried Nell. 'Do you want to be bombed?'

'Yes, yes, I do!' her mother screamed. 'And who the hell is this?'

Mrs Bunting darted past them to launch another pailful of water that sizzled and hissed ineffectively amid the flames.

'We've got to put this fire out!' ordered the airman. 'Do you have a stirrup pump?'

'Yes,' said frantic Mrs Bunting, 'in the kitchen. We haven't been able to—'

He raced towards the house.

Nell tugged at her mother's arm. 'Oh, come

151

away, please, Mother. Let's get inside. We should call the fire brigade.'

'Leave me alone,' she hissed. 'You're on your father's side, I know it. You're with him and that slut with her fur coat and no knickers.'

'Really, Mrs Garland,' admonished Mrs Bunting, 'there's really no need for that kind of talk.'

Nell heard Sylvie at the back door. 'Thank goodness you're here! It's all tangled up... We simply couldn't–'

He took control. He grasped the pump – on standby in case of air raids – and lugged it over the step. He expertly began to repair it, check its workings. In a flash, it seemed, he'd fixed it.

'Don't you *dare* interfere!' Mollie screamed at him.

'Mother, please. He's trying to help.'

'As for you!' Mollie yelled at Sylvie. 'You're deserting me, too. Going to London. Too good for this place, are you? Everyone's leaving!'

'No one is leaving, Mother,' Nell uttered, suddenly hopelessly tired. 'Please come away, so Mr ... so Flight ... so he can deal with the fire.'

'You, you're going to go too.' Her mother turned on her. 'You're going to live with your father, too, aren't you?'

'How can I when he hasn't told me where he is? Oh, please stop this.'

Mollie bent to the pile of fragments that were once her father's paintings. Nell saw the incomplete watercolour of the dog rose, exquisite still, just a moment from obliteration.

Mollie lifted it up and held it to the peculiar light from the fire. 'Half done. Half-hearted.

Half finished, just like him.'

Mrs Bunting pulled the painting out of her mother's hands. 'You are finished, here, tonight, Mrs Garland. You must stop this, and come inside and calm down and have a cup of tea.'

'A cup of tea?' Mollie heckled her. 'That's all you think about, you stupid woman. Is that going to mend all of this? All this damage? A nice cup of bloody tea!'

Mrs Bunting's hand flashed out and slapped Mollie's cheek. In an instant, she was silent. She hung her head with a whimper. Her shoulders sagged and her knees buckled. Nell caught hold of her and drew her away. They trotted across the lawn together towards the kitchen door, just as the airman, his jacket discarded, his face glowing and concentrated, passed them, spraying water from the stirrup pump in a huge quenching arc.

Sylvie came close to Nell, helped her with Mollie. She was nearly in tears but she was smiling her secret smile.

'Nell, *Nell*,' she whispered in admiration. 'Where did you find Rhett Butler?'

Sylvie

She surveyed the clothes in her wardrobe, dividing them in to 'keep' and 'discard' piles. Nell, lounging on the bed, watched her with barely suppressed eagerness. The mews cottage in town hardly had any storage space and so Sylvie had to leave lots of things behind. She had two good suits, a pair of wool trousers and a jacket. She'd definitely take them and buy some new blouses in Selfridges. Her best black shoes looked a little crumpled across the toes, but perhaps they'd do for now.

'I didn't wear this skirt last season,' she told Nell, tossing it onto the bed. 'And this blouse has a scorch mark from the iron on the cuff. Mrs B thinks that I haven't noticed. You can always turn it up. No one would ever know.'

Her cousin thanked her, her eyes round with appreciation.

Sylvie delved into the wardrobe and realised with a start that, as well as her Uncle Marcus, Diana Blanford had also run off with her blue silk dress.

'Oh, the piffling liberty!'

From along the landing they heard the wireless in the study hum and then crackle into life as Auntie Mollie tuned it in.

'Is it nine o'clock already?' Sylvie glanced out-side at the light evening sky. 'Time for the news. How I hate the news.'

The clipped tones of the BBC announcer barked from the study, *London calling*.

'It's become a bit of a ritual for her,' said Nell, fingering the burnt cuff of the blouse. 'Going into Dad's study every evening.'

Sylvie glanced at her cousin. 'You'd think she wouldn't want to, wouldn't you? I tried to cheer her up earlier. Mrs B told me some frightful gossip. Did you hear? Miss Hull and Miss Tren-ton forgot to close their bedroom curtains one

154

evening, as reported by Mrs Oliver in the village. Saw something she said she'd never seen before and never wanted to see again.'

Nell smiled. 'She told me too. What did Mother say?'

'Well, she certainly didn't laugh. She said live and let live, or something. In the old days, she said, she would have been completely affronted and then hooted with laughter. But she said the war is changing everything. And how awfully right she is,' Sylvie sighed.

Truth was, the sound of the radio news made her feel sick. She'd sat through the reports of the soldiers being evacuated from France by a fleet of 'little ships'; and she listened while Mr Churchill told them it was their finest hour. She refused to believe the newscaster when he said that the Nazis were parading through Paris. When the headline stated *Allies Blow Up Cherbourg Docks As They Retreat* she stood by the radio and cried, 'But why don't they stay and fight? Cowards. They're all cowards!'

Her aunt and cousin did not know how to comfort her. The thought of her mother stuck there in Montfleur was brutal. If Uncle Marcus had still been at Lednor, he'd say something, anything, to make her feel all right again.

'I am desperate to start this job, Nell,' Sylvie confessed, pulling her suitcase from under the bed. 'I can't sit around here while all this is going on. I've got to get up to London and start *doing* something.'

There had been nothing since early December, no word over Christmas. Her last letter to her

155

mother was 'returned to sender'. She had a mad idea about heading for the south coast. Just for one day, to stand on a beach, somewhere in Hampshire, or Dorset. She knew it'd be all mines and barbed wire, but she would stand and watch the tide go out, draw itself away from England. Across the water in Montfleur, the tide would be coming in. The harbour water would be deep and still and the fishing boats resting at anchor. Along the sea wall, seaweed would be floating; and along the coast, waves would be breaking across the long white Normandy beaches. *Je veux être au bord de la mer. Je veux sentir la mer.*

'What was that, Sylvie?'

'*Rien*, ah, nothing.'

Down in the hall, the telephone grumbled into life, ringing shrilly up the stairs.

'Quick!' cried Nell. 'It might be Dad. Every time I think it might be Dad.'

Sylvie followed her cousin quickly along the landing, stopping at the top of the stairs as Mrs Bunting puffed along the hall and picked up the receiver.

'Lednor House. Ah, bad line. Sorry. Please repeat. Oh, Mr Hammond. Yes. Certainly. Hold the line.'

'Sylvie, my love, it's for you. That fellow. The airman.'

She exclaimed with surprise and a bubble of excitement and thundered down the stairs.

Mrs Bunting and Nell both stood by, arms folded, watching her.

'Hello, hello?' the line crackled abysmally. 'Sylvie speaking.'

Alex Hammond's voice was small and far away. She pictured him straight away: his blue smiling eyes and softly handsome profile. She remembered his calm efficiency in dealing with Auntie Mollie when she went temporarily round the bend. The way he took tea with them after the bonfire incident with such charm, such good humour. The way he made them laugh in the face of all the commotion. How even Auntie Mollie had been quick to smarten herself up and return to the drawing room for another cup of tea in his company.

Down the line, he said, 'Hello, Sylvie. Awfully sorry. It's Nell I wanted to speak to. Is she there?'

Sylvie's heart dropped like a stone. Her flesh felt peculiar and cold with shock. Speechless, she held the receiver out to her cousin.

'It's for you,' she said, unable to mask her disappointment. Nell just stood there, her mouth gaping.

'Come on, lovie,' cried Mrs Bunting, shoving her forward. 'You only have three minutes.'

Nell

She sat next to Alex in the darkened cinema, aware of his arm close to hers, stealing a glimpse or two of his profile in the flickering light of the screen, thinking that perhaps this was not the best choice of picture. They should have seen a comedy or a musical, not the slow-burn, intense mystery of *Rebecca*. The first thing she'd said as they waited in the queue was, 'This is Sylvie's favourite book.' And had then wittered on about how many times each of them had read it, as if it was some sort of competition.

Alex Hammond then asked if she really would like to see the film and she had said, but of course. She wanted to see how well they portrayed the book. And that, aside from Clark Gable, Laurence Olivier really was her ideal man.

How smart, buttoned up and composed Alex was in his blue uniform, the colour of which made his eyes extraordinary. He hadn't told her how old he was, but she guessed he was over twenty-five. After all, he had come up the ranks. He fell quiet then, miles away, she thought. And then pondered that perhaps he had meant to ask for Sylvie on the telephone after all. Perhaps it was one big, awful mix-up.

They emerged from the matinee to a pretty, sunny afternoon.

'Goodness,' she blinked. 'The sunlight always surprises me. I expect it to be night-time, after all that time in the cinema.'

'Would you like some tea?' he asked.

She felt as gauche and as awkward as the child bride in the film, and then thought of the awful buns in the tea room. How could she let him eat them? And how could they have the inevitable conversation over tea about their respective families, the usual way people find out about each other, when she'd have to admit her father was no longer at home. All that, and God-awful tea.

'Oh no, I think I'd better go back,' she said. 'I'll

158

get the bus. There's one in ten minutes.'

And so she thanked him for a marvellous time and left him.

As soon as she sat back for the ride, her loneliness returned. The thought of being taken out by the flight lieutenant had sustained her for a good many days. It had distracted her, and gave her a spring in her step, made her love the start of summer and all its sweet promise.

And now their date was over, all she felt was disappointment. Perhaps she wasn't who he thought she was and maybe he wasn't the person she had expected him to be.

'Hurry up, Nell,' urged Sylvie. 'Your mother and I are going for a walk, and you're coming too.' She lowered her voice. 'We need to get her out of the house. She cried all yesterday afternoon, while you were out at the cinema.'

Nell felt her guilt blossom as Sylvie filled her in. She told her that her mother had been brushing her hair in front of her bedroom mirror and that Sylvie had offered to do it for her. Mollie told her that, in the old days, Marcus would brush it for her at bedtime.

'She broke down. Wouldn't stop. Kept talking about calculated duplicity. What was I supposed to do, Nell? It was Mrs B's afternoon off, and you were out cavorting with your airman.'

Nell was about to tell her that it was hardly cavorting when her mother came downstairs, ready for the walk, and took her by surprise. She had applied lipstick and combed her hair. There was a brightness in her cheeks; her skin looked less fragile, less transparent, although her eyes darted a little fast for Nell's liking.

She linked her mother's arm. 'You look well, Mother. How are you feeling?'

Mollie replied, bluntly, 'I've sent Mrs Bunting off with a letter for the post. I've just instructed my solicitor.'

A dense fist of sorrow ground inside the pit of Nell's stomach as they stepped out into the balmy June morning.

'Breathe that air, Auntie Mollie,' Sylvie said kindly, 'Isn't it plain *merveilleux*.'

'There was a time when I would have told you off for that, my girl, using your language so casually. But it makes me appreciate how very clever you are. Even though you will be leaving me for London, I realise now it's all for the good. But at least Nell is staying, aren't you?'

Nell looked at her and felt tenderness shift inside her. She calmly told her mother that yes, of course, this was her home.

'Well,' said Mollie, 'I can tell you now, Nell. I know where your father is. Living with *her* parents in Harrow. They don't mind that he's married. They are quite the bohemians, it appears. She's been thrown out of her job, of course. Miss Trenton and Miss Hull couldn't express their disgrace and embarrassment more vehemently. But then, she said, what do you expect from suburbanites?'

Nell's eyes wandered over the serene valley, the green sea of undulating copses and fields, and felt that she had been ambushed, forced to take sides. They had reached the ford with the water meadows beyond. She absorbed her mother's flippant imparting of information about her father, gathering the scattered pieces as they were thrown.

'And now I am going to shatter their sordid little world.' Mollie breathed in with a drawn-out shudder. 'I am going to be bloody.'

Nell was trying hard to understand her when Sylvie grabbed her arm and urged her to look up. 'There, there! Can you see it?'

They all stopped and squinted over the treetops into the wide sky where far-off flashes of metal sparked against the blue. Two tiny planes, over Aylesbury way, were trailing vapour in great swoops and curves.

'My God, a dogfight,' said Mollie, in wonder.

Nell stared, mesmerised. The curling streams of cloud looked incredibly beautiful against the lucid summer sky, like some sort of macabre ballet. The sudden spectacle of battle – amid the quiet solitude of their valley – struck her, compelled her.

'It's coming closer and closer,' she said.

She turned then, hearing an odd sound of hissing. Her mother stood next to her with a peculiar expression on her face. Mollie's eyes were frozen, fixed on the sky, wild with excitement. She seemed to transform from elegant woman into something rather grotesque as she spat through her teeth, 'Win! Win! Damn you, win!'

The Sunday afterwards, Nell set out with her pannier containing her secateurs and trowels to tend the September Garden. She had an urgent desire to make up for its neglect so far this year.

She saw it as a way of working through sadness, keeping busy. Mrs Bunting had suggested, referring darkly to the war effort, that she herself was digging for some sort of victory. Dahlias were still tight-budded, sleeping, but the chrysanthemums were coming on, boosted by the hot sun. Sunflowers were stretching upwards, their stalks thickening by the day, with their faces still curled over and blind. She plucked at the weeds, and eased out dandelions, while bees serenaded her, congregating over the pink flowers of the brambles.

On the drowsy air she heard the sound of a car on the drive and wondered lazily if Mrs Oliver or Miss Trenton were paying a visit. But they would walk, surely, on a day like this?

Then came the clunk of a car door, footsteps shifting the gravel. She turned, peeling off her gardening gloves, to see Alex Hammond standing at the entrance to the walled garden. His hands were in his pockets, his smile bright and expectant, his head cocked to one side in humorous anticipation.

She thought how lovely he looked; she wondered, then, how tall he might be, before asking herself why he was here, and not at the airfield. And why here, at Lednor, and not with his crewmates in the pub? After all, it was Sunday lunchtime.

In a flash, Nell got to her feet and cried, 'Oh hello, I'm so glad you came,' astonishing herself with her own unexpected delight.

'Sorry if it's a bit rich, me turning up out of the blue.' He strode over to her. 'But the day is so perfect, and, don't you think, so much nicer

162

for not sitting in a hole of a darkened cinema?'

She smiled warmly. Oh, she was so glad he had felt the same.

'I had a day pass going begging, was idling about the mess and I thought, I know a girl who–'

He stopped himself. Nell wiped the back of her hand fearfully over her forehead, worried there might be a smudge of dirt there or something.

'Who might like to take a walk with me.'

The way he suggested it gripped Nell with joy. Of course, a walk. Why didn't they think of it before? She left her gardening stuff where it lay, and went out with him, across the gravel and up the lane.

'What's in your bag?' she asked, matching his strides and feeling buoyant in the sunshine.

'I've brought a flask of tea, and some sandwiches. If you hadn't been home, or didn't want to come out, then I'd have sat in the car like a lonely old soul, with a full stomach and not much to say for himself. I must say, it is sublime around here, isn't it?'

'This is where I go cycling. Not so much now that my job gets in the way of my fun.' She felt proud to show him her valley. They climbed up, away from the Bottom. 'This is where I once saw a little yellow bird.'

'With a brownish rump? A yellowhammer? I've never spotted one.'

They stood by the stile at the oak meadow where the sheep grazed. The ford was a distant chunk of silver; the hillside was green and brilliant.

'I wonder how long she has stood there, that

163

oak, being home to so many blue tits,' mused Alex.

'Three hundred years, so my dad reckons,' said Nell and then swallowed her shock at mentioning her father so casually. It didn't feel normal to do so. 'He always said how strange it is to stand in one place and look over one view for all those years. The things she must have seen. And look,' Nell indicated the miniature oaks springing up in the meadow, 'see her children are all around her.'

Alex looked at her. 'Sorry if I am speaking out of turn,' he said, 'but I do hope that everything is settled now. That your mother is quite well after ... after the rather unprecedented bonfire.'

Nell thanked him and said she appreciated that. She dipped her head, blushing, crushed into silence.

They walked on. It seemed to Nell that there was a relief settling over both of them; that they had at last mentioned the deranged episode of their first meeting where her mother acted fit for the lunatic asylum.

He opened his canvas bag and drew out a pair of binoculars.

'Now I know you are a fellow birdspotter, let's set ourselves a challenge. Five different species in half an hour.'

'You're on. Have you pen and paper, to write down the score?'

'I do indeed. What do you take me for? And we have both to stay in one place, or it won't be fair.'

Nell waded through the flat-faced daisies on the verge and climbed over the gate into the

164

wheat field. The ears were tender, tight and green and, as the breeze caressed over them, stirring them, they whispered at her quite crisply. Alex followed her and they sat, as were the rules of his game, side by side in the short grass at the field bounds, their backs to the hedge of hazel, to watch for birds. He'd torn his notebook so they each had a piece of paper, and he produced two pencils from his pocket.

She teased him on how well prepared he'd come for an outing that may have proved completely fruitless. He assured her that, as an RAF man, he came prepared for anything.

'Not sure this is the best of places,' he said, lifting his cap to scratch his head.

'Rubbish,' she answered. 'I know all the best places.'

They sat in silence, glancing this way and that like birds themselves, perched on a branch. Nell felt a little breathless; she was determined to win. Their companionable silence made her confidence fly. Each moment sitting next to him in the glorious sunshine was like a gilt-framed picture, captured for her for all time inside her head.

'Well done. You win. I think it was the nuthatch that did it,' conceded Alex, glancing at his watch a little while later. 'Quite a scoop.'

'I do work on a newspaper, you know,' she laughed.

'You know a great deal about birds, don't you?'

'That's my dad,' she said.

He'd taken off his cap and swept his dark hair back from his forehead. He looked sleek and far too good-looking, Nell decided, feeling shy again.

They retired to the shade of the hedge where curls of honeysuckle nudged through and spires of luminous wild pink foxgloves nodded a welcome. He broke out the sandwiches and poured the steaming tea. He lay down on his side, sleeves rolled up, propped on an elbow. She told him she'd wished she had brought her hat, for the sun was making her squint. He let her borrow his cap. It felt heavy, warm and rather comforting on her head.

'Don't let Winco see you,' he smiled. 'I'll be booted out.'

They both fell quiet as they munched sandwiches.

Alex surveyed the field. 'So beautiful, so brittle.'

She glanced at him and asked him what he meant.

'What I mean is there's a hard edge to all of this glory. The sky up there looks so benign ... but things are hotting up. I don't need to tell you, or anyone.'

Nell felt the war tap its finger on her shoulder. 'But if you want to tell me ... then I will listen.'

He looked at her with such open honesty that she was compelled to glance away.

'Life expectancy is not good,' he said. 'For the likes of me.'

She struggled to form her next question into one worthy of his profound declaration.

'For pilots, you mean?'

'Yes and no. I mean, yes, I am a pilot and we have certain prospects that we have to accept go with the territory. And I always say I never want to be in tail-end Charlie's spot. But, the *no* is

166

that I am due to be posted elsewhere. Not as a pilot. For something ... altogether different.'

'You can't tell me, can you?' she said.

He shook his head.

The birds continued their business around them, instilling life into the air, the very fabric of the countryside. She thought of her father then, and experienced a spark of anger.

'I think it's horrific,' she said. 'Horrific that people have to go away. They are here, and then they go.'

'Nell. I am so very sorry.'

She looked at his face and saw misery walk across his features.

He asked her if she was free next Saturday.

'Mother needs me at the church fête. So not till after teatime.'

'Will you meet me then? I will telephone every evening so we can talk. So I can talk to you.'

'Whatever for?' she asked, bluntly, rudely.

His laugh was a delighted bark of surprise. 'Because, my love, I'm falling for you.'

Sylvie found it incredibly hilarious that Mrs Bunting was in charge of the bunting. In the meadow beside the churchyard, the Lednor housekeeper held reams of red, white and blue pennants in her arms, while she ordered the young boys of the parish, up stepladders, to hang it straight and hang it well.

'Come and give me a hand, you two,' she called out as Nell arrived with her cousin carrying between them a basketful of cakes.

Sylvie collapsed with the giggles. 'Please tell

167

me I have the translation wrong.'

The stalls were being set up in the long golden grass. There was even a beer tent.

'We're expecting the RAF,' explained Miss Trenton.

She and Miss Hull were manning the white elephant stall, and Nell was under strict instructions from her mother to look out for any of her father's paintings that the villagers might be trying to sell off.

'And if I find one?'

'Put your fist through it,' said Mollie. 'The painting, not the person.'

A banner was strung up over the beer tent: *Lednor/ Bovingdon munitions benefit.* Men in air force blue were arriving, along with a scattering of WRAFs.

As Nell got the tea urn going, she wondered if Alex might come along early. Her fingers fluttered with nerves as she set out a battalion of cups and saucers on the table. And then she told herself to put a sock in it. How can he have fallen for me after seeing me just three times? It was just plain silly. Even so, she'd thought about him a great deal in the past week. She'd been excited about their three-minute telephone conversations, although he hadn't managed to call every evening. She got used to his voice; liked to ask him questions. She found out he was from Kingston in Surrey and was an only child, like her. She had qualified this by saying that since last summer, with Sylvie living with them, that could no longer be true. He'd been to Marlborough, he told her, and had read geology at Cambridge. He

168

had a sweet tooth and liked chicken gravy the best.

She smiled to herself, glancing up at the entrance to the meadow where the vicar was greeting the parishioners from near and far, wondering if she'd spot his face. She knew she'd know him in an instant from right across the field. Conscious that he had only ever seen her in trousers or her work skirt, she chose a summer dress with a print of tiny seashells on it. Her shoes, donated to her by Sylvie, were cream with navy-blue polka dots, and made her ankles look slim and delicate.

'How are things at home, Nell, dear?' Mrs Oliver was milking the cups. 'I'm so awfully sorry about everything.'

'There are worse things,' said Nell, bravely. Good God, she thought, at least she wasn't Sylvie with her parents in danger stuck in Normandy, or even the Androvskys. Who knew how they were coping?

'Ah.' Mrs Oliver set down the milk jug. 'Yes, there are worse things, Nell. But not for you.'

Nell's stomach contracted with the essence of grief. How can this woman know this about her?

'I do hope people don't put a wet spoon back in the sugar,' Nell said in a voice far too high-pitched to be necessary. 'That really annoys me. Doesn't it you, Mrs Oliver? Lumps in the sugar?'

'As for that teacher woman,' Mrs Oliver came close, 'doesn't it make you spitting mad. Who does she think she is? I was only saying to Miss Trenton–'

'Please, Mrs Oliver...'

'Well, good riddance, that's all I'm going to say.'

'But he's my father.'

Mrs Oliver stopped herself. 'So sorry, my dear. You're a lovely girl. You deserve better than this. Chin up. Here comes Miss Hull. She's brought her own mug with her. And it's enormous.'

The evening began to fall, like a warm comforting quilt. It was made for cherishing. The light across Lednor valley was exquisite and, on soaking in its beauty, Nell felt her skin begin to crawl with frustration, a yearning like she'd not felt before. The pleasurable fluttering in anticipation of Alex arriving tangled up into tight knots in her belly.

She couldn't stop thinking that he'd told her he'd fallen for her. She felt helpless with it, unaccustomed, as if it was a newly hatched bird suddenly landing in her lap. Even so, she met him, as arranged, by the lychgate at six. It was as if it was the first time she'd ever seen him. She'd grown familiar with his voice through the week, and yet had somehow forgotten how attractive she found him. There he was, splendid in uniform. Heads turned among the general setting-down of the fête and Sylvie called out yoo-hoo, waving. Nell waved back discreetly, anxious to get away from the eyes of the village.

They wandered back down the lane along the valley. The air was rare and balmy, clotted with the pink perfume of may and a deeper, green, more earthy scent from the undergrowth of fern and nettle. The basking hills on the horizon were the colour of damson plums, and looked as close

170

to her as the end of her fingertips.

'Divine, isn't it?' she said. 'We've been so lucky with the sunshine today.'

She flinched. How idiotic she sounded, talking about the weather.

They reached the ford and crossed, as Nell explained to him, using 'Sylvie's sensible way' on the stepping stones, keeping their shoes on.

'How did the fête go?' he asked, sounding a little nervous, on edge.

'Oh, not bad. I think we made ten pounds for the munitions fund. It's all a good bit of fun. Keeps everyone on the up.'

He took her hand, then, and she jumped in surprise.

'Sometimes, though, it isn't much fun, is it?' he said, mildly.

She glanced at his face in an effort to gauge his seriousness.

'Shall we sit by the river?' she said as an unusual confidence trickled through her, stealing her anxiety away. 'I'll show you my favourite spot.'

They picked their way along the riverbank beyond the ford to where the reeds were dense, thick with green, and the water trickled like music over the stones in the shallow bed. Sitting with their backs against a robust willow, beneath a silvery canopy of leaves, he once more took hold of her hand. His thumb chafed gently over her wrist bone. She liked him sitting there beside her. Her settled feeling was ringed with a tight, new certainty that she could hardly account for.

But then Alex sighed heavily and said, 'I'm not sure I want to put you through all of this, Nell.'

171

She couldn't respond for she felt him venturing deeper than she'd ever expected or imagined. Resting her head back against the trunk, she hoped her silence was generous enough to encourage him to continue.

'I'm not always sure how I go on, really,' he said eventually. 'If it's not 3 a.m. sorties, maps and targets, then it's long training flights, hours on the gunsights with the firing teachers. Those Brownings are nasty pieces of work. Tiring, exhausting.'

'But you do go on; you have to, don't you?' She wanted to find out what made him tick, but she was scared of it, and what the underlying truth of it would mean to her.

'Yes, we all do,' he said. 'But I begin to fail when I link the two: the weight of the bombs in the hull, with what, and especially who, is way down below us. That's when it gets dangerous, for then I start to think too much.'

He turned to look at her, struggling with his smile, and said, 'I think the answer, really, is that I shouldn't think too much.'

The sun was slowly peeling away in the west, but the moon had yet to rise. Swallows still pitching against rosy-pink clouds hadn't realised that the day was done.

This man likes me, Nell decided, watching his face in the reflected half-light, but he will leave.

Alex put his arm around her shoulder and she drew herself up close to him. When he turned his face to her, his breath traced her cheek. She wanted to give him strength, to be kind to him. She whispered, 'But you will go on, Alex, I know you will. You will not think too much. And you

172

will be fine.'

He kissed her, then, with a gentleness that seemed to rock her in a lullaby. A thrill caught at her, and took her breath away. Presently, she noticed the unearthly light gradually beginning to extinguish itself. The birds, finally convinced it was nightfall, grew silent.

They sat close together, their heads resting against one another. The moon rose as a great silver globe. High mackerel clouds swept in against the navy sky and the moon drifted between them, illuminating them. A breeze rushed past her ears. Alex kissed her again, and she fell deep into him, wanting him. The moon was a million miles away, she thought, silent, cold and beaming down on her. Something flew fast, like black lightning, over her head.

'Bats,' she whispered.

He kissed her forehead through her curls.

'I know this moon,' he said. 'It lights my cockpit, ebbing and flowing through the clouds. It's a world of black and white up there. The black night, the light of the moon. Even sitting there in front of all the instruments and dials, the roar of the engines, there is such a strange serenity.'

Hot tears sprung into Nell's eyes, shocking her. She must not cry in front of him, for that would be such a weakness, compared to what he had to do. She stared straight ahead, concentrating hard to spot another bat, which she knew was impossible. She only ever realised they were there once they'd gone.

Alex tried to explain what it felt like, to be on his way home, home from the target, and to see landfall. There below him: fields and trees. England.

His hands pressed together over hers, held her solidly. He bent his face and kissed her knuckles.

'And now I am in danger of thinking too much again,' he laughed softly.

She inhaled deeply on air punctuated by the dark, unearthly scent of the night by the river, growing colder with every breath. She thought of the Spitfires as they were scrambled, the bombers made ready for their journeys through the sky, all in the defence of her beloved world. Down here by the trickling river, and its dripping stones, and mossy bark, she felt the tug of gravity. Close to the earth, close to Alex, she felt safer than she ever had done before.

'Nell,' he said, finally, when it was really quite dark. 'I want to ask you to marry me.'

'But how can you?' she blurted out and then clamped her hand over her mouth in shock.

'I know what you're thinking,' he said.

She searched his face, searching for the humour; the sign that he was jesting. That he didn't really mean it. In the gloom, his face was steady, grave and deadly serious. She watched as his eyes flickered to and fro between hers. A fear began to build up against the void of shock that had emptied her insides out.

'Well, Alex, what am I thinking?' she asked eventually.

'That we know hardly anything about each other. We've only just met. You don't know me, really, from Adam. But I want you to know how I feel, how it is for me, from my point of view.'

She fought hard to gather herself, to be grown-up and sensible.

'Alex, you are right. That is what I'm thinking.'

'The times we have spent together have been so dear.'

She nodded in affirmation. How could she tell him how exquisite they were?

'The station is being closed down – meaning no one can leave or come onto it, all leave cancelled – the day after tomorrow, for a big operation. Christ, listen to me. I will be drummed out of the force, telling you that. What I am saying is, that I won't be able to see you or speak with you for a few days. And I might be losing my nerve–'

'Please don't,' she said. She unhooked her hands from his and stood up. Her dress felt crinkled and damp from the ground. She realised, suddenly, how cold she was. 'Please, Alex, don't say any more. You are right when you said it was a mistake to think too much.'

'Nell, wait a moment, Nell wait–'

She began to push her way back along the path, stray ferns tripping her legs, branches whipping her face. Dampness slapped her bare arms, thorns tugged at her hair. She was out of breath by the time she reached the ford.

She waited for him, not understanding why she ran, had to get away, but knowing that her reaction was true and real. She heard him swear mildly as he stumbled out of the undergrowth and then laugh a little as he brushed himself down.

'Does this mean you are saying no, Nell?' he said.

'How can I, Alex?' she said. She was glad of the half darkness of the midsummer night, the kind of darkness that blurred but did not obliterate, for tears coursed silently down her cheeks. 'How can I marry you, when you are most certainly going to leave me?'

She slept late the next morning. Her night had been wakeful, her body restless and twitching. In the dead quiet of the small hours, she felt exceptionally lost and lonely. She had only just had her bath and got herself dressed when the RAF jeep rolled in over the gravel.

'Great heavens! Nell, are you up yet?' she heard Mrs Bunting call from downstairs. 'It's the airman.'

She met Sylvie at the bottom of the stairs who gave her a playful little smile. 'He's a persistent man, Nell,' she said. 'What on earth have you said to him?'

As she opened the front door her fingertips froze and sharp shame prickled her scalp. He was standing beyond the doorstep, his hands clasped in front of him, his uniform pristine, his peaceful face gazing at her from beneath his cap. He smiled his hello, questions and confusion flashing in his eyes.

'Hello, Alex,' said Nell, trying for cheerful. 'I'm surprised you're here. Oh, Alex, you see I...' She closed the front door behind her and stepped onto the gravel. She wondered how awkward, how painful this was going to be. 'I want to explain myself. I really don't know...'

'I want to ask you a favour,' he said.

176

She recoiled in surprise, absurdly disappointed.

'It's just this,' he said. 'Last night, I told you about everything that is going on at Bovvie at the moment. But this morning there has been a further complication. I am not taking part in this latest operation...'

As he said this, the relief in Nell's mind felt like a physical rush of cool air. It nearly floored her.

'...but I am being posted away sooner than I thought. Remember the op I mentioned? These posts often come like this, at the drop of a hat. I won't be at Bovingdon from now on. And because of the various changes in the crews and suchlike, which I can't go into, you understand, there is no one available to look after Kit.'

As Nell opened her mouth in perplexed dismay, Alex pointed behind him. The dog's long, expressive face gazed through the passenger window of the jeep, his panting breath misting the glass.

'I've taken the liberty of bringing him down here with me.' He sounded rather breathless. 'You see, we'd really like you to adopt him. We'd appreciate it very much indeed.'

'*We* being...?'

'The boys in the squadron. They all remember your visit so fondly. They loved the story. A few of them cut it out from the paper and it's pinned up all round the mess.'

Bashful at the accolade, Nell cried, 'Just look at him,' and rushed over to the car to open the door. Kit leapt down and padded around her, nudging her leg with his wet nose. 'Oh, he is such a pussycat.' She ruffled his great shoulders, scratched between his ears.

Alex was by her side and his closeness brought back the excitement, the tingling in her bones that she'd felt down by the river, moments before she spoilt things.

'So, you will, Nell? He really took to you before. You look after him. And he will look after you.'

Alex's eyes were as bright and as blue as periwinkles.

She said, of course she would, how could she refuse? She was sure her mother wouldn't mind at all. With that she glanced back at the house and saw that Sylvie was watching them through the dining room window.

'When will you be back?' she asked, keeping her voice as steady as she could.

'I can't tell you. Not just because of official secrets, but because I really don't know.'

Nell squatted down and buried her face in Kit's coat, making a huge fuss of the animal to hide the grimace of disappointment on her face.

'Everything I said before remains.'

'Alex.' She looked up at him as a dreadful pain wrenched inside her. 'I'm so dreadfully sorry. I don't think I'm strong enough to love you.'

'I have to go.'

He turned away, got into the jeep and shut the door. He called out quickly, 'Goodbye, Nell. Please take care,' and pulled his cap firmly down. She could not read his face. He executed a deft three-point turn, putting his arm out of the window in a farewell salute.

The jeep slipped away around the corner and

the engine faded into the distance. She was left standing there while the silence of the morning returned and Kit tugged gently on his lead, wondering where his master had gone.

Adele

Standing at the kitchen sink, up to her elbows in water, Adele smiled at a memory. Jean making love to her in his bedroom in the cottage by the sea wall; the two of them, grasping their fervent exchange while his mother was out. She knew her own mother – God rest her – along with Madame Ricard would also have disapproved of Adele not waiting for her wedding night. But these days, everything was different. And every moment, every chance, mattered.

Jean had proposed two weeks before Christmas while they dined at the Petite Auberge. Since then, as the fate of France unfolded before them, they stole whatever happiness they could. They planned to be married in the autumn, when they had both saved enough for the deposit on a little cottage on the road into Montfleur. And yet every day that had passed since then had become shocking, taut and almost unbearable.

The British had left them to it, embarking from Dunkirk. The retreating units from Cotentin had destroyed Cherbourg docks. They'd left the place in pieces, sunk their ships in the harbour, scuttled any seaworthy vessels. Oil,

179

Jean told her, still floated like an iridescent infection over the waves.

She upended the washing-up bowl and tipped the dirty water down the drain, thinking of the water beyond the harbour, the deep of *La Manche*. She thought of what lay across the sea, on the far side, beyond white cliffs and green fields, in some unimagined English village: Mademoiselle Sylvie in exile.

'Heavens, it's Saturday. I need to change her sheets,' Adele cried out loud.

She dried her hands on the linen towel, picking up her engagement ring from the window sill and slipping it back on.

'The safest place for a ring is on a finger,' Madame often told her.

Even so, Adele always took Jean's ring off when she washed up. She feared it slipping from her hand under the water unnoticed.

She squinted through the lace curtain at the garden baking in the heat. Madame was out there, harvesting the runner beans from the frames, plucking with fury. She saw Madame glance suddenly over her shoulder at a sound coming from the street. Adele cocked her head to listen for whatever Beth could hear. She caught unfamiliar voices calling; children crying. Adele ran up the stairs and up again to the first-landing window that looked out over the front courtyard and beyond the high gates. A straggle of people wandered by the front of the house. A wretched, weary crowd, their petrol having run out many miles ago, their cars probably abandoned by the roadside. Some were pulling their own farm cart,

180

as if they were a beast of burden, loaded with bundles of possessions, a precious secretaire that could not be left behind, some lace curtains, a ticking mattress, a standard lamp with swinging tassels. And *grandmère*, inevitably in black, beaten and head lowered, sitting on top of it all.

Adele was used to crowds in August in Mont-fleur, for this was the month for *les vacances*. Paris would be empty: the boulevards serene and quiet, left to the shade of the plane trees, the sparrows and the stray dogs. The small towns en route in the dozing countryside would be shuttered and sleeping. August was a drowsy month where all industry came to a halt. But on the coast, in the seaside towns of Normandy, of Brittany, of the Côte D'Azur, people would stroll along the promenade, gather under parasols with their best hats and take off their shoes on the beaches. They chattered; ate ice cream. Fairs came to town. Everyone laughed and they drank wine. But this August was different. The people arriving in Montfleur were not on holiday. They were shattered people. Refugees in their own country.

Adele went back down to the kitchen and caught sight of Madame through the window stuffing the last of the beans into her basket and hurrying back along the path towards the house.

Like the steady stream of people who first appeared two months ago, during that terrible June – the month of the inevitable, dreadful downfall – the truth of it all dripped through her mind. Jean had been wrong and it was not often that he was. The might of the grey army marched like a machine across *La France*, penetrated

Paris, and reached them here, yes, even here, Jean, at the very tip of the Cotentin Peninsula.

Adele pressed her hand to her belly where an emptiness gnawed her. She was so hungry her bones felt hollow. Lack of provisions and empty market stalls were now their lot. She had learnt to quiet the rumbling of her stomach by drinking lots of water. She'd lost weight, as all brides-to-be do. But it wasn't due to happiness or excitement. It was hunger and subtle, creeping fear.

Madame burst through the back door, along the stone passageway and into the kitchen.

'These are the last of the beans, Adele,' she said, out of breath. 'I want them washed and out of sight in the cellar. I want you to preserve them somehow. In salt? In vinegar? As a conserve?'

'I'll see what I can do. Perhaps in salt. Do we have any?'

'*Merde!* The soldiers took the sack when they came to take our potatoes. Did you know, that Monsieur Androvsky next door had to give up all his cabbages? His wife told me this morning. The soldiers just got out a spade and dug them up, happy as you like.'

Adele wondered if they had paid him and Madame said that she didn't know.

'They're *supposed* to pay us,' Adele said. 'Didn't Monsieur say that the *Kommandant* had put it out to his men that they must do good business with us, whenever, wherever.' She took a handful of the beans and spun them under the running cold-water tap. 'But then,' she realised, 'if we do business with them, we are disloyal to France. Disloyal to de Gaulle.'

'Huh, that perfect idiot.' Madame took the beans from her and laid them on a red striped tea towel on the table. 'He can't help us from London, can he? I think you are listening too much to Jean Ricard. Loyalty is all well and good, Adele, but we have to *live*. We have to eat.'

Adele glanced out of the window. Edmund and Estella had let themselves in the back gate and were running up the garden path. It was time to feed the rabbits. But what on earth with? She bent down to the bucket under the sink where a stump of cabbage and some carrot tops, remnants of yesterday's stew, had been discarded.

The children knocked on the kitchen door and crept in quietly, their faces twitching with trepidation. Adele knew that they worried what sort of mood Madame was in.

'Here you are, children.' Adele handed them the bucket. 'See what Sylvie's rabbits make of this.'

Madame turned her back on them, muttering how she could see them all eating cabbage stumps soon.

Estelle thanked Adele, her dark eyes behind her huge glasses glistening with expectation. Adele noticed a scab on Edmund's knee, the muddy smudges of a playful, unbridled boy. He piped up, addressing Madame Orlande. 'Excuse me, Madame. Have you heard from your Sylvie yet, at all? We were wondering how she was. And her cousin, little Nell?'

Adele shook her head at him. Estella nudged her brother in the ribs.

Madame spun around, her eyes blazing. 'How *dare* you ask me about my daughter. Impertinent boy. We will tell you when we hear from her, if it pleases us. *Only* if it pleases us. It's none of your business.'

The children sank back together, clutching the bucket in front of them. Estella was bewildered. Edmund whispered his apology, his eyes wide with shame.

Adele urged them to go and go quickly, that the rabbits would be hungry.

'I want those children to stop coming here,' snapped Madame, as their footsteps receded up the passageway and into the garden. 'It's too much for my nerves. Isn't it enough me missing Sylvie without them bringing it up like we haven't a care in the world? And also, another thing. Monsieur thinks it's best we don't fraternise. Do you know what I mean?'

Adele watched Estella and Edmund run up the path, swinging the bucket between them.

Madame lifted the kettle onto the range. She sighed. 'Monsieur Androvsky is a communist. He needs to be careful. But nothing surprises me any more, Adele. Look at the state of Montfleur. I just heard another rabble walk past not five minutes ago. Did you see them? Where are we going to put them all? You should hear some of the things Monsieur tells me. How is he going to deal with it all? And what about the harvest? Half the men have gone to munitions factories in Germany.'

Everyone must do all they can to preserve France, Monsieur had said, the France they loved. And if this meant working for the enemy, working in a factory in Bavaria during the armistice, then, he said, so be it.

Madame looked at her. 'Jean Ricard is lucky he can stay. And Monsieur Androvsky too. As a teacher. He should count his blessings. That's what Monsieur says.'

Adele watched her employer rub her hand fiercely over her forehead. She noticed how pale she was these days. She speculated if Monsieur would be back for supper.

'I do hope so. He was summoned to the *Kommandant's* office at the *mairie* for a meeting. That was over two hours ago. So, no doubt... What have we got?'

Adele told her she planned to do fried potatoes and omelettes. Plus a little ham. And tarragon, of course. Plenty of tarragon.

'Yes, the soldiers seem to leave the herbs behind. I wonder if they think they are weeds. Ah, is that him? I just heard the gates. Bring us coffee to the salon, will you?'

Adele rested the tray on the console table outside the salon and tapped on the door. Monsieur, still in uniform, sat with his boots on the fender, his hands clasped over his rounded stomach. Adele set out the cups, poured the coffee.

'I hear you are going to delight us with omelettes tonight,' Monsieur said to her, his eyebrows arched in some sort of suppressed amusement.

She told him that's what she thought. There was not much else at the market to be had.

'Never mind the market, take a look at this.'

Claude Orlande reached down to a canvas bag that was resting by his feet and pulled out a whole

185

naked chicken by its feet, its feathered head dangling like an obscene gesture. 'It's plucked and ready to go,' he said, evidently pleased with himself. 'All thanks to the *Kommandant.*'

Madame exclaimed how marvellous it was, as a flush bloomed over her face. She couldn't have faced omelettes *again,* even though Adele's were very nice.

Monsieur thrust the chicken towards Adele. 'It won't bite you. The *Kommandant* wrung its neck himself.'

She asked where it came from and Monsieur tapped the side of his nose.

'We don't ask questions like that. Some farmer out near Valognes, perhaps. Take it, girl. What are you waiting for? No, just take it in the bag. Here, take the bag. It's dripping a bit. Look.'

'Oh, clean that up will you, Adele?' said Madame, glancing at the drops of blood on the parquet. 'And have you aired Sylvie's bedroom today? I'm not sure I've seen the windows open.'

'I'm sorry, Madame. I meant to do it earlier. And change her bed. I forgot.'

Monsieur grumbled at her. How could she possibly *forget?*

'Oh, *Claude,*' Madame laughed uneasily, trying to tease him. 'Why don't you go upstairs for your bath? I will run it for you ... scrub your back... I hope you thanked the *Kommandant.*' Madame pressed her hand on Claude Orlande's knee.

'Of course I did, woman,' he said, his voice deepening. 'But there will be a better way to thank him than that. And thank him properly.'

Adele began to walk out into the hallway

carrying the bloody bag gingerly in front of her, but paused when she heard Monsieur speaking. He was telling Madame how the *Kommandant* had reminisced about hunting rabbits as a boy. Loved to give them to his *Mutter* to cook up in a pot. And so, he knew exactly how to thank him.

Madame's voice turned high-pitched. '*Sylvie's rabbits?* But just one of them, surely, Claude? We will need to breed from the female.'

'No, give him both. Show him we are serious. When one's wife is an Englishwoman, it is even more pertinent, don't you think? Oh, don't look like that, Beth. I'm joking. God damn it, woman, can't you take a joke? Now where is my hunting knife? I'll do it right now. They'll need to hang for a few days...'

Adele shut the door behind her.

She had a quick hour before the curfew. Hurrying along the sea wall she watched the waves lifting seaweed from the rocks and settling it back down with every charge and retreat. Behind her, in the east, the placid sky was deep azure as the sun sank low, sending shafts of light breaking over the choppy waves.

At the squat granite cottage built just behind the sea wall, Jean's mother opened the door to her furtive knock and let her in.

'He's upstairs with Simon,' she said, her hard, long face straight, folding her arms.

'May I go up and see him, Madame Ricard?' Adele asked, unpinning her hat.

The woman cocked her head towards the staircase. 'You know the way. But be quick about

187

it, I don't want any gossip.'

Adele watched Madame Ricard's thin back as she scuttled back into her parlour. She knew that Jean's mother did not trust her. She was, after all, housemaid to Claude Orlande, gendarme of Montfleur. Orlande who had signed away his soul to Pétain and Vichy France. Orlande who hobnobbed with the *Kommandant*, who had turned his back on the fight, the *real* fight.

She ascended the dark stairway, her shoes clipping away on the stone steps.

They had the curtains drawn against the evening. By the greenish glow of the oil lamp, they hunched over the table in the corner, tuning Jean's wireless transmitter. Simon, frowning, had the earpiece held close against the side of his head. Jean was squinting in concentration, turning the dial. He was saying something about the state of the battery when Adele slipped into the room. He looked up and his face softened.

'Adele, come and listen to this.' He held out his arm to her and she went towards him and perched on his knee, encircled by his warmth and his familiar scent. He tugged the earpiece off Simon's head and handed it to Adele.

She held it to her ear and listened. A signal rang deep into her brain, resounding, unfaltering. The same sound, over and over again. It was reaching her, she guessed, across many hundreds of miles of sea and sky. From somewhere in England, all the way to Montfleur and the bedroom of Jean Ricard.

'It sounds like Beethoven's Fifth,' she whispered. 'Three short sounds, then a long one. It

188

keeps repeating.'

'That's London,' whispered Jean. 'GCHQ.'

'GC...?' Adele began and faltered over her English pronunciation of the letters. 'What is it saying?'

'It's Morse,' said Simon. He dipped his head as he ran his finger down a cipher list. 'It's the same signal, isn't it? They fill that frequency with it. All day and all night.'

Adele closed her eyes and listened again. The signal, metallic and mechanical, rang in her head like a chime. 'But what is it, what does it stand for?'

'It's the signal for "V",' said Jean. 'They are sending us "V" in code. Over and over again.'

V for Victory, Simon told her.

Adele turned and looked at Jean.

'*Our* victory,' he said. His face was grave and stubborn.

Adele removed the earpiece and gave it back to Simon, who hunched back over the table, squeezing his eyes shut, listening.

Jean whispered to her, 'Monsieur Androvsky came to see us today. Did you know that he is also a chemist, as well as being a maths teacher? He taught chemistry at a boys' school in Paris. He can make explosives. He wants to help us. Join the network. He certainly has an axe to grind. We trust him. He seems all right.'

Adele put her hand over his mouth. 'Don't tell me any more,' she whispered. 'I don't need or want to know.'

She got up from Jean's embrace and knelt beside him on the floor, resting her arms over his legs.

'How is the gendarme?' asked Jean, touching her hair. *'L'homme collabo.'*

'Jean, don't frighten me. I hate it when you say that. It's so hard to know what to think. But I can't think *that.*'

Jean ran his hand down her back. 'I'm sorry, *ma petite.* I am being harsh. It is his job. He has always been the gendarme. Except nowadays, it takes on new significance.'

'He despatched the rabbits today,' she said, leaning into him, shuddering at the thought of how the children would take the news; the empty hutch, the limp carcasses hanging by their feet from the rafters in Ullis's stable. She said, 'God knows how Sylvie will take it. I will write again but how can I tell her? How can I tell her *this?'*

'The letter won't get through anyway,' said Jean with confidence. 'Believe me, Adele, none of your letters have reached England.'

Adele glanced at Simon. His pen was scratching over the sheet of paper in front of him. He wrote down letters in sets of three. He looked up, his eyes blazing with excitement.

'It's just come through. I can't figure it out.'

Jean reached forward and grabbed the earpiece. 'Let me listen.'

Adele said, 'I must get home. The curfew...'

Jean waved his hand at her, he did not look up. He took the pen from Simon's hand.

Adele left the room and made her way back down the stairs. In front of the mirror in the dark hallway, she set her hat on her head and listened. From the back parlour came the muffled, disembodied tones of an English voice. Jean's mother had found the World Service.

Outside, the sky was deep navy, fragments of elderly stars hung over the sea. It would be dark in less than ten minutes. The tide was coming in, racing in over the narrow shingle beach, whispering over scattered pebbles. Beyond the waves lay the half-submerged barriers strung with wire, which glinted as cruel teeth in the dusk. They had no place here, she thought, no place at all.

Her footsteps rang on the cobbles of the harbour. A group of German soldiers were lighting cigarettes by the war memorial. The German flag, hoisted at the church, offensively, a few weeks before, hung limp in the still air. The soldiers were tall, broad-backed, imperious. Rifles were slung casually over their shoulders. She averted her eyes from the upright collars, the rounded helmets, the high boots – the sight of which made her stomach churn with loathing. One of them had taken off his helmet and his blond hair shone out in the darkness.

'*Bonsoir, mademoiselle*,' he said, his accent surprisingly good. '*Voulez-vouz une cigarette?*'

'*Non*,' she snapped, and increased her pace, her heels noisy and rebellious in the silence.

She heard another of them command that the curfew was in place, that she must return home. His voice barked hard at her: *Schnell, schnell!* Their laughter followed her as she hurried along the harbour front.

I will make a fur collar, she thought, shivering, thrusting her hands in her pockets as the wind picked up and the night turned a corner from balmy summer's evening to an autumnal chill. I will use the rabbit fur and make a collar for Estella. The winter is going to be very cold.

Part Three

1941

Sylvie

The new sunlight brought them out as if from nowhere: stems of lanky buddleia, pushing blindly
through jagged rubble and hanging off gaping
broken walls. Their dusty leaves were a soft contrast to the innards of the terraces, houses and
offices, the streets that were mapped out so inno-
cently under the sharp sight of the bombers. But
Maman always said that butterflies love buddleia,
Sylvie thought. In the summer, here in the broken
streets and squares of the West End, the droopy
buddleia flower heads will be dancing with them.

She realised how used she was getting to the
smell of grime and ashes; occasional whiffs of gas
from an unstoppered tap in a wrecked, exposed
kitchen. The filth of destruction latched on to her
as she stepped quickly past the remains of the
blasted buildings. But every now and then she'd
turn a corner, and there was the tranquil beauty
of Berkeley Square with its towering plane trees,
or the white-stucco sweep of Pall Mall, resplendent and defiant.

Blossom painted the trees and, in recent weeks,
the sirens eased off, the raids receding. The nights
could be spent sleeping, if not dancing. But Sylvie
knew deep sleep could never return. The sky
remained ominous, day or night. Auntie Mollie
still worried, asked her during every telephone
call to come home. But this was Sylvie's time to

be defiant. Every day she worked hard, every word on every chit of paper she translated with speed and accuracy helped someone, somewhere.

As she waited to cross Marylebone High Street, two forces girls came out of a newsagent's and chatted together beside her. Sylvie squared her shoulders against envy. In her civilian suit and hat, faced with the dignity and esteem that the Wrens' uniform invoked, she felt isolated, far from home.

'Sylvie, *ma chère*, there you are. Bless you. You ran off sharply.' Henri bounded up to her, catching her by surprise, and went in for the double-cheek kiss. 'Thought I'd ask you. We're all going to the Lamb and Flag. Come along, please. Will make my rotten old day.'

Henri's accent and his handsome bony face drew surreptitious glances from the Wrens. Their eyes then fell on the fine collar of Sylvie's silk blouse, the cut of her suit, and they went opaque with admiration. Sylvie cheerfully linked her arm through Henri's.

'All right, then. I'm rather tired today, so just the one.'

The pub was noisy, shoulder to shoulder. Framed mirrors were stacked decoratively and precariously up the walls, gleaming darkly under the 40-watt bulbs. The walls, papered and painted many coats of emerald green, had soaked up years of tobacco and body heat. It was about fifty-fifty here, Sylvie guessed, of forces and civilians. Her colleagues from the Ministry had taken over a red velvet booth, so there was no room for her and Henri. They stood instead near the bar and chinked their half pints of ale together. She spotted the two Wrens come in, ravenous, she suspected, for the company of War Office chaps.

'*A la vôtre*, Sylvie,' said Henri. '*Vive la France.*'

'Here's one in your eye. I heard that for the first time the other day.'

Henri laughed with her, drawing closer. She'd seen that look on his face before.

'I had been meaning to ask you,' he said, 'would you like to go to the picture house to-night? It's Laurel and Hardy.'

Sylvie patted his hand. 'I've already told you, I'm tired.'

'Tomorrow, then?'

Sylvie shrugged and scanned the room, taking in the bright laughter and the brighter lipstick. The fact of the matter was that she was *very* tired. She was weary of the gaiety which she, and every one else it seemed, wore like a shield around themselves. Two soldiers moved from their corner, making a beeline for the Wrens, and revealed in their wake an empty expanse of upholstered bench.

'Quick, Henri,' she said, 'let's sit down.'

A man was sitting at one end of it, nursing a pint. She glanced at him, and a fraction of memory hit her, made her pause. He was alone, his own shell around him, she thought, just like the rest of us.

She mentioned to Henri that she was sure she recognised him, as they made their way over. But then it couldn't be. He was a civvy, wearing a pinstriped suit. It wasn't him, surely.

She hotched along the bench and told the man

197

excuse me. But the inkling was still there: the turn of his head, his profile.

'*Ça alors!* It *is* you!' she cried.

Alex Hammond set his pint glass down and looked up at her.

'I'm terribly sorry... What?'

'Oh, it's you, it's just that your hair is a bit longer and you're not in uniform.'

She stared at him full in the face, expecting him to gape with amazement at her. He was non-plussed and took another draught of his bitter.

'It's Sylvie Orlande,' she insisted. 'I'd know you anywhere. We met once or twice, briefly, but I'd never forget.'

His eyes flicked past her to Henri, who told him, 'Don't worry, old man, she's only had one stoop of ale.'

'I'm Nell's cousin,' said Sylvie, crestfallen. 'Remember?'

Alex Hammond pressed his fingers either side of his lips, deep in thought. The skin on his face flushed. Sylvie saw a sweat break out on his forehead. He rummaged in his top pocket for a handkerchief.

'Surely you remember. The newspaper report? The dog?'

'Of course I remember,' he spluttered, trying for a laugh, which came out in a choking sound. 'Of course I do.'

'It's nice to see a friendly face,' observed Sylvie, indicating the room. 'It all gets rather busy, doesn't it? Do you live in London now?'

'I certainly do. Look, it's been a pleasure.' He made to get up, but Sylvie, by occupying the

198

bench, had trapped him in his corner.

'Oh, do stay.' She faced him and gave him the full blaze of her smile. 'I remember how you put out Auntie Mollie's bonfire.' She lowered her voice and turned her body closer to his. She noticed the fine quality of his suit stuff and wondered again why he was dressed in civvies. 'You were rather the hero that night.'

His attention was drifting past her shoulder to where Henri was suddenly besieged by the two Wrens, who'd shaken off the soldiers. Henri was entertaining them gamely. A sting of annoyance rattled Sylvie's demeanour. She felt the need to take out her lipstick and apply some more. Both men, apparently, were ignoring her. She took a breath and said, 'She talks about you often, you know.'

With that, Alex Hammond swung his focus back to her.

'Would you like another drink?' he asked. 'I'm going up to the bar.'

As Sylvie waited she checked her face in her compact. Henri peered over one of the girls' shoulders at her.

'It's so transparent,' he said, on the edge of laughter. 'I'm almost ashamed of you.'

'Take the girls to see the film, Henri,' she told him. 'Mr Hammond is an old friend.'

She watched Alex push his way back with the drinks, wondering what on earth Nell had been thinking to give him the brush off last summer – or 'shoot him down' as the boys at the Ministry would say.

'How is Nell?' he asked, with a dip in his voice.

He licked a bubble of ale off his finger.

'Ah, well I haven't seen or heard from her in a good few months,' said Sylvie, enchanted suddenly by his fingertips.

'But you just said she has mentioned me...'

Sylvie hotched a bit closer to him and exclaimed brightly, 'You know I could never work out what happened between you two. Tell me to mind my own business but...'

Sylvie looked at his face and knew he was thinking exactly that. She pressed on.

'To be honest with you, Nell simply shut herself away. Would never talk about it. Auntie Mollie and myself thought it such a shame. Kit the dog has been a godsend to Auntie Mollie. To us all at Lednor. We never really got to thank you.'

Alex's polite smile revealed the strain. His placid expression twitched over his face, and finally broke away, leaving an impression of sharp pain around his eyes.

She tried harder for a reaction. 'All she did for months was walk that damn dog.'

'Of course,' he said, with a drift of longing. 'The damn dog.'

He rubbed his hand over his face, his eyes searching the far corner of the room for something. He picked up his pint and very nearly sank all of it.

Sylvie suddenly had a breathtaking idea. 'Alex, come and have supper with me. It's only veg soup but I made a vat of it yesterday and will be eating it all week.'

He looked bothered, ready to flee.

'Oh come on, Alex.' She wondered if she had

lost her touch. 'Better that than your landlady's offerings. Am I right? Tell me I'm right.'

Her little mews house was only five streets away, she assured him.

They walked along dark blacked-out streets, along high, looming, faceless terraces. She kept her eyes on the luminous white marks along the kerbs, letting them guide her along in the darkness, wondering why Alex did not offer her his arm, or hold her hand. A warden doffed his cap to them and said good evening. Alex did not respond. His face, Sylvie saw, was closed and blank. He was not with her.

As she let them both in, she was pleased to see that her char had been, for the sitting room was tidy and the kitchen wiped down. She lit the coal fire, sensing Alex's discomfiture. The room was cold but would soon warm up. He sat on the edge of the armchair, drumming his fingertips.

'Nice place you have here,' he observed, looking everywhere but at her.

'Thanks to my parents. They had the foresight to send money for me to Switzerland when war broke out. Most of it, it seems,' she shrugged, 'because I must say, I am rather comfortable.'

Alex admitted that he was going to say as much, what with the rent on a place like this, so close to the West End.

'But then I think, what the hell,' Sylvie called from the kitchen where she set the pan of soup over the gas ring. 'A bomb could drop on my head tomorrow and I'd never know anything about it. Doesn't it make you think, Alex? The way we are now. Each day is a gift, isn't it?'

He did not answer her, so she stirred the soup and brought him a bowl on a tray with some sliced bread and butter. He accepted the tray, his attention once again drifting.

'Stop thinking about her,' she said, leaning against the door to the kitchen.

He glanced up, spoon held in mid-air, briefly alarmed. Sylvie felt her heart jerk at the sight of his face: defeated and vulnerable and so peculiarly attractive.

She laughed lightly. 'You know, I have been lying to you. She has never breathed a word. Not to me. I have no idea, really.'

He dabbed his spoon at the far edge of the bowl.

'Except, of course, she's walking out with another chap now, someone from the paper.' The real lie was so easy, it slipped across her tongue.

Without delay, Alex reasoned, 'It's the war. She is young. She doesn't want to get involved with the likes of me. I told her, last summer, my life expectancy is not good.'

'And yet, here you still are,' mused Sylvie.

He continued to eat. 'I wonder if the whole thing was a misunderstanding. A wrong footing from the start maybe? This is very good, by the way.'

Sylvie smiled in confusion, expecting dismay from Alex. A heart broken. If he felt any pain, she thought, he was very good at hiding it. Exactly the same as Nell. She crossed the room towards him.

'I remembered this recipe from our maid Adele back home. Her cooking was rather

202

legendary. Far better than my mother's. She was awfully good at rustling things up. I hope she's–' Sylvie stopped and sat down abruptly. A surge of cold fear gripped her shoulders and surprised her with such violence that her bones seemed to fall away. 'Oh goodness. *Sacré bleu,*' she muttered, feeling in her pocket for a handkerchief, not finding one and then trying to catch her tears with her fingertips. 'That wasn't meant to happen. Not now. Not like this. Oh, sod it!'

Alex put the tray on the table with a crash and knelt by her chair.

'Oh dear. You seem so composed just to look at you,' he said, his own shield falling away, it seemed to Sylvie, as hers had done so cruelly. 'But really? You're as much as a wreck as any of us. Here, do you need a dry one?'

She took his pristinely folded handkerchief, embroidered with A.H. in the corner. As she pressed it to her eyes she tried to laugh. She smelt a delicious scent of cologne, like the grass in the meadows around Montfleur.

She breathed on it, as a smile stretched her lips. 'Oh heaven.'

Alex kissed her, suddenly, his hand gently cupping the base of her skull. The kiss was like velvet.

'Really,' breathed Sylvie, letting her fingers rest on his hair. 'I don't think you ought...'

He pulled away. 'Sorry, so sorry.' He stood up abruptly. 'That should not have happened. What am I thinking?'

'Of Nell?' Sylvie felt sadness fold around her.

'I ought not to, should I? I really have tried to

forget.' He strode to the other side of the room, as if to remove himself from the situation, to shake Sylvie off. 'I have a duty. I have my job to do.'

'I can help you forget.'

Alex sat back in his armchair, agitated. He did not answer her. Would not look at her.

Presently, she said, 'Your soup is going cold.'

He asked her if she was having any.

'I'm simply not hungry much at all these days. I think worry clean wipes out my appetite.'

'Perhaps you should move back to Lednor, where it's safer.' He was trying to make polite conversation. The crucial moment had passed by.

'Oh no, it's nothing to do with the bombs,' Sylvie told him. 'I was here all through the Blitz. Sounds a dreadful thing to say, but I felt thrilled some nights. Fear brought me close to some sort of wild hysteria. No, not that. It's the continuous worry about my parents, and what might be happening to them. And that won't go away if I return to Lednor. In fact, I might feel worse. Auntie Moll is hard to live with, wrapped up in her own troubles. My mother's her sister, you see.'

'I remember your auntie.' Alex became uneasy again.

'Anyway, I am leaving London soon. I've been posted to somewhere in Berkshire. Intelligence, you know. Can't say much more.' She smiled, her tears drying, drifting away. 'Couldn't tell you even if I knew any more about it.'

'I can guess where you are going,' he said. 'Your knowledge of France, your language, must be an absolute godsend to the chaps. And until such time, I would like to look after you. Make sure you eat something. Here,' he smiled then, his tension breaking away, 'at least have some of my bread.'

'Well, thank you. It's new bread. Rather good in the circumstances.' She took a slice and nibbled a corner reluctantly, her stomach feeling full and brimming with curiosity and desire. A God-awful state to find herself in.

'Alex,' she said, then was stopped by a memory: a dead rabbit and the turn of the handle of her bedroom door. Her mouth went dry with the return of an old old fear. She had to conquer it with the next breath she took.

'Alex, does looking after me extend to staying tonight?'

Adele

A cold late afternoon, and the clouds were low over Montfleur; the sky dull, like a bruise. Adele decided that spring had forgotten to come to this corner of Normandy as she opened the gate to the Orlande house, flinching at the sound of its brittle squeak. She glanced briefly at the tall facade as she crossed the courtyard. All shutters were closed. The house looked dead.

She opened the front door with her key and stepped into a gloom of chilled grey light. Furniture in the disused *salle à manger* was shrouded in dust sheets, ghostly in the shadows. Along the

205

quiet hallway, doors were shut. Even the clock on the console had stopped. Monsieur no longer bothered to wind it up.

Adele set to performing her duty just as she did every day. She no longer lived at the Orlande house; her home was with her husband Jean and his mother at the cramped cottage under the sea wall.

Downstairs in the kitchen there was a pile of Monsieur's shirts to iron; some potatoes to peel. He had sausages and onions in the pantry. There was a flagon of wine on the table and rotting apples in a bowl. Adele did not want to continue to work for Monsieur now that she was expecting a baby, and now Madame had gone. But Jean had the notion that it was better if she could get past the door of *l'homme collabo* every day; it might help their cell one way or another – information might be dropped from Monsieur's lips during his careless wine-soaked moments. Aside from this, Adele wanted to continue to perform Madame Orlande's parting wish: that she would look after Monsieur and the house. And keep it nice for when Sylvie came home.

Madame's fate, as an Englishwoman married to a Frenchman, was to be interned. Monsieur's bribery could not be sustained for ever, could not be indulged longer than seemed appropriate. One dark January morning, two months before, the *Kommandant* had politely and efficiently sent a black car to pick her up. She was to be taken to the station at Cherbourg to travel by train with a British family who lived in Valognes and who had been flushed out by the Gestapo. Their destination, the camp for enemy foreigners at St Denis, Paris. In all honesty, Monsieur said, after being allowed to visit her a month later, life there was tolerable.

'She is resigned but comfortable,' he told Adele. 'She will be able to write a letter once a month.'

He mentioned the extra rations, food parcels from the Red Cross, plenty of fresh air and exercise, even if the yard was surrounded by barbed wire. There was even a theatre. A library.

'She is knitting,' Monsieur had said. 'Socks for soldiers. *German* soldiers. She has made some new friends. They play cards. At least I know she is safe there. It helps...' he had swallowed on his words, his face haunted with shame, brushing his moustache with his fingers '...it helps that I am who I am... She will be looked after.'

'Keep Sylvie's room aired and dusted,' Beth Orlande had whispered that morning to Adele as she put on her coat in the hall and picked up her small suitcase. Her slender frame had taken on a stooping, hardened look, as if the spirit inside her was trapped and tormented.

Adele had glanced past her, past the open front door, across the courtyard and through the gates to the black car waiting by the kerb.

'Go carefully, Adele. Take care of everything,' Madame had said, her voice tiny, her face shrinking with fear, and yet she'd walked out to the car with a dignity and poise that was beyond her duty.

Adele picked up the iron and set it on the range to heat up while she contemplated the pile of

Monsieur's shirts. She felt sick with the relentlessness of it all. A continuous stretch of days sunk with creeping fear and loathing. What was to keep her here, really? A pipe dream of Madame Orlande's concerning the imagined return of her daughter? Adele indulged her fantasy: her and Jean setting sail in the *Orageux Bleu* and heading out into the choppy waters of *La Manche*, just like the Allied soldiers had done nearly a year before. They would head for England, with Jean navigating, Adele at the helm, escaping the hunger, the degradation, the chains of occupation. Adele envied Syivie her freedom. But Jean would hear nothing of it. We fight, he says, we fight them every step of the way. He would never abandon his country, he assured her. And neither, it seemed, should Adele.

A hard, violent thumping on the neighbour's front door startled her from her thoughts. There was a commotion outside in the street. Adele ran up to the front landing window to see a lorry pull up and soldiers opening the back of it with a hard crash of metal and hinges. The thumping on the Androvskys' door continued, German voices shouting orders. She hurtled back down to the front door and across the courtyard in time to see two soldiers, rifles slung over their shoulders, pushing a speechless and compliant Madame Androvsky up and into the back of the lorry. Monsieur Androvsky was being shoved by two other soldiers, holding their rifles at him like battering rams. He, too, was forced with indignity into the truck, like an animal on his way to market.

Only then did Adele notice Monsieur Orlande

standing on the other side of the road, watching, preening his moustache. She went to open the gate, to run out, to protest, when he stopped her with his bark: 'Stay where you are, girl. Stay where you are! You will only make it worse.'

From the kerb, she saw Madame's face pale against her red headscarf. Her eyes, from that distance, were unreadable. She heard Monsieur Androvsky shout from the belly of the truck: 'I am a schoolteacher. Just a schoolteacher. We are French citizens. *Vive la France!*'

The doors were slammed shut on the couple, truncating his protest, and the truck roared off, swaying as it went, over the cobbles. It was all over in a matter of seconds.

Monsieur Orlande muttered something about getting back to work and strolled off.

Adele peered down the street. Doors were closed, windows shut as the truck drove past. Finally, it disappeared around the corner and the subsequent descending silence pressed on Adele's ears. She froze in shock, standing in the middle of the road with an awful thought spinning around her head: *The children? Where are the children?*

The day drifted on and the people of Montfleur went about their business. Adele sat indoors, her nerves shredded, her baby thumping her; her mind wild with fear. It was not until nearly dinner time that she felt brave enough to go round to the back of the Androvsky home. Through the back door she could see chairs upturned, breakfast plates smashed on the floor and left where they fell. Monsieur Androvsky's morning paper was still propped against the teapot.

She stepped in and tentatively called their names. An immense, horrific thought filled her mind: that they'd been murdered, their little bodies left to be cleared up later, or that the Gestapo were coming back for them and would be here any moment.

Her calling became quieter and quieter, ever more desperate and pathetic through the empty rooms.

But then she heard a shuffling and a weeping and stooped to open the understairs cupboard door. Estella and Edmund were cowering, their dark heads together, crouched in the corner.

'Papa told us to hide,' the boy whispered, his face as sharp and pale as a crescent moon. Estella had wet herself. She was mute, clutching her doll, running her finger over its face. Her eyes were huge behind her wonky glasses.

Adele hurried them down the garden, behind the back wall, past the stables and through the Orlande garden. She tapped on the salon door as they clung to her skirt, sniffing, flinching, trembling with fright.

'Monsieur, the children ... the children were left behind...' She was panting with fear, needing his guidance. Imploring his help.

Claude Orlande looked up from his paperwork, his brow furrowing with anger and unease. She expected him to bellow; she braced herself for it. But he pondered, his eyes opaque and unreadable. Eventually, he exhaled through his moustache.

'Take them upstairs, out of my sight,' he told

her, dismissing her with a wave of his large hand. 'Hide them in the spare room, the one little Nell stayed in, until I decide what to do with them.'

Nell

She had not been to London for a long while. Her job was frantic and consuming, as was her mother with her sorrow and her need for attention. Nell was trapped at home with her, her horizon severely truncated, and she experienced a rather foul twist of envy when she considered Sylvie's escape to the city.

As her train sped through the outskirts, she saw the thin church spire atop Harrow-on-the-Hill, the trees shrouding the old school up there and, close to the railway's edge, suburban bay windows and gardens. She wondered whether her father, now ensconced with Diana Blanford up on that hill, was able to paint still; whether he missed the lanes and fields of Lednor. Were there enough birds for him to spot here among the streets and avenues? She could barely imagine so. Travelling so enticingly close to her father's new home, his new life, she sensed the distance yawn even greater between them.

She walked from Marylebone station, following Sylvie's directions: cross over the Marylebone Road, go past the wrecked shop on the corner of Dover Street with the Union Jack outside and a sign that says *Bombed but not beaten*. The church with the air raid shelter sign on it will be on her left. The mews was opposite, down the cobbled lane off Montague Place. Look for the one with the green door. Sylvie greeted her in her dressing gown, with her face covered in cold cream and huge curlers in her hair. She looked rather harassed, her expression quite startling.

'Plans have changed,' she said, beckoning Nell inside. 'Quick, shut the door before my neighbours see me. I look a fright.'

Nell walked straight upstairs into a neat first-floor sitting room, put her overnight case down and commented on what a lovely little place it was.

'It's not mine for much longer, that's why it's so tidy. I've packed away all my knick-knacks,' said Sylvie. 'I catch the midday from Paddington tomorrow. And so much for my farewell party. My department has some urgent crisis on. I told them, what crisis isn't urgent? Anyway, none of them can make it to the supper club. So it's all going to be a bit quiet.' She walked into the tiny kitchen, filled the kettle and set it on the gas ring. She called out. 'Just four of us, in fact.'

Nell said that it was no matter. In fact, she was relieved that there was not going to be a large crowd. These things happen all the time, she supposed. You can never plan for anything. 'It's something Mrs B moans about the most,' she told Sylvie. 'That and the quality of the tea.'

'I have a good little stash here,' said Sylvie, bringing in a tray. 'Courtesy of some contacts who shall of course remain nameless.'

'Mother sends her love,' said Nell, accepting a

cup and taking a sip. It was, in fact, exceptionally good tea. 'She was awfully worried about me coming up to town, as she has been about you living here for the last year. But I kept telling her the raids have eased off.' Nell pondered on how the raids had become the least of her worries. 'And at least you'll be out of it tomorrow.'

'Have you heard from your dad?'

'He writes occasionally. I had a letter, a month ago. He seems quite well. Quite settled. I'll show it you.' Nell drew the letter out of her bag and Sylvie scanned it briefly, glancing at her.

'Don't be sad,' she coaxed. 'I hope you've got your best dress and dancing shoes in that suitcase, for tonight we are going to dance away that look on your face.'

Nell smiled gratefully at Sylvie. She hadn't seen her cousin for months and was struck at how much more beautiful she looked. Despite being shiny with cold cream, her face was as divine and inscrutable as ever.

Upstairs in the bedroom, Nell changed into her long silk evening dress and dancing slippers. At Sylvie's dressing table she applied her lipstick and rouged her cheeks. The slate grey of her dress made the green of her eyes shimmer. She tucked a smokey-jade corsage behind her ear.

Not too bad, she decided. If only she could extinguish that little shadow of despair in her eyes.

Hearing a knock at the front door below, she leant over to the window, straining to catch sight of whoever it might be. All she could see was a few puddles on the cobbles and the top of a man's head, sleek with Brylcreem.

Sylvie opened the door, exclaiming crossly in French and saying that he was too early, her voice ringing along the mews. The door shut and Sylvie rushed upstairs.

'Henri's here,' she said, peeling off her dressing gown and wiping furiously at her face with a tissue. 'I've told him off for being premature, but his excuse was that he needed to put the champagne on ice.'

'Champagne!' cried Nell in delight. 'And who is Henri?'

'From the department. He managed to pull some strings and get away. He's always a good old egg.' Sylvie hurriedly combed out her hair so that it fell in inky waves over her shoulders. 'Very attractive, as you will see in a few moments. I thought, perhaps, you might like him.'

'Might I?' Nell sat on the bed and folded her hands on her lap. She glanced at herself in the mirror and saw a look in her eye that she did not like: a touch of fear, a shimmer of regret. 'I will see about that. Oh, what a lovely dress.'

It was scarlet, as bold and beautiful as its wearer. Ruched and pleated, it skimmed Sylvie's bosom and hips, a slit revealing her long legs to just above her knee.

'Lend me your powder puff, Nell,' she said. 'I need to take some of this shine off.'

Someone else knocked at the door.

'Oh, who else?' asked Nell, as she heard Henri's footsteps going down the stairs to the front door.

Sylvie blazed a swift look at her from beneath her eyelashes.

'Come on, are you ready, little Nell?' She

214

grabbed her hand. 'Let's get to that champagne.'

As she stood up, Nell heard the male voices of greeting below, and felt a shadow cover her heart.

'Who is it?' she asked, disbelieving her instinct.

'Champagne!' cried Sylvie, pulling her towards the stairs.

They reached the sitting room, just as the two gentlemen came up the steps from the front door.

'Nell,' said Sylvie. 'Dear Nell, look who I found.'

Something cold and hard gripped her round the throat as Alex Hammond walked into the room.

'Nell, it's so very good to see you.' He walked forward and grasped her hand to shake it with delicate courtesy.

His touch lingered and her hand trembled. He was there, right there. She stared openly, immobilised. Her memories from the last year, all the desire and the wondering and the regret, spun together making a whirlpool in her head.

'But how?' she asked, her voice distant and weak. 'Alex, how?'

Her cousin and Henri were laughing. 'See what happens in these strange and dangerous times,' Sylvie said. 'I bumped into him in a pub a few months ago. Isn't that absolutely marvellous?'

Nell sat down, hardly able to breathe. She continued to gaze at Alex, fascinated by him, her thoughts spinning. She plucked restlessly at the strap of her gown as Henri handed her a glass of champagne.

'Take a sip,' said Alex, sitting opposite her. 'It will do you good.'

She did just as he said, automatically, because she trusted him, she knew him, but now, suddenly enormously shy, she could barely look at him.

'I simply don't believe it,' she whispered.

Alex leant forward. 'Are you all right?'

She lifted her head to look him full in the face, and it was like looking into the sun. His ebony-black evening suit was sublime; she'd forgotten how blue his eyes were. He was smiling.

'How's Kit?' he asked.

Her shock burst out of her in a tremendous, earthy laugh.

'Oh, that old blanket. Very well indeed.'

Alex's expression was mercurial: sorrow chasing delight.

'You look beautiful in that dress.'

She wanted to say, *and you look beautiful too,* but her astonishment kept hitting her in hard waves and it was enough to stay sitting upright, holding her champagne glass steady.

Sylvie bounced onto the arm of the chair and put her hand on her shoulder.

'See?' she said, clearly delighted with herself. 'See how you can never plan for anything these days?'

As they glided up the escalator to Piccadilly Circus ticket hall, Nell became giddy with excitement, her stomach jittery. Alex was near her, Alex was with her – and she had thought she would never see him again. Even though the lights had been switched off all over the country and gloom settled so deeply that it was hard to recall a time when it

216

wasn't all dreariness, she enjoyed taking in the jolly couples, the glint of medals pinned to pockets, particularly splendid make-do-and-mend hats.

The sky over the West End was as pink and as luminous as the inside of a shell. Warm mid-summer evening air settled over crowds out in search of merriment. The four of them crossed Regent Street and plunged into the streets of Mayfair, where grand stucco houses glowed white in the soft light.

'Ha,' said Henri, 'I see they've all still got their railings. This is how it is, with you British. Only the poor people give them up for Spitfires.'

'Oh, shush,' Sylvie said. 'As well you know, Henri, you and I might as well be classed as British now, so you better get used to the whys and wherefores of this strange nation.'

She linked her arm through Henri's, leaving Nell to walk behind beside Alex. They had not spoken much amid the flurry of the champagne and the trot off to Baker Street station. On the crowded tube train, Alex had kept a polite dis-tance from Nell and she was grateful to him. She was struggling, but little by little, as her shock faded, or at least, as she got used to it, the memory of last summer returned as a reality. And her guilt embraced her. She had inexplicably, brutally, sent Alex on his way. She looked at him now in the evening light of the Mayfair street and wondered over and over again – *why?*

'Here we are,' said Sylvie, lifting her gown and stepping carefully down some steps. 'The Velvet Rose.'

'Oh good,' said Alex. 'A basement, where we can feel nice and safe.'

Nell glanced from her cousin to Alex and back again and was struck suddenly by panic: why had Sylvie never mentioned before that she'd met Alex in London?

The doorman doffed his top hat and opened the door onto the marble lobby where walls were hung with drapes of berry-red velvet. There were little gold crowns embroidered onto the corners of the fabric and engraved onto the opaque glass doors.

'They have a royal appointment, no less,' Sylvie confided, handing her coat to the attendant. 'Wonder who will be in tonight?'

'This girl never ceases to amaze me,' said Henri. 'She takes you to all the best places, doesn't she, Alex, old man?'

Nell paused as she unbuttoned her coat. What Henri said and the way he was laughing was loaded with meaning. She glanced at Alex.

'Well, we have to make the best of everything, these days, don't we?' said Sylvie, blandly.

The maître d' held open the double doors and Nell found herself in the half-light of a hexagonal room, muffled by sumptuous plum velvet. The air was heady with cigar smoke and perfume, and tinkling with conversation. Lamps were suspended over tables edged in shimmering mother-of-pearl. Couples sat close, leaning in to one another; parties were gay, animated, raising their glasses. On the dais a five-piece in smart evening suits dashed out a light swing tune.

They sat in a plush semicircular booth and the

218

waiter brought champagne and oysters. Alex was next to her, and his closeness made her insides float and then knot with confusion. While Henri and Sylvie whispered and giggled next to them, tucking into oysters, Alex politely asked her about her job.

'I am enjoying it very much, thank you. I have filed quite a good many stories. My editor seems pleased,' Nell told him hesitantly. 'They reduced the size of the newspaper again this week, to save paper.'

'And there's no lemons to squeeze,' interjected Sylvie as she scooped up another oyster. 'Same old story. Here goes. Bottoms up.' She threw her head back and tipped the shell against her mouth. Henri reached over to dab the drip of juice on her chin with his napkin.

The lights dimmed and a sharp spotlight hit the dais as the singer came on to a ripple of applause. Her soft, deep voice breathed into the microphone, sending shivers down Nell's spine. *'I get along without you very well...'*

Unexpected tears stung her eyes. In the rose-pink half darkness, she felt Alex take hold of her hand and rub his thumb around her palm. A sudden thought trapped her. In the bedroom at the mews house Sylvie had said that she had Henri in mind for her. But why say that, when she knew her and Alex's history? It was as if it no longer mattered. And when Henri spoke just now by the cloakroom, he seemed to know more about Alex and Sylvie than Nell could ever imagine.

Alex's touch in the darkness was beautiful and

219

excruciating, but completely inappropriate. She couldn't quite believe what was happening. An evening with Sylvie's colleagues to say goodbye as she was leaving for her new job was what she'd expected. And now here she was in seductive light, listening to a sentimental song with Alex Hammond holding her hand.

She pulled away from him and clasped her hands firmly in her lap. She lifted her chin and tried to concentrate on the beauty of the song, sensing Alex looking at her in the soft light. And, once again, she wanted to flee.

She woke with a crick in her neck and eased her eyes open slowly as slivers of memory fitted themselves together. Sylvie's sofa was just that little bit too short for her. She stretched her legs, thinking of the champagne, oysters and the dancing. Dancing with Henri, then with Alex. To dance with Henri was a whirlwind of banter and flirting; to dance with Alex was torture. He'd held her politely at a distance. Suddenly, he was a stranger again, neither of them knowing what to say to one another. A hundred questions poised and unsaid between them.

As she danced, her feet foolish and leaden, Nell had glanced occasionally back to the booth and wondered why Sylvie enjoyed meddling so much; setting up the evening and watching her subjects circle one another. As it was, the club closed earlier than expected because, as one was wont to hear all the time, there was a war on. Henri started to talk about a little drinking den he knew off Neal Street but, to Nell's relief,

220

Sylvie declared she was tired, and needed her bed – after all she still had some packing to do in the morning. Henri hailed a cab for them. Alex stood by and waited, saw Nell into the cab. His face was unreadable as he said goodbye. Nell in her inexperience and confusion didn't even acknowledge him, but laughed instead at Henri running off to flag another cab and then falling over the kerb and onto his backside.

And now, this morning, as she peeled herself up from the sofa and padded into Sylvie's kitchen to make the tea, she wondered at Alex, wondered at the whole scenario. In the hazy mid-morning light, it all seemed so remote, like a faraway dream; a play watched from the very back of the gods. She heard thumping up above and the latches on a suitcase snap. Sylvie came down in a pristine navy suit with a grey felt hat, looking far too good for someone who had drunk champagne until after midnight.

'Oh, you look the part,' Nell said. 'That is, for whatever it is you are going to be doing.'

'Put it this way, it's pretty darn safe. You must reassure your mother,' she said. 'It's a desk job in an office. Languages, you know. Just with a few more knobs on than I have in London.'

Nell braced herself. 'Sylvie, I wanted to ask you about–'

'Look, sweetie, my cab will be here any moment. Train's at midday and the traffic is always bad on Praed Street. Help yourself to whatever you like. In fact, take what you can from the larder. Mrs Char will be in later to finish up. Why don't you use the time? Go down to Oxford

Street? Have a browse round Selfridges? I saw a really pretty evening dress in there the other day; black with white piping. Delightful. Would suit you well.'

'The thing is, I really want to know why–'

A vehicle rumbled up the cobbles and tooted.

'Here I go!' cried Sylvie, leaping forward for a hug and a kiss. 'Be a good girl, keep digging up those scoops. I'll see you soon. Love to Auntie Moll, love to Mrs B!'

And in a commotion of suitcases, a delicious waft of Chanel No. 5 and a slamming of doors, she'd gone.

Nell sat with her tea in the rather bare, Sylvie-less room, and wondered. Yes, she should certainly use her time well. She'd telephone her father, try to arrange a visit. Perhaps take the train as far as Harrow, drop in for a cup of tea. The telephone sat on a fat directory. She placed it on her lap and turned to G for Garland. Halfway through the names beginning with 'Ga' she stopped, took a breath and turned to 'Bla' for 'Blanford'. She had no idea of Diana's father's initials, but the surname was not common, was it? The listing could not be too hard to find. But this, she realised in defeat, turning to the front page, was the *London* directory. As if it could be *that* easy.

Someone knocked at the door. The cleaning woman was here already, and she still not dressed.

'Just a moment,' she called, and quickly ran a comb through her curls in front of the mantle mirror and hurried down the stairs.

She opened the door to Alex.

'Oh crikey,' she uttered.

'Can I come in? I really want to speak to you.'

'Sylvie's not here. She left half an hour ago.'

'Nell, I want to speak to *you*.'

She stood back, steeling her nerves and let him pass her.

'You better put the kettle on,' she said, 'and make some more tea while I get dressed.'

Upstairs in Sylvie's bathroom she washed quickly, squeezed the last of the toothpaste. She thanked herself privately for packing the summer dress with the little shells on it, and its link to their beautiful sacred evening by the river. As she buttoned it up, her mind unfolded tentatively to a possibility, a way back, or even better, a way forward. A strange peace settled within her. Perhaps they would talk, work things out. Perhaps the impossible could happen.

As she popped back into her cousin's bedroom to get dressed she noticed that Sylvie had forgotten her handkerchief. She went over to the bedside table and picked it up. It had been pressed carefully into a kite shape and on its corner was a monogram in deep navy.

Downstairs, Alex was setting out the cups, whistling faintly. He seemed pleased, contented.

'Not one of my greatest skills, making tea, so you'll have to take a chance. And I don't know yet if you take sugar, but you won't be today; there is none, I'm afraid.'

'Is this what you came back for?' she asked him bluntly, and gave him the handkerchief.

He looked surprised, wondered where it had

got to.

'What was it doing up in Sylvie's bedroom?' Nell's voice hit a shrill note of rage. 'I think you need to tell me what's going on here.'

'Going on?' he said, coming towards her. He opened his arms to her. 'Nothing is *going on,* not from my part.'

She stepped away from him and flung up her hands. 'Oh no, you see, this is where I go. I'm leaving now. I'm going.'

She ran up the stairs to grab her case and rushed back to find herself face to face with him, barring her way.

'Not again, Nell. Don't run off again.' He looked bewildered, frantic, his eyes watering. 'Please, I want to talk to you. It's complicated, it's–'

'I don't want to hear any of it. When you held my hand in the club, it didn't feel right, and now, well now all of this makes me feel sick. Oh, where the hell is my coat, my handbag? I need to get out of here. I can't look at you now.' Her breath was coming hard and fast. 'You're not who I thought you were.' She was ranting now, incoherent with fury. 'You said your life expectancy was not good – and yet you're still here!'

She saw her words hit him like a blow, his face crumple. She bundled up her belongings and ran down the stairs to the front door. To turn the latch, she had to put everything down on the floor at her feet. The door fumbled open, breathless and urgent, she stooped to pick them all up again. And the moment she slipped out the door, once more, her conscience told her, she was running away from Alex.

As she stumbled outside onto the cobbles the air raid siren suddenly started up, keening through the air, ripping apart the sunshine. She darted along the mews, clutching her belongings, and hit the main street. People were hurrying; cars tooting, swinging to the sides of the road. A bus rumbled by, with passengers hopping off the back as it turned the corner. A coalman perched on his cart was urging on his mare; someone official was blowing a whistle.

She stood still, breathing hard. Where on earth should she go? What should she do?

'Is there a shelter round here?' she asked a man in a suit as he panted past her, his eyes wide with terror under his trilby.

'Down there, miss. Down the road. Under the church. The crypt.'

She remembered seeing the sign yesterday. Could it have only been yesterday?

She hotched up her case and took a step to the kerb when a hand fell heavily on her shoulder, pulling her back.

'There's no time. The mews has a cellar. Come back with me.'

The roads were emptying of people, front doors were slamming shut. She glanced in fear up at the sky. It was an empty blue summer's sky. The audacity of it, she thought, in broad daylight.

'It's all right, Alex,' Nell trembled, her thoughts jumbled. 'I'm going to go to the church, or the underground. It's that way, isn't it? I want to go and visit my father. I want to see him, you see.'

Alex was peering at her, his eyes puzzled.

'Seriously, Nell, we need to get to the cellar.'
His hand gripped her arm. 'Now.'

She twitched her arm ineffectually to try to release his hand. They stood together for a few moments more, the siren wailing, surrounding her, urging her.

'But there aren't any planes, Alex. It's a false alarm. We have them out at Lednor all the time.'

And then she heard them, the engines humming. She dipped her head in fright as the droning grew heavier and heavier by the second. The sound folded up the air, making it uneven and full of metal.

And then she saw it, high up, between a gap in the buildings at the far end of the street: on the horizon, the squadron, like a fleet of black arrows in perfect V-shape, regimented and in control. Advancing, tearing open the sky.

'Christ, Alex,' she uttered.

He pulled her along the mews in such a desperate rush that she turned her ankle on the cobbles. He opened the little door under the stairs and she followed him down concrete steps, dipping her head under low beams. There was a battered sofa, blankets, an oil lamp. Alex quickly struck a match and the lamp glowed feebly, highlighting the dusty brickwork, reams of cobwebs, the green line of damp creeping up the wall.

She slumped into a corner of the sofa as cold, blood-freezing realisation filled her guts. The unmistakable uneven beat of the engines swooped low, over their heads, and the first bomb fell like a crunch of thunder into the ground, then again, and again. Again.

The foundations flinched. It's my turn, she thought, cowering on the sofa, holding her head in her hands. It's all over. Alex sat beside her, put his arm over her shoulder. The deep thuds continued in hideous, punishing rhythm, as if a giant was kicking a keg of beer over and over again. The earth rocked with every one, a trickle of dust fell from the joists over her head. In the corner, dust poured down like water.

She moaned, pushed her fingers deep into her hair. When she dared, she looked at Alex. His face was white, startled, his eyes like black pools in the lamplight.

'Whatever you do, keep the light going,' he said, opening his arms wider to her, pulling her close. He wrapped his body over hers, shielding her. 'Keep the light going.'

She felt his heart pounding through his shirt, his grip on her tighter and tighter. Pressure pushed down on her body. Her guts were cold, twisting. She wanted to speak to him, but couldn't form words in the mess of her terror. Her throat was hot and tight. They were bombing them blindly, any old how. One, two, three, count them. They were degraded together, she and Alex, cowering in their hole.

The silence then was like death. She slowly became aware of the stench of drains and damp. The horror, the nightmare cramped close to her in the darkness.

Alex moved away from her, to sit upright on the sofa. She heard him say, 'Are you all right, Nell?'

227

She wanted to answer him but her mouth was dry, her tongue stuck to her gums. She found his hand and pressed her own into his. She brought his hand up to her mouth to kiss it.

Presently he said, 'Can you move?'

'Yes,' she managed, 'I just want to get out of here.'

Alex tried the door and she saw his relief that the hallway was intact, that the building had not been hit. But, as he opened the front door, the stench of burning hit her. Clouds of smoke blocked the sun and forced the afternoon into evening. The sky was on fire. An angry light glowered down on them, smoke billowed upwards. She came and stood next to him on the cobbles, not wishing to leave his side for a second.

She breathed fire and brick dust as they stumbled in shock to the end of the mews. Hosepipes snaked along the centre of the road, firemen were at work, ambulances parked with back doors flung open. Thick white dust covered cars, lampposts, everything. Three houses along from Sylvie's mews was a shattered, gaping void. A neighbour, in dressing gown and wellies, was stumbling over rubble, calling for her cat. There was a gathering of activity around another smoking ruin at the end of the street. Men stood in lines passing buckets of debris, some with masks and goggles on, others coughing with every other breath. A bedstead protruded rudely from the ruins.

'There but for the grace of God,' muttered Alex.

She gazed up at him, reappraising him. Her

fear no longer choked her. Dust filled his hair, and his eyes were bright red and watery against his ashen, exhausted skin. She knew that she would look exactly the same to him: almost unrecognisable.

But then someone hurried past them and said hello to her. It was the man in the suit from earlier, transformed by dust and shock. He seemed to have lost his hat.

He blurted, 'Hello again, miss. The shelter was full, so some kind soul took me in. Did you know, the church took a direct hit? I just went past there. It is full of blood and flesh...' He paused, thinking about what he had just said. 'Hats and shoes, slippers all over the place, like a jumble sale... I couldn't look. I couldn't stomach it. I suppose one must try to help but...'

She turned from him and pressed her face into Alex's shoulder.

'I need to take you home,' Alex said into her hair. 'I need to get you home to Lednor.'

But still, they stood and stared, deep in shock at the glowing horizon, the flames over the West End.

Alex sighed, devastated, 'London is well and truly burning.'

Nell suddenly cried, 'The moon! See Alex, the moon is pink.' She pointed at the faint crimson disc rising sedately over the ruined and bloody horizon. 'They even changed the moon.'

She came off the telephone to her mother and left the fuggy confines of the public call box. It had been the fifth one they'd stopped at on their

229

way, the first one which had a working line. She told her mother that she was all right. Her mother replied that Sylvie had called safe and sound earlier from Berkshire; she had caught her train well before the raid. But why was she, Nell, calling at three in the morning?

Now, curled up in the passenger seat, Nell stared out of the window, waiting for Alex to finish stretching his legs. They were parked on the country road somewhere near Amersham, some eight miles from Lednor. The indigo of the short summer night was becoming paler by the moment. Nell glanced behind her to see the flaming glow on the eastern horizon like a bloody sunrise. In contrast, the hawthorn hedgerows along the verge were pure and white with star-like blossom. She wound down her window and breathed the peaceful sweetness of cow parsley, drinking its balm like an elixir. Moths fluttered around the dipped car headlights. Dawn would be with them in less than an hour.

'It looks stormy up there, over in the west; can you feel the humidity?' said Alex getting back into the car. 'But never mind, we've not far to go.'

Nearly six hours earlier, they had made their way back through streets of chaos and confusion to Alex's digs on Baker Street and found that his car was intact and his landlady safe. He had insisted on giving Nell a tot of brandy and then filled the flask with tea. His landlady gave them some sandwiches and a mothballed cardigan for Nell, who was shivering, her bones aching with a residue of terror.

The landlady pressed Alex, telling him that

Nell should stay there and rest up.

'I just want to get out of here,' Nell replied. 'I want to go home.'

He drove as fast as he could through the night, negotiating roadblocks, police signs, slowing for the ringing ambulances, being bellowed at by an air raid warden for nearly running him over. Alex knew his way out along the short cuts out of town, through the tight grey suburbs and onto the A-road deep into Buckinghamshire.

Parked by the verge now, Nell could indeed feel the sultry heat of the storm approaching. She felt as if the heat of the fires of London was still upon her. Burning into her mind, her clothes, singeing her hair. Those people. Those poor, wretched people. Cold sweat broke down her back. She took the landlady's cardigan off and tossed it out of the window.

Alex fired the engine and turned down a lane. The narrow unclassified road unfurled before them like a rich purple ribbon as they meandered through dark beech groves.

'I want to cry, Alex,' she said in the gloom, 'but I just can't.'

'It's the shock, my love,' he said, reaching for her hand and pressing it tightly in his.

It took her a few moments to realise he'd called her *his love,* and yet in her turmoil, her earlier confusion and doubt began to reform and grow like a filthy stain.

'Nearly there,' said Alex, cheerfully. 'Nearly–Oh.'

The car shuddered, the engine made a whining noise and cut out.

'Don't tell me,' he said. 'Run out of petrol. What a fool.'

Nell stood in the blanketing, dark silence under the trees, while Alex unloaded her coat and suitcase from the boot. She decided that it would do them good to walk. They needed to breathe some good Chiltern air.

They began to walk down the lane. Meadows and hedgerows emerged from the gloom, their shapes shifting, and shadows melting and re-forming at every switch and turn in the lane. All the time, a great billowing bruise of cloud rose against the darkness of the western sky. A breath of cold breeze was chased by warm, stifling air. Nell could feel her forehead grow sticky and then cool in another instant.

'Hear that?' Alex asked, cocking his head. 'That's a nightjar.'

She wondered aloud if they were going to have another birdwatching contest and told him she hoped not for she was shattered and her skills were compromised.

'Don't you miss being a pilot?' she asked out of nowhere, her mind leaping among a thousand thoughts.

He told her no, that his new job was far more interesting and suited his background.

'And that is?'

'Do you remember that I told you I read geology at university? Well, I was called upon to lead a study in that field.'

'A study of utmost importance to the war effort,' she said, blandly, 'as you were posted away from Bovingdon last summer in the blink

232

of an eye.'

'I'm going to tell you, Nell,' he said, his voice grave in the stillness of the dawn, 'for I would trust you with my life.'

'You know me better than that,' she said, cockily. 'You can trust me with your soul.'

He stopped her and turned her towards him. 'Nell, it seems an age since I arrived at Sylvie's house, with this on the tip of my tongue. I wasn't there for a night out on the tiles. That was my perfect excuse. I was there because I wanted to see you. Was desperate to see you. I was there to say sorry and to try to explain everything. Will you let me do that now?'

She told him of course. She looked up at his face and her doubts shut themselves away again. She began to love every angle of his face, every curve of his lip. Everything.

'Last summer, I was tasked with the audacious mission of crossing the Channel and collecting samples of sand and earth from the beaches of Normandy.'

She nodded along, understanding the premise of what he'd just said. And then she froze and gripped his arm tightly. And then whispered in breathless disbelief, *'Normandy?'*

He pressed his finger playfully over her lips.

'Shush now. Careless talk.'

'But, but how...?'

'It's been a whole year in the planning. That's all I can say. I went to ground, really, stuck in a darned office near my lodgings on Baker Street mulling it over. Building the team, poring over the intricate details: weather, tides, prevailing winds. My team is in the Highlands now, training.' He urged her to walk on, his arm over her shoulder. 'And quite soon it will be time for us to cross the Channel.'

Nell put her hand over her mouth to try, ineffectually, to smother her distress.

'Let's just get you home,' he said. 'Number one priority for the moment.'

He took her hand and began to lead her.

Nell's scalp prickled then with fear, and her instinct caught a sudden change in the air around them. Deep in the sky there came a rumbling.

'Oh God,' she whispered. 'Not again, please.'

Her body began to tremble, her bones turning to ice. Alex was going away again and the storm was approaching. She was helpless. She pressed her hand to her throat. A flash of light signalled over the rolling hill like a silent beacon, and immediately a great crack of thunder exploded overhead.

'Christ, Alex... oh God.' She pressed herself to him and he began to laugh gently in her ear.

'It's thunder, that's all.'

Warm air billowed around them, shaking the treetops. Eddies broke over the meadows at the bottom of the valley, stirring it like a sea. A great drop of water hit Nell square on top of her head, another on the end of her nose. The breaking dawn grew dark, suddenly, and they began to run. They hurried through the village, where flashes of lightning repeatedly lit the roof of Miss Trenton and Miss Hull's cottage, past the church which looked surreal in the strange yellow light, and plunged on down the lane to Lednor

Bottom. Rain bounced back off the tarmac, and shattered the leaves in the hedgerows.

Another crack of thunder and another followed, as brutal and as violent as the air raid, and yet Nell suddenly laughed, turning her face up to the quenching rain, letting it wash through her hair and over her skin.

'It's scaring the life out of me!' she cried as they reached the ford. 'But it feels wonderful. Come on, don't bother with the stepping stones, straight through!'

They splashed through the shallow water, both still in their shoes and then stopped, both panting, as another rumble bowled across the sky like a great iron ball.

Nell pressed her hand to her chest. 'I'm alive! I'm alive!' she cried, jumping up and down and giggling. 'My God, I'm alive!'

Alex was laughing hard, his hair plastered to his head, his shirt almost transparent with rain-water.

'I can't go any further,' he said. 'You feel alive, I'm half dead.'

She grabbed his arm and urged him on.

'Round this bend, nearly there, here we are.'

She opened the gate to Pudifoot's cottage as the rain continued to pound them, lifted the doormat for the key and unlocked the door.

She was greeted by the tranquil, still air of the kitchen, with a lingering scent of vanilla and coal dust.

'Not too bad, considering it's been empty a year and a half,' she said. 'There's no electricity, though.'

Alex shut the door behind him and told her to come here.

The little cottage was in darkness, its tiny windows unable to afford them much of the dawn light at all, as the clouds continued to roll over. The rain was hammering on the roof. They heard a scuffling of tiny claws behind the dresser.

'You're not afraid, are you?' he asked her.

'Not of mice, no,' she told him.

She felt his fingertips touching the collar of her dress. He remarked how the fabric was sticking to her body. His hands moved around the back of her neck and lifted her sopping hair free. The cool air breathed onto her skin. Her instinct was to close her eyes but she dared not for she wanted to look at Alex and watch his face.

His lips found her throat and he breathed on her that he was sorry.

'For what, though, Alex?' she whispered.

'I'm sorry, but I need you. Have always needed you. There seems to have been a perpetual catalogue of misunderstanding between us, I–'

She laughed then and pressed her finger over his lips.

'Now who is talking carelessly.'

He held her shoulders and told her to stop joking.

'I know I can dance a lot better than I did last night.' He was laughing gently.

He kissed her softly first, as they reacquainted with each other, re-explored each other. And as he pulled her wet dress open, excitement ran like a hot dart up her body. She cried out and tears sprung from her eyes. She whispered to him that she was crying; at last, she was crying. He wiped her tears for her, and held her, rocking her.

They lay down together on the rag rug in front of the cold, dead range and he cradled her while the rain continued to beat down and the clouds finally rolled away.

The morning light was fresh and quenched, and found its way through Mr Pudifoot's windows and onto Nell's naked shoulders. Alex caressed her skin with his fingertips, moving in tiny, exquisite circles.

'This is no way to treat a lady,' Alex said quietly. 'And this rug has seen better days. You must be longing for your bed.'

'Alex I am, but nothing matters when I'm with you. I'm perfectly fine when you're here.' She felt honesty spilling out of her. 'So fine that I don't understand why I keep walking away from you. Look at me. I have just come through the worst day and night of my life, when my fear could not have been any greater than it was ... but here you are, still beside me. And I feel fine.' She sat up to get a better look at his face, confident in her nakedness. 'But the lesson is, I suppose, I should not fall in love with someone so very important.'

He was watching her with barefaced longing.

She asked him, 'Do you understand at last how I feel?'

'I know now how *I* feel,' he said, his voice choked with sorrow. 'And now I have to do it all over again: this *being important*. Of all the bad timing, I have a meeting today in town. In a bunker no less.' He reached for his watch. 'Christ. The meeting is in two hours. I have to go *now*.'

'With all those other important people,' said Nell, willing herself to smile. She reached for her dress and slipped it over her head.

'You are so brave,' he said. 'So very brave, and I just keep leaving you. The assignment is imminent. In the next week or two.'

She smiled at his earnest face. 'Alex. It's all right. I don't like it, but I understand.'

He sat up and reached for her, held her face tenderly in his palm, cupping her chin. He kissed her eyes. 'But it's not all right, is it?'

She watched his face suddenly close in shyness.

He hesitated, then said, 'Sylvie told me you had a boyfriend?'

'*What?*'

'A newspaper man? She didn't mention a name. That's why I left you alone. Let things go. I thought you should grab your chance of happiness with someone steady and sensible. Someone whose life expectancy–'

'She didn't mention a name because there *is* no newspaper man.' She laughed then. 'Oh, Sylvie.'

Alex got up and stretched, deep in thought, not mindful, Nell decided, of his effect on her. She gazed at him with total and assured certainty that she loved him.

He tugged on his shirt and began to sigh. 'It's wretched,' he muttered in agitation. 'So damnably wretched.'

'It is,' she said, sensing an enormous bravery at her core. She sat on Mr Pudifoot's fireside chair, registering a vague scent of mildew from it. 'But you will get through this one, and we will see each other again. After last night, I think we're invincible, and we will–'

He squatted beside the chair and grasped her hands.

'Nell, please, listen.'

The tone of his voice stopped her mid breath. She waited. The look on his face sent an acute arrow of pain through her chest.

'What is it?'

'I had relations with Sylvie.'

A laugh yelped out of her. She put her hand over her mouth and stared at him. When she could no longer bear to look at his eyes – their clear blue veneered with torment – she gazed beyond his shoulder at the bare little kitchen. There was the stove blacked by Diana Blanford, the dresser where Mr Pudifoot's medals had been found; on the floor, the rag rug where, two hours ago, she'd made love for the first time ever. Made love with Alex. And her father had stood right there and broken faith with her mother, broken faith with *her*, by kissing Diana Blanford. And then heaped betrayal upon betrayal.

'It was a mistake. She was weeping,' Alex was trying to explain, dragging his hand through his hair. His mouth was loose with regret. He looked dazed with sorrow. 'She was sad for her parents. I was lonely, I admit, amazed at the coincidence of bumping into her. London these days is a minefield of frantic liaison and passing strangers. But I drink alone. I keep myself to myself. To see her was a link back to you. To *you*, Nell. She had told me that you had this boyfriend. I actually felt sorry for her.'

Nell put her hand up to stop him. 'This is true to form,' she uttered, chilled and hard. 'Sylvie's brazenness knows no bounds. I expect it was a beautiful performance. Beautiful.' She covered her hands with her face, rested her knees on her elbows. 'She is sick. She must be ill. She deliberately toyed with us. Got us to meet again. She left your handkerchief where she knew I would find it. Strange how her mind works. Strange how she wants to play with our misery.'

Nell's mind drained of its despair and a calm steady glow of compassion replaced it. She looked up at Alex.

'But I won't let this happen again to us. Not this. Never this.'

'Nell, you are–'

'This is the story of our lives. Sylvie and me.'

'You don't know how lovely you are.'

Alex gripped both her hands in his and rested his head submissively on her lap.

His voice was lacerated. 'This has been killing me.'

Nell sunk her fingers into his hair, looked down on to the top of his head.

'You are with me, Alex,' she said. 'No one and no one thing is going to remove you now.'

As they slowly got dressed together, gathered their belongings, Alex remarked that he needed to retrieve the Ford from the side of the lane. That he'd probably get done for obstruction if the Bovvie RAF came trundling through.

'Olivers will have petrol. We can buy a can

240

from them.' She smiled at him. Her clear-mindedness about such practical matters made things seem easier for a moment or two.

'Dear, secret little cottage,' she said as she shut the door and hid the key back under the mat.

But just half an hour later, as he screwed the petrol cap back on and wiped his hands, took a breath of the new rain-washed air, considering his journey back to London, she felt her old fears trickle back and freeze across her chest. They stood under the trees where it appeared to be still raining. Drops fell randomly from the leaves, making her shiver. She wanted to tell him, come back to me safely, but knew that would jinx him. Curse him to disaster.

He told her again that he was a fool and took her in his arms. They stood, both unable to speak. Blood rushed through her ears, the warmth of his body so familiar now to her. Above their heads came the plaintive cry of a kite but she could not see it through the canopy of beeches.

'Alex,' she said. 'I know we will get through this.'

'I love how strong you are,' he said. 'Give Kit a big cuddle, or failing that, a big thump on the rump from me.' He laughed into her mouth as he kissed her. 'I love you.'

Yes, Alex, I will be strong, she assured herself as his car bumped away along the lane. She kept the flavour of his kiss on her lips for as long as she could. She would be strong enough for both of them.

Sylvie

It certainly wasn't her idea of heaven. Henri had assured her it was bliss out at Manor Park. No raids, peaceful countryside, interesting work, plenty of officers on site and at least four pubs within striking distance. Birdsong in the morning could be an idea of perfection to some, she thought, but a draughty cramped Nissen hut with a smoking oil lamp certainly wasn't.

She missed the city, the Velvet Rose, the strangely comforting, brown smell of the Underground; and the girl she shared her quarters with, Kristen from Oslo, snored like a sawmill. Still, Henri was visiting this weekend and promised her lots of fun. Fun? If he called dragging miles down rutted lanes on a pub crawl fun, then he was certainly in for it.

Frustrated, her energy sapped, she braced herself to get ready for her early shift. She pulled on stockings donated in exchange for a kiss from the spiv at the Horse and Groom, buttoned up her second-best suit and checked her reflection. A new and now permanent frown creased the space between her eyebrows. She drew out her Elizabeth Arden powder puff and dashed it over her face. The frown remained. Ticked off, she slammed her drawer shut, forcing the bulk of sleeping Kristen to flinch, turn over and resume her vibrato snuffling.

Sylvie opened her diary between the pages of which she kept Auntie Mollie's letter. She scanned the pages of her aunt's correspondence quickly again, taking in the begging for a visit to Lednor one weekend soon. Sylvie would reply later that day: 'not until at least September'. She'd have to drum out the cliché that 'things were hotting up', something she'd heard numerous people saying in the corridors and mess halls of the establishment. But then, things were always hot under the collar at Manor Park. It was the perfect no-questions-asked excuse.

She simply didn't feel like going back to Lednor. There was something about guilt, she decided, that turned her stomach, made her not want to see those responsible for making her feel it. Lednor, in its quiet little valley, did not hold any sort of allure for her. It had never been her home.

Sighing, she leafed over a few more pages of her diary, working out if she could possibly meet Auntie Mollie in London for an afternoon. She paused, frowning, and then turned the pages back.

She looked at herself in the mirror, put her hands on her hips and said quite loudly, 'Oh, I see.'

Kirsten opened her eyes and muttered in Norwegian before flinging her arm over her face.

And then, a few shocked moments later, Sylvie said, once again, 'I see.'

Henri roared up in his little Austin, beaming with smiles, his hat cocked over one eye.

'Your *voiture* awaits you, mademoiselle.'

'I hope you've got a full tank,' she said, ducking in and shutting the door.

'*Bonjour* to you, too,' said Henri and patted his stomach in a manly way. 'A full tank? You can bet your life on it.'

'Yes, very funny. You're taking me to Beaulieu.'

Henri stuck the car in first and pulled away from the Manor Park gates, protesting that it was mucking miles away.

'You mean, *Beaulieu?*'

'It's where Alex Hammond is now stationed. I have to speak to him.'

'On a matter of national urgency?'

Sylvie insisted that it was, in a manner of speaking.

As the Austin hurtled down the B-roads, Henri commented on his government-issue petrol ration and that he'd have some explaining to do when a week's worth disappeared in a day. And, quite frankly, you couldn't just bowl up at Beaulieu and ask to take tea with one of the 'inmates'.

'You have your contacts, Henri,' Sylvie said. 'I'm relying on you to reel them in.'

'*Merde*, you think me more capable than my commander does.'

That went without saying. Sylvie allowed her fingers to walk across Henri's knee.

'Get off, Sylvie, who do you think I am? I thought Hammond was your chap, anyway? He of the Baker Street Irregulars? He kept that quiet that evening at the Velvet Rose.'

'I wouldn't know. It's all classified information,' said Sylvie sweetly. 'Put your foot down.'

Trunk road followed trunk road and, by late afternoon, the little Austin, now snarling and wheezing with the effort, crossed the undulating heathland of rural Hampshire that rolled down to the coast. Sylvie relished the tremble of excitement in her stomach whenever she caught sight of the distant sea, a surreal blue segment between a cleft in the New Forest scrub. How she had hungered for it since her exile in England.

'Just across there, Henri, is home,' she sighed, giddy with the intangible thought of it. 'Just across *La Manche.*'

Henri agreed and warned her that it might no longer be as she remembered. Sylvie fell silent as he muttered on about his own home, in deepest Lorraine, being very much further away. He laughed because, he said, many of his fellow countrymen felt they had always belonged to Germany anyway.

'Your sarcasm is not endearing, and your loyalty to *La France* questionable,' said Sylvie as they pulled up by the formidable gates to the station disguised within a rambling stately home. 'But this is where your negotiation skills come in. Come on, this is why Churchill employed you.'

Henri got out of the car and went to speak to the guard at the barrier. He became ensconced, so Sylvie used the time to check her lipstick and reassert the position of her hat.

His thump on the roof of the car made her jump.

'Chops away, Sylvie,' Henri announced. 'Checkpoint Charlie is summoning him. He's a top man in there, you know. And, by all

245

accounts, extremely busy.'

'Can you make yourself scarce?'

Henri agreed that he would if he had to and indicated that he'd seen a nice little *auberge* of some description in the previous village.

'I'm going to take Mr Hammond to the pub, so keep out of our way,' she told him.

She waited, leaning against the car. The guard kept his eye on her and she expected that he thought her a spy. She let her mind wander back to Lednor and the reasons she resisted visiting. She could hardly look Nell in the eye at the best of times, but after this, how could she ever go back? She felt adrift, then, as the minutes passed and Alex Hammond kept her waiting. She was alone, but the idea hardly surprised her. Everything she ever did, she did on her own.

The sound of an exchange of greeting and the click-clunk of the gate drew her attention, made her tilt her chin in expectation.

'Hello, Alex,' she said, her smile sweet and contrite. 'Isn't this a lovely surprise?'

He strode over with the gait of a man far too busy for surprises, and far too important to even pass the time of day. His grin was taut. 'Don't tell me, you were just passing.'

'I must say, the tone of your voice isn't what I would expect from a dear old friend,' she said.

'I'm in the middle of preparing for an immensely crucial briefing. Your timing isn't perfect, Sylvie.'

'I admit, timing never has been my strong point. A quarter of an hour of your time is all I ask. And perhaps a little snifter.'

They walked quickly to the nearby pub in spiritless silence. Alex bought the drinks and set them down, glancing at his watch.

'What is this, Sylvie? I really have to...' He paused to temper the irritation in his voice. 'Nothing wrong, I hope? Nothing wrong at Lednor?'

'Depends what you call *wrong*,' she said.

'Spit it out, Sylvie.'

She sipped at her half pint of local ale, wincing at its bitterness, and watched his face closely as she told him she was expecting his child. His eyes glazed, their blue fading to grey. He dipped his head, momentarily stupefied.

'You're sure?'

She told him she was as sure as any girl could be.

'But I used, but we...'

'These things happen, Alex.' The ale was making her eyes water. 'It's never foolproof, now, is it?'

Alex took a large draught of his own drink, wiped his hand over his mouth. He cradled the empty glass loosely in his hand, staring at it. There was a cleft between his brows, as if his agony was manifesting right there.

'I have got the most important operation unfolding ahead of me, I have men relying on me and everything I can give them, men's lives, my life ... how can I...?' he muttered. 'Oh, my Christ.'

Sylvie sat upright, her hands folded demurely on her lap. 'Alex, what are you saying?'

'Can't you go back to Lednor, to your auntie...' Alex's head snapped up and he stared at her. 'Oh

God, Nell.'

'Do you think they'll want anything to do with me now? Especially Nell? After all, she had a thing for you, didn't she?'

'A *thing*?' His blanched face cracked as he laughed bitterly. 'A thing, you say?'

'You're not angry, are you, Alex?' she asked.

He pressed his lips together so hard that the skin around his mouth went pale.

'We will marry once your mission is over?'

Sylvie let the question float between them and watched the man's attractive potency disintegrate in front of her. He glanced around the pub, his eyes flinching and flickering with each desperate idea that cleaved his mind.

'Sylvie,' he uttered, like an enquiry. He sat back in his chair and regarded her as if seeing her for the first time. A hopelessness haunted his face.

She stared at him openly, aghast, registering the hell in his eyes.

'Alex,' she said, earnestly, and reached forward to take his hand. 'Alex, I have no one.'

Nell

At the *Bucks Recorder*, Nell was on to the story that a great deal of aluminium was still needed to replace the fleet of Spitfires destroyed the summer before, and so the people of Buckinghamshire were being called on once again to clear out their

248

cupboards. *Don't forget Grannie's attic,* Nell tapped into her typewriter, *and think how proud your young son would be if he knew his toy cars were going to be part of one of the great machines that defend the skies over Britain, and our very freedom.*

'Is your filler ready yet, Miss Garland?' Mr Collins called across the office. 'The leader page is ready to go, bar that space. Do we have a picture? We need a picture of saucepans. Do we have one? Can you size it up?'

Feeling unduly harassed, Nell pulled her finished copy out of the typewriter, handed it to Mr Collins and hurried over to the filing cabinet. She began to leaf through the buff dividers, the A to Z files of photographic prints, searching under P for pans, S for saucepans and scrap metal, trying to ignore her sudden giddiness from standing up too quickly at Mr Collins's bidding. She took a deep breath to steady herself. Her fingers shook as she plucked at the paperwork, a steady chill pricking her blood. She'd felt all right this morning. Perhaps she was coming down with something. Anthea had had a bad cold last week, which had wiped the smile off her face for a while.

'Preferably one with people standing around a big haul of it,' Mr Collins insisted from across the room. 'You know – housewives, children, old men.'

She was used to his voice now. His perpetual badgering ensured that the newspaper always went to press on time, and near-as-damn-it perfectly typeset too. But just then, as she concentrated on the task, she felt her patience

249

stretching and annoyance bit her right there.

'All right, Mr Collins, I'm on to it now!' she cried.

Anthea's head snapped up.

'Nell, you're looking in the wrong drawer. Those files only go up to 1938. You need to look over here.'

Nell pushed the draw shut with an angry bang, catching her finger. She stuck it in her mouth, her eyes smarting. Anthea was at her side.

'You look very pale, my dear.'

Nell whispered, tears in her eyes, 'I think I'm going to be sick.'

'When you're ready, Miss Garland,' called Mr Collins.

'Oh, put a sock in it, Collins,' muttered Anthea, taking Nell by the arm and ushering her outside.

In the toilet, Nell knelt down on the hard ceramic floor, expecting the inevitable.

'Must have eaten something,' she tried to call out to Anthea, as the juices in her stomach lurched, and cold sweat lapped up her throat.

Anthea tapped on the door. 'Are you all right in there?'

'Nothing's coming up,' she said. 'Just feel so awful.'

After a bit, she unlocked the door. Her colleague handed her a soaked hand towel. 'Have a dab down with this and go and see your doctor.'

Nell would have her know it couldn't be anything serious enough for that.

Anthea smiled in her enigmatic way. 'I'll come with you if you like. It happens more often than you think.'

'Anthea, I don't know what you mean...'

'Just one look at you, my dear. I can tell. I'm an old married woman, remember. And he can marry you as soon as you like. Because you know what people will do. They'll start counting on their fingers, but won't say anything as they are generally too polite. And these days, well, anything goes.'

Nell put the lid down on the toilet and sat on it. She stared up at Anthea, her mind emptying in a peculiar and precarious way. Anthea leant nonchalantly against the cubicle door, examining her nails.

Through a mouth dry as cotton, Nell maintained, 'I don't know what you mean.'

'Speak to your sweetheart, my dear. It's Mr Hammond, isn't it? I knew you were made for each other, I saw it, way back then,' said Anthea. 'And when he gave you that brute of a dog ... well – it was like he gave himself to you.'

Nell was stubbornly silent, her insides barricading themselves firmly against the utter wonder of that idea.

Anthea insisted, 'You know exactly what I mean.'

Nell bowed her head. A pellucid comprehension of her situation grabbed hold of her by the scruff of the neck so hard that she flinched.

'I can't tell him,' she murmured. 'For I don't know where he is.'

'Story of our lives, these days,' said Anthea. 'The men come and go as easy as breathing.'

'Oh no, Alex is coming back,' rallied Nell, prickling defensively. 'I love him and he loves me.'

251

'I know, I can see by the look on your face. Oh, bless you. Look at you.'

'It's just that he's at a secret location preparing for a God-awful mission. How can I tell him *this*? He will be distracted and so, so worried. I can't do anything to jeopardise what he's about to do. It's so important. He's on a knife edge. By God, the last time I saw him... So many men are relying on him. It's so, so *deadly*.'

Anthea held out her hand. 'Come on, miss. Let's get you some fresh air. See if we can't coax a cup of tea out of that grumpy waitress at the tea room. Mr C can find his own damn photograph.'

As they left, Mr Collins was bent over the filing cabinet, muttering expletives.

On the stairs down to the street, Anthea stopped suddenly and whispered, 'Shall you tell your mother yet?'

'Oh no,' Nell replied. 'She has far too much on her mind. You know how indisposed she is. I won't burden her with this. Just an announcement of my wedding when the time comes. She can do the workings out later if she likes.'

'That's more like it, girl.'

A fine mist of rain was falling from a milky summer sky as Nell linked arms with Anthea and they trotted across the cobbled square. She turned her face up to the droplets, relishing their coolness on her cheeks and brow. She remembered the soft touch of Alex's fingers, his breath on her neck. The wash of rain felt like a baptism; something almost like ecstasy. She and Alex were going to have a baby. They were going to have a life together when all of the horror was over.

Her mind did an about-turn and the years seemed to unfold before her in an open and welcoming winding road. I'll save the good news for him, for when he comes back. And he will. For he promised me.

'When Alex is back and safe, then, Anthea,' she giggled, as an uncertain euphoria took hold of her, 'you will be dancing at my wedding.'

Nell kept to her promise to herself and declined to tell her mother anything; but she wrote some of her news to her father in a letter the following day. It had been a while since she'd written, and a long while since he'd replied, so a shyness swept over her and stilted her words. She told him, *Dad, I have something wonderful to tell you. I have met a flight lieutenant in the RAF and he and I want to be married.* She wrote, *Everything is so difficult at the moment, for I am unable to see him. But he is a magnificent man, and loves to birdwatch. He is better than I, but not as good as you, Dad, I'm sure you'll like him very much.*

She folded the letter, and registered a sudden, unsavoury trickle of fear about Sylvie and Alex, then watched it fade away. Addressing the envelope, she speculated about the house her father lived in on Harrow Hill. She wondered at Diana Blanford's parents and their thoughts on the whole matter, their daughter's relationship with their soon-to-be-divorced house guest. To all intents and purposes, Nell decided, he was their lodger. She longed to go there, and find out what kept him away. She wanted to take a step towards understanding him, to tell him how the Sep-

253

tember Garden was doing, now that it was about to bloom and run riot. And tell him all about Alex.

How her dad must miss the valley, she thought, as she set out down the lane with the letter to the postbox in the village. He had missed two spring times. And now the summer was turning another corner. And he would miss that too.

When she stepped back into the hallway, her mother was on the telephone, her voice singing with astonishment and laughing with joy. 'Oh, my dear, well that is wonderful, I must say, if not an absolute surprise.'

Mollie pressed her hand over the receiver and hissed to Nell, 'It's Sylvie. Calling from Berkshire.' She tapped her nose with her finger.

Nell stood by, her scalp tingling with irritation. Her mother had been drinking, that was obvious. She revelled in the clandestine nature of Sylvie's work, all the *ask no questions* and *keeping mum*. And now she was hooting, 'Sylvie, you have made me so happy; why, that is wonderful news.'

Nell could not help but shrug, wondering at Sylvie's latest escapade. She sat on the bottom stair and did not have to wait long, for the telephone call was soon cut off by the operator.

'Blast this three-minute thingy,' cried Mollie. 'I need a good drink after that!'

Nell followed her swiftly into the drawing room, wondering why.

'Our lovely Sylvie is ... wait for it ... going to be married.' Mollie's glee was radiant, her eyes wide and bright. Her hand clutched the heavy crystal decanter and she splashed whisky into a

254

cut-glass tumbler.

Nell kept her smile fixed. She was surprised but mildly pleased for her cousin. Sylvie was perplexing and unpredictable and forever out of her orbit. But, perhaps now, she would settle down.

But then, Nell beamed inwardly, didn't she have her own surprising news to impart? But not yet, for it wasn't quite the right time to tell her mother. Let her get over this news first. As for Sylvie, who had she bagged now? Poor Henri?

Her mother's tongue was loosened by the whisky. 'My dear,' she said to Nell. 'Do you remember that lovely man? Oh, when I had that to-do with the bonfire, burning your *dear* father's paintings.' Nell ignored her mother's sarcasm. 'You remember, don't you? Oh, of course you do. Didn't he take you to the cinema once?'

Nell shrugged childishly, thinking only of Alex and their secret. Their soft, warm secret. She burrowed down with it, held it tight.

Her mother was laughing. 'This is the way it goes, these days; there's no need to get high and mighty about it. As long as it's born before the wedding night, no one seems to care, do they?'

Nell flinched, thinking, does Mother know about *me?* Why is she talking about *Alex?*

Mollie blundered on. 'Our Sylvie is going to marry ... wait for it ... that very same Mr Hammond.'

'Mister...?'

'Yes, oh now, Nell, don't be so prudish. I can see what you're thinking. She's a game girl, got caught out, that's all. Yes, dear, she's pregga. And going to be Mrs Alex Hammond, rather quite soon, I think.'

Nell's mouth gaped in horror. 'She *can't* be!'

Mollie declared that no one can afford to dilly-daily, not these days.

Nell's skin contracted in shock, tightening over her bones. Her jaw slackened, she felt her heart crushed by a fist. She stood rigid, staring at her mother, who was still speaking, her voice bizarre and joyous.

'Ho, now Nell, you know what she's like. Our darling Syivie. When she's on to something, she really is. "Soon", she said. Oh, so very soon. I wish to God I could find a way to tell Beth. How she would love it – she'll be a grandmother.'

Adele

A sudden thump from upstairs, and something rolling across the floor. Adele looked up from her pile of potatoes to the ceiling. Easing herself up from the kitchen chair, she winced. She only had a little while to go and her baby would be born. And then? What then for Estella and Edmund? She panted her way up two flights of stairs. She walked the long landing and grasped the handle of the spare room – the one that little Nell had stayed in when she had been their summer guest just three years before – and opened the door.

The children were already in their dressing gowns, their heads bent over their schoolbooks. Adele taught them to be ready for bed when she came to give them supper. It saved her time.

She glanced quickly at the windows; the shutters were closed, the curtains drawn. Not one chink of light would show to anyone standing below in the street. The lamp was dim and, at her insistence, set away from the window by the bed. With a dull nagging fear she wondered how much the neighbours knew; how much they turned a blind eye.

Edmund looked up from his homework and beamed at her, his smile brightening his pale, narrow face. 'I have learnt my nine times table today,' he said cheerily. 'Estella tested me. Will you test me again, Madame Ricard?'

'Yes, all right. I will,' Adele murmured, distracted, wondering, as she always did, how the children managed to exist, and still be *children*, shut away in this stifling ill-lit prison.

Estella already squinted, complained of headaches. She probably needed new glasses. Edmund often chatted about the outdoors, the harbour, the billowing green fields, the *bocage* beyond, as if he was reliving a recurring dream. And yet, they complied, obeyed Adele daily in the confines of their stuffy bedroom.

Estella, sitting at the desk, piped up, 'Adele, will you tell us a bedtime story? The story of the horses again?'

She wanted to chastise her with *It's Madame Ricard to you*, but hadn't the heart to when she looked at the little girl's open expectant face.

'Yes, yes,' she said. 'But first, I must tell you something else. Something else very important.'

'Is it *Maman* and *Papa?*' Edmund leapt

forward, bright and eager as always.

Adele ruffled his black hair with the tips of her fingers. 'No, my dear. No, it's not.'

'But you still think they are with Madame Orlande?' said Estella. 'That's what you said, didn't you? They've all had to go away to the camps, to work, to help *La France* through the war. Isn't that so?'

'Yes, that's right,' Adele said quickly.

'I wanted to go too,' Estella said.

'Nine times one is nine. Two times nine is eighteen,' quoted her brother.

As Adele took some clean sheets from the armoire, nausea rose in her throat. She stayed perfectly still while the boy's confident little voice recited his tables. The sickening worry of the last few months had changed into something even more precarious.

She glanced around, unable to look them in the eye. 'We are going to play another game, children. You wanted a story about the horses, Estella?'

The little girl nodded, her tired, pinched face pitifully eager.

'Well, when it's darker, when it's quieter, we're going to go down to the stable and climb up to the loft. You are going to sleep up there, above where Ullis and Tatillon used to live. And I'll tell you the story there.'

Estella was wrapped in innocent rapture. 'We're going outside? In the night-time?'

Edmund, ever studious, asked politely, 'Can I leave my lessons now, Madame Ricard? Did I do well in my times table test?'

'Yes, Edmund,' Adele said, not remembering a

single sum. She bundled up some bedding inside the sheets and gathered some pillows with trembling hands. Her back was aching, the skin on her pregnant belly taut, her patience sharp. 'I'm going to make up a nice bed for you in the attic, but you must be very quiet and very still. It's all part of the game.'

What a risk she was taking, she thought, what an utter, dreadful risk. But she loved her husband and would do whatever he asked of her. Last night he told her about the rumour: there were whispers about the children in the bistro. The Gestapo had a suspicion they were here. If she could get them out of the house, then Jean and the maquisards could spirit them away overnight and send them down the lines.

'All the way to Spain?' she asked him, her murmuring hoarse under the bedcovers.

'All the way to Spain,' he replied.

Adele had thought, then, of the irony of the sea just below their window, and freedom beyond, just within their grasp. But the dangers of going that way were far worse.

They would take them from the stable loft, Jean had revealed. They would come for them in a few nights' time. When, he would not tell her.

'And what about Monsieur?'

'That is the hardest part,' Jean said. 'We have to rely on his humanity. We are at his mercy.'

Dusk was falling rapidly as Adele climbed the steep stone steps between the two stable doors each with its own sign nominating the long-dead horses who fed the children's imaginations. She

259

made up a bed in the dark on the dusty attic floor. The air smelt musty, of vegetables, of earth and old straw. It was a cold, grim place for *her* to be, let alone two small children. A keen draught blew through the missing tiles on the roof. She could barely stand under the low sloping ceiling. It would be for just a few nights, she told herself, shivering. They would be fine.

Hurrying back down the path, she realised she would risk breaking the curfew by returning to the sea wall cottage after dark. But she decided, if she was stopped, she could claim she had been busy making the gendarme's *déjeuner*. She, as his housekeeper, had certain privileges, just as he did.

'Now, children,' she said, opening the bedroom door. 'This is very important. You must not say a word. You must follow me. And do exactly as I say. In fact, you must do exactly what any French person tells you from now on,' thinking of when the maquisards would come for them. 'Do you understand?'

'Madame Ricard,' Edmund stood in front of her, his face very solemn. 'Will the soldiers find us?'

Estella wondered, 'Are you going to stay with us in the stables after you've told us the story?'

'No, my dear,' she said. 'I have to go home.' She watched her face fall. 'Are you both ready?'

'Can I take my doll?'

'Yes... yes...' Tears stung at Adele's eyes. 'But that's all.'

The little girl held on to the doll, tucking it beneath her chin.

'I want to take my schoolbooks and pencils,' announced Edmund.

'All right!' Adele shouted in frustration. 'Put your hats and coats on, put your thick socks and boots on.'

She helped the little girl tie the rabbit fur collar she'd made her around her shoulders. She told Edmund to go first; to run along the path. Thank goodness, she thought, that his clothing was dark; he disappeared into the evening. She held Estella's cold little hand and they hurried after him. By the time they reached the top of the attic steps, Adele was panting with a great stitch ripping at her side; Estella was in tears.

'Don't leave us here,' the little girl begged. 'Please don't leave us.'

Adele did not look at her.

'Here is some bread and cheese.' She showed them a basket in the corner. 'And some milk. There's enough for a day...'

'Aren't you coming back? Stay, please stay.'

'Get into bed and I will tell you the story,' Adele said, sitting uneasily on the splintered, creaking floorboards over the empty stable below.

She listened to the profound silence of Montfleur beyond the stone walls; the subjugation, the tedious fear. She whispered her story to the children. She told them of the brave horses – one white, one chestnut – and how they went so eagerly to Flanders to help their masters win the Great War. They triumphed over the shells and the bullets, the mud, the wire and the wasteland. They helped take the wounded soldiers back to the hospital barracks; they helped take the great guns forward to strike at the enemy.

'Our same enemy,' Edmund whispered in the dark. 'Even now.'

Adele looked over at him, but in the pitch-black she could not see his face. She could barely see her own hands in her lap.

'That's right, Edmund,' she said. 'And now, as you settle down to sleep, as you drift off – you too, Estella – if you listen very carefully, you can almost hear Ullis and Tatillon below, snorting and snoring in their straw. They'll keep you safe,' she said. 'They will look after you tonight. Don't be frightened. And soon, very soon–'

Adele stopped herself, for she realised she had no promises to make.

'Very soon,' she told the children, 'you will fall asleep.'

Adele woke, alone, in her own bed, to a flat, cold dawn. This was not so unusual, as the *Orageux Bleu,* when night fishing, often didn't come back into harbour until six, and then there was the unloading of the fish, the work still to be done. But this morning was different. This morning *felt* different. For Jean and Simon had not set sail.

She turned over in the bed. As the chilly depths of the heavy covers shifted around her, she felt the continual yearning in her blood, the craving that had stayed with her ever since that dreadful June last year: a desire for peace, for safety, for a life. How unprepared we all were, she thought, to give up France, to give up our lives. The baby stirred and dealt her a wakeful kick. She thought of the children and whether they had slept; she prayed that they were not as fearful as she was.

Her mother-in-law was at her door, tapping. 'Are you awake? Simon's been here already. You must get up.'

Adele hauled herself upright against the headboard, feeling a swell of panic in her chest at the tone of the older woman's voice.

Madame Ricard walked over to the window. She opened the blackout and stared at the sea.

'There have been explosions, out on the railway line near Cherbourg.'

'So,' Adele ventured carefully, 'it was a success?'

Madame Ricard turned and stared at her. The grey light from outside gave her wrinkled face a ghostly demeanour. Her eyes, blue like her son's, were like ice. 'Depends which way you look at it. Switch on the radio.'

Adele moved swiftly to the wireless in the corner of the bedroom, tying the cords of her dressing gown as she went. She fumbled with the earpiece. Electricity hummed in the wires, an airwave crackled. Static snapped around the room.

Madame Ricard informed her, 'Simon came here to tell me, we must send a message. Urgently.'

'Where is Jean?' Adele asked, as she bent her head to listen deeply into the earpiece, her fingers on the dial. She heard it immediately: *V for Victory* tapping through the airwaves, a constant covenant; part of her consciousness.

'He is hiding. Somewhere beyond Valognes. In the *bocage*.'

Adele looked at her mother-in-law.

'Quickly, quickly ... this is what you must send.'

Madame Ricard unrolled a scrap of paper. Adele recognised Simon's handwriting.

Pole Star sighted. Moon behind the clouds.

Adele flexed her fingers against the cold and began to tap out her appeal. *Do you read? Over. Do you read? Over.* She listened hard for the response. At last, an acknowledgement. She signalled the message slowly, methodically into the airwaves. Over and over again.

'Please tell me what has happened,' she asked, as she continued to send the message.

'I'm not sure that I should.'

'Is it best that I know nothing about it? Is it that serious?'

Madame Ricard's dreadful sigh made Adele look sharply at her.

'I'll tell you what everyone else in Montfleur will know within the hour,' she said, her features drooping with unspoken dread. 'We blew up a troop train near Cherbourg. It did not go as well as expected. The explosives were not the right mix and not enough damage was caused. Not enough damage compared to the risk that we took. Simon just told me he wishes that Androvsky was still here. He knew his dynamite. He knew how to do it properly.'

Adele shook her head. She didn't want to waste her time absorbing Simon's opinions when her husband was not home. When her husband was in danger.

'Is Jean all right?' she demanded.

Madame Ricard looked down at her. 'Yes, but he made a dreadful mistake.'

Adele hurried along the Montfleur streets, her heavily pregnant stomach and grimacing face rousing the startled interest of passers-by. She was desperate to get to the Orlande house quickly to check on the children, take them some food. They were certainly not going to be the maquisards' priority today, or anytime soon.

In the marketplace small groups of people gathered around the stalls, fingering the scanty produce, and in the bistro, drinking dregs of coffee. Caps and hats were pulled down against the cold. Collars were turned up and glances directed over shoulders. There was a murmuring, like the static from the radio in the bedroom. Adele kept her head down and hurried past, not wishing to catch anyone's eye. She could not risk a single *bonjour* and give herself away. The news must be filtering through to everyone, as if the shock waves from the bombs on the railway line had infiltrated Montfleur.

As she stepped down the kerb to the side street that led to the house, she felt, more than heard, a heightening of voices, a rippling through the square. Everyone began to face the same direction, jerking their heads for a better view. She, too, stopped and stared. Around the corner of the *mairie*, a small company of German soldiers marched into the square. They advanced in perfect formation, faceless under rounded helmets, inhuman behind the grey uniform. Shoulder to shoulder, they carried their weapons with chilling command. Not such an unfamiliar sight, Adele told herself, and yet her panic sharpened as the broken-engine sound of a posse of motorbikes followed them, a motorcade for the *Kommand-ant's* car. It parked outside the *mairie*. The *Kommandant* got out. The soldiers stood in their ranks, facing the people of Montfleur.

Monsieur Orlande in his gendarme uniform appeared at the door of the *mairie* and hurried down the steps. He saluted the German officer, his demeanour solid and confident.

A man next to her muttered, '*Collabo*,' and spat on the ground.

The *Kommandant* began to speak to Monsieur, and Adele, hoping the spectacle in the square would prove a distraction, turned to walk towards the Orlande house.

She paused. The whistling of a megaphone sliced through the cold air. The *Kommandant's* hard amplified voice split her ears.

'...for the crime committed last night against the German army, there will be certain retribution. The citizens of Montfleur will pay the penalty for the actions of the rebels, the communists, the criminals who have perpetrated this deed. Fifteen German officers have been injured. I am required to tell you that two have lost limbs.'

Adele stared. Her employer, Monsieur Gendarme, stood shoulder to shoulder with the German officer as he continued his address: 'This is inexcusable, and will be punished accordingly. Whoever carried out this crime may or may not be flushed out from among you, but you, the citizens of Montfleur, must and will pay.'

Villagers collectively gasped in shock, threw violent glances between themselves. A woman cried out. A man shouted. On the steps, the gendarme stepped forward and began to talk earnestly with the *Kommandant*.

Adele thought, hopelessly, *perhaps he is trying to reason with him. Make him change his mind.*

'No soldiers were killed,' someone behind her said. 'We should not be the ones to take the blame.'

'The most damage was to the train and the tracks,' said another. 'What can he mean, we will pay?'

'It's obvious. No one is immune from this.'

'Orlande better be persuading him otherwise.'

'About time he protected his own people.'

Adele turned away, their panicked voices receding into a blur of anxious speculation. Her hand shook as she unlocked the gate but a strange security enveloped her once inside the silent void of the Orlande house. She felt removed, suddenly, from the announcement in the square – and its horrific reality.

In the basement kitchen she sawed the loaf of bread and found a dab of butter, something to feed the children. Her mind turned its way to Jean. *A dreadful mistake,* his mother told her. Adele presumed he had become separated from the cell and was hiding out in the cold, misty dampness of the *bocage*. Was he injured perhaps? She would not let herself imagine the pain, the frustration of the man she loved. She must do her duty here; do what she could for the Resistance, for her comrades, unknown strangers to her, and yet still worthy of her very best.

The front gate creaked above and Adele jerked her head, her eyes suddenly smarting with confusion. A clump of a footstep overhead; Monsieur must have come home. What can he want? He was on duty until six tonight. Why should he come back now? Surely he'd be busy with the *Kommandant?* She heard him come quickly down the stairs from the hallway to the kitchen. She rose to greet him, to enquire at his unexpected return. And yet, instead of the kitchen door opening, it was shut fast. From the outside, the key turned in the lock.

Adele ran to the door, tried the handle. Thumped on it.

'Monsieur? Monsieur? What's happening?' she cried.

Her appeal was met with silence. Monsieur's footsteps retreated back up the stairs. Adele stepped back, astounded.

She ran to the kitchen window and squinted up into the garden to see Monsieur walking down the path, past the straggling, overblown lavender plants, past the naked bean frames. He opened the back gate wide and left it ajar. And it was then, through the gateway, that she saw them: three German soldiers, their rifles drawn.

She stood on tiptoe over the sink, reached up and fumbled with the latch on the window; she hauled down the sash with the stupid idea of climbing out, of running to the children. She wanted to scream, to scream her protest, but stopped. As Monsieur had once said, it might make matters worse.

All too quickly, she saw Edmund and Estella emerge and stand on the cobbles, which once rang to Ullis and Tatillon's hooves. They were bedraggled after their night and hungry morning in the stable attic. Edmund's hair stood on end. Estella was fastening her skirt, trying to tug her long socks up with one finger. Her rabbit fur collar over her shoulders. Monsieur had his hand on Edmund's shoulder, talking earnestly. The soldiers stood back, awaiting command.

Monsieur continued to speak to the children. Adele watched his mouth, aghast. A sheet of ice adhered to her insides. She'd told Edmund; she'd told Estella: *you must do exactly what any French person tells you.* She saw Edmund nod. She saw him breathe deeply and look up at the sky, as if he knew he, at last, would be free.

The soldiers moved in, towered over them, blocked them from her view. In an instant, they disappeared around the corner and down the alleyway to the street. They'd gone.

Adele ran again to the kitchen door and hit it madly with the heel of her hand. Tears sprang from her eyes and she covered her mouth. Sheer futility hit her like a heavy wave of cold seawater.

She sank down onto a kitchen chair and rested her head on the table.

Why did it take four grown men to round up two small children, she wondered, as she wiped the wetness from her cheeks with the palm of her hand? Didn't they have anything better to do?

An hour passed, and the morning moved on. Who knew what had happened beyond the confines of the Orlande house? Who knew what had transpired in the streets of Montfleur? What retribution had been exacted? The key scraping in the lock of the kitchen door woke Adele from her stupor. Footsteps retreated again.

Slowly, she unpeeled herself from the chair and stood up stiffly. Her baby was quickening, protesting. She went in a daze up the stairs to the vestibule and opened the back door. She didn't know, didn't care, where Monsieur was. She was glad that he was hiding his face, somewhere in the house.

Adele forced herself to walk the path and through the back gate which had been left carelessly open, swinging in the wind. She braced herself for the steep stairs of the stable attic.

There she found the chaos of the children's night: rumpled bedding; the basket containing bread and cheese crumbs, apple cores. The chamber pot was brimming.

She pulled at a quilt, thinking that she must tidy up, make everything straight; to keep house, just as Madame Orlande requested.

Edmund's schoolbook fell out from within the quilt. As she picked it up, two sheets of paper fluttered to the floor: the children's drawings. They were crude, innocent, their odd proportions familiarly pleasing. Estella had drawn her mother and father side by side, and written their names beneath their feet; her own name with a flourish in the corner. Edmund had drawn an outline of the stable. He imagined it with two figures lying asleep on the top floor, on the rough, broken lines of the floorboards. Beneath them stood two lanky horses: one white, one chestnut, chewing on golden hay.

Surely, Adele thought, *I am as culpable as the*

270

Kommandant, *as Monsieur, as any one of the people of Montfleur who shut their doors and closed their shutters*. Her realisation crept like disease through her bones; her association with the Resistance, with the radio transmissions, the coded messages, with the battle for France, all sealed her guilt.

Adele held the drawings in her hand, dipped her head and wept.

Nell

The avenue off the hilltop high street under the shadow of the school and the ancient church was pretty, shaded by sycamore and untouched by bombs. Along the way, right at the end, was a red-brick villa with a chequerboard path littered with the husks and leaves of a sheltering horse chestnut. *Rather impressive, the Blanford household,* thought Nell; her father's new home. It all looked very tasteful and stable and yet the broad, dusky maroon front door, with its stained glass panels of dancing medieval ladies, hinted at a certain artistic eccentricity.

And her father had been right, when he wrote to her, that the view was good, if not as lovely as at Lednor. French windows in the back parlour offered a glimpse of the rambling garden and, beyond the brick wall, the school playing fields, which stretched a long way to the railway line, and the smudge of the London suburbs in the distance.

271

She sat in the parlour, where a clock ticked comfortingly, while downstairs in the kitchen, the housemaid was making a pot of tea. She wondered how Mr and Mrs Blanford had kept her on, with most staff leaving to go to the factories; she also wanted to discover that her tea would not be as good as Mrs Bunting's.

She waited for her father, stupefied, in a dream. Pale sunlight rippled over the soft green of the Willow Bough wallpaper pattern, swirling it before her eyes until she felt as if she was immersed in water. Leaving Lednor behind did not absolve the shock that still had stiffened her body and made her want to weep. Somehow, being here in a new world, in this strange house of her father's, made Sylvie's news even more unbearable.

'Nell, Nell,' her father mumbled as he darted into the room and as his quick wiry embrace found her. 'I'm so sorry. I should never have left it so long. You know how difficult things have been. I've left you out, neglected you. But look at you. So glad to see you. Are you well?'

She sank back into the chair, despair ringing like a heavy bell in her head. 'Dad, can I stay for a while?'

'Of course you can. Diana will be so pleased. She is due back from work at six. Getting her hands dirty, she is, in munitions down in Wembley. Teaching's out of the question, of course.'

Nell looked up at her father. She had not seen him in over a year, and yet was astonished how much he was still himself, still Captain Garland standing before her. He was still the man who left her and her mother without looking back. Still the man who paints and birdwatches. He of inestimable talent. And yet his eyes were not so haunted as they had once been. They seemed to focus on her like they'd never done before.

Under his scrutiny, she thought she'd better enquire politely about Diana's parents, Mr and Mrs Blanford.

'Gone to Norfolk for the duration. There's some connection. An elderly aunt, a cottage by the sea. Sounds idyllic, doesn't it? Left us to it here. A nice couple. I'd like you to meet them one day. Oh, you do look done in, my dear. Where is Marion with that tea?'

Nell gathered her wits, trying for a normal conversation. 'So you have a maid.'

'You're lucky to catch her. She comes in one day a week. Can't you tell by the state of the place?'

She glanced around at the dusty piles of books and papers, the film over the framed mirror above the mantel.

'Once she gets to work,' Marcus granted, 'the house is in order, for about a day.'

'Mrs B is spending more time at her sister's these days,' Nell told him. 'We don't use so many rooms. The house seems rather large – larger than ever before. And the September–'

Her father dipped his head. 'Tell me about it another time.'

A painful silence stretched between them. Marcus walked to the window and pointed out the direction of the city on the horizon. Nell made a polite noise, choking back on her disappointment. She wanted to share the garden with him.

The maid came in with a rattling tray, set it down and bobbed a curtsy before leaving.

'That's Marion. She'll do,' said Marcus, picking up the teapot.

Nell saw that his hand was shaking. 'Leave it to brew, Dad,' she said.

They sipped and crunched on some inferior home-made biscuits.

Her father waved his half-heartedly in the air, scattering crumbs. 'Diana's.'

'Dad...' she blurted, 'I'm in an awful fix.'

He looked at her, and such was his intensity that she felt she'd never been the subject of his gaze before.

'We'll cope with it. After the year or so we've had, there's nothing Diana and I can't get through. Whatever's the matter, we'll get through it together.'

He handed Nell his handkerchief and she wept while the tea grew cold.

Diana came home with her hair still wrapped in a turban and a sparkle of happiness in her gimlet eyes. Nell was immediately reacquainted with her tiny pretty face, her plump manicured fingers and perfectly straight nose.

'Welcome, Nell,' she said. 'I am so glad you have come to visit us. Has your father been looking after you? Well, of course he has. Marion has left us a hotpot in the oven, but before dinner we always like to have a glass of wine upstairs in the studio. Has he shown you his studio?'

Nell thought the woman who had run off with

her father possessed the confidence of someone who was truly content. It was as if the last year and a half did not matter: her loneliness, her mother's grinding distress. But she realised then, with a jolt, as she watched Diana Blanford greet her father, that if she was to be restored to his life, then she must honour Diana's part in it, too.

'We were waiting for you to come home, Diana,' Nell said, generously.

After putting her suitcase in the guest bedroom, they all walked up the second flight of stairs to her father's studio. He had converted the attic soon after he moved there and had builders in to add a huge arched window, facing south, to bathe it with light. Nell hesitated at the door, registering the same smell, the same atmosphere, the same dust as her father's study back at home. Chunks of sunlight fell over the parquet, highlighting motes in the air and the sheen of grey over the familiar clutter of books, tubes of paint and stacks of curling paper.

'Come and sit,' her father indicated the group of armchairs near the window, 'and we will partake.'

He went over to a sideboard to pour some wine.

Nell sat beside Diana. While watching her father with a glow of passion, Diana leant over and said quietly to her, 'I know what you're thinking, Nell. I am the woman who was capable of stealing a fur coat and also a husband, and a father. I know what I have done. I hope we can be friends, you and I. We are happy, but, believe me, our happiness is sometimes soured.'

Not knowing how to answer her, Nell turned to look through the arched window. The school playing fields and park swept away from the foot of the hill to the suburban streets beyond. A Metropolitan Railway train, appearing to her as small as a toy, caught a flash of the setting sun as it trundled along the line sweeping on its curve through Wembley. A murky smudge hung in the air over the city in the distance.

'Has there been a recent air raid, Dad?' she asked. 'I can see a pall of smoke.'

'Yes, one or two nights back. We get a good look at the fireworks from up here. Good show some nights. We feel somewhat removed. Sometimes you think it's not quite happening.'

Nell took the glass of wine from him, thinking of the cellar below the mews, thinking of Alex. She felt, for a moment, the sheer terror, and the realisation that love transformed her that night.

'I so wish the view was clearer now,' she muttered, close to tears.

Her father was busy stoppering the bottle and didn't notice. But Diana laid her hand on her arm.

'Tell us when you are ready, my dear.'

Furtively wiping her eyes on the back of her hand, Nell spotted the half-finished watercolour of the dog rose, now framed and tacked to the wall by the window. She got up to look at it, to distract herself. Peering closely, she saw its singed edges.

'I didn't realise you had this,' she said.

'What? Oh that,' Marcus said. 'Your mother sent it on to me. A sort of peace offering, I suppose. Rescued from the bonfire. Anyway, I always liked the dog rose. Always liked the fact it was unfinished. And saved.'

'Quite a nice gesture from Mollie, really,' Diana observed, kindly.

Nell tried to smile but was prevented by the constant drizzle of sadness, like a perpetual dripping tap, inside her.

'How is she, anyway?' asked Marcus.

Nell glanced at him, confused.

'Your mother, dear,' he smiled.

'Poor and sad,' she answered him succinctly. 'Mrs B looks after her.'

Her father did not appear to hear her.

'Sit there and drink your wine with us,' he said. 'Sit right there in the window. That's it. With the last of the light on your face.'

He reached for a large sheet of cartridge paper and pinned it to his easel. He picked up a chip of charcoal and began to sketch. Then he stopped and walked over to the gramophone.

'Oh please, no, Dad!' cried Nell. 'If that's *"Clair de Lune"*, I can't stand it.'

'Yes. Sorry. Right you are.' He returned to his easel and settled himself on his stool.

'Shall we talk about it, then?' he asked, not looking at her but frowning at his work.

Struck by the thought that she'd never sat for her father before, she couldn't answer him. She listened to the scratching of charcoal on paper, and watched through the window as a girl and a dog ambled across the playing field way, way below, followed by two long, faithful shadows. Alex again walked into her mind. Despite herself, the remembered sound of his voice, suddenly, inexplicably, consoled her. She wished, with all her might, that she was that carefree girl with her dog out there in the park. It could easily be her and Kit.

'Your father tells me that you have fallen in love,' ventured Diana. 'With a birdwatching flight lieutenant.'

Nell glanced at her in surprise, suddenly very afraid at the absurdity of her situation.

'I have,' she managed, her shame beginning to bind her words. 'But I have since learnt that he is committed to someone else.'

'Oh hell,' uttered Diana.

Nell's voice rose a pitch in bitterness. 'And he is gone, anyway. Gone on some dreadfully dangerous mission. Unlikely to come back alive, so I believe. I haven't heard from him. He could be dead already. So there was never any hope. Not really. I don't know why I ever thought it. How would such luck come to me? I lose everything.'

Her anger faded in an instant, like a snuffed-out flame, to be replaced by the familiar slow-burning sense of betrayal, the misery that had woven its web around her since the day Sylvie had telephoned.

Marcus continued to sketch, a frown deepening between his eyebrows.

'I blame this damn war. Puts the mockers on so many things,' Diana said.

Her flippancy annoyed Nell.

'Well it's not just the war that puts the mockers on, Diana,' she snapped. 'Not when I am expecting his child.'

Diana's eyes rounded in surprise. She looked, after a fashion, almost pleased.

'Oh, my dear.' She slipped her cool hand, pale and plump, into Nell's and held it.

'Ah, now,' said Marcus, after some moments passed. 'No tears, please. You'll spoil it.'

He turned the easel towards Nell and she stared at his work. The portrait could have been Mollie, at a much younger age.

'Do you like it?' asked Marcus.

'I didn't realise how much I look like Mother,' Nell whispered. 'I always thought I looked like you.'

Sylvie

The doctor removed the cold instrument with a rather hard tug. Sylvie winced, wishing that, as in every other walk of life these days, from fire-fighting to welding, there were more women in *this* profession. She dressed behind the curtain while he washed his hands over the basin and buttoned the cuffs of his shirt. A fresh drop of her blood had landed on the lino floor by the examination couch.

'Do come and sit down, Miss Orlande,' he said, indicating the chair by his sleekly polished desk.

He took out his fountain pen and began to write laboriously.

Sylvie sat and waited, feeling ruffled and peculiarly vacant, watching sunlight glimmer on his bald head.

'It seems to me, miss, that you have been suffering from amenorrhea for some time. Now, no need to worry. This is often brought on by shock and distress. And perfectly understandable, under the circumstances, don't you think? Try to keep calm, and continue as normal. Should be right as rain in no time.'

Sylvie laughed with relief. 'Do you mean I should just keep my tin hat on and my head down?'

'That's the spirit. I suggest you are fitted with a Dutch cap in the meantime. Keep babies at bay, I would.'

She walked down the russet-brick steps of the Harley Street practice on rather shaky legs, to see Henri waiting for her, leaning against the railings.

'Have you had the all-clear, *ma chérie?*' he asked.

'Just some female silliness.' She linked his arm, feeling frivolous. 'I need a drink. It's time for champagne at the Ritz, Henri, my boy. Let's take a cab.'

The doorman held the door for them and they entered the hushed, gilded reception. An enormous vase of lilies exuded a heady perfume, making Sylvie think of births, brides and death. Her heels sank into the carpet; she should not breathe or she would break the tranquil spell, crack the elegant vacuum of the hotel's interior. She walked across the salon and up the steps into the Palm Court and all eyes – behind newspapers, spectacles, false lashes – turned and followed her.

Henri often teased her that she had the looks of a film star and a figure that men would kill each other for. She wanted, desperately, to giggle.

'I can't tell you how relieved I am. It must be for the best. Bombs and babies don't go together very well,' she confided in Henri as the waiter topped up the champagne flutes and twisted the bottle deep into the ice bucket.

'And what of Alex Hammond?' Henri asked.

Sylvie lowered her eyes, concentrated on the bubbles in her glass. The light feeling that had followed her from the surgery turned a sharp corner into sadness.

'I have no idea.'

'You know that fellow has a short life expectancy. Special Operations are our best men, but they are generally doomed.'

Sylvie leant forward, cigarette between her lips, while he offered her his lighted match.

'There's been no word,' she agreed. 'But then why should there be? I'm not his next of kin.'

Henri was watching her. 'You really have the most exquisite retroussé nose.'

'Stop it, Henri,' Sylvie bristled. 'I'm thinking about Nell.'

'Cousin Nell?'

'She took herself off to her father's place in Harrow before I could get down to Lednor last month. Left me to spend three whole days on my own with Auntie Moll. Didn't see her at all.'

'She must be cross with you.'

'She liked Alex Hammond, you see.'

Henri sucked hard on his cigarette. 'He's out there in the field, expecting to marry you, expecting to be a father. I hope he keeps his mind on the job.'

'Dear God, so do I.'

'Forget him.'

Sylvie drained her glass and held it out for more. 'He was mine, you know. For a short while. He still could be.'

'Don't talk rot.'

His words stung her as if he'd slapped her cheek. She had known many men, had known many lovers, including Henri. But Alex Hammond had such a fascinating potency that it made her want to kick up her heels and call off the search. But, then, was that just what he was like with every lady? Was that why Nell had fallen for him, too? Right now, there may be another girl somewhere out there, succumbing to his distinguished allure, to his deft touch. Truth was, he was different to all the other fellows, because *she* had cared.

Henri looked grumpy. He waved his hand in front of her face. 'Sylvie, my dear, you were miles away. There is nothing more to it, we should do this for *La France* more than anything else.'

He'd interrupted her thoughts just as she was uncovering a truth, admitting to herself the depth of her feelings. How irritating he was.

'Do what for *La France*? What are you talking about?' she snapped.

'Marry me.'

'Don't be ridiculous, Henri. I'm going to wait for Alex.'

Part Four

1942

Nell

She woke up to the bleary vision of Strawberry Thief wallpaper surrounding her bed as if she was sleeping in a medieval bower. Drowsily following the green and pink tendrils where thrushes perched, stealing fruit, she longed to have awoken amid the fairy tale inside her mind. She was still wrapped in a dream of velvet wonder: she and Alex, birdwatching in Lednor valley, picnicking on a rug, with cheerful little John-James, his baby flesh chubby and pinchable, sitting on a fat nappy. Her father's framed watercolours of birds on her bedroom wall, including, she noted with a half smile, a yellow hammer, created their own little menagerie and became the stuff of her dreams. The sound of an alarm clock along the landing broke up her slumber. And the little snuffling from the cot drew her from the bed, as if the child was made of metal and a magnet was attached to her heart.

He was tiny, *scrawny*, Diana had said. He could not see her yet, she guessed. His eyes were blank and dark, his skin peppered with blemishes, his hand as wrinkled as an old man's. And yet, he was beauty.

She shuffled her fingers under his ribs and lifted him; he was light and empty, curling onto her shoulder, wheezing mindlessly, as yet unaware of the love that oozed from her bones into his tiny, kitten-like frame.

Her father tapped on the door. He looked flustered; nicks of blood on his chin.

'I'm leaving now. Getting the eight-thirty.'

'What time will you be in Norwich?'

'God only knows. It's such a hazard these days. Never mind that, how is the little man?'

Nell tucked the knuckle of her little finger into the hard opening of his mouth.

'Hungry, I think.' She rested her nose gently on his scalp and inhaled.

Her father said, 'I'm sorry I have to go.'

'Diana needs you. Give my regards to Mrs Blanford, won't you? At least you can rest up before the funeral tomorrow.'

'It's still a shock, you know, even when a person is quite old and has been ill.'

'I know, Dad.'

'Marion will be here at midday. She's to come in every day. Listen, Nell, wouldn't you rather go back to your mother's?'

'I don't want to traipse all the way up there. He's settled here. Too tiny to travel.'

'Diana is worried. You know how sodding bad those public telephone lines are. But I could tell from her voice. She won't say.'

'She's got enough on her plate. She's just lost her father. Dad, it's eight o'clock.'

He walked over, his embrace enveloping both Nell and John-James, a tear in his eye.

Marion made her a lunch of cold meat and potato salad and brought it in for her on a tray in the back parlour.

It tasted reasonably good, Nell conceded, but she had no appetite at all. She ate what she could, battling with the clogging cloth of misery that filled her insides.

'How's the bubba?' the maid asked as she came to take the tray away, peering into John-James's cot.

Nell told her that he was not feeding too well at the moment.

'Well, to look at you, miss, seems like you aren't either.'

Nell smiled brightly and said that she was all right. She found it peculiar that this girl who hardly knew her was cooing over her son, calling him *bubba* and offering her opinions, when her own mother knew nothing about him at all.

A hard point of disagreement between Nell and her father. He was worried that her mother would think he'd forced her not to tell her, to keep her in Harrow all to himself. But, all Nell wanted to do was keep her head down and try to ride out the storm facing her; abandoned and unmarried, a fallen woman. It would drive her mother mad with shame. Wherever she was, she decided – at Lednor or in Harrow – she was on the wrong side.

'Mother thinks I'm working in a factory here, making parts for Spits,' Nell had reminded her father. 'Doing my bit.'

'She has to know sometime,' Diana reasoned and Nell had agreed but insisted that that time was not now.

Her mother's letters to her were sporadic, rambling and barely coherent. There was never any news about Sylvie, but she understood from her mother that Mrs Bunting was spending far more time away from Lednor with her sister, who had lost her husband in the North Atlantic.

'It seems everyone has their troubles,' Nell told Diana. 'I don't want to add to anyone's.'

'Don't tell me you consider yourself a burden,' said Diana. 'For you know that would be a right ruddy lie.'

'What about Sylvie?' her father had asked. 'Didn't she start doing something very secretive and important out in Berkshire?'

'She did, Dad,' said Nell. 'Last I heard she was getting married.'

'Such a shame to lose touch, isn't it?' he observed.

'We weren't that close, really.'

He told her she surprised him. 'Be nice to tell her about little John-James.'

Once Marion had left the room, Nell went quickly to the cot, prickling with possessiveness that the maid had stood over him and breathed on him. She let her finger touch his fluffy dark hair. So new, he was, so fragile. His infant breath was pure and soft and rhythmic. 'Yes, it would be nice to tell her about you,' she whispered. 'For you will also have a second cousin by now ... or is it first cousin, once removed, or–'

'Just off now,' Marion called from the hallway.

Nell returned her 'cheerio'.

'And one day, John-James,' she whispered to her baby son, 'it will be nice to tell your daddy about you.'

She settled into the armchair and picked up

her father's newspaper from yesterday. She read the headline, before folding it away and deciding that the war was an absolute brute. Brings out the worse in everyone.

She allowed Alex to sit by her for a while. Her mind swayed like a pendulum between her memories of him. He had told her of his mistake with Sylvie and she had forgiven him. After all, the war had made him do a stupid thing, and she knew that once Sylvie had a hand in any dealings they tended to muck up for everyone else. And she had forgiven him. It made her love him more, his confession in Pudifoot Cottage. But then, his duplicity was like a horrific jack-in-the-box rearing up to mock her. Of course he chose Sylvie in the end, who wouldn't?

Her thoughts degraded her, wearied her. At last, she dozed, and they disappeared into the clog of an ill-remembered dream.

When she woke, the springtime sunlight had shifted and a shower was sparkling silver over the garden. She went to the french windows and stretched, relishing a brief moment when her head wasn't full of Alex and of Sylvie. Glancing at the clock, she realised John-James would need another feed. Her breasts felt heavy, she noted with pleasure. She was ready to feed him up.

'Here we go, little man,' she told him softly as she reached into the cot, tucking her fingertips under his back.

It was wrong, immediately. So fiercely, incredibly wrong. She withdrew, her hands still poised in the air. She heard the moaning; it surprised her, as if it was coming from nowhere, and then above her head, *inside* her head.

'Not this little one,' a voice said. *She* said. 'Not now.'

She fixed her eyes on his cheek where a bloom of red flushed like an angry burn. Above it, his eyes were closed and sunken far too far. Eyelashes skimming rosy cheeks. The snuffling had ceased, the fragile breath no longer the rhythm that had measured her days and nights. He'd curled up his little body, as if he had fought it. The sudden hush of the afternoon was absolute and rotten with horror. Rain drizzled onto the window and she dragged her eyes away from John-James to stare cold and hard at the drops coursing down the panes. Beyond, bright daffodils in her father's naked-earth flower beds dipped their faces under the downpour. Cold and hollow, she remained at the window. Not one ounce of her strength would make her turn again and look at the cradle and face the truth. She shivered, shaking, as reason began to drain from her. Her face tingled with creeping, icy horror. The springtime evening began to fall, like a veil around her, to darken her sky.

She bought her ticket, asked for a single.

'Last train to Aylesbury. Platform one,' said the railwayman. 'Leaving in five minutes.'

She'd left the note, *Gone to my mother's,* propped up against the kettle where Marion was sure to see it in the morning.

She thought of Kit, and how he might have missed her. How he might have forgotten her. Picking up her overnight bag she walked down

290

the steps with a sure ringing sound at her heel, and waited on the echoing midnight platform. Flagrantly dim lights hardly cut through the darkness, made the world unreal. The tracks glistened in the last of the rain, curved away into the night, into nothing. She breathed the scent of new rain on tarmac, new rain on concrete. Seeking shelter in the waiting room, she was confronted by a poster on the wall shouting at her: *Is your journey necessary?* She decided that she'd prefer to wait outside.

Her coat wasn't adequate. It was an old one of Sylvie's: a summer rain mac, really, and not thick enough for the brittle spring night. Her shivering that had started a few hours before seemed to seep inwards now, so that her insides quivered with sickening persistence. At last, the train eased in beside the platform with a noisy, swelling head of steam. The carriages were jammed with soldiers and sailors on their sing-song, snoring way home on leave. She found a corner in third class and sat, her thigh pressed against a snoozing private, her bag heavy on her knees. One kind soul offered to put it above her on the luggage rack, his words mixed up by the cigarette at the corner of his mouth. She thanked him, refused him, and held on to it even tighter.

There were no buses at Aylesbury. She was hardly surprised: it was quarter past one in the morning. Olivers taxis would long be in bed. The train cruised on through the night with its blackout down, into the Midlands, where the men and boys would find the salvation of homecoming at dawn. She began to walk.

The night was so black, the sky so deep above her, that she decided that the stars had drowned in it. On the silent main road, hardly a car passed her. And when she turned into the smaller country road, she had the darkness to herself. She talked to John-James and told him all about the kites that ruled the air. How, now, they'd be in their treetop nests, waiting for that first sight of pale eastern sky when they would rouse, stretch their wings, fly and shriek. That call. The frightened child. She told him to listen, for there was the voice of a tawny owl, spine-chilling and tremulous from the wood. She told him how his daddy would know that voice. Any bird voice; he knew them all.

She stopped in the centre of the lane, as if she suddenly realised where she was, her legs trembling, her mouth gaping with the silent sobbing that rose from her chest. Tears washed her face, and she took a step, and then another. Soon, the walking became easier, the endless striding, the journey, became easier, as the gaps in the hills – like black sleeping beasts on the shadowy horizon – grew more familiar.

There was the rumble of a plane up above and then another to join it. Listen, John-James, do you hear that? Are they leaving or coming home, I wonder?

Great Lednor appeared out of the gloom as a familiar tableau, the cottages huddled and pale in the now dusky light before dawn. The churchyard was thick with yew and the evergreen smell was heartbreaking in its seduction. Beyond it, the meadow where the fête had been held was lightening, its rolling contours reversing out of the night.

The first birds were piping by the time she reached the ford. She took the stepping stones – Sylvie's sensible way – mindful of how cold the Chess would be. She reminded John-James that his daddy had enjoyed his evening with her by the stream. 'We even saw a bat,' she told him. 'Fancy that.'

She hurried past Mr Pudifoot's cottage, as quickly as her savaged feet would allow her. The pain caused by her pressing shoes shot up her legs, and the small of her back was burning. Yet, still, she kept up a good pace, up the gravel as dawn began to feel her way through the sky, coming down from above, so that pockets of night still lingered among the trees.

Her key turned easily in the lock. Her home's very own soul cloaked her in clock-ticking, coal-fire, furniture-polish familiarity. From the depths of the kitchen, she heard a cough from Kit in his basket, and a stirring. She hurried then. In the darkness of the hall, she stooped quickly to take what she needed from the cupboard. Then she slipped back out and followed the path around the west side of the house and into the September Garden.

It was a cold place, during an April daybreak. The bulbs were not as advanced as they were back in Harrow, and tight-budded narcissi glowed like baby angels in the half-light. The ground was compacted, firmer than she expected, and she worked hard to break it with the little trowel, all that she could lay her hands on in the cupboard. When she decided, finally, that the hole was big enough, a beam of new sunshine found its sleepy, pale way into the garden. Broken winter-dead plants and grasses formed skeletal shapes around her as she sat back on her haunches and wiped the sweat from her forehead. Even though digging had made her hot and exhausted, she shivered still, inside Sylvie's inadequate coat.

She sat there, breathing, and finally turned to John-James. She took him from the overnight bag, a horribly impromptu cradle, and wrapped his fragile form in her father's forgotten rubber coat, found by her groping in the cupboard.

'Warm and dry, at least it is,' she breathed on him. 'It is the best I can do, little man.'

The moment slipped past her, too fast for her ever to be able to remember it properly. And far too soon, far too finally, John-James was tucked away.

She could scarcely feel the warmth on her cheek from the early sun as she made her way back to the house. The morning revealed the peaceful red-brick facade and comfortable windows snug under the roof but, illuminated in the grey, tranquil light, her home looked like a painting, flat and rather unreal.

Inside the hallway, the gentle light revealed to her a letter, there on the telephone table. She'd recognise the neat curling handwriting anywhere. As she reached her hesitant hand to it, she realised it was covered in a film of dust. It had been there so long it left a ghost of an outline on the polished wood. The postmark was dated last August.

She glanced up the stairway, and put the letter deep into her coat pocket.

'Mother,' she called, her voice breaking. 'Mother, are you awake? I'm home.'

Sylvie

'It's good to see St Paul's still standing,' she told Henri as they walked together across Waterloo Bridge. She stopped for a minute to take in the sweep of the river, curving past the Houses of Parliament and the ruins of St Thomas's Hospital on the opposite bank, under the bridge and round the bend to the City. She breathed in the whiff of exhaust fumes from the buses and cars rattling past her north to Covent Garden. 'The most perfect view of London,' she said.

Henri took her hand. 'Some say, the most romantic view of London,' he replied. And then, 'Oh, you're still wearing that damn thing!'

Sylvie laughed, pulled her hand away from his and touched her fingertips onto the modest diamond of her engagement ring. 'He *did* propose rather reluctantly, as well you know.'

'And yet here you are, still waiting for him,' Henri snapped. 'You might as well be engaged to a dead man.'

Sylvie looked at Henri sharply. She hadn't seen him for a good six months, but that was how it was. War work kept everyone apart. He was always there for her, trying too hard, she conceded. But now, in that instance, she'd had enough.

'Henri, thank you for picking me up from the station,' she announced, 'but I really have to go now.'

'Oh, come on, Sylvie.'

'No, it's getting pretty tiresome. You and me. Pretty tiresome.' Sylvie stalked off, heading north over the bridge.

'But we're going to go to the 400. I've booked a table.'

'Go on your own, there'll be plenty of girls there who I'm sure would like to share your champagne.'

'But it's your first night back in the city. We have to celebrate.'

'Don't feel like celebrating.' She was out of breath now, her suitcase weighed a ton. She'd not had to carry it since she left the headquarters in Berkshire. One of the officers there who was keen on her carried it out to her taxi; the porter at the railway station loaded it onto the train. Another unloaded it at Waterloo. And then Henri had taken care of it for her, eager as always, overwhelmed, as always, to see her. Dear Henri, she thought as she heard him hurrying behind her, how he took care of everything.

She'd grown bored of Berkshire and had requested her old job back. A year in the sticks was enough for her. She'd given her tenant at the mews notice, was pleased it was all still standing after that really heavy raid last summer, and couldn't wait to get back into the swing of parties and nightlife. The London crowd were more jolly, more daring, more up for anything, she decided. It was time to get back into the fray.

A bus rumbled past her, slowing to stop for the lights at the junction with the Aldwych. She quickened her step and, as it pulled up, she hopped on board, leaving Henri pacing after it along the pavement, his disgruntled face red with exasperation. She stood on the backplate as the bus swung round the corner, her suitcase at her feet, and lifted her hand in wry apology.

Sylvie was impatient to be home, but the bus crawled along through the traffic. She had to change buses at Holborn to go west and it was eight o'clock before she stepped onto the cobblestones of her mews. The evening shadows were dark, the blackout heavy. But all at once, she felt at home as her heels rang on the stones. Her own little mews was intact, just a couple of windows boarded up next door. She smiled softly, humming to herself, and it took a while for her to realise that the pinprick of red light she saw ahead of her was the glow of a cigarette.

She wondered, who could be there to welcome her? It could be any of the fellows from the office. They were expecting her back today, after all, and were all very much looking forward to it. It was just like any of them to be there to greet her.

Her suitcase slipped from her hand, landed with a thud and tipped over into a puddle on the cobbles. She felt pinned, like a butterfly in a case, her arms stretching out to her sides as she tilted her head and cried, 'Alex?'

He stepped out of the shadows and ground the

cigarette under his heel.

'Sylvie? Is it you?'

She ran, giggling with shock. 'Of course it's me. Of course it is.'

She expected his arms to open to her, but he stood rigid as she went to him, put her hands on his shoulders. 'But is it you, Alex?' she asked, half joking.

Opening her front door, she ushered him in and up the stairs. She hurried from window to window in her living room to make sure the blackout was down before she could switch on a lamp and see for herself.

'Poo,' she said. 'Smells a bit musty. You'll have to forgive this, I haven't lived here for a year.'

He stood by her empty hearth, his cheekbones angled and tanned. His temples were flecked like a badger, a streak of grey swept back through the dark hair over his forehead. His eyes were still that same burning blue.

'You've lost weight, my dear,' she said.

Alex looked around. 'Not been here for a year? So where's the baby? Where is...? I don't even know. Boy or girl? No one has told me. You haven't told me. I don't even know.' He was bewildered.

'Let me fix you a drink. See if my tenants have left anything by way of spirit or wine... Ah, yes.' She opened the kitchen cupboard. 'A syrupy bit of port. Do you fancy it? Oh Christ, that's never the siren?'

Alex stood by the window and peered round the blackout as a muffled whining resounded outside. 'It's at least three miles away. I thinking

298

they're stonking the East End.'

'No need to worry, then,' said Sylvie. 'Marvellous isn't it? My first night back in town and I'm grounded.'

He turned to her, his eyes blazing. 'Stop your nattering, Sylvie, and tell me. Where the hell is our child?'

'Alex,' she retorted, her hands on her hips, suddenly ferocious. 'And where the *hell* have you *been?*'

Sylvie poured another round of port and lemon as they sat cross-legged under the kitchen table.

'There's the cellar,' she told him. 'But I'd rather not.'

'Me neither. And we're perfectly safe.' He reached up and knocked the underside of the table. 'Good solid English oak.'

'I'm so sorry. I couldn't let you know,' she said quietly. 'Seems I have had these *women's* problems for years, the doctor said. It was, as old wives would have it, a phantom pregnancy.'

Alex rubbed his fingertip obsessively on the rim of his glass. 'So there was never...? Never a...? And you are quite well?'

'Never felt better,' she smiled. 'Although you don't look so good. It's a shock, isn't it? All this time, you thought...'

He knocked back his drink and winced.

'All this time...'

'And that is quite a suntan you have, Alex. Are you going to tell me about it?'

His smile was crooked on his face. 'I want to tell you how wonderful your fellow countrymen are. Absolute unfaltering heroes. I would not be sitting here under this excuse for an air raid shelter,' he laughed wearily, 'if it was not for *le pêcheur*, code name *Esprit Fort*.'

Sylvie sipped her port as a crump of bombs landed a mile away and smiled at Alex. 'It's okay,' she said. 'The curtains didn't move. That means its incendiary and a long way off. If the curtains suck inwards, and the windows rattle, then we're in for some trouble.'

'I was in trouble,' he said, 'almost as soon as I shuffled onto that damnable beach.'

It was a perfect night. Many months of planning to reach this stage. A deep, black night, he told her, with a huge starless sky. Everything was going according to plan. Samples of sand collected, the reach of the waves, the pull of the tides monitored and recorded. It took hours. A survey of the dunes was taken as he lay on his stomach and peered through binoculars in the dark of a Normandy night and dictated measurements to his corporal.

'Remember, Sylvie, I have a degree in geology. And this is what it leads me to.'

The sentries, he said, dug into the sand, warned him that they'd heard a German patrol on the beach road.

'"Back off", I gave the order,' Alex said. '"Day trip's over."'

As he turned to shuffle back to the encroaching waves, he felt a muscle pull hard in his thigh, a flash of pain that paralysed him, so intense he couldn't breathe. His leg, stiffening, useless. He'd been lying so long in cold, wet sand that his muscles had clenched in protest, pretty much disabling him.

'Sir,' whispered his corporal. 'Ready to go. Awaiting orders.'

'Carry on,' he said, his teeth gritted in agony. He ordered his men to leave, to struggle along the lines of rope through the waves to the waiting boat, out there in the rocking darkness. He thrust his bag of equipment at the corporal and watched his astonished, mute face recede into the night.

'I kept my head down. The patrol passed by, oblivious, leaving me with some pretty foul jokes in German. I hadn't reckoned on the cold, and I knew I had to move soon. Any rate, by then, the dawn was breaking. I managed to crawl up the beach and hid in a fold of the dunes.'

'Which beach?' asked Sylvie.

Where the Seine estuary feeds out, he told her, at the base of the Cotentin Peninsula.

'I know it.' She smiled at Alex, feeling a soup of emotion swell inside her. Her months of worry and resentment had faded, and her old desire, her old longing for Alex resumed.

He had to wait for nightfall again, and in the darkness turned his face north and hurried along the coast, ducking through hedgerows and skirting the fields. He followed the streams, kept close to wherever there was water, always the lowest point.

'Your leg?' she asked.

'Right as rain.' He slapped his thigh. 'But I could not have my men waiting on that beach for it to get better. Even for five more minutes. I could not jeopardise them.'

And this, he told her, was how he met *le pêcheur*. Word had been radioed through via Special Operations, via intelligence, to the cell, and the man intercepted him, let him rest in a safe house, kept him away from Montfleur where there was a high concentration of Germans. 'Bit of a head-quarters there, I understand,' said Alex.

'The village,' breathed Sylvie. 'My village. How is the place? Oh, but I think I know who the fisherman is. Mother once mentioned that our maid Adele had a sweetheart, Jean Ricard, who fished out of Montfleur harbour. She told me that in her last ever letter. Before the first Christmas of the war.' Her voice cracked. 'How is she, did *le pêcheur* say?'

'I have no idea. He barely spoke to me. That's the rules. The least we know about each other the better. If indeed it's the man you are think-ing of.'

Sylvie breathed out long and hard, shuddered. 'I can't believe you were there, so close to my home. It seems absolutely incredible. And here you are.' Her smile broke as tears watered her eyes. She sipped the last of her port and glanced at her empty glass.

Alex told her how the fisherman gave him food and water, and false papers. He was to become a French peasant and travel, sometimes alone, sometimes accompanied, south-west, heading for Brittany and the Vendée, down the lines, all the way to the Pyrenees.

'I stayed in various farms in isolated hamlets, in bastides, in gîtes, sleeping next to cattle, in barn lofts, in bales of straw. The risks these people took were humbling. I was speechless with fatigue some days, with reverence on others. Way down in Gascony, with the mountains on the horizon, I remember the aged couple who insisted on giving up their bed for me. This peasant farmer and his wife, all bandy legs and deeply lined, tanned faces, were happy to die, they told me, as long as *l'anglais* made it across the border safely.'

'And then into Spain?'

It was another long, arduous journey, he said, through mountain passes, and long, hot, dusty roads, but eminently safer. Olive groves became his bedrooms, and wine cellars, too, he smiled. The organisation was stupendously efficient. Finally, he said, Gibraltar, and the dubious delights of a debrief and a bunk on the ship of His Majesty's Navy.

Alex stopped, exhausted. The all-clear had sounded, and yet Sylvie did not feel like moving out from under the table. Here, she felt safer than she had in a long long time, now that Alex was back.

He glanced at her hand. 'I see we're still engaged.'

'We are,' she said, brightly. 'I told myself I'd wait for you.'

Alex shuffled out from under the table and stretched hard. 'Let's sit down in the armchairs,' he said. 'God, it must be the middle of the night.'

'I was hoping,' said Sylvie, following him into the living room, 'you were going to say "let's go to bed".'

She saw that his face was tired and pale, but

that his eyes were bright and guarded.

'I think we'd better talk,' he said.

'Oh no, not that.' Sylvie almost laughed. 'Not that old chestnut.'

She gazed at him in the dim light of the lamp and waited.

'It's very delicate,' he said, courteously.

'You're telling me!' she snapped.

'We got engaged because we thought you were expecting a baby.'

'And now?'

'Now,' he sighed. 'Now, everything is different. Except one thing.'

Sylvie waited again, her heart hammering. He said one word that broke her world apart: 'Nell.'

She wanted to laugh it off, to try to pretend how much she didn't care, but her cousin sat like a ghost in the room. Over there, in the corner. 'All this time, through your great escape across France and Spain, you thought I had had our baby, and yet, you still thought of her.'

'I thought of you both, constantly,' he replied. He coughed to hide a sob in his voice. 'But Nell–'

'Oh, don't give me that pathetic noise,' Sylvie snapped. 'So you came here, to check me out first. I bet you're over the moon, aren't you? No more need to look after Sylvie. Aren't you the lucky one? Well, I have no idea where she is, if that's what you're wondering. She's disappeared on us. Went a bit funny about a year ago. Around the time you left, actually. But then, I suppose that wasn't surprising in the circumstances, when she heard my news. Stayed at her father's

304

for a good while, went home briefly to Lednor, so Auntie Moll tells me, then went into nursing. And don't ask me where, because I have absolutely no idea.'

Sylvie stood up, ferociously rummaging in her handbag for her pack of cigarettes.

'You know, Alex, when I saw you on the doorstep,' her voice quivered too hard for her liking, 'I thought it was a miracle. You were safe and my happiness had returned. And now, you just ruin it all again. You better work this one out for yourself.' She turned from him, not wanting him to see her tears. 'Shut the door on your way out.'

She stood with her back to him, breathing hard as she inhaled on the cigarette. She heard the rustle of his overcoat, his step on the stair. The front door below closed quietly. She stubbed out the cigarette and slumped back into the chair, her hand over her face, squeezing her eyes tight in an attempt to stop misery bubbling out of her. Her head snapped up when she heard the front door knocker rap gently. As she leapt up, she felt her agony fall away, as if shedding a skin. She hurried down the stairs, her happiness rising, simmering in her throat. Her love for him still blooming in her chest.

Alex stood on the doorstep, the street lightening with the dawn behind him, his hat low over his eyes.

'Your suitcase,' he said, handing it to her.

He turned and walked away.

Part Five

1944

Two years later

Nell

Rain drummed on the pitched roof of the nursing home, sending silvery rivulets snaking down the grime and dust on the roof light windows. She lay wakeful in bed and watched as streams of rainwater met one another on the glass, collided and divided. Outside the drainpipes were rushing, gutters spluttering under the deluge. The unseasonal storm – it was only the middle of May – was passing overhead, washing away the dirt, cleaning the air.

Her bedroom was in the converted attic, with a little dormer window facing north. She could look straight over the rooftops to the city, and what was left of it. Getting out of bed, she washed quickly in the bathroom along the corridor and, back in her room, dressed in her uniform. There was a rumble of thunder and a flash of lightning over the West End. *Not the Luftwaffe this time,* she thought. *Just plain old weather.* And, at any rate, these days they were all terrified of buzz bombs. She made her bed, then opened her dormer wide to let in the cooling early dawn air just as the bell clanged along the corridor. Six in the morning. Time to get up.

Someone tapped on her door and Violet, in her dressing gown, poked her head round.

'Might have known you'd already be up and dressed, Diana,' she said. 'Can I please borrow some stockings? Mine could be used as a fishing net and I got the most frightful rocket from Sister yesterday for walking over to the hospital without my cloak on. Can't risk it two days running. I'll pay you back soon as I can.'

Nell handed her her last pair.

'Thanks ever so, Di. See you at breakfast.'

Nell knew she had exactly twenty minutes before she had to be downstairs in the nurses' dining room. This was the only period of the day when she truly had time for herself. As the nurses' waking, chattering voices grew steadily louder along the corridor and in the rooms next to hers, she pulled out Alex's letter. She curled up on her crisply made bed to read it, even though, two years after she'd first opened it, she knew each line by heart.

Nell wondered how any of the patients got any rest or proper sleep. The morning bedpan round, with its scrubbing and sluicing, produced deafening and offensive clatter, assaulting both senses of hearing and smell. And all had to be in order and shipshape for the consultant's daily visit on the ward when he swooped through, white coat-tails flying, followed by Matron and Sister in terrified flutter. The work was exhausting but good, always good, Nell decided, for it helped her forget, gave her no time to think. At King's College there were no babies or children, no little ones to remind her. Just men, badly injured, horrifically burnt young men, some who came in, still alive, with labels tied to their feet for identification.

While she worked she sometimes allowed herself to think of Alex. As she scrubbed bed legs to ensure against bed bugs, it was as if she was watching a film at the picture house, another girl playing her. Alex's letter had been desperate in his contrition, but whatever his appeal, it became meaningless in the face of what actually happened. He loved her, he wrote. And she knew that. But he had thrown her away.

She dared herself to think of Sylvie and, moments later, stopped to stare at the red marks on her hand ingrained by the scrubbing brush.

Around midday, Sister asked her to feed the patient in bed five. Pushing aside the curtain, she saw a charred head against the white pillow. The familiar smell told her the soldier had been roasted.

'I've come to give you some lunch, sir,' she said.

The eyes were bloodshot and strangely alive amid the dead flesh; the split mouth grimaced in what she suspected was a smile. He let out a faint wolf whistle.

'What a cracker.' His voice was hoarse, trapped in his throat. 'What an absolute cracker. I bet your sweetheart is head over heels. What's your name?'

She helped him sit up, feeling ribs and shoulder blades beneath his pyjamas. He grunted, hissed with pain.

'I'll ask Sister about your drip,' she told him. 'It looks like it needs topping up.'

How hard it was to keep her nerve. The first year had been difficult, of course, but she'd hoped things would have been better by now. Last week, a consultant had asked for a patient's

X-rays. Off she'd trotted to fetch them and handed them straight to him. Afterwards, Sister had called her to one side and in no uncertain' terms told her that she should have given them to her, so that she could pass them to the doctor. And then Sister had wondered if Nurse Blanford should take a hearing test, as more often than not, when she was summoned, it was an irritatingly long while before she responded. *It's as if you don't know your own name.*

Nell sat on the chair at bed five, poised with the spoon of liquefied vegetables and gravy.

'You haven't told me your name,' the patient said.

'Nurse Blanford,' she whispered, mindful of Sister's strictness about being too friendly with the soldiers, for it only caused heartache in any of the so many inevitable outcomes.

'Pleased to meet you, Blanford.'

If the soldier had still had both of his eyelids, she was sure he would have winked.

On her day off, she was free to leave the hospital and all of its nauseating odours and claustrophobic racket behind her. She would often watch the other nurses hurrying off, linking arms and giggling, their capes billowing, with a mixture of curiosity and envy. The thought of doing as she pleased, without the structure of routine and work, sucked Nell through a void of confusing dread. She would fight it by sitting in the cinema in Peckham, or walking around Brockwell Park. Some days, she even went as far as Greenwich Hill, where she could look over the bombed and ruined docks, all the while alone and with a mind to forget, or at least to fill her head with something other than John-James.

How she longed for her valley, her place under the willows by the river. How she longed for the September Garden, where bees bumbled over his scented cradle, wriggling over the clover. It was early June and the dog roses would be out along the lanes, festooning the hedgerows, and the air would be soft with birdsong.

That day, for a change, she caught the train from Denmark Hill to London Bridge. She walked, still in uniform, her cape fluttering behind her, across the bridge, the churning, dirty river below her. She plunged into the city, her flat, sensible nursing shoes negotiating the cobbled alleys in the grey shadow of mighty and inviolable St Paul's. She circumnavigated the bomb sites of the ancient quarter, darting down alleys and passages, relishing the sense of being lost; that no one on this earth knew where she was.

She reached Charterhouse Square and, sitting on a bench under a plane tree, she watched the lawyers and city men in pinstripes and bowlers, faces behind newspapers, come and go around the quiet medieval enclave, and contemplated how they simply carried on ashen-faced amid the chaos and ruin, just like she did. And yet, she supposed, those city workers got back on the Underground each evening and went home to their families, their lives, cherishing them for who knew what tomorrow might bring.

Nell knew she could never go home again. Her lies, her forsaking of the truth, would follow her there and break the spell that she had cast around her. Impervious the spell was, and solid. It should stay here with her in London, where it protected her. Inside it, she floated in a senseless dreamworld where her parents were strangers, to each other and to her; and they did not know her any more.

A man said *good afternoon* and sat down on her bench. She shifted her bottom along, mildly irritated, wishing she'd brought a book, always a good way to prevent conversation. There were plenty of other spare benches around the square, why didn't he go elsewhere? She sensed him looking at her, askance, and she turned her face away, concentrating on a squirrel bouncing around the roots of a tree. Sunlight found its way through the branches, dappling the path. How clear blue the sky was, she thought, tilting her head. Such a lovely day.

'My, my, you're a difficult girl to track down.'

Turning in surprise, Nell saw a familiar profile, a long Gallic nose.

He doffed his hat, his grin wide.

'Surely you remember me, Mademoiselle Nell,' he said. 'Henri. Sylvie's friend. Well, I say *l'ami*, but we are so much more than that. I am forever asking her to marry me. She still refuses, you know. She runs off to Berkshire, and she comes back, and still she does not want me. She's a stubborn one, that cousin of yours. Very stubborn indeed.'

Nell glanced around her, embarrassed and on edge, wanting to take flight.

'*Track down?*' she said, with a shake. 'Who is

314

trying to track me down?'

'There are many people looking for you,' he said. 'And I see you have disguised yourself rather successfully as a nurse.'

'I *am* a nurse. In training.'

'Where?'

Nell opened her mouth to tell him, and then snapped it shut. She saw the mischievous glint in his eye.

'Not even my mother knows where I work,' she said. 'So why should I tell you? I've only met you once before.'

'Ah, I see. So you have. And so you have run away from home?'

'I wouldn't say that.'

'Run away from *something*, then?'

'Perhaps you are right.' She stood up and gathered her handbag with a little huffy show. 'Good day to you, sir.'

'Not so hasty, mademoiselle. What would you say if I buy you a drink, and I tell you news of Mr Hammond?'

Nell's legs turned to straw. A great whoosh of pain blew out her middle. She sat back down, hard, on the bench.

'I'm not surprised Sylvie refuses to marry you,' she muttered, staring at Henri through eyes cloudy with tears. Her mouth was as dry as chalk. 'Why would she want to marry you, when she is married to Mr Hammond? Because who would not want to be married to him? And she has a baby. She is so very lucky.' A sob broke from her chest. 'I'm sure they are very happy together – why should you break them up?'

Henri's calm voice slipped below the storm raging in her head. 'She is not married to him or anyone. Do you think me an utter, pathetic fool to chase her if she was? Come and have a drink with me.' He took her hand and held it as if that would stop it shaking. He linked her arm through his and pressed it tight to his side as she leant onto him. 'Brandy is good for shock. I know a little place. A nice old tavern just round the corner in Smithfield.'

She sat in the ill-lit pub, resplendent with stained glass and oil lamps, and pictures of hunts and shoots, sipping at the drink Henri gave her. It tasted like blistering fire. He sat by her, earnestly peering at her face while he told her that her cousin had never been pregnant, it had been a false alarm, and that she had not married Alex. But, he said, she had been engaged to him for nearly a year.

'There, you see.' Nell's words stumbled and rose to a pitiful pitch. 'She means a great deal to him, for them to be engaged for all that time.'

'Mr Hammond did not come back from France for nearly a year. Put it this way: Sylvie stubbornly wore her ring for the whole time. We can deduce from that, that she was *sweet* on Mr Hammond. He was delayed in France. Something went wrong on the beach. He was left behind and became a guest of our Resistance; he escaped down the lines to Spain.'

The bones in Nell's hands stiffened, her fingertips went cold. She murmured something about chance and danger and terror, shaking her head to try to understand what Henri was telling her. To think that had been happening to Alex, and she'd had no idea.

'He is safe?' she asked at last, her bravery finding its way through the clot of fear in her throat.

'He is now.'

She sat back against the pub chair and tried the brandy again, breathing hard with relief. She remained silent for a while, trying to find a way through her thoughts, force it all to make sense: Alex and Sylvie did not get married; did not have a baby.

She glanced at Henri and saw his compassion and patience.

'He wrote to me before he went to France,' she told him, 'but I did not get the letter for a year. I went to live at my father's house, you see, and my mother never forwarded it.'

'What did he write?'

'His regret, his deep love for me. His sorrow. But his duty to Sylvie. His duty to "the cause". He said all of that. I read it every day.' Her voice was barely a whisper. 'But in the meantime, I sent him a telegram from my father's house. Sent it BFPO. This was before ... before I went into nursing. I don't even know if he ever received it.'

Henri waited. Eventually he asked her, what did the telegram say?

'It was four words. *Never contact me again.*'

She choked, then, as a helpless sob filled her throat.

'Why did you hide yourself away?' Henri asked her. 'You've worried a lot of people. Your mother and father, Sylvie tells me.'

Nell looked at him, and saw a gentleman in a

pristine suit, the cut of which was divine. His haircut suggested the military, and yet she knew he was in intelligence; Sylvie had hinted that he was very well connected, very brainy. He knew far more secrets than anyone should do in this war.

'You probably know already?' she asked. 'Why I had to hide.'

'You were in love with Alex Hammond. And Sylvie got there first.'

'She didn't,' Nell retorted. 'I got there first.'

Henri grinned, and then his face fell. His high cheekbones reddened. He looked mildly embarrassed at her confession. 'How did you manage to evade everyone?' he asked. 'They knew you'd gone into nursing. We've established that. But you've managed it for nearly two years.'

'I knew that my mother wouldn't talk to my father. And my father wouldn't talk to my mother.' Nell considered how her father and Diana would assume John-James was being cared for at Lednor by Mrs B and her mother. And yet her mother did not know he'd ever been born. Her deception was cruel and it terrified her. One more reason never to go back. 'I wrote at Christmas and at birthdays. I told them I was perfectly happy.'

'But, I can see you are not.'

Nell pressed her fingernails into her palm, desperate to stop the tears. She did not want to cry in front of this man.

'More recently,' Henri said, 'Mr Hammond approached me. He knows my skills.'

Nell glanced through the high pub window distracted by the pearly June sky – just like it was on the evening of the village fête. That delicate light, so precious. It filled her with delicious memories. *Alex wants to find me.* She held the idea in the palm of her hand and it felt like an exquisite charm.

She suddenly glanced at her watch, realised the time. She had to sign back in at the nursing home at 9 o'clock sharp and the light summer evening was confusing her.

'Don't worry,' said Henri, watching her, 'I'll get you back on time.'

Nell swallowed another tot of brandy.

'I'm not proud of what I did. I am a thief and a liar.'

'Oh, *ma chérie,* we are all both of those things.'

'I took my stepmother's school certificate and her ration book. That's all I needed. I had to buy my own uniform.'

'Your *stepmother's?*'

'She's only about five years older than me.'

'What about your identification papers?'

'I pretended they'd been lost. In the chaos, it seemed so easy. They were desperate for nurses. Somehow, it was never resolved and I was lost into bureaucracy. I often wonder when they'll rumble me.'

Henri congratulated her, raised his glass of beer to her.

'You're in the wrong job, my dear.'

She sat for some moments in silence, longing to know the answer to the question that had plagued her, driven her senseless, made her reckless with grief.

'Where is he?' she finally said. 'Where is Alex?'

'Ah. I cannot tell you.'

Infuriated, she asked, 'But is he safe? Is he in London?'

'He is not in London. But he is somewhere safe,' said Henri. 'Safe, at least for tonight.'

Adele

It seemed to her that deep midnight had only just passed, yet already the sky in the east on such a short summer night was awakening with soft luminosity. The full and radiant moon hung just out of her reach. Below the cottage she could hear the waves licking languidly at the sea wall. She'd never seen a spring tide so high or the water so deep and heavy. The air was still, the night was tender and tranquil, like a muffling blanket. Moonlight silvered the barbed wire twisting out of the sand.

For weeks now, her nights had been disturbed by sporadic Allied raids further along the coast, on Caen and on Merville. The explosions and flares lit the horizon like ominous flashes of lightning; and the retorts from the Panzer units' anti-aircraft guns brought rumblings and vibrations. But up here by the sea, at the apex of the peninsular, Montfleur had been left in relative peace. Even so, despite this, life every day was corrupted by fear.

Standing by the bedroom window, Adele reached her hand down a fraction to touch her fingertip to her sleeping daughter's cheek. She could see the little girl's face, oval and pale in the half darkness. Sophie, now three years old, was tucked in Jean's passed-down truckle bed, snoring in dreamless sleep. Two-month-old Pierre, in the crib next to her, had been an underweight baby, underfed by Adele's own lack of food and aching hunger.

Incredibly, too, Jean was fast asleep in the bed. The doctor had at last been able to give him a sleeping tablet; they had been hard to get hold of in recent months. Her husband had hardly slept since that night three months ago when the maquisard blew up a convoy on the road to Cherbourg; since the German machine gunner keeping watch on the roof of one of the trucks had strafed the hedge, shattering both of Jean's ankles and destroying his feet. Two nights later, the doctor, under cover of darkness in his own salon, in danger of the arrest of himself and his family, had removed the splintered bones, fractured toes; he'd sliced through and stitched severed tendons.

'You will be lucky if gangrene doesn't set in. Watch out for blood poisoning,' he warned Adele as Jean, reviving from the first dose of ether, began to spit through his teeth in screaming bloody agony.

Adele now watched her husband sleep. They'd run out of morphine two weeks ago, and his wretched torment had returned with fresh onslaught and carved itself into his wide, handsome face. But, thanks to the sleeping pill, he lay in the mercy of sleep, his dark hair ruffled against the pillow. The covers at the end of the bed were raised by one of Madame Ricard's small tables so the weight of the sheets and blankets would not press on her son's destroyed extremities.

The crutches, leaning in the corner, helped Jean get down the stairs and to the outside lavatory and back. That, in months, was as far as his strength would allow him to go. Simon took the *Orageux Bleu* out with the help of a lad from the village. The people of Montfleur had expected Simon, Jean and the rest of the cell to be flushed out and lined up against the *mairie* wall to be shot. But inexplicably, Jean had been left alone, and Simon to continue with the fishing. The elder and the younger Madame Ricard had sat in terror of the Gestapo's knock on the door. It never came. Adele wondered if Monsieur Orlande had used his influence this time.

In the past few months, as the weather eased itself into the warmth of summer, she had noticed that German soldiers began to outnumber the population of Montfleur. Units seemed to be on the move, colonising the surrounding fields with their camps, building makeshift kitchens and digging foxholes and commandeering people's doors to cover them. There was an incessant rumble of trucks up and down the country roads and a more frequent hard marching of boots across the square. Perhaps, Jean had commented, this was in response to an intelligence that they had no hope of even guessing at. Their radio had been down for weeks, the cell disbanded.

It was only tonight that her mother-in-law had managed to obtain a new battery for the radio, but when they tuned in just before bedtime they heard a babble of incoherent messages that were impossible to decipher. They switched off.

Adele glanced down. Pierre was stirring and uttering plaintive mews, his little gumless mouth nuzzling the back of her hand. Fearful of both Sophie and Jean waking, Adele plucked him from the crib and headed downstairs to the parlour to feed him. She sat by the banked-down fire. Even in June, the stone house did not feel warm and she shivered under her shawl as her baby suckled.

Pierre was a slow, lazy feeder; he had no energy to try. Adele, realising she would be sitting there for a long time, felt in the pocket of her dressing gown for Madame Orlande's letter which had arrived a week ago. She reread it, feeling a sting of pathos as she perused her old employer's hand. Such a marvellous letter writer she had once been. And now reduced to a few lines on a fragment of pilfered paper.

Her eyes fell heavy as Beth Orlande's words drifted through her mind. *Pray for my dear Sylvie ... my dear sister and her family ... how are the cabbages and the beans, Adele? ... how are the neighbours? Our camp is truly intolerable ... we have one stove between ten of us and ten books between about sixty of us. I have been rereading* Rebecca, *darling Sylvie's favourite book... All fine old fillies here ... we've become quite a rabble ... English, Dutch ... an American woman who was something at the consulate in Paris. Wrong place, wrong time, she keeps saying. She's been saying that for months. She bores me. We sew uniforms and make socks for German soldiers. They will have the warmest feet in the war. I have taken up table tennis... Quite unladylike. What would Sylvie say? I hope for a visit from Monsieur if things quieten down. Can't believe it has been three years. Three years in this hole... Pray for Monsieur... He takes it all very hard.*

'She knows nothing of you, little one, or of Sophie,' Adele whispered to Pierre's oblivious little face. 'She knows nothing at all.'

She folded the letter away and dozed. The small square window, cut into the deep stone wall, grew lighter. The night, she sensed sleepily, altered and the silence was suddenly being consumed by a deep rumbling. It came closer and closer by the second like processional thunder. Adele, suddenly alert, knew that it was aircraft. She was used to the sound, but *this* grew so immense and so embracing that the air was bracketed by metallic vibration, stuffing her brain and blocking her ears. And then she jumped up; the engines were droning in over *La Manche*. Allied bombers, covering the sky, coming their way. She clutched Pierre to her chest.

And then cannon fire, like she had never heard before, from way out at sea. The thunderous roar tore up the air. Windows rattled, the shutters vibrated. The explosions thumped in fury onto the land to the south of Montfleur over and over again.

She turned in shock. Madame Ricard appeared at the parlour door in her white nightgown.

'Oh, *Maman!*' cried Adele. 'What is it? What on earth is it? This is worse than ever.'

'It's over at the Bay of the Seine. I'll try the radio,' said the older woman. 'See if I can't find some news.'

Madame Ricard bent to her radio set but the airwaves were strangled and merely spluttered an awful whining, then silence. 'I can't find any frequency,' she sighed. 'All hell has been let loose,' she muttered, glancing up at the ceiling, out of the window. 'This is appalling.'

'Hold the baby,' said Adele. 'I need to get Jean and Sophie downstairs. We should go to the cellar.'

In the upstairs bedroom, above the protection of the sea wall, the weight of the bombardment was phenomenal. Adele stood in the doorway, petrified. With each insane salvo, she felt as if a train was passing over her, emptying her body, demolishing her senses. Sophie was crying, clutching at her father, as Jean struggled to reach his crutches.

'You know what I think this is,' he said, eyes bright in the half-light, his fingers clutching at Adele's arm. The air raid siren began to howl, ineffective and drowned instantly by the thunderous noise. 'Those are naval guns. *British* naval guns. Adele, my love. We've fought for so long. This is what we've been fighting for. Waiting for. This is *it*.'

During a moment of quiet in the cannons' terrible voice, Adele heard thumping on the front door. She went up the dark cellar stairs and was met with a morning of light and lucidity; an exceptional summer's day. As she opened the door the bouquet from Madame Ricard's rose bushes by the step was immediately swamped by the acid scent of gun smoke on the breeze.

Monsieur Orlande stood on her doorstep. Behind him, on the street, a handful of harassed soldiers hurried along banging on front doors of the other sea wall cottages with the butts of their rifles, barking orders.

'These houses are to be evacuated,' said the gendarme, gruffly, his eyes roving, unable to meet hers. 'It will be safer for you all to come inland. Into the village.'

Adele folded her arms, and looked up at him. Her anger, her loathing fixated on his droopy moustache and the bulk of his stomach bulging his uniform. She noticed two buttons had popped off. Of course, he was alone and had no woman – wife or maid – to take care of such things. Surely, she thought, one of his Nazi subordinates would do a little tailoring for him?

'And you've come here especially to tell us yourself?' she muttered. 'Why didn't you send one of your minions from the *mairie?* Why didn't you leave it to the Bosch?'

'I want you all to come to my house. Away from the sea wall. I have a better cellar.'

'We don't want to come to your house, sir,' retorted Adele, aware that Madame Ricard was at her elbow.

Monsieur Orlande glanced over her shoulder at the older woman. 'By the look on her face, I think Madame wants to, very much,' he said. 'You have your family. Don't be a fool, Adele.'

'A fool? Is that what I am now?' she snapped. 'Better that than *collabo.*'

Adele went to close the door. Her mother-in-law put her foot in the way.

'Adele, shut up!' she cried. 'Stop this now.'

Adele turned away, her throat tight in frustration, in anger and the grinding fear that she had grown so used to.

She heard Jean's mother say, '...of course, Monsieur, we are so very grateful...'

Her voice was swamped by the sound of another round of salvos, thumping over the sea.

'What on earth is going on?' Madame Ricard asked.

'We are being invaded,' said the gendarme.

Adele glanced at him, drawn by the tone of his voice. His face was pale; his moustache twitching.

'Invaded, sir?' Madame Ricard responded.

'They're landing.' He was distracted, his eyes wandering down the street, up to the sky. 'The coastline is under fire, I've been told; from Quinéville to Arromanches to Ouistreham.'

'The Allies!' breathed Madame, incredulous.

'Here is my key,' Monsieur barked. 'Take it or leave it.'

In the distance the guns boomed. Passing through the melee of activity around Montfleur harbour, Adele held onto her limping husband. Beside her walked Madame Ricard with her grandson in her arms. Sophie trailed behind them.

German soldiers, their features tight with fatigue and fear, lined up in platoons, and began to march. They were ready for action but quaking, it seemed to Adele, at the prospect of it. What a change, she thought, to the cocky, self-assured men who had harassed her, teased her, after the fall of France. Yet, still, they were immaculate: boots shining, rifles gleaming.

The residents of Montfleur, Adele noted, had other, more complex expressions as they responded to the sudden and undisputed transformation of their day: restrained glee, a glimmer of hope, and yet still, not daring to speak of it.

As they passed the *Orageux Bleu,* Simon, thought Adele, was less restrained. He was whistling, packing up some nets, winding some rope. He nodded to them all, first of all wary; but then he realised that now, perhaps now, he could say what was on his mind. He stepped onto the quayside.

'This lot are being deployed south where the heavy fire is.' He motioned towards the soldiers. 'I reckon they are short of men. I've heard that the divisions are depleted because of the Eastern Front. The timing is right. The message was on the radio last night: *the dice have been thrown.* Did you hear it?'

'We couldn't make it out,' said Adele, glancing over her shoulder in fearful reflex. She flinched as the guns out to sea roared again. She wondered at the mayhem, the chaos of battle, what the men were *doing* beneath all that noise. Allied soldiers on French soil? It was too astonishing to comprehend.

Jean, leaning heavily on Adele, was gazing down at his boat, idle on the high water in the harbour.

'I long for the end,' he whispered, his face unrecognisable with pain. 'I so long for it all to end.'

'Jean, here, look at this.' Simon rummaged in a box on the boat and drew out a *tricolore,* folded and bound with rope. 'Take heart because, any day soon, we shall unfurl this and fly it from the top of the *mairie*.'

Adele helped her husband lie down on the chaise by the empty fireplace in Monsieur Orlande's salon. He winced as she lifted his legs onto the cushion, his throat drenched in sweat. Hobbling the kilometre over rough cobbles from the sea wall cottage to the Orlande home had taken its toll on his savaged feet. His eyes swam; his jaw was fixed.

'I will call the doctor,' she said. 'He might have something he can give you.'

Jean grabbed her hands and made her sit by him. She knelt on the carpet and rested against the *chaise*. 'Not yet,' he sighed, despairing. 'Don't go.'

Pain made him breathless. Adele looked around the room, knowing Monsieur kept his brandy in the small cabinet. The sunny morning made mockery of the dust, revealing it lying thick on the *buffet* and the secretaire where Madame used to write her letters. There were empty bottles of wine discarded in the fireplace and crystal glasses lined up in a row stained with telltale smears of red, long evaporated. Next to Monsieur's chair was a plate of cheese crumbs, manna for the mice; old pipe tobacco reeking in an ashtray. A grey cobweb extended from one corner of the mantelpiece to the wall.

She got up and found the brandy, poured a small tot for her husband. With her back to him, she herself took a sip. Kneeling back down beside him, she held the glass to his mouth.

He sipped, his eyes not leaving hers.

'Look at me. I'm useless to you. To everyone. Lying down in this salon. *His* salon.'

'Monsieur is being very kind,' said Adele, feeling disloyal for saying so. 'Your mother just told me, there is a good ration of milk down in the kitchen; some dried fish; some tins. But even so... I also don't feel this is the best place for us.'

Madame Ricard came into the room. 'What are you talking about?' she cried. 'The cellar is deep, safe from the bombs, the garden is full of vegetables. Doesn't he have some chickens down there in the old stables?'

Adele reminded her that there used to be rabbits.

'What more could we ask for?' Madame sat down in an armchair and ran her finger over the coffee table, examining the pleat of dust she made.

'But, *Maman*, this is the house of a traitor. A traitor to France ... the people of Montfleur know what he has been doing for the last four years. Hobnobbing with the *Kommandant*.'

'But his own wife was carted off to prison,' cried Madame Ricard. 'I can only feel sorry for him. A man in his position. Whatever he does, he cannot win.'

'But now...' muttered Jean, 'but now the tide is turning. Adele, you take care of Sophie, Pierre and *Maman*. If something happens. If the hell we're expecting reaches us ... you leave me here. If I can't manage it ... whatever happens. You leave me here.'

'But what *can* happen?' Adele lifted her face to look him in the eye. 'The Allies are here.'

'Tomorrow might be different once again.'

They all glanced in the direction of the hallway. The front door was opened and shut with a slam. A curious rattling and squeaking came down the corridor towards them. Monsieur appeared in the salon, pushing before him a wheelchair.

'It's got broken springs,' he said, 'and it needs some oil. But it will do, don't you think?'

'Oh, Monsieur, thank you,' breezed Madame Ricard. She leapt up and pushed the chair into the room. 'Look at this, Jean. Isn't this wonderful?'

Adele's stomach contracted in embarrassment. Her mother-in-law's simpering reaction to the gift – just one more confirmation of the gendarme's corruption, for which they must all be so grateful – was unforgivable. She held her husband's hand tightly on her lap, feeling his sweat drench both their palms.

Jean coughed, and tried to draw his legs up, tried to stand. He gave up.

He said, 'Thank you, Monsieur.' And his voice was flat with defeat.

Monsieur Orlande's parlour radio was not as robust or as capable as the one they left behind in the sea wall cottage, but Adele managed to trace the World Service and pressed her ear to the fabric speaker to listen to the news.

'Tommies are in Caen,' she told Jean. 'Carentan is taken. They are joining the Americans via the Valognes to Cherbourg route.'

'They're getting closer,' her husband said.

Adele glanced out of the Orlande salon windows at the benign summer sky, quiet now. Sporadic shelling punctuated their days, like a depraved and tuneless symphony along the horizon. The missiles had not yet reached the town, but Adele felt their presence over her head, as if she constantly wanted to duck. Out in the *bocage* the Germans were fighting a rear-guard action, defending the peninsula from the invaders, the liberators. And the people of Montfleur were either trapped, cowering in their homes, or they had left to find a place of safety. But where, in the besieged peninsula, could they possibly go that was safer than anywhere else?

'I'm not leaving, Jean,' she told him stoutly. 'I'm not going without you.'

Jean glanced at the wheelchair parked in the corner of the room. Monsieur had left it with them, and then moved into the *mairie*. He had a camp bed there in his office, he told them. He said he had to be on duty twenty-four hours a day.

'Damn that man,' said Jean, 'but I want to use it. I want to get out. I want to breathe fresh air, blow away this awful ... frustration. Will you take me out?'

She dressed her husband in a clean shirt, and found his Sunday trousers. Thick socks covered his damaged feet. She eased him into the chair and set his cap on his head. He had shaved that morning and his eyes were bright, his forehead smoothed by the rare shot of morphine she'd

332

managed to get from the doctor that morning. She kissed his lips.

'You are a fine-looking man,' she told him, 'and I love you.'

He had no need to say anything to her – his eyes told her.

'Where is Sophie?' he asked as she manoeuvred the chair through the front door.

'*Maman* has her with her down in the kitchen. Pierre is fast asleep. I told her we won't be long.'

'But I want to be,' said Jean.

Adele pushed her husband over the cobbles, through deserted streets. Occasionally a shutter would open, she would see a timid face, and she would utter *Bonjour*. Montfleur was holding its breath.

Out on the smooth tarmac road sweeping around the low-lying coast, the wheelchair was so much easier to push. Adele began to giggle, she began to run. The chair nearly flew as she propelled it before her.

Jean laughed, 'I need to fasten my safety belt! But this thing doesn't have one.'

'You should have stolen a Bosch helmet for extra protection,' she laughed, panting. 'You know what a bad driver I am. I haven't run so fast for years. I feel like I am back at school, tearing round the playground.'

The beach lay to their left, perfect with crisp white sand tickled by gentle waves. *La Manche* was a pure blue, reflecting the sky, with streaks of gunmetal grey where the waters were deeper, darker. The sun was hot overhead. The stupendous green of the fertile green blanket of fields nearly blinded her. Birds fluttered through the rambling hedges where big white cows poked their soft faces over. Adele stopped the wheel-chair and she and Jean both reached up to stroke their noses. A vile stench hit her suddenly and she stood on tiptoe to see where it was coming from. In the field beyond, three dead cows lay in the long, lush grass, their bodies bent and ravaged by shrapnel injuries. A bleating calf bent its head, trying to nuzzle its dead mother's teats.

Without a word, Adele grasped the handles of the chair and pushed Jean away.

A puff of wind blew his cap off and Adele ran along the road behind it as it bowled along. She caught it and planted it on her head.

'Hey, Adele,' he cried, laughing. 'Give that back. That's mine. It's the only one I've got, remember.'

'Unfortunately not any more,' she cried. 'I have commandeered it. I haven't visited the hairdresser's in months. In fact, I think they all left Montfleur weeks ago. My hair is a mess and I need to keep it covered. You're fine without it.'

They reached the bottom of a slope that led up to the headland, the apex of the eastern edge of the peninsula. Adele braced herself and pushed hard, steering her husband up to the top.

'Put your back into it.'

'That's right,' she wheezed, 'you do all the huffing and puffing, I'll do all the hard work.'

She stopped at the top, applied the brake and wiped her face with a handkerchief. She put Jean's cap back on his head, knelt beside him, took his hand and gazed out over the bay. They both fell silent, awestruck by the enormity of the sight before them. The sea swept wide to the distant south where Caen lay, marked on the horizon by the shroud of black smoke over it. The Allied armada lay at anchor, colonising the bay. Countless warships and destroyers, surrounded by flotillas of smaller boats, imposed their strength and their will on the sea, on the land, on the war.

'Here,' Jean drew his field glasses out of his pocket and handed them to her. 'Take a look and tell me what you see.'

She squinted through the lenses. The terrifying mechanical bulk of the warships came into sharp view, with a blur of activity between them as small boats flitted, conveying supplies, conveying men to the coast.

'They keep on coming,' she said. 'They just keep on coming.'

She spotted planes in the sky over the land, protecting and monitoring. She swallowed hard at the power – the sheer audacity – of it all unveiled before them.

'Do you feel safe now?' Jean asked her, as she handed him the glasses.

'It's as beautiful as a dream. It's as frightening as a nightmare.'

Jean fell silent as he, too, watched through the glasses and took in the magnitude of the fleet. He put the glasses away and Adele watched him wipe his eyes.

'If only we'd waited,' he said. 'We should have waited. We shouldn't have ... we shouldn't have carried out the raid. You know... I mean the one years ago, when the children were taken. We should have waited. They were taken because of us.'

'Jean, please.' Adele rested her head on his shoulder and stared ahead of her at the might of the Allies, feeling the twist of pride, of delight in her gut, and the sharp guilt that raked over her heart. 'Oh Jean, you're shivering. You're so cold.'

'My legs...' he said. 'The pain is creeping up them.'

'I'll get you back home.'

'Wait a moment. I want to look at the ships for a few minutes more. I don't want to forget this.'

The sun beat down. The dune grasses rustled and whispered peacefully. Summer clouds jaunted across the sky and, beyond the wire that guarded France, that suffocated France, the sea looked perfect for bathing, the sand ripe for children to build their castles.

Jean lived for just a few days more, but not long enough to see the first Tommies walk into Montfleur.

As British tanks streamed up the road from the south, Adele tried to call the doctor but the telephone lines were down, the electricity cut off. In the Orlande salon, they guessed at blood poisoning. Jean was delirious, his fever intensifying; he cried, he whimpered like a child with the pain. And then, very suddenly, he became incredibly quiet. His eyes glazed over as the first shells screamed in over the rooftops and blasted holes in the houses around the square.

'Tell them to stop,' cried Adele, clutching

Sophie in her arms as an obscene blast rocked her bones. She crouched by the *chaise*, shielding her daughter and burying her face into her husband's shoulder. His face was tilted away from her; his sweat felt ice-cold under her fingertips. As the blistering explosion faded, the deathly quiet returned and she dared to lift her head, she realised how still he was. 'Tell them, Jean, tell them,' she whispered into his sleeve. 'There's hardly any Germans left here anyway.'

Simon appeared suddenly at her side, his eyes staring wildly, his face white, his clothes encrusted with brick dust.

'I just made it across the square. Oh God, get down to the basement with that child, Adele. Go.'

'Simon, I'm not leaving him.'

'Do as I say!' Simon gripped her arms and picked her up as she held onto Sophie and dragged her away from the *chaise*. A stream of plaster trickled down from the ceiling. Glass could be heard falling, breaking somewhere in the house.

'I want to stay! I want to stay with Jean!'

Madame Ricard hurried in and grabbed Sophie from her arms.

'The baby is downstairs. Now come with me,' she commanded. 'He can no longer hear you.'

Adele looked at her mother-in-law. Her hard wrinkled face was broken with emotion and yet her cold voice sounded so reasonable and natural that Adele dumbly obeyed her.

Sheltering in the basement kitchen, Adele sensed the hours drag by, the sunlight change outside the window. The noise from the shells slowly eased to be replaced by cracks of gunfire from hand-held pistols in the streets.

'They're fighting house to house now,' said Simon. 'They're flushing them out.'

She wondered where the Germans might be hiding. The stables at the end of the garden, or the shuttered house, empty and ghostly, next door? She held Sophie close and spoke gently to her, listened to her muffled weeping. She, too, longed to cry but was too empty, too shattered to even try.

A spell of silence passed and Madame asked, 'Will they retreat to Cherbourg, Simon?'

'They might try but I hear that Cherbourg is surrounded by the Allies.'

Madame made a satisfied remark.

Simon said, 'Someone told me this morning, the gendarme's gone missing. Disappeared last night. I hope he's done the honourable thing.'

'One can hope,' said Madame.

Adele said nothing. She lowered her head, longing for sleep. She wanted to crawl up the stairs and find Jean and look after him, to comfort him, to at least cover him. But she knew she must stay here and stay safe for Sophie and Pierre. She must stay alive for her children.

'And guess what else, Adele,' said Simon. 'You know the *tricolore* that I kept hidden on the boat?'

She lifted her face and tried to smile at him.

He said, 'I grabbed it just before I ran for cover in here. I hung it on the gates outside. For Jean. For you. For all of us. *Vive la France.*'

The front room of the Orlande house was a special room, for special occasions, Madame Orlande had always said. The grand *salle de diner* with dusty crystal chandelier, exquisite panelling – now bearing cracks from the impact of the bombardment – a marble fireplace and rose-pink drapes at the windows, had been shut up and shrouded since Madame was taken away. With the shutters closed and the candles lit, it became Jean Ricard's chapel of rest. He lay in his open coffin on the dining table, his eyes closed, his face sleeping.

Adele knelt by his side in the golden, smokey half darkness and prayed. She pressed her hands into her face and forced out the words, yet they were muffled by her tears and by the wrenching of her heart. How quiet it was, in the room, in the house, in the village. She did not want to breathe for she might break the peace.

The window was open behind the shutters and she heard through it a scattering of jovial voices. *English* voices.

'This is what you wanted, Jean,' she whispered. 'This is for you.'

She left her husband and quietly closed the door behind her. She went out of the front door and crossed the small courtyard. She opened the blue gates, hearing the familiar squeak of metal against metal.

'What the blazes...? Oh, you made me jump!' It was a British man, sitting on the step, unlacing his boots.

He was alone. A ragged platoon of Tommies was patrolling further along the street, their uniforms in a shocking state. Rifles looked cumbersome and old-fashioned. Revolver holsters were made of thrown-together webbing, and their pockets were torn. *What a rabble,* thought Adele. But then, a shock of compassion sliced through her. Those young men were far from home.

'So very sorry...' the man muttered as he pulled off his boots. 'My perishing feet are killing me.'

The boots were split at the toes and looked like a comical flapping mouth, or something Charlie Chaplin might wear. His socks were torn and his toes poked through.

But he wasn't a soldier, that much was clear. Somehow, he was altogether more refined and Adele could not work out why. His flecked grey hair had a short cut, but he was in sober civilian clothes that looked rather dilapidated. For a moment, a desperate fear seized her. *Who the hell is he?* Jean had said how the tide could turn and turn again. The war was certainly not over and even now, with British soldiers on the street, her uncertain heart failed her. But when this man smiled at her she felt suddenly, immensely safe, as if he'd earned her total and unexpected trust. He glanced up at her before rummaging in his canvas bag. She blushed as she found herself hypnotised for a moment by the depth of his brilliant blue eyes.

'Here you are, madame, cigarettes and chocolate,' he said. His French was good and educated. His inflection perfect.

'Thank you,' she said, thinking of Simon, who would be in dire need of them.

'I think I have my bearings wrong. Last time I was here it was the dead of the night and I was rather worse for wear. You heard me right, madame, worse than I look now. Am I at all near the headquarters of *Esprit Fort?*'

She sat down on the step next to him.

'The cell has been disbanded,' she told him. 'We had an unsuccessful operation in the spring and have not been much help to the cause since then.'

'*Esprit Fort* helped me in 1941,' he explained. 'I wanted to let them know that, this time, I would be at their service. I parachuted in a few days ago and mustered with this regiment for the time being,' he nodded down the street where the soldiers had disappeared, 'before I rendezvous with my unit and begin my work. But, to cap it all, these boots have let me down somewhat.'

'Will you come into the house?' she asked.

He looked sharply at her, and stood up as she did, but did not speak. She noticed that he'd seen the crude swastika chiselled into the stone gatepost, legacy of Montfleur's opinion of Monsieur Orlande. As they crossed the small courtyard, she saw him fingering his revolver, glancing up at the windows. She understood. It could be a trap. There were reports of renegade German soldiers hiding out in buildings all over the countryside. She might, for all he knew, be affiliated with one or more of them.

She left him in the hallway and went upstairs to collect Jean's fishing boots and his thick knitted socks that were waiting to be packed away. She picked out his jacket and good trousers from the wardrobe, too.

The man was waiting, tense and alert, at the

bottom of the stairs, his eyes large in the semi-darkness of the shuttered house.

'Here you are, monsieur,' she said. 'Will these be any use to you? My mother-in-law is outside in the garden with the children so please, get changed here in the hall if you like. Or upstairs if you prefer. Would you like some coffee? We have some coffee. Come down to the kitchen when you are ready.'

'You have a fine house, madame,' he said, entering the kitchen looking extremely comfortable in Jean's clothes.

Adele laughed briefly. 'It is not my house. We are merely sheltering here. It is my employer's house.' She stopped herself. She was going to say that the house belonged to the gendarme and Madame Orlande, but did not want to share the bitter shame of the situation with this British man. This extremely brave, special man.

'Well, thank you, I can't tell you how grateful I am. And this coffee…'

'Is not good?' Adele smiled.

'Is the best I've tasted, after what I have been through, since I landed off target in a field of cows, four nights ago. I must say, these socks are exceptional. They will keep me warm for many a night.'

'That's because they're fisherman's socks,' Adele said, overbrightly.

She busied herself at the table, cutting bread and butter, hoping the man would not see her distress, or her sharp tears, remembering that Jean was lying upstairs in the darkened *salle à manger*.

'Here, sir. Please take some food with you. We are so grateful to you. To all of you.'

'Thank you, Madame ... er?'

'Ricard.'

'Ah,' he said, a recognition falling over his face. 'Ah, *le pêcheur*.'

She felt him staring so hard at her in such absolute deference that she had to look away.

'How the coincidences occur,' he mused. 'In all this chaos and destruction, a beautiful coincidence. Is your husband–?'

'The least we say about it the better, don't you think?' Adele broke in quickly. 'Please, don't say any more.'

The sound of Sophie laughing in the garden drifted through the basement window of the kitchen. The man walked over to the window, and looked up, smiling. The older lady was dozing in a deckchair, Sophie playing on the rug. Pierre's pram stood in the shade of the high garden wall.

He turned back to Adele and she saw his eyes glistening, his mouth widening, not in a smile, but in an effort to stay straight and to hide the torment behind his eyes.

'I thought that I, once, was going to have a baby. But then, it was with the wrong girl and it all turned out to be a false alarm.'

'The wrong girl?' Adele was confused and a little flustered by this man's confession and its translation. She thought perhaps she'd misunderstood him. She wrapped the bread up and filled a bottle with milk for him. 'False alarm? The *wrong* girl? I'm sorry, sir. I don't understand.'

'It all happened with the girl that I didn't love,' he said. He picked up the bread and milk and stowed it in his bag. He spent a long time checking through what else he had in there, tucking some paperwork safely away, fastening the buckles, placing the strap over his shoulder. At last he looked up at her. 'You know when someone is ... sorry, I'm struggling ... I'm trying to find the correct French words to say it. When someone is under your skin?'

Adele looked at him blankly.

'Someone is inside you. Part of you?'

She nodded and turned her face away. This man was standing in front of her wearing Jean's clothes. She wanted to shriek with the madness of grief.

'The girl who I betrayed, she's the one who is under my skin. I am a fool. An utter bloody fool. And I wish to God everything had been different.'

As Jean had warned her, the tide did turn and turn again three months after the British man left, three months and a day after Jean's funeral. Madame Orlande came home, liberated from her prison near Paris by triumphant Allied soldiers.

She stood on the doorstep, frail, a bag of bones, her once dark hair a mass of grey. Adele took two steps back, such was her surprise. Madame's eyes were sunken, her cheeks hollow and lined. She had lost some teeth. What remained was her defensive demeanour, the hesitant but forceful presence that told Adele that her mistress was home.

'I expected to see him at the station, I expected to see him here. I've not heard from him in so long. Where is he?'

Adele followed her into the salon where she looked around, surveying the cracked plaster, boarded-up windows.

'So you had it rough here?'

Beth looked at her, expectant, waiting for Adele to explain herself.

'Madame, you have had such an ordeal, please take some refreshment, some wine perhaps?'

'Where is my husband?' she demanded and then folded meekly onto the chair. 'Oh, don't tell me. Don't tell me he is dead.'

'No, Madame.' Adele sat down opposite her. She spoke carefully, precisely, the way she used to try to explain things to Estella and Edmund. 'He was accused of collaboration at the time of the liberation. The Allies arrested him. He has been in custody in Paris, as far as we know, since then.'

'But I've just come from there! This is ridiculous. Who is in charge here? Who is the gendarme? The prefecture?'

'There is an American general at Cherbourg,' said Adele. 'He is pretty much in command of the area. But as for Montfleur, they are trying to rebuild everything. Get everything in order. It's rather chaotic.'

Beth Orlande leant forward, grabbed Adele's hands.

'You will stay here with me?' she demanded, her eyes huge in her ashen face, her bony fingers shaking. She rubbed at the swollen knuckles. Her hands, once so pale and soft, were ruddy, the skin

345

broken, the nails flaking. 'Will you stay?'

'Of course. Madame, we actually live here. We've been here since the invasion; Monsieur allowed us to. It seemed safer, somehow. My children, Pierre the baby and Sophie, and my mother-in-law Madame Ricard also...'

'Ah, of course, your fisherman. Yes, I think I can tolerate Madame Ricard. And the Androvskys next door?'

'Gone,' said Adele. 'Years ago.'

Beth Orlande flinched.

Adele broke the silence with the words she dreaded to speak; they always sounded like a lie, trapped in her throat. 'My husband is dead.'

Madame muttered her sorrow. So many had died, so many gone, it hardly seemed to be a surprise any more.

'Let's drink that wine, Adele.'

Adele helped Madame Orlande settle in as best she could. Her fussing and weeping were a timely distraction to the grinding agony of losing Jean, and the questions from Sophie, the little girl's tears because Papa wasn't there to read a story, and her own silent weeping deep into the night.

By the time that a week had passed, Madame had managed to put her firm stamp on the household again; organising but never really understanding. As Madame Ricard whispered to Adele that morning in the kitchen, 'I've never met anyone so self-absorbed.'

'She's distraught about her husband,' Adele said kindly.

'Her husband isn't dead.'

346

Adele looked at her mother-in-law for a moment too long. Their mutual grief blended, grew bigger. Adele turned to the kettle, her voice brittle. 'Madame Orlande is going to go to the *mairie* this afternoon, to, as she says, get some answers about the gendarme.'

'Barking up the wrong tree,' muttered Madame Ricard, her hand twisting through the tea cloth. 'Not sure I can live here for much longer with her. Let's go back to the sea wall cottage.'

Adele nodded and picked up the tray of coffee to take to Madame in the salon.

On her way up the stairs, she heard raised voices from the street outside, the distinctive humming noise of a crowd.

'Oh, listen,' said Beth, cocking her ear to the window as Adele placed the tray on the table, 'can you hear the shouting in the square?'

'Perhaps some news has come through. Another push on the Western Front, perhaps? I'll ask Maman to tune in the radio. Oh, I can hear Sophie crying downstairs. She is so sensitive. Hates any noise from outside, I'll just go and—'

There came a tremendous hammering on the door and Adele heard Sophie burst into louder crescendos of terror.

'I'll answer the door,' Madame Orlande said, 'you go to your child.'

As Adele hurried towards the stairs the front door was opened and she heard barking, urgent voices and then Madame Orlande's sudden startled cry from the hallway.

Adele turned to see Beth Orlande, her arms pinned to her sides, hauled out of the house and across the yard by three men of Montfleur, one of whom was Simon.

'What are you doing? What on earth are you doing?' she yelled, hurrying out of the house. 'Simon!'

The other men continued to frogmarch Beth away down the street, while Simon paused to wipe sweat from his forehead. His eyes were bright with strange and violent pleasure when he looked at her.

'Justice,' he panted. 'Justice for France. Collaborators like this one are not going to get away with what they've done. They have to be taught a lesson.'

'But, this is Madame *Orlande!* She has been in a prison camp for four years. How can you do this, Simon?' cried Adele. 'She's a lady, a tired, shattered lady. She's only just been released.'

He waved her away and ran off down the street, along which the frail prisoner was propelled so fast that her feet, still in her slippers, began to drag on the cobbles. Beth was mute, her mouth pressed tight with terror. She glanced frantically over her shoulder at Adele, her eyes opaque with disbelief. Adele followed, bewildered, not knowing what else to do.

Around the square, on buildings broken by Allied shells, the *tricolore* was flying. Some of the flags were ragged, had seen better days, others were crisply pressed, fresh out of armoires. All were signs of pride, defiance, jubilation. The people of Montfleur were cheering, drinking. They started pointing, turning to look, and jeering as Madame Orlande was marched to the centre of the square.

Upright chairs from someone's *salle à manger* were set out in a row. Her captors forced Beth to sit down. A sign was slung around her neck. Adele pushed her way to the front of the crowd to read the crude scrawl: *collaboratrice putain*.

'But she is innocent!' Adele cried, her voice obliterated by the baying crowd. 'For goodness' sake, Simon. What are you thinking? Jean wouldn't do this.'

'She's guilty by association. Keep out of it, Adele,' he snarled at her. 'You don't know the half of it.'

The baker and his wife, and the hairdresser, too, were marched forward and made to sit. How absurd these people looked, dumbfounded, beaten, terrified, sitting on someone's Sunday best furniture in the middle of the square.

Adele felt her limbs shake, her blood run cold. This wasn't to be a summary execution, surely? They couldn't be so barbaric. Surely not Simon, who had been Jean's friend, had been her hero.

'This is madness!' she cried, pulling on Simon's arm. 'It wasn't her fault. Her husband ... it was Monsieur who–'

Somehow Beth heard her words amid the melee. Her head snapped up and her look silenced Adele. Her eyes, sharp and dark, burnt with fury.

'Quiet, Adele,' she hissed. 'Don't mention my husband here.'

Adele was helpless, incapacitated by terror. Her mistress trembled, her mouth wobbling in a scream that no one could hear, as someone came up behind her and hauled her head back. A whirring noise began and, on the chair next to her, the baker's wife began to howl.

The barber's clippers worked roughly over Beth's straggling grey hair, shaving to her scalp; clumps of hair fell over her shoulders, onto her lap. Her tiny bowed head was crudely naked. The people of Montfleur, her friends, her neighbours, cheered. Some gasped and some looked away. And yet Beth Orlande did not make a sound.

Part Six

1945

Nell

The firecrackers woke her from her afternoon-off snooze on the bed, cracking and whizzing like rockets, like bullets. Children were letting them off near the hospital and the noise echoed around the courtyard below her window. And so the celebrations continued around her, without her. She pressed her hands over her ears.

Violet rapped once on the door, startling her, and poked her head round. 'Come on, Di, shake a leg and get dressed. I'm bored of bobbing around here. Some of us are going to cut over to Piccadilly Circus, see what's going on. Come with us. Do you good.'

'That was all of yesterday and the day before,' said Nell. 'Surely the party's over by now.'

'I don't think it ever will be.' Violet hugged herself and twirled around on the spot. 'Everyone jumping in fountains and getting drunk. I'm still soaring, I tell you. I have never been kissed by so many fellas in all my life.'

Nell would have her know that she didn't quite believe it. She told Violet that she was feeling under the weather.

'Oh, suit yourself. You know, I've never known any one as plain miserable as you.' Violet flounced out, slamming the door.

Nell lay back down on the bed. Violet was right. She was miserable. Bloodless. Her skin an empty husk. There was no joy, no reason to celebrate. There was nothing inside her. As her tears fell, soaking her ears and her hair, and finally her pillow, she wondered how many more she would have to shed before her mourning would stop. It was, quite frankly, getting beyond reasonable.

Another tap on the door. 'What is it this time?' she called.

A wide-eyed ward maid looked in.

'Sorry to disturb you, Nurse, but you have visitors. They're waiting in Matron's office.'

'*Visitors?*' Nell glared at the girl who shrank away and closed the door behind her.

'For crying out ruddy loud,' Nell muttered, as she slipped on her uniform, realising she had to dress correctly if she was being summoned to Matron's office, and then she paused mid button. Who on earth had found her *here?*

She knocked on the big oak door with its opaque glazed panels and slipped in. There was no Matron, or any other member of nursing staff there. Just her mother, sitting in an armchair by the grate, and Sylvie, pacing and agitated by the windows, her tailwind positively shaking the pot plants on their stands.

As soon as Nell closed the door behind her, Sylvie pounced on her.

'This is where you've been! All this time – why have you done this, telling people the wrong name? Why are you *here?*'

Her cousin gripped her shoulders, her face, close to Nell's, pinched with anger.

'Sylvie please,' said Mollie, quite calmly, rising from the chair.

Nell looked from one to the other, not comprehending for a painfully stretching moment that these two women could actually be standing here, in an office at King's College Hospital, speaking to her, demanding answers from her.

Bewildered and giddy with panic, Nell spluttered, 'Have you been down for the VE celebrations? I heard it was quite a party.'

'What the perishing hell are you going on about?' Sylvie cried. 'We haven't seen you for years and you are making small talk.'

'I think VE day is quite *big* news actually,' Nell remarked. She rested her trembling hand on the back of a chair by Matron's desk, registering the relatively warm wood against her icy flesh. Her mother moved towards her. My, thought Nell, *how grey she is now, but looking much better.* There was colour in her cheeks and a fire behind her eyes.

'Nell, we have been out of our minds. We had no idea where you were.'

'Well, now you do.' Nell tried for a smile, but was stifled by nauseating shock.

Sylvie huffed and sat down on the chair, folding her arms, crossing her leg and kicking her foot out sharply. 'Henri told me in the end,' she said. 'You know you've broken the law.'

'Probably more than you realise, Sylvie.'

Mollie glanced nervously between her daughter and her niece, let out an awkward laugh and settled her thin hand on Nell's arm.

'You do look lovely in your uniform,' she said. 'Of course, we knew you were nursing. It's just been so confusing. Not being able to contact

355

you. Not knowing where you were. I've spoken to your father.'

'Finally,' Nell sighed.

'Yes, and he told me something that utterly shocked me. So utterly, that I could not speak.'

'Is it true?' Sylvie pressed. 'What your father tells us?'

Mollie interjected, 'You know that isn't in question, Sylvie. I believe it to be true, because it is what Uncle Marcus said. And, even though he is a prize spineless cad, I would not allow that of him. He would not lie about such a thing, it's ridiculous. Nell, my dear...'

Nell looked at mother, drawn sharply by the unprecedented kindness in her tone, the concern in her voice. 'Please, oh my dear girl, did you have...' her whisper was as soft and as vulnerable as Nell's memory of cradling John-James '...a baby?'

The blank wall in her mind began to crumble, her empty body to fill with the pain that she had stuffed behind it. Her mother's question echoed, like a voice, long lost from years before. The scolding of Miss Hull, perhaps, or a telling-off from Mr Flanagan at the paper.

'He would have been four by now.'

'What?' Mollie's face wobbled. *'Been?* We thought perhaps you'd had him adopted...?'

Sylvie cried out and leapt to her feet. 'Are you saying the baby's dead?'

Nell groped her way to the armchair her mother had vacated and sat down. Mollie perched on the arm, and pulled her head to her lap.

'There now,' she said, stroking her curls repeatedly and saying over and over again, 'there now.'

Nell stared, dry-eyed, over at Sylvie whose face was disintegrating through realms of disbelief and horror. Her mother's words in a soothing voice just above her ear meant nothing to her, and yet they seemed to resonate with her, to pave the way for her to begin some sort of journey.

Nell swallowed dryly before she could speak, searching for her voice: 'He's called John-James.'

'Ah.' This from her mother, and a convulsing weeping made the strokes of her hand through Nell's hair ever more agitated.

Sylvie started to sob with her face quite still and her mouth wide open.

Nell stared at her cousin for a moment longer and then squeezed her eyes tight.

'He's in the September Garden,' she said.

She heard her mother's shuddering breath above her. 'Well then, that's where we must take you. Take you home.'

She hadn't seen the harvest for years. Each morning she woke at Lednor that summer, under the cool first breath of the day, the countryside was remade. A field of barley, of oats, had been cut down, reshaped by the men working on it, gathering it in. There was a ripening glow like golden mist on the horizon, orchards were plump with plums and apples and there was plenty in the larder for Mrs Bunting to make the meals that were so comforting and familiar to Nell that she found it hard not to cry as she ate.

In her numb and meandering state of mind, she

observed the skies change too, the stars shift in their bed. She watched the mean slice of crescent moon rise and alter, waxing undiscernibly every night. She watched her become fatter until the true harvest moon revealed her full, shameless, naked glory to light up the entire deep night.

And her father came back to Lednor, 'just for the afternoon, mind,' her mother was quick to add.

Nell met him on the lane near Pudifoot's cottage, taking Kit with her, off the lead, for he clung to her side, her unquestioning companion. Her fears had been unfounded: he had never forgotten her.

She and her father walked the way they used to walk, around the curve of the valley, up the steep hill to where the oak meadow lay, now under plough and the old tree's spindly offspring grubbed up to make way for it.

While Kit sniffed around roots of trees and thrust himself through hedges, they leant on the gate and talked about John-James. As Nell struggled to explain, her father, perplexed and muddled in his deferred grief, assured her she didn't have to.

'Should I have a word with the vicar, Nell?' he asked. 'It's best I do. He can sort something out. Something fitting for him.'

She was weary beyond belief, but one thing she fought over was the need to leave him in peace. 'But it will be questions upon questions, Dad. Questions I can't answer for I did not know what I was doing. It is so true when people say it: *I lost my mind.*'

Her father's face reddened, his eyes glowed with water. He looked away.

'I can't bear to dig him up, Dad, even to put him in the churchyard,' she whispered, her words clumping together. 'And he is perfectly safe. He is wrapped in your old rubber raincoat. You remember, the one with the big poacher's pockets.'

'She drove me mad,' Marcus uttered, suddenly, bitterly, as if Nell had not been speaking. 'I had to go. I didn't want to – but she told me to go.'

Nell waited and acknowledged her father's guilt; his disjointed admission. She listened to the cranking of a tractor engine, reaching them way up here from the valley floor. It stopped abruptly and a curiously heavy silence fell on them, the whole weight of the sky.

'Listen, Dad. Did you hear that? A yellow-hammer?'

'I do believe it was,' he said, sounding strangely shrill. 'Now if only I had my field glasses.'

They strolled back down and walked up the gravel path, her father saying that he'd like to take a stroll in the September Garden. Nell waited for him, perched on the bench under the dovecote, Kit spark out in the sun at her feet.

Moments like this, when she was left to herself, Alex inevitably walked through her mind. She let him, giving in to him, for all of her energy was spent on the basic activities of sleeping, eating and putting one foot in front of the other.

She thought of the starry convictions of that first summer, and of the following year when they were caught in the raid and the rain together and had sheltered from both. How the love they created was now transformed like the land around her, into something teetering on the boundaries of madness.

His letter was ragged with her fingerprints; his explanations known by heart and absorbed painfully into her mind. His great love for her, and yet his duty to Sylvie. And then, there was his duty to King and country. He'd described the intense course in the Highlands, back in '41, where, even in training, they expected five per cent fatality. And yet Henri had told her he wanted to find her. She deduced now that that had been simply to check she was alive and well. After all, who could blame him when her telegram warned him to never contact her again?

Sitting by the dovecote, that August afternoon, it was easy to feel angry with him, for that gave her a sense of reality she simply could not find anywhere else.

Her father approached her, his face transfigured in a way she had never seen before. She decided to distract him from it.

'I forgot to ask, Dad. How is Diana?'

'Well, after her lengthy stint moonlighting as a nurse,' he said, and Nell's sudden laugh surprised them both, 'things have settled down a bit for us. She has left the factory, of course, now the munitions race is over. She is expecting a baby.'

The front door opened and Mollie came out onto the step.

'Marcus, would you care to come in for some tea?'

'Er, oh, yes, if you like. Of course. Thank you. Yes.'

Nell held back and watched her father's meek progression towards the house that had once been his home. Her mother stood back, dignified, with an air of courtesy as he went through the door, ducking his head as if the entrance was lower than it really was.

Her mother glanced at her, enquiring, and Nell held up her hand in negative response. *Let them talk about me,* she thought, *let them consider John-James.* She sat back down on the bench beneath the lullaby purring of the doves and pushed her foot under the dog's breathing rump as the front door softly closed.

The news of Uncle Claude a few days later threw the consequences of war right onto the doorstep of Lednor House. When word came through from Montfleur in the winter of 1944, Auntie Beth had written of their ordeal – of her own shocking stint in prison, that Uncle Claude had been incarcerated by the Allies and was awaiting trial.

And then, that August, soon after VJ day, they heard of his attempted escape, the guards shooting him on the wire. Auntie Beth wrote that she was packing her suitcases, she was leaving the damned despicable, ungrateful country for good. And would someone get the steamer over to bring her home.

Sylvie was hysterical, telephoning from the mews.

'I want to go, I *have* to go, and I wanted Uncle Marcus with me. What a perishing idiot he is! Breaking his leg falling down the stairs. Carrying the new cot from Peter Jones. That's what delivery men are for! I turn to Henri, but, oh no, he is ensconced in some military intelligence. Something to do with the Russians, although I screamed at him, I thought they were our friends. Nell, Nell, will you come with me? I need you. I need to get *Maman* home.'

No mention of her father and his crude demise, Nell thought, as she put down the telephone.

Nell pressed her hand to the strip of grass. It felt springy, alive. She whispered to it, to the patch of earth, *It is time to go.*

Sitting in the back of the Olivers' taxi taking her away from Lednor, she watched the smouldering beech woods captured in the velvet wonder of the autumn morning. She stared at their stupefying beauty until the colours blurred and shifted out of focus. Tears splashed down onto her empty palms.

What on earth was she doing? She had vowed never to desert her baby again. When she gave up nursing and returned to Lednor she'd promised him: that was the last time she'd ever leave. And what was a vow worth if she could break it so easily like this? She wiped her eyes, leant forward and opened her mouth to say to the driver, *Stop, please turn around,* but Mr Oliver spoke first.

'I know, lovie. Always hard to leave this place, isn't it?' She saw the taxi driver's kind eyes glance shyly at her in his rear-view mirror. 'Must be the most beautiful valley in the whole of Bucks, if not the world.' He winked. 'But just remember, it'll all still be here when you get back.'

The taxi was passing Mr Pudifoot's cottage and

Nell was struck by a strange glimmer of hope. Blind, stupid and futile her optimism might well turn out to be, but she suddenly decided that this was her last chance to patch things up with Sylvie. Her cousin needed her. The trip to Normandy would give her a purpose, give her strength to keep going. Give her strength to forget.

She'd said her goodbye to the valley, to Kit, to the September Garden, and promised to be home soon.

Stay like this, she told her valley as the taxi chugged on. Look after him, won't you? Stay just as you are, in all your blazing glory, until I return. Then the leaves can fall if they want to.

Sylvie

She stood with Nell outside the gates. The blue was flaking to reveal the dull metal beneath. She remembered her father painting the railings in the spring before Nell came to visit, the year before the war. He had spent hours sanding down, stepladder out, shirtsleeves rolled up. Meticulous movements of his rather fat fingers getting into all the angles, all the tight corners. Her mother had said, 'Let's pay someone to do it: Simon the fisherman, or Jean Ricard.' 'No,' said Papa, 'I want to do it myself. Then I know the job will be done properly.'

She glanced at Nell with an urgent desire to thank her for being at her side, to tell her how sorry she was. But her cousin's inscrutable expression made her mouth dry, her tongue a dead weight. Nell was dressed in a pale-green suit and looked as pretty as a button; she'd done something different to her hair, twisting it up inside a new hat. They had never spoken of Alex, and they had only skirted around John-James. Nell's tragedy had done away with her childlike nature. Her new-found maturity placed a mask over her face which Sylvie could not see through.

She grasped a railing in her fist and peered across the short courtyard to the porch with the tall shutters either side, all so shabby now. Some tiles had slipped and fallen. Fragments of them lay scattered like rubbish in a corner. The shutters on the *salle à manger* were slightly ajar and she saw that the windowpanes were cracked. Behind the glass was darkness, a void. And yet behind that very glass had been her life, her childhood, her memory.

She opened the gate and stepped forward, with Nell mute beside her. There were cracks and pockmarks in the facade, the scars of the war. Someone had scratched a swastika into the wall by the front door. Beneath was carved one word, crude and misspelt: *colabo*. The door opened and her mother stood on the step, her arms outstretched. She looked weak and ill – more than ill, as if the light had been taken out of her. A weight of dread pressed hard on Sylvie's back, like a heavy hand, pushing. She walked towards her mother, saw the opaque torment in her eyes and held her bony frame in her arms without speaking.

In the six years she'd been away, in her dreams she had returned to Montfleur. She walked the rooms and the staircases of her home as it had once been: gleaming parquet, slender windows, elegantly faded Louis XV chairs. The dreams often unfolded long into the night with a smothering sourness. Her unconscious journeys projected her here like a shadow on a wall. When she died, she thought, *I will haunt this place, just like I do in my dreams.* Now, the house she knew from childhood was gone. The bricks and mortar may remain, but the essence of it was gone. And yes, she thought, this was to be applauded.

As she hugged her mother, she was aware of Nell making her way past her, along the hallway and into the salon at the back. Sylvie's ears pricked when she heard a familiar voice exclaim from within, 'Ah, little Nell.'

She pulled away from her mother and looked at her.

'Adele Ricard is here to help me pack,' Beth Orlande informed her.

'And you, *Maman,* are coming home with me,' Sylvie said. 'Thank God, you are.'

The salon was as she remembered: chairs placed just so, facing the large stone fireplace, the *chaise* at an angle, *Maman's* secretaire in the corner. But everything looked bruised, Sylvie thought, an inferior copy of itself.

'Now, we will have coffee,' Adele announced briskly, bearing a tray, 'and my apple cake. I expect you have missed the Calvados apples, Sylvie?'

'Among so many things,' said Sylvie, sitting on a fireside chair. She fumbled with the knot of her headscarf, her fingertips shaking.

Nell was by the window, peering at the wall that divided the gardens, finishing a conversation she'd been having with Adele.

'They had a ladder, do you remember? Kept popping up, with their little faces. They were such naughty little beans.'

Sylvie's mother interjected, bristling defensively, 'Well, you know, Nell, the Androvsky family were taken away. But that was after I had gone so I don't really know much about it, really.'

'We can all take a good guess what happened, Madame,' Adele said. 'I expect they ended up in Drancy. Trains left there, we know now, for Auschwitz.'

'No need to be so brutal,' scolded Beth. She poured coffee with a pale-knuckled, shaking hand.

'The *children?*' Nell exclaimed.

'When their parents were sent away they were left behind. They came to live here with Monsieur Orlande. We hid them in the spare bedroom. Your room, actually, Nell, do you remember?'

'See, there you are.' Beth's voice was shrill with justification. 'He did what he could. Claude was a good man. Of course,' she said, handing a cup to Nell, 'we have no sugar.'

Sylvie stood up suddenly, desperate for a change of air. '*Maman,* will you take me upstairs, for a moment? Show me my room? I really want to—'

Her mother's face broke into a broad smile.

'Oh, *ma chère*. Of course.'

Sylvie trod the stairs with care, as she had always done – in an attempt not to make any noise. She hurried along the long landing past the closed door of what had once been her parents' bedroom. Up another flight, and the sickness in her stomach began to churn.

She opened the door to her old bedroom and walked over the Paris carpet, looking around the serene white-painted walls, at the bed with its French Grey drapes, and the little armoire in the corner. Her dolls, her ribbons, her shoes were in tidy rows, the bed made up, the crisp sheet turned down. A pain settled over her heart as her mother began to speak.

'Adele kept the room aired and clean for you, all through the war,' Beth was saying proudly. 'I'm afraid it could do with a bit of a going-over now, but everything is still here. Everything you own, Sylvie. I wanted to keep it for you. For when you came home.'

Sylvie's memories bubbled like poison under the surface of her skin.

'You needn't have bothered.'

She walked to the window as her mother's open-mouthed, shocked silence bore down on her. The garden was forlorn, left to rack and ruin, but she remembered clearly the rows of beans, the mounds of lavender, the stables at the end. Poor old *Monsieur le lapin*. It wasn't Nell's fault. She knew that then, and she knew it now. If only she could tell her so.

'I had hoped to slip through Montfleur without attracting attention,' she told her mother.

'Thought my headscarf might do the trick, but no such luck. I saw them looking. The intakes of breath, the raising of eyebrows. I heard them say it. *La fille du collabo.*'

'But that's why I am so desperate to leave,' said her mother, wringing her hands in agitation. 'I take it that you are settled in England, and would not want to return here? I wasn't sure what your plans were. I am so glad you came back for me.'

Sylvie turned to her. 'I never wanted to set one foot in this place again. I'm only here to bring you home.'

An understanding filtered softly over her mother's features. 'He wasn't a bad man, Sylvie. He was caught in the middle. Damned if he did. Damned if he didn't. And for it to end like that. So barbaric. He didn't stand a chance.'

She stared at her. '*Maman*, I don't want to sleep in this room tonight. I'd rather sleep on the *chaise* in the salon.'

Her mother recoiled. 'But we kept it all for you. We have it all laid out. Fresh sheets. Every week.'

Anger simmered inside Sylvie's bones. She stared at her mother's pathetic face, at her broken tooth, and had to look away. Through the open window, Adele's and Nell's voices drifted up as they stepped out of the vestibule and lingered on the path below.

'... the old fort at Cherbourg was the German headquarters ... soldiers in the cafés, asking girls to dances. We refused, of course. Always said we were washing our hair.'

Nell pondered on the unimaginable dangers

and prompted Adele to continue. Sylvie found herself smiling – her cousin, forever the reporter.

'We'd tune into the Free French in London,' Adele went on. 'The World Service. My husband was in the Resistance. He died just after D-Day.'

Hearing Nell's sudden exclamation of sorrow, Sylvie glanced angrily at her mother. 'Just because my father is dead,' she said, 'it doesn't transform him – suddenly – into a good man.'

Leaving her mother speechless, she hurried down the stairs and along the garden path, catching up with Adele and Nell outside the stables.

'Monsieur Androvsky once told me about Ullis and Tatillon,' Nell was saying. 'The two horses that used to live here.'

Sylvie looked at the faded signs above the twin stable doors.

'We never had horses, Nell,' she gently chided. 'Only rabbits.'

Nell protested, 'No, there were horses here a long time ago, when Monsieur Androvsky was a young man. Oh, I can still smell it.' She was standing where the narrow stone steps disappeared up into darkness. 'That faint whiff of straw.'

'Nell, you're being too ridiculous,' said Sylvie. 'How can you smell it when there haven't been horses here for years?'

Adele put her hand on Nell's shoulder. 'You were always so fanciful, so sensitive, little Nell,' she said.

'Will you tell us what happened?' Nell asked. 'To the two children?'

369

Sylvie's mother had followed them out to the yard. She now stood with her arms folded, her face downcast. A twitch had appeared above one of her eyes. Sylvie thought how sunken she was; how she was crumbling away.

Adele said, 'The night we planned to send the children down the lines, I hid them up there in the stable loft. We thought it would be easier that way.'

Nell said that she wanted to go up and take a look. She'd never dared to before.

Sylvie followed her cousin and Adele up the steps. She sensed her mother climbing silently behind her.

'*Sacré bleu,*' Sylvie muttered, her eyes blinking in the darkness. 'I was never allowed up here as a child, and I can see why. It's a positive death-trap.'

'Can someone help me, please?' came her mother's plaintive voice from below.

'Here, allow me.' Adele stooped, gripped her under the armpit, and with one strong pull, hauled her up.

They stood close together in the half darkness. Sylvie's nostrils were warm with timber dust and the musty scent of confined air, her head almost touching the sloping ceiling. As her eyes adjusted she began to make out the pale faces of her mother, her cousin and Adele, their eyes like dark pools. She saw pinpricks of daylight through the roof tiles. They looked like stars in a night sky. She remembered the tree house at Lednor and how it had been the most wonderful place. This loft was draughty, dusty and festooned with cobwebs. It was not a place anyone would want to stay for very long.

'The same night Estella and Edmund were hiding in here, there was a Resistance operation,' Adele whispered, as if she might wake the children. 'It went terribly wrong and it was not possible for us to deal with them. It was a dreadful mix-up. We should never have...'

The break in her voice scratched at Sylvie's nerves. She felt her heart quicken with dread.

'And then, Monsieur Orlande betrayed the children.' Adele's shoulders shuddered.

Nell covered her mouth with her hand and looked away.

'How *dare* you!' Beth cried out.

'I'm afraid it's true, Madame. That dreadful morning, to save the cell, the town, himself, he sacrificed the children. He redressed the balance. And I watched him do it.' She wept in the gaping silence. 'We are guilty. All guilty.'

Sylvie's legs turned to liquid. She span around, sat down hard on the dirty floor. She leant forward, her chest sinking, her head collapsed under the weight of the shock that came at her like a physical blow.

'He *betrayed* them,' she hissed, 'like he betrayed *all* children.'

'Oh, Sylvie.' Her mother was there in front of her, her face aged with distress, her eyes bright with tears. 'It's awful. So awful. I am so sorry.'

'Why are you sorry?' screamed Sylvie. 'You will forgive him, like you always forgive him and, again, forgive him!'

Her sobs filled the rafters and the dark corners

371

where the children had crouched and waited.

She felt Adele's hands scrabbling for hers in the half darkness, placing in them some crumpled folded pieces of paper. She stared down at her lap in the gloom, trying to make them out.

'These are pictures that the children drew the night they were here, Sylvie. I'd like you to have them.'

In the gloom of that stable loft, Sylvie could hear Nell weeping and the footsteps of her mother as she hurried back down the steps. She felt a soft puff of relief, as if someone just then had breathed gently on her throat.

She gazed down at the pictures, smoothing her fingers over the wrinkled paper but unable to see clearly what the children had drawn for all she could think was that he was gone.

At last, at last. He was gone.

Nell

She barely noticed her Auntie Beth drifting around the house at Lednor, such was her plaintive withdrawal into her own shadow. But whenever Nell did encounter her, on the stairs or in the garden, she saw grey hair unwashed and tangled, slippers mismatched, heard her muttering to herself, fingertips twitching in unconscious agitation. And she could not help the compassion that lifted out of her chest for her frail aunt. Even more so, because Sylvie refused to visit Lednor.

After the revelations in the stable loft in Montfleur, Nell explained to her mother, the two women had barely spoken to each other. The journey home to England had been awkward, arduous. Nell had watched the choppy heavy-grey waves from the prow of the cross-Channel steamer, urging England to appear out of the drizzling horizon, longing for it to take shape, craving for Lednor, for home. She'd done her duty in accompanying Sylvie back to Montfleur and left her cousin and her aunt to prowl the ship like strangers.

Her mother begged her to become arbitrator, to telephone Sylvie and ask her to reconsider. After all, Auntie Beth was contrite and suffering more than she needed to, was desperate to make amends with her daughter. Nell reluctantly dialled the number for the mews.

'I'm glad you telephoned,' Sylvie said, quite calmly, surprising her. Her voice contained an edge of humour. Nell braced herself. Sylvie making jokes was lethal; a symptom of something much darker brewing underneath. 'Yes, I will come up to Lednor. Just to warn you, however, I will be liaising closely with Mrs B to ensure no *lapin* for dinner.'

She arrived the following afternoon just after their mothers had left for the cinema.

Nell was nervous of Sylvie, skirting around her as she took off her coat and put her suitcase upstairs, wishing her mother and aunt had stayed in to shield her from the hardness that veneered her cousin's face, those beautiful, unreadable eyes.

373

'They've gone into Aylesbury on the bus,' Nell explained. 'Even Mrs B decided to join in. It was Mother's idea, an outing to cheer your mother up. And the perfect day for sitting indoors in a cinema, looks like it's going to tip it down.'

Sylvie followed her into the kitchen, unusually reticent, and sat herself near the warm Aga, pushing her hands up the sleeves of her cashmere cardigan. Outside, the day grew blustery and rain started to fall from voluminous grey clouds.

'I'm glad they're out, and we have the place to ourselves,' said Sylvie. 'I've always liked good old Mrs B's kitchen. Most comforting.'

Nell agreed that it was and offered to make some hot chocolate. She talked about the weather, wondered what the film would be like, asked about the mews house, anything to stop Alex rising between them.

Sylvie politely took the steaming cup of milk and, dipping to her bag on the floor, said, 'I have something in here for you, Nell. You didn't get a chance to see them properly at Montfleur. I've brought the drawings.'

Surprised, Nell took them, unfolded them, smoothed them out over the table.

They sipped their hot chocolate in silence, contemplating Estella and Edmund's innocent imagination. When Nell dared to look at Sylvie she saw that she also had tears in her eyes.

Nell said, 'I know what we should do with these.' She went to the dresser and found an empty biscuit tin, saying that it would do and that Sylvie should put the drawings in it. 'Make sure the lid is tight. That's it. Come with me.'

Sylvie protested that it was raining, but Nell chivvied her up, putting on a raincoat of her mother's and handing Sylvie her own old hand-me-down mac from the hall cupboard.

'I'm surprised this old thing hasn't been given to Miss Trenton for the jumble,' she protested.

They left the house and ran together across the lawn through the rain, wet beech leaves blowing in their faces, their hair whipped madly by the saturated wind. Breathless, the shoulders of their coats wet already, their shoes soggy, they stopped by the bourn under the big willow tree.

'Can you do it, Sylvie? I think you should do the honours.'

'Hold the bottom of the rope ladder for me, then. Merde, I'm surprised it hasn't rotted away after all this time. Ouch, that's my stocking gone.' And then, 'You're right, I can't fit through the entrance. Six years ago it was a bit of a struggle – but now certainly not. It's definitely built for children.'

'Push the tin in as far as you can.'

'Have done,' she called down. 'It's over by the eaves, away from any gaps. It is rather dry up here, surprisingly so. That's good. Job done.' Sylvie made her slow way back down the ladder, swinging over Nell's head while she held it steady.

Sylvie landed with an elegant thud on the ground and the cousins faced each other under the shelter of the branches where the raindrops barely reached them.

'They're safe up there,' Sylvie said. 'No adults will ever find them there.'

Later, in the lamplit drawing room, Sylvie opened the trunk that stood in the centre of the Aubusson rug. It had arrived yesterday from Normandy for her mother. Nell poured them both a sherry and busied herself perusing the shelves in the alcoves, chancing upon some of her father's old books. With broken spines and yellowing pages, they should, she decided, have been thrown out years ago. Kneeling down to peer along the bottom shelf, she was surprised at what he'd left behind – most of his life, it seemed. He had walked out of the house five years before with the clothes he stood up in.

She commented as much to Sylvie, saying she ought to clear them away, and wondered why her mother hadn't.

'Hanging on to him, isn't she?' said Sylvie. 'I think we can all be guilty of doing that. How is Uncle Marcus, anyway? And his young teacher bride?'

'Hasn't been a teacher for years. Drummed out of the profession for running off with a married man.'

'Well, *they're* married now, aren't they?'

'Their baby is due in a few months, and he is on crutches. Has to sleep downstairs, Diana tells me. She hopes he will be better by the time the baby comes.'

'He won't be much use around the house, will he?'

'I don't think he ever was.'

They laughed dubiously.

'Ah, here we are,' said Sylvie, drawing out a pale-blue photograph album from the trunk and wiping the silk cover with the cuff of her sleeve. 'Come and look at this, Nell.'

She sat beside Sylvie on the rug as her cousin carefully opened the wedding album. The dust made her sneeze delicately and Sylvie commented that even her sneezes were pretty. Between the thick wax-paper leaves half a dozen photographs had not seen the light of day for years. Uncle Claude stood in the studio in front of a curtain, while Auntie Beth sat on the edge of an overstuffed chair. She was demure in a cloche, her white gown trimmed with a band of fur. Claude held his gloves and bowler hat in front of him. His moustache in those days was neat and small.

'Why did they bother to include this one?' Nell wondered. 'Uncle Claude must have moved as the shutter closed. His face is a blur.'

'Just as well, I say,' said Sylvie, snapping the album shut and burying it back in the trunk. 'Who wants to look at him, anyway?'

Nell wondered and then bit her tongue. She said cautiously, 'Of course, my mother burnt her own wedding album on the infamous bonfire.'

'The first time I met Alex. The day we both met him.'

Nell looked at Sylvie, braving the full force of her intense and contrite violet-blue eyes, and then turned her face away.

'Thank you for coming with me to Montfleur,' Sylvie said quietly.

Nell blurted, 'I left John-James when I didn't want to. I don't want to do that again in a long time.'

She felt Sylvie's hand on her arm. 'I asked a lot of you. I only did that because I needed you.'

Nell shrugged, unable to contemplate this notion.

'Nell, it's not your fault.'

'Oh, it is,' she said, her own voice drilling painfully through her head. 'I fell asleep. I should have watched him, always, watched him. The vicar's been up to bless him, you know. Everyone has been so kind. But it's so cold out there. So cold.'

Sylvie knelt up and her arms went round Nell. Sylvie's sweet, powdery perfume enveloped her. Tears raced down her cheeks.

'I knew Alex loved you,' she heard Sylvie say in her ear, 'that's why it drove me mad.' She drew back. 'I was under the influence, completely, but hadn't a cat in hell's chance. And yet still I clung on. Where's the dignity in that? I wouldn't give up for a whole year. Not until he came home from Gibraltar. At last he came home, and finally I took off my engagement ring. There was no fight left in me. That was the night I knew. He loved you. He wasn't interested in me. Nell, you are made for each other.'

'But how can I do it to him, Sylvie?' Her words were shredded with pain. 'Don't you understand? I have left it far too long. How can I tell him about his baby? He will hate me. John-James would have been four. *Four.*'

Rain darkened the window, the evening was falling fast. A splatter of drops hit the glass hard, water poured down the drainpipes and gurgled along the gutters. The storm pounded in her head, making her remember dawn in Mr Pudifoot's cottage, the watery light through the little window. Alex holding her as if she was a precious thing, as if he would never let her go. 'How can we ever even try...?'

'Open the door to him,' Sylvie said. 'Because, by golly, when you were with him, however briefly, you were truly Nell and I want Nell back. The girl I remember.'

'But you hated me.'

'I hated myself.'

This alarmed Nell, silenced her. She looked at her cousin's beautiful, rigid face.

Sylvie said, 'I wanted to be like you.'

'But my parents always said I should be more like you.'

Sylvie crowed, *'Parents?* What do they know? Look what they've done!'

Nell pondered, staring at the pile of her father's books, registering the sweet whiff of dust, of disintegrating paper.

'Come with me,' said Sylvie, snatching at her hand. She pulled her out into the hall, sat her on the telephone stool and rummaged in her handbag.

'I expect the Hammonds still live there.'

'Where?'

'The family home in Kingston. He stupidly gave me his parents' telephone number.'

Nell looked in awe from her cousin's face to the battered little black book she was holding open, the page turned to GHI. This was the girl who had tormented her, who had terrified her and yet had tried to love her. Clarity switched on in her head, like a light, opened her mind to a startling reality. Not daring to think of what she was doing, her fingertips trembled as she lifted the receiver and waited for the operator. She dictated the number and listened to the rhythmic clack-clack-clack of the exchange whirring, imagining the wires suspended through the wet darkness across the fields.

The shrill ringing started and she mouthed to Sylvie that the call was going through. Her cousin got to her feet and left her to it, shutting the drawing room door behind her.

A click and a hard echo billowed in Nell's ear. Her heart rapped in her throat, choking her. Her blood pounded cold and visceral, deafening in her temples. She did not hear the car draw up outside the front of the house.

'Hello, hello. May I please speak with Alex Hammond?'

The front door burst open with a thump and clatter, and Auntie Beth stumbled in, her face crumpled with grief, wet with tears and rain. Her hair was a halo of grey around her head, standing on end. Her chaotic voice pitched high to the ceiling as she shouted, 'I didn't know, I didn't know what he did. How could I know? I didn't *know!*'

Nell bent her head, crushing her finger into her ear to stopper the sound, to listen hard down the telephone line.

'Hello? Hello?' she said, deep into the receiver.

Mrs Bunting and her mother hurried in behind Auntie Beth just as she fell to her knees in front of Nell. 'He sent them to the camps. *He* sent them, *not* me. But they still shaved my head, did you know, Nell? They shaved my head.'

Nell looked up to see her aunt right beside her, looming maniacally close, her face in tatters. 'And now my daughter hates me. Where is she? Where is she?'

Behind her, Nell's mother gesticulated furiously for her to put the telephone down and help her.

A voice in her ear said, 'Nell, is that you? Are you still there?'

Mrs Bunting said, 'It was the newsreels. We had to leave the cinema.'

Auntie Beth pressed her face to the floor and wailed, 'They thought they were going to take a shower. They had no idea. They trusted him. They trusted me.'

Sylvie emerged from the drawing room and knelt down by her mother, placing a hand gingerly on her shoulder. Sylvie looked up at Nell, bewildered. 'Please help me.'

Nell flinched at the pain, sheer translucent pain, masking her cousin's face.

She replaced the receiver.

Next morning, the storm had passed. At first light, Nell opened her eyes and looked across to the twin bed where Sylvie was sleeping. She had intended to sleep in the Lavender room, but then, at the last moment, at bedtime, they had decided to share. Kit was scratching at the door and gave a rough bark. It was not like him at all, he was normally such a good dog and stayed downstairs in the kitchen.

Nell walked over to the window and opened it a fraction. The woods were dripping, drenched, but the sky was clear, the green scent of moss reached her as she shivered in her dressing gown. Kit howled.

'*Sacré bleu*,' Sylvie said, waking. 'What on earth...?'

'He wants to go out. He sounds rather desperate. Do you fancy an early walk?' Nell asked, expecting a negative response. But, again, Sylvie surprised her.

Vaporous mist lay across the valley bottom like a whisper. The ascending autumn sun was breaking through. It was going to be a beautiful day. They plunged into Lednor woods, glorious in gold, as Kit bounded ahead, seemingly tracking a rabbit, or a fox. Every so often he'd glance back to check they were still there. The silence was absolute. The spaces between the trees chilled, breathless and still.

'I always think of trees as such lonely figures, shedding their leaves every year,' said Sylvie. 'Known only to the rain and the wind.'

Nell almost laughed. 'Sylvie, you are getting rather sensitive in your old age.'

'Still in shock from last night. I think we should have called the doctor.'

'But Auntie Beth insisted she was all right. Once she'd had a bath and one of Mrs Bunting's hot toddies. We tucked her in, didn't we? She would have been out like a light.'

'She would have got through the night, yes,' said Sylvie. 'But there are all the days and nights, and many hours to come. To get through.'

'It takes time. Lots and lots of time,' Nell said bravely. 'We know that, don't we?'

Kit crashed through the ferns sending a shower of fallen raindrops over them. They exclaimed, they laughed.

'What have you found, Kit? What is it?' Nell scolded him. 'Should have brought his lead. It's as if he's having another adolescence.'

They'd reached the deepest, most secret depths of the wood where the air was no longer fresh, but tangy and wood-scented. Daylight had escaped, leaving behind an eerie green gloom.

'This is where Auntie Moll comes 'shrooming,' observed Sylvie. 'I recognise that big old tree.'

Nell pressed her hand onto her cousin's arm. She saw the knife first, a harmless little penknife lying brightly on the leaf mould in a cleft of the thick root. Beside it, a crop of fungus. Pure-white Destroying Angel. *Neither vegetable nor animal,* she thought. Such inert devilish things.

Auntie Beth lay curled beneath the tree, her brown coat disguising her within the depths of the undergrowth, her back to them, her face buried under her arm.

'*Maman!*' Sylvie screamed.

They ran, and knelt, tugged at her arm. Auntie Beth's face turned as Nell hauled at her sleeve. Her head dropped sideways, unnaturally. Her cheeks were white, bright with a film of sweat, her eyes tight. Her lips were dried, shaped appallingly. By Nell's knee was a matted pool of blood-black vomit.

Auntie Beth's face was monstrous. Her body contorted.

'*Maman,* what have you done? What have you done?' Sylvie shrieked, her voice bouncing

383

around the glade, scattering pigeons. There was no answer; never any answer. She simply wasn't there any more.

Adele

She arrived earlier than expected. The taxi driver, a Monsieur Oliver, dropped her off by the shop in the little village and she walked towards the church. *So this is Great Lednor,* she thought: a row of cottages bowing under undulating red-tiled roofs. It was, as these things always are, so very different to her expectation. Smaller, somehow, than it had been in her mind's eye. Everything, from the lane, to the doorways, to the casement windows, was more petite, and a little worn and ramshackle. There was not a soul around. Respectful silence behind the closed front doors. The church stood up on its rise, serene in the slanting sunshine. She breathed the dark scent of woodsmoke. So this was an English village, an English autumn. This was the sort of day Madame loved. Yellow light patterned the leaves in the sycamore canopy over the churchyard; leaves were like jewels against the sky. Fallen winged seeds crushed under her shoes.

Mollie Garland had written to her. The coroner had stated: *Amanita. Death cap.*

Her mistress's knowledge of mushrooms was outstanding. Adele remembered the foraging expeditions in the *bocage.* Madame had eaten,

384

deliberately, the most deadly she could find. She had walked the woods of Lednor, the coroner had deduced, bided her time, let the poison seep through her body. *A punishing death*, thought Adele, opening the lychgate, feeling the damp of its wood through her glove. *A penitent's death.*

She found a bench under a spreading yew and waited. Mourners started to arrive in little groups. Two ladies of a certain age, almost identical in tweed suits, left the slate-roofed cottage over the way together and walked, with arms linked, up the church path. The taxi driver arrived with his wife. Other people congregated with hushed voices: an older, tall, wiry man in uniform, with a very young and very short pregnant wife beside him.

And then the hearse. Adele stood and watched its silent black shininess invade the space beyond the brick and flint wall. The pale-wood coffin in its rear looked small and humble.

The murmuring voices in the churchyard quieted. A large-bottomed woman got out of a car behind the hearse, hurried through the lychgate and bore down on her.

'Are you Madame Ricard?' she asked. 'I am Iris Bunting. So glad you could make it. How was your journey? Are you quite well?'

'Ah, Madame Bunting,' Adele said. 'Where is Sylvie? Oh, Sylvie.'

Mademoiselle hurried up the path in heels, severe in a jet-black suit, a veil of lace over her ghostly face. Lips redder than they should be. A tall, good-looking, sharp-suited man trailed her.

'Oh, ma petite, je suis désolée.'

385

Adele felt Sylvie dig her chin into her shoulder as they embraced.

'This is Henri,' said Sylvie, breaking away. 'And Nell's here, see.'

Adele shook hands with the Frenchman and hugged the little cousin in turn. 'And Madame Garland? Oh, shall I meet her later? Afterwards?'

'Yes, yes, let's get inside,' said Sylvie.

'After you,' said Adele, holding back. Someone had caught her eye. Behind the hearse, on the other side of the road, a large expensive-looking car had parked in front of the cottages. Adele squinted, retrieved a memory. Greying temples, extraordinary blue eyes, boots that had seen better days. Her mind swayed in confusion.

'I know him. *C'est lui*,' she whispered to herself. 'It's him.'

Sylvie

The church was pretty full for the funeral of a non-parishioner. Behind her the congregation was breathing as one, like a many-eyed beast. All the cold familiarities of the place of worship dripped reality and mortification into her: the carved pews, the smell of old books, the tombs in the ground. She knew that if she stayed here much longer, the chilly air would seep into her heart and stay there. Henri, comforting and solid beside her, put his hand on her knee. Sudden and totally inappropriate desire sliced through her body. She recalled his lovemaking over the years. She had always allowed him to drive Alex out of her mind. Did he know that of her? Even so, if he did, here he was still, by her side.

She bowed her head in shame as she remembered the desire that had made her take Alex away from his love, from his life – just for that moment. She felt a cynical laugh bubble in her throat.

'Are you all right?' Henri whispered in her ear.

She shivered, couldn't look at him.

The coffin was born aloft up the aisle. She lifted her face to watch the vicar walk to the pulpit and take a breath. Over her mother, he boomed, *'I am the resurrection and the life.'*

The service was over. The church emptied but Sylvie remained sitting in the pew, her back against the hard wood. She kept shivering.

'How are you, *ma chère?*' Henri asked her.

She picked up the service sheet: *In loving memory. Elizabeth Annabel Orlande. 1905 to 1945.*

'Not all right,' she said. 'Not all right at all.'

'Of course you're not.'

She glanced at him, at his kind questioning face. Minutes seeped by. A long yawning silence.

'They're burying her now.'

'Do you want to go out there?'

She did not know how to answer him. Instead, she said, 'I was happy when I heard that my father was dead.'

Henri's arm came round her shoulder.

'I know.'

'But even then, I did not know the full extent

of what he had done in the war.' She twitched involuntarily as memory bit her. 'He made me bad. He made me misbehave. I'm glad he's dead. But not *Maman*, for she didn't deserve this.'

Henri's lips pressed her temple.

'Oh, Sylvie.'

'We all know now that my father was a Nazi sympathiser. The whole of France knows it. But no one knows about this.' She balled up her fists and crushed them to the centre of her chest as her insides began to boil. 'It is *unspeakable*. Yes.'

She glanced at Henri. His expression questioned her, but he didn't press her. She knew, then, that she loved him.

'My father...' she began, and her mind was sharp and bloody. 'He called it *le petit sommeil*.'

'*Pardon?* The little sleep?'

'The days he was not working, the days he was at home, he insisted everyone had an afternoon nap. He visited me in my room. I'd be curled up, a tight little ball. I'd pretend to be asleep. It didn't work, though. It never worked.'

Henri held her hands tightly. She felt his whole body shudder in shock.

'Your mother?' she heard Henri ask quietly, as if his mouth was full. 'Did she know?'

'I don't know if she knew.' A sob tore at her voice. 'But now I'm older I think, how could she not have known? She bought me rabbits. I always had a rabbit.'

She listened, strained her ears for more of Henri's words of comfort. When he did not – could not – speak, she tried again.

'That summer, the year before the war, I was

so worried he'd go for Nell,' she whispered. 'So I did what he said, always what he said, so he wouldn't go into her room. Perhaps I deserved it. I am such a spoilt little bitch.'

Henri held onto her shoulders, turned her to him. She shied away from his eyes because she knew he was about to speak the truth to her.

'You don't deserve it. You deserve to be loved,' he said, incredulous. 'Do you know that?'

Sylvie could not speak.

'Do you *know* that?' he insisted. Now he was angry.

'Show me, Henri. Because I don't know how. Please, will you show me?'

Nell

She always thought the view from the churchyard was sublime. Through a chink in the trees, Lednor valley was dozing, making ready for the winter. Above the hills, rising pale and indistinct, the moon was fully grown but feeble-looking. It was an interloper, like a ghost appearing in daylight. The evening star shone steadily like a benevolent old friend.

As the chief mourners gathered around the hole in the ground, she wondered where Sylvie was.

Her mother, reading her thoughts, hissed in her ear, 'She's missing this. How *could* she?'

The clods of earth slammed on to the top of

the coffin, the mourners peeled away. All around them, the sycamore trees were giving up their leaves to the breeze.

Nell felt someone slip their arm through hers and turned to see Anthea Challinor.

'Hello, my dear.' Her ex-colleague's warmth reverberated in her voice.' We read the report in the newspaper. Such a sad affair. Your poor aunt. I said to Syd, "we have to go support that girl". I don't think you have ever met my Syd, have you?'

Anthea introduced her to a smiling, suntanned man wearing a camel coat. He doffed his hat.

'I see you have a visitor,' said Anthea, her face so close that Nell could smell her toothpaste. 'So we'll leave you to it. See you afterwards in the village hall for the sherry and sandwiches.'

She left behind a waft of perfume. Nell glanced around her in bafflement. A visitor? All she saw was Miss Hull and Miss Trenton in their tweed suits and hideous hats buttonholing her mother.

'We are so sorry, Mrs Garland,' Miss Trenton was saying, her eyes bright behind her smudged specs.

Miss Hull put her hand on Mollie's arm. 'If there's anything we can do, anything at all, you know where we are.'

Nell's father came close and put his hand on her shoulder.

'Listen, Nell, Diana's done in. And we think it rather inappropriate to stay on. Give my best to your mother.'

'Come and see us soon,' said Diana.

She watched them hurry away in thinly veiled relief, believing that no one would notice, and then she walked over to Adele who was sitting alone on a bench under the yew, dabbing her eyes. She'd travelled so many miles on her own, leaving her young children with her mother-in-law, to pay her respects to a former employer of whom she had lost all respect. Her broad-beamed body looked robust and capable, as it had always done. *Her glorious skin,* thought Nell, *just like uncooked dough.*

'Adele, do you know where Sylvie is?'

'Mais oui, ma petite. Still in the church with Henri.'

'I'll go and fetch her. See if she is all right. Wait here for us and we'll go over to the hall together if you like. I think we can all do with a bit of a drink.'

'Oh Nell, but I think there's someone ... someone there...'

Adele's teary eyes focused past her shoulder with a confused blend of surprise and recognition.

'This is all rather puzzling.' It was Alex's voice, behind her. 'Madame Ricard? From Montfleur? Can it be?'

'I'm sure, yes. It could be. But I think I really must find Mademoiselle at once. She must need me. Please excuse me.' Adele stood up quickly and walked towards the church door.

In a daze, Nell took a step back as if to get a better view of the man standing in front of her. Alex wore an immaculate suit. His face bore deeper lines than she remembered. But his smile was as familiar and as devastating as ever.

'You're here?' Nell croaked. 'You're *here?*'

He stepped towards her. 'When you telephoned, to hear your voice was unbelievable. After all this time. I thought I'd never hear it again, let alone see you. The telephone call was rather bizarre, so then, of course, I had to come up to Lednor. Is this for Sylvie's mother? Oh, I am so very sorry.'

Unable to speak, Nell glanced instead over her shoulder to see Sylvie leave the church and walk towards them down the path. She turned on Alex. Anger – illogical and frenzied – snapped inside her head.

'Are you sure you're not here to see Syivie?'

'Oh God, no. Oh Nell, *no.*'

Sylvie stopped in her tracks, still some way off, with Henri and Adele either side of her. Adele began to speak to her in hushed tones as Henri leant in, talking quietly. Sylvie shook her head at them both and then beamed at Nell, her face oddly serene, the beauty of it coming like a light from within. She nodded and lifted her hand to salute Nell, her eyes glistening, then turned and walked away towards her mother's grave.

'I was a fool with Sylvie.' Alex was breathless, speaking quickly. 'Wrong place, wrong time. I was, frankly, beside myself.'

She felt his hand touch hers, delicately by the tips of her fingers. She saw the pain on his face and knew, then, that she was going to make it worse.

He tried again. 'You told me to leave you alone – to quite frankly get lost. And so I did, I suspect. I did get lost. The years, the war, just created that dreadful breach. But I can't tell you, your telephone call made my head split with delight, with hope, I...'

'Can we walk, away from here? I want to get away.'

He assented and they hurried together in silence out of the churchyard, along the lane, and left the village behind. The light of the November day was failing, and the damp air over the Chess spread its thin chilly breath to reach them on the lane. An owl called prematurely from the depths of the copse.

'I remember this way,' said Alex, endeavouring to be conversational. 'When we walked back after my petrol ran out. What a night. I am so sorry that it has been like this. I have never forgotten.'

'And neither have I,' she said. With a jolt she understood that whatever had happened between them, however long the years had taken to turn and turn, none of it had any bearing on how she felt about him.

Alex cleared his throat. 'It must have been a horrible shock when you heard Sylvie's news,' he said cautiously. 'And by the time it was all resolved, the misunderstanding between Sylvie and I, well, you'd gone. I wrote to you and you waited a year to send a telegram—'

'Alex, please stop,' she held up her hand. 'You don't have to explain. I know what happened. But you don't know my side of it. What happened to me.'

'I understand you threw yourself into nursing.'

'I failed you, Alex.'

'No, no, no.'

'I lied to everyone. I lied to you.'

She pulled on his arm to make him stop walking. In the deep silence of the dusk, the cold river babbled in the shallows, and she breathed on the chill, her eyes adjusting to the gloom under the trees. She felt the air refresh her, restart her heart. Something changed inside her; shifted out of the way. She suddenly was profoundly grateful that Alex was standing before her. That they had both survived the war. It seemed like an absolute bloody miracle. She gazed up at him and held both of his hands. His face was expectant and rather placid. She could barely look at him and watch his expression fall away as she told him that she had borne his child, and that his child had died, and that his name was John-James.

Alex placed his hand over his eyes, resting his other on her shoulder. His chest shuddered as he suppressed a cry. She waited, her veins pumping ice.

After some moments he found his voice, and it cracked in his throat.

'You must have been in hell.'

'I was on the edge of it. I was blind crazy.'

'Why didn't you...? You must have needed me. Why didn't you tell me?'

She could not answer him.

Instead, she took his hand and they continued on up the lane, negotiating the ford by walking carefully from one stepping stone to another, helping one another, using touch and instinct to cross safely. The memory of them splashing riotously through the water the night of the air raid, the night John-James was conceived, nudged her. How the closeness of death and terror had made them heedless, had made them laugh.

'Your own hell would have been in France,' she said. 'I hear that you went twice?'

'That woman. The French woman, back at the church, I...'

It was no use, the phantom of John-James rejoined them.

A numb silence fell around them. His arm went round her and she rested her head on his shoulder. It felt like a profound anchorage, as if she was home.

The house was in darkness at the end of the drive, except for the lamp in the hallway window.

'Who's this?' asked Alex. 'Oh, I know who this is.'

Kit, having taken to sleeping on the front step when no one was at home, lifted his long-snouted head and whimpered in recognition.

'Oh, what a good lad.' Alex knelt down to receive the sniffs and nudges and grunts of delight from the dog.

'Come, Kit,' said Nell.

As she pushed open the wooden door to the September Garden, the slow moon brightened suddenly inside a corridor of milky stars. The shapes within the garden slowly became apparent: the gnarled apple tree, drifts of spent dahlia, lanky sunflowers buckled and broken, silhouetted in the gloom.

Alex exclaimed and stumbled. 'It's too dark,' he said with an edge of panic, disguising the fall of his tears. 'How will I ever see?'

Nell gripped his arm and walked with him.

She felt embalmed in comfort, floating alongside him. And his arm about her told her all she needed to know.

'It's all right, Alex,' she told him. 'Kit knows the way in the darkness. Let's follow him.'

Acknowledgements

The September Garden has been four years in the making and proves what they say: that the second novel is often the hardest. There have certainly been a few setbacks, including two titles and two rewrites, and I'm so grateful to my agent Judith Murdoch for always believing in me and encouraging me along what has been a very long journey.

The first spark for the story came from *The Normandy Diary of Marie-Louise Osmont* (Random House), which I picked up in a second-hand bookshop. This feisty and independent Normandy château owner gives her firsthand account of living in occupied France and through the hopeful and desperate days of the Allied invasion. Haunted and inspired by her shocking experiences, I went from there, linking the story back to England with the idea of two cousins who were caught up in the dark, uncertain days of the conflict.

A huge amount of research has gone into creating a convincing background for my characters, including days spent at the Imperial War Museum, London, and the Liberation Museum, Cherbourg, plus devouring many articles and books. I'd like to thank Neil Wood for lending me his 78-volume *Images of War, The Real Story of World War Two* (Marshall Cavendish), which gave me valuable insight into what people would have known at the time (through newspaper headlines and reports) often in contrast to how much more we know now.

To write truthfully about a place, I have to see it with my own eyes, and I'd like to thank my mother Coral for coming with me on my recce trip to Normandy and navigating so patiently while I drove our hire car so erratically through the French countryside. We arrived, coincidently, on the 65th anniversary of D-Day and everywhere we went, through towns and villages, we saw Allied flags and *Welcome to our Liberators* banners. We stayed in Valognes in the Grand Hotel du Louvre, a turreted building of silvery stone on a narrow cobbled street. It was there that I discovered, in the quiet courtyard behind, the stables of the long-departed horses Tatillon and Ullis.

Other books that have inspired many aspects of my novel include: *Forgotten Voices of the Second World War* by Max Arther, *Debs at War* by Anne de Courcy and *Wild Mary: The Life of Mary Wesley* by Patrick Marnham. Plus the writings of war-time correspondent Edward Murrow, *This is London*, and the books of two great novelists who experienced the war: Nevil Shute's *Pastoral* and H.E. Bates' *A Moment in Time*.

The publishers hope that this book has given you enjoyable reading. Large Print Books are especially designed to be as easy to see and hold as possible. If you wish a complete list of our books please ask at your local library or write directly to:

Magna Large Print Books
Magna House, Long Preston,
Skipton, North Yorkshire.
BD23 4ND

This Large Print Book for the partially sighted, who cannot read normal print, is published under the auspices of

THE ULVERSCROFT FOUNDATION

THE ULVERSCROFT FOUNDATION

... we hope that you have enjoyed this Large Print Book. Please think for a moment about those people who have worse eyesight problems than you ... and are unable to even read or enjoy Large Print, without great difficulty.

You can help them by sending a donation, large or small to:

**The Ulverscroft Foundation,
1, The Green, Bradgate Road,
Anstey, Leicestershire, LE7 7FU,
England.**
or request a copy of our brochure for more details.

The Foundation will use all your help to assist those people who are handicapped by various sight problems and need special attention.

Thank you very much for your help.